HONEY AND THE LEOPARD

L. T. KAY

MJB

To Maggie

With my love and thanks for your continued support and encouragement that enabled me to write this book

ACKNOWLEDGMENTS

I am indebted to all those who helped me in writing this book. These include my beta readers who comment on grammatical and structural errors that have slipped through the net.

My thanks also go to Melody and Russell for their line edits, picking up several small omissions and typos, and for their suggestions adding to the story.

I especially want to thank Maggie, my editor-in-chief, who read and re-read the manuscript several times, pointing out typos and other errors affecting the flow of the narrative.

Any remaining errors are entirely my responsibility.

Finally, I'd like to thank you, my reader, for taking the time to read this book. If you notice any typos or errors of fact, no matter how small, please let me know through my website or my email address ltkay@ltkay.com, so I can improve the reading experience for those who follow.

L.T. Kay

Author website https://ltkay.com

Strange how long the minutes last

When the years go by so fast

L. T. Kay

PROLOGUE

In August 2014, Grace Mugabe, the president's second wife, started a campaign to undermine Joice Mujuru, the vice-president of Zimbabwe. Grace and her husband, Robert, conspired to establish a dynasty by stealth. Critics labelled the plan *Grace Mugabe's Bedroom Coup*.

Grace's first goal was to take over the leadership of the powerful ZANU-PF Women's League. False accusations against Joice Mujuru, questioning her loyalty to the president and the regime, led to her dismissal by the president, who then appointed Emmerson Mnangagwa as one of two vice-presidents. This was possibly a ploy to prevent Mnangagwa from becoming the obvious and sole contender for the presidency, post Mugabe.

ZANU-PF split into two acrimonious factions. Mnangagwa led the Lacoste faction, so named to represent his totem, the crocodile. The Generation 40 (G40) faction favoured Grace Mugabe to succeed her husband. The battle for the future, post Robert Mugabe, had begun, and all eyes focussed on the 2018 elections.

To complicate matters, the Movement for Democratic Change (MDC), led by the ailing Morgan Tsvangirai, also planned to contest the forthcoming elections. Senior members of that party jockeyed for the leadership position upon Tsvangirai's demise.

Zimbabwe was set for the perfect political storm.

CHAPTER 1

How did it come to this? Paul Tinashe, compounding chemist, was top of his class at Wits University in Johannesburg. Voted the student most likely to succeed. The clever one. He made good money and had a lovely wife and two beautiful children. One little mistake shouldn't put his life in danger and his family and career at risk.

Paul left Harare in a hurry. He'd warned them that the powder might not work. It was way beyond its use by date and stored in conditions bound to affect its efficacy. A higher-than-normal moisture content reduced the chances of it being inhaled when disturbed.

The newspapers said the minister's secretary breathed in a small amount and lay in hospital with respiratory difficulties. The minister remained unaffected. Paul warned them, so why should they now blame him for the failure of the mission? Perhaps the plan was meant to fail, and he'd be the scapegoat. He should never have got involved with those state security guys. They promised gratitude from high up, and the temptation blurred his judgement.

Paul's father owned a house in Lupane, near the Hwange National Park. It mostly stood empty, so Paul, Millie, and the kids holidayed there as often as possible. They'd always stayed inside the house, but without Millie and the kids, it would feel too quiet and ominous. He didn't want to advertise his presence, so the outside veranda room would serve as his hideout for a few days.

On the drive from Harare, he'd only stopped once, in Bulawayo, for a quick toilet break and to buy food items for his stay in Lupane. Paul carried two jerry cans of petrol in the boot of his Volkswagen Golf to counter uncertain petrol supplies and long service station queues.

Now, as he approached the house, he switched off the headlights and crawled up the driveway to limit the vehicle's engine noise. He stopped in front of the garage and eased open the doors to minimise the loud creaks the old hinges made. After driving in, he took his carry-bag and supplies from the back seat and locked the garage. With luck, no one would realise it concealed his car. He blessed the dark, moonless night.

The single, self-contained room at the end of the broad L-shaped veranda which ran along the front and one side of the house felt more secure than the house's interior. The veranda ended towards the house's rear, with a wall made from vertical timber boards. A close-fitting door, also made from vertical timber boards, camouflaged the room's existence. With no door handle and an inconspicuous keyhole, it was an ideal hiding place. In normal times, it served as a guest room or change room for the swimming pool, but for several months, it lay locked and unused. As he opened the door, Paul found the stuffiness overpowering.

The room incorporated a shower and toilet and space for a single bed and bedside table. The shower and toilet backed on to the bathroom inside the house. A single, horizontal, narrow window near the ceiling served both the bed and bathroom areas, and mirrored the window of the indoor bathroom. An observant person might notice the extra bathroom window, and that would betray the veranda room's existence. The vertical timber boards covered both the small veranda room and part of the indoor bathroom. A casual observer might think the timber wall covered only the latter.

Paul was relieved the caretaker was nowhere to be seen. He didn't want anyone to know about his arrival. Potato chips and cold baked beans did for supper. The generator lay idle, but he did not intend to switch on the lights. The book he'd brought would see him through the daylight hours. For now, his portable battery radio, with the volume turned right down, would keep him company.

Tomorrow he'd decide his course, but he was too tired to worry about that now. His food supplies would last three or four days if he was careful, but at some point, the caretaker would discover his presence. The caretaker's kia stood on the edge of the property, about one hundred metres outside the garden's fenced area. It was the likely reason the caretaker did not notice his arrival.

Paul lay back on the single bed with his hands behind his head. It was so quiet here. He adjusted his battery radio's volume to the lowest level, listening to a distant-sounding, unidentified station.

The peace reminded him of the old days, when he visited his grandparents in their rural village in the Buhera district. He'd lie in bed at night, listening to soft music on his crystal set. That was thirty years earlier, when he was ten, and his whole life lay before him. With The Gukurahundi in full swing then, Mashonaland was quiet. Comrade Mugabe was in charge, and it was different back then.

Now the politicians vied for position, and ZANU-PF, the governing party, was splitting down the middle. The question of Mugabe's successor occupied everyone's mind, as they did not expect the frail old president to last much longer.

The Lacoste faction supported Emmerson Mnangagwa to succeed Mugabe when he vacated his position as president. Mnangagwa, nicknamed *The Crocodile*, headed the faction named after the Lacoste clothing brand's logo. The faction comprised the old guard, including those who fought in the Bush War.

The G40 faction supported Mugabe's wife, Grace, to replace him. Its name stood for *generation40*, a reference to the approximate age of many of the younger party members dominating the faction.

Paul regretted his minor part in the assassination plot, but received assurances the very highest authority backed it, and he would be well rewarded for his cooperation. Until he read about it in the newspaper, he didn't even know the target's identity. He was reluctant to help the plotters, but they made clear the consequences of refusing.

The anonymous warning phone call only told him to get out of Harare urgently. The caller didn't reveal who threatened his life, so he could only guess who hunted him. Would it be the disappointed conspirators, realising he might give evidence against them, or perhaps the target's faction looked for revenge?

Locked in the stuffy little room, Paul wondered if he should stay in Lupane? Would they be able to find him? Did anyone realise he'd fled Harare? It was fortunate his family were visiting relatives in South Africa. He'd got word to them to stay there until he advised them it was safe to return. Perhaps he should drive to Victoria Falls and make his way to South Africa, through Zambia and Botswana. Yes, that sounded like a good idea.

A sudden noise from inside the house interrupted his thoughts. It wouldn't be the caretaker. He didn't have a key. A burglar, perhaps? Paul strained his ears, listening for any other sound. All quiet! Then a loud crash! Someone knocked over something in the house.

The soft music on the radio now sounded way too loud. In his haste, reaching for the knob to turn down the volume, Paul's finger accidentally knocked it, turning up the volume. In a panic, he turned the knob, switching off the radio. The volume blared for only a second. Did the intruder hear it? If the indoor bathroom door was closed, it was possible the radio may not have alerted the intruder, but if it stood open....

Paul sweated in the little room's confines. The heat or the tension? All now silent. The radio may have frightened off the intruder. In the moonless night's darkness, the high, horizontal, narrow window prevented any ambient light from entering the room. Paul lay in the darkness, listening for any sound. Long minutes passed. All quiet!

Just as he breathed more freely, footsteps approached on the veranda. The radio hadn't frightened off the intruder. This was the worst of all possibilities. Someone searched for him!

The footsteps halted near the door. Paul stopped breathing. After a few moments, the footsteps descended the nearby steps to the garden.

Time to breathe again. Paul lay on his bed, hoping and praying the intruder would leave.

For a quarter hour, he waited. Nothing! Not a sound. Wait! Was that a noise in the house? Hard to be certain. Paul's imagination played tricks on him. Then someone walked up the garden steps and stopped in front of his door.

CHAPTER 2

DAN Scott sat at his computer working on his third novel. His desk faced the front garden with its green lawn surrounded by trees. Autumn now, and with each gust of wind, a shower of yellow leaves would catch his attention as they floated to the ground. He looked at the pretty garden bordered by a high brick wall. The camellias bloomed; their splashes of pink and red, breaking up the expanse of green. But Dan found no inspiration there yesterday, and none today either. He sat, pondering the structure of the next chapter in his latest novel, when the phone rang. 'Hello, Dan Scott speaking.'

'Good morning, Mr Scott. My name is David Jones. I work for the Zimbabwe government.'

It was an educated voice, but it put Dan on his guard. His first published novel, *Dead Heat in Zimbabwe*, was critical of the regime. As a result, the authorities banned his books, and he needed to get out of the country fast, with state security nipping at his heels. 'Yes, what can I do for you?'

'Mr Scott, you've been busy writing your novels over the past three years. I've read the first two, and I understand you're working on your third, but it's your first book that interests us. It's quite a work of art. I'm visiting Melbourne next week, and I wondered if we could meet for a cup of coffee.'

'Oh! What do you want to discuss? If you've read my novels, you'll be aware they don't paint your government in a good light.'

'Yes, that's true. Your books are banned in Zimbabwe, but we're not worried about that. What interests us are your ideas, and I'd like to discuss them with you further. You live in Brighton, I believe. How about the Half Moon in Church Street, at eleven o'clock on Tuesday? Would that suit you?'

'Hmm, yes, that would be OK, I suppose.'

'I can assure you, Mr Scott, you needn't worry about anything. It may even be in your best interest.'

'How will I recognise you, Mr Jones?'

'Don't worry, I'll recognise you from the photo in your book, sitting here in front of me.'

'You know a lot about me, Mr Jones.'

'I know all about you, Mr Scott. We keep a close eye on our friends, as well as our enemies, of course.'

'No doubt, I'm in the latter category, Mr Jones.'

'Oh no, we don't see you as an enemy. Let's just call you a critic. That can work to both our advantage.'

Dan worried about the meeting. Would they threaten him? Perhaps try to sue him? Mr Jones was well spoken. Was he their lawyer? Anyway, better to get it over.

Tuesday came around all too soon. Dan made sure that he arrived early for his appointment with David Jones. He sat fiddling with his glasses case at a quiet corner table in the hotel bar-lounge. How did Mr Jones gain so much information about him? Did they hack into his computer? If so, they might already know where his third book was heading. That would be a concern.

A deep voice interrupted his thoughts. 'Mr Scott, you look just like your photo on the back cover of your last book.'

Dan looked up to see a hulking black man standing in front of him. Tall for a Zimbabwean, and well built. He had a friendly face and an affable manner. Dan was just over six feet tall, but he felt dwarfed by the man.

'Mr Jones, I wasn't expecting—'

'A black man; you weren't expecting a black man?'

'Well, your voice—'

'I went to school in the UK and college in The States.'

'Please excuse me for saying your name doesn't fit with your appearance, Mr Jones.'

'You're right, but hey, you write under a pseudonym. David Jones is not my real name, either. Work requires me to use an alias.'

'So, what's this about, Mr Jones?'

'Please call me David, and I'll call you Dan. So much simpler!'

'Fine by me.'

They ordered two coffees, and David Jones leant forward in his seat, lowering his voice. 'I'll get right to the point, Dan. In your first book, you write about a clandestine secret police unit in Zimbabwe.'

'Yes.'

'Of course, it's a fiction.'

'Yes, of course.'

'Your ideas interest us, and we believe they can improve the way we work.'

'How does that involve me?'

'We wondered if you'd care to work with us in a consultancy role. Initially, it would be a six-month stint based in Harare. Depending on how it goes, they may offer you an extension. And of course, you would be free to resume writing your novels. We would pay all your fees here in Australia.'

'That's flattering, David, but you're talking to the wrong man. Can you imagine me supporting the work of your security services? Beating and intimidation is not my line. Critics of the government have disappeared without a trace. I couldn't countenance such behaviour.'

'Perhaps, Dan, but you wouldn't be involved in the day-to-day operations. You'd simply be helping us to streamline our systems. Your work would make people more accountable. That would lead to a reduction in those abuses that concern you. Like you, I abhor the abuses.'

'And what if I got opposition to my ideas?'

'Ah, that's a good point. No one will oppose you. My instructions for recruiting your services come from the very top, so you'd have a free hand.'

'You mean from the president?'

'Please understand. I can't answer that question. You'll have to trust me on that. There'll be no written contract. This arrangement must stay between us.'

'When I was last in Zimbabwe, the police had a warrant for my arrest. I had to get out fast. What if they exercise that warrant when I return?'

'You have my guarantee no one will try to arrest you. Not when you're working for us.'

Dan was keen to revisit the land of his birth, and the offer tempted him. Well, why not? 'OK David, you have a deal, but there's one condition. They must pay me monthly in advance. It will cover my out-of-pocket expenses, and insurance in case someone at the very top changes their mind.'

'That's agreed then, Dan. We would like you to start as soon as possible, but it probably won't happen before September. I'll be in touch and give you all the details when I have them.'

* * *

Dan's parents were aghast.

'You're crazy,' said his father. 'They want to get you there and stick you in jail. You should have said you'd think about it.'

'Dad, I trust David Jones.'

'What! You trust someone who won't even tell you his real name? And what sort of name is that? I ask you! He's just using the name of a department store.'

'As he pointed out, Dad, I use a pen name.'

'Did he call you by your pen name?'

'Uh, no, he called me by my real name.'

'So, he knows your real name, but you don't know his. Marvellous! Never let your ego make your decisions for you. Have you forgotten? You escaped the country by the skin of your teeth? Criticising the president is a crime, and the authorities also wanted you for subversion.'

'David Jones has guaranteed my safety.'

'And what about Maureen? Are you planning to just leave her in the lurch?'

'Dad, I've told you before, we're good friends. Nothing else.'

'Well, I still think you're taking an unnecessary risk.'

'I've been feeling stale recently and haven't done much writing. It would be an opportunity to get inspiration and material for the book I'm writing.'

'If anything goes wrong, don't come crying to me about it.'

'I'm not a child anymore, Dad. If anything goes wrong, it will be my responsibility.'

* * *

Three and a half months later, despite last-minute pleas from both of his parents to reconsider, Dan found himself in a taxi headed for Tullamarine Airport. It was only two years since his last trip, but it seemed much longer. As the taxi dodged through the fast-moving traffic, he reflected on the change in the Tullamarine Freeway. Each time it was different, so it pleased him he wasn't driving. He could easily take a wrong turn and arrive late at the airport in a flustered rush.

As they neared the airport, the traffic slowed. There was some hold-up ahead. Dan looked at his watch; plenty of time before check-in. Soon, the taxi pulled up in front of the international departures. The taxi driver sprung open the boot and jumped out to retrieve Dan's travel bag. Dan thanked him and walked across the pavement and through the sliding doors into the high-ceilinged hall.

The buzz of excitement and anticipation of the travellers washed over him as he stood examining the departures board to see which check-in counters handled his flight. Like his last trip, he was flying Etihad. On that occasion, the check-in counter stood at the end of the hall.

Dan also arrived early on his previous trip, but he made the mistake of going for a coffee. He was quick, but when he returned, the short queue had grown a long tortuous tail. After he checked-in and passed through immigration, he'd no time to browse in the duty-free shops. Instead, he needed to hurry to the boarding lounge, where his flight was already being called.

Today was different. Dan kept his position near the front of the queue, though the wait seemed interminable. When, at last, the check-in counters opened, and the queue moved, he passed smoothly through check-in and immigration and into the large duty-free shopping hall. He wanted to buy pressure stockings and adaptors for his computer, electric shaver, and toothbrush. The mystery of those purchases was that he bought them each time he travelled overseas, but could never find them when he packed his bag for the next trip.

With his purchases done, Dan browsed through all the exciting duty-free shops. He perused the cameras, watches, and liquor, and marvelled at the prices. The opulence was on full display. Scotches and cognacs with price tags running into thousands of dollars. When he returned to the shelves displaying affordable liquor, he picked up a one litre bottle of Johnnie Walker Black Label, but then thought better about it and put it back on the shelf. He'd buy a bottle in Johannesburg.

Dan made his way to the circular departure area, where he paced for half an hour before settling in a seat at the edge of his departure gate. He sat back, watching the other passengers arrive in their twos and threes, looking for vacant seats. At last, the gate hostess called the flight to Abu Dhabi, and Dan gathered his bag and joined the queue. He showed his boarding pass at the gate, where the air hostesses checked it against the passenger manifest, and then he made his way down the long aero bridge to the plane. Now it was almost nine o'clock at night and dark outside.

At the plane's entrance, the air hostess directed Dan to the second aisle, where he found his window seat seventeen rows from the front. He placed his bag in the overhead locker and settled back to watch the other passengers board the plane. Most passed through to the next section.

Close to departure, the passengers continued to trickle in. The lengthy queues at the check-in counters seemed to have evaporated. The plane was half empty. Where was everyone?

Soon, a hostess asked the passengers to fasten seatbelts and make sure their seats were upright and their tables secured. The plane moved backwards as the truck pushed it away from the aero bridge to give it room to turn. Then, under its own power, the plane taxied to the runway. At the runway, it turned ninety degrees and trundled to the end. There it turned one hundred and eighty degrees to prepare for take-off.

The roar of the engines increased as they built up power and fought against the brakes. A vibration and shaking signalled the plane's readiness to break free from its leash. The release of the brakes set the plane in motion, picking up speed as it hurtled down the runway in tune with the engines' rising scream. Dan always thrilled at the power and roar of the jet engines. Then suddenly, as the plane lifted-off, the engine noise subsided into a comforting hum. Soon the air hostesses wheeled their trolleys down the aisles, offering the passengers pre-dinner drinks. By the time dinner arrived, he was starving. The meal wasn't great fare, but the attractive multi-national hostesses were a little compensation.

After dinner, Dan took out a copy of his first novel to reread it. What was it that impressed 'the very top?' He thought it strange that he'd forgotten so much about his first novel once he immersed himself in the second and third. As he read, he found what he'd written disturbing. It surprised him he hadn't been aware of the detail in his writing. It was dark stuff. What use would a brutal regime make of it?

Dan became so absorbed, paging through the book, he forgot all about the on-board screen entertainment. That would be a first for him.

Time for a rest. Dan switched off the overhead light, pulled the airline blanket around himself, and reclined his seat to get some sleep. It seemed like only minutes later; the lights switched on and the air hostess announced they would serve breakfast. He slept well and felt refreshed.

After the usual early morning rush of toilets, breakfast, and hostesses clearing up the mess, the fasten seatbelt announcement and lights prepared the passengers for landing. With the sun kissing the horizon, Dan assessed it would be a sweltering day in Abu Dhabi.

A long taxi to the terminal followed the smooth landing. When the seatbelt lights turned off, the passengers scrambled to retrieve their hand luggage from the overhead lockers and choked the aisle in an impatient queue. Dan, in his window seat, fancied there was little to gain by joining the crush. He relaxed until the aisle cleared. Then, he retrieved his hand luggage and walked from the plane, through the aero bridge, to the terminal.

A queue had formed for immigration and customs, but he had ample time for his connecting flight to Johannesburg. The connecting flight would leave from terminal one, with the old, picturesque, mosaic tiled roof. After a quick round of the upper and lower levels, Dan walked back to a cafeteria in the corridor he'd passed through earlier and ordered a coffee.

Following another slow tour of the upper and lower levels of the terminal, he walked to the departure lounge to wait. As a writer, he was a keen observer of people and their habits. It helped keep him occupied and add to his list of characters for a future novel.

Soon, the speakers announced the flight, and this time, Dan claimed a spot near the front of the boarding queue. Once again, the plane was half empty, and he had a window seat row to himself. The next time he passed this way, Dan thought he might spend a couple of days in Abu Dhabi. Always keen to return to Africa, he hadn't considered that possibility on this trip. Too late to worry about that now.

The plane landed at Johannesburg's O. R. Tambo International Airport around six in the evening. David Jones had booked Dan into the InterContinental Johannesburg O.R. Tambo Airport Hotel. Expensive, but David Jones was paying for it.

Dan spent half an hour wondering around the shops at the airport. As he left the arrivals hall, an African man in a navy blue uniform called out, 'Taxi, Sir?'

'No thank you, I'm walking.'

'Not safe to walk, Sir.'

'The hotel is only seventy metres away. What can happen in that short distance?'

The man shrugged.

CHAPTER 3

OUTSIDE, darkness had fallen. Dan left the terminal and walked past the Gautrain railway station and headed for the nearby Intercontinental Airport Hotel. No one else walked in his direction, but it was only a two-minute stroll. He had a spring in his step, happy to be back in Africa.

Soon he turned into the hotel's u-shaped entrance road, with trees and hedgerows growing on both sides. Without warning, a large African man stepped out of the shadows in front of him, raising one arm, signalling him to stop. Dan froze. The man brandished a long screwdriver. Then Dan noticed a second African man standing on the road to his right, waving a handgun in an agitated manner. Dan worried the gun might fire, even if the man didn't intend to fire it. His nervousness made the situation most dangerous.

'Don't look at our faces! Put your bag on the ground! And your cell phone!' said the large man in a menacing voice.

'My bag has only got clothes in it.'

'Just do it!'

Dan put his carry bag on the ground and reached into his jacket pocket to retrieve his cell phone. As he put his phone on top of his carry bag, a car came racing around the corner, hitting the man standing in the road. The big man holding the screwdriver turned and ran into the shadows. The car showed no sign of slowing or stopping as it raced away. Dan saw the second man lying motionless on the road. Was he dead? Dan didn't wait to find out. After a moment's hesitation, he picked up his phone and carry bag and ran to the hotel.

The surprised concierge stopped him at the front entrance. 'What's the matter? Is something wrong?'

'Outside, on the road, a car knocked down a man but didn't stop. I think he's dead, but be careful, he's got a gun.'

The concierge didn't go to check on the accident victim. Instead, he called the police, who appeared in a few minutes.

'Who reported this?' said the police officer in charge.

'I did,' said Dan.

'What is your name, Sir?'

'Dan Scott.'

'There's no one lying on the road now. Are you sure the car hit him?'

'Yes, it sent him flying.'

'Can you describe the car? Did you get its number plate?'

'No, I didn't. It was a dark colour. Maybe black or dark grey.'

'Did you recognise the make of car?'

'No, they all look the same. It was a saloon.'

A policewoman interrupted her senior officer. 'We found this, Sir,' she said, holding up the handgun.

'Two men tried to mug me,' said Dan. 'The one the car hit carried a handgun. The other had a screwdriver. He ran off after the accident, and I ran into the hotel.'

'If you can't give us more information, there's little we can do,' said the senior officer. 'In Johannesburg, too many criminals have guns. We'll check it for fingerprints, though we'll be lucky to find the culprit. You must be careful here, Mr Scott. You can run into trouble anywhere in this city.'

'Perhaps you can find the driver of the car. They may have booked the hotel for dinner or the night. Then, when they hit the man, they just panicked and drove off. I'm sure the hotel would record last-minute cancellations or no-shows.'

'Yes, thank you, Mr Scott. We're aware of that.'

When the police left, a hotel receptionist checked-in Dan. 'We've upgraded you to one of our best rooms, Mr Scott. I hope it will help you forget your unfortunate experience here.'

Dan remained calm and clear-thinking throughout the attempted mugging, but now, as he tried to fill in the registration form, his hand shook with delayed shock.

A porter showed him to his sumptuous room on the seventh floor. In South Africa, there was no skimping on luxury. The porter explained how everything worked, and after getting his tip left with a cheerful smile.

The room faced the runways, but its soundproofing eliminated the engine noise of the planes taking off and landing. Dan found the scene mesmerising. Now he felt hungry. After his traumatic experience, he stayed in the hotel. He examined the room service menu and then picked up the phone and placed his order.

He enjoyed the room's comforts. Who knew what accommodation he'd have in Harare? Following a tender steak dinner, he relaxed under a long, hot shower. It had been a tiring day, so it was early to bed.

* * *

Dan slept well and woke refreshed. Yesterday's experience was like a bad dream. It was a beautiful sunny morning, and outside everything looked the picture of a busy commercial hub, with travellers coming and going on the big international flights. He thought it odd how the normal world sat so close to this troubled city's violence.

In the hotel dining room at breakfast, the previous evening's events played on his mind. He wondered why the two muggers lurked on the hotel grounds. Could they have been hotel staff? He'd always been alert and watchful of his surroundings in Johannesburg, and it just showed one couldn't be careful enough. Crime in South Africa was a constant threat and compared unfavourably with Zimbabwe, where the government appeared to be the major risk to a person's unfettered enjoyment of life.

Dan had booked a mid-morning flight to Harare, arriving just before lunch. He had time to brush his teeth, pack, and explore the hotel before checking out. On his return to his hotel room, in the corridor, he passed a large African who looked similar in size and shape to the big man who accosted him the previous evening.

When he stopped to open his room door, he glanced back and caught the man watching him. 'Good morning, Sir,' the man called.

'Good morning,' said Dan as he hurried to open the room's door. Should he mention the possibility to the concierge? No, he didn't have any evidence. In the darkness, it was hard to distinguish the man's features. He couldn't be certain if it was the same person.

Dan left the hotel entrance and stepped out for the airport terminal. In the hotel garden, a worker trimmed the hedge with a pair of garden shears. Dan almost broke his stride. That man also resembled the big mugger who blocked his path, though he couldn't be sure. Was he seeing the mugger in the face of every big African he passed? Perhaps the experience made him a little paranoid.

It didn't seem likely that the muggers would be hotel staff, but why were they hiding on the hotel grounds? If they were hotel staff and anyone else saw them, they'd have the ideal excuse for being there. Would anyone risk robbing a guest at the hotel where they worked? He thought not.

At the Gautrain railway station, a crowd was building, while inside the airport terminal, travellers hurried in all directions. The airport cafes were crowded with people.

After checking-in, Dan walked through the crowded terminal and caught an escalator down to a busy departure lounge. The area looked dated and worn. Rows of plastic seating led to several departure gates. The signs at each departure gate suggested the terminal was for travellers to other African countries. With few seats vacant, Dan walked around the large room, observing the crowd. A few travellers dressed in their country's traditional clothing.

Before too long, the speakers announced the Harare flight, and Dan joined the queue at the departure gate. Outside on the tarmac, an airport bus waited to take the passengers to the South African Airlink plane.

The bus was jammed full of passengers before it began its leisurely drive to the plane parked a fair distance from the terminal. The lucky ones found seats, but the majority stood, holding on to the handles dangling from the overhead rails. Soon, the congestion warmed the bus's interior to an uncomfortable level.

Which was the Harare plane? Each time he thought they'd arrived at their destination, the bus circumvented the plane and sped towards another. The standing passengers needed to hold on tight to the handles to keep their footing. When at last they reached the waiting plane, everybody poured out of the bus and rushed to join the boarding queue. Dan was one of the first to board the bus, and the standing passengers crowded in front of his seat. When the bus doors opened, he was amongst the last to disembark and join the queue.

On board, he found his window seat and placed his luggage in the overhead locker. To his pleasant surprise, no one sat next to him. The plane was much smaller than Etihad's large international jets and didn't induce quite the same thrill as the take-offs in Melbourne and Abu Dhabi.

Soon after the smooth take-off, the fasten seat belts light switched off, and the drinks trolley rattled its way down the aisle. Dan ordered his usual tomato juice and relaxed to watch the passing countryside far below. The dusty light green and yellow colours of Southern Africa tugged at his heart. It was the sign he was nearly home.

CHAPTER 4

THE one hour and thirty-five-minute flight passed in a flash, and soon Dan obeyed the fasten seatbelt sign and craned his neck to get a view of the Harare skyline. The plane banked and lined up with the runway. It was a smooth landing, followed by a slow taxi to the terminal. Dan's seat near the front of the plane enabled him to be amongst the first to disembark.

It was a short walk to the terminal building, where an immigration officer offered him a form to complete. Dan had done this several times before, but would the circumstances of his last visit cause a problem? He'd no need to worry. The filled in form, and his work visa, helped him pass through immigration without difficulty. Now it was just customs to clear. With only a limited amount of clothing and toiletries in his bag, and nothing to declare, he wasn't concerned.

A custom's officer walked over to him at the counter. 'Good afternoon, Sir. Please open your bag for inspection.'

Dan sat the bag on the counter and opened it. The customs officer rummaged through the clothing in the main compartment and then searched the smaller side compartments. A safety razor and manual toothbrush in one, and travel documents in another. 'What's this?' said the customs officer as he pulled Dan's book from the third compartment. He flicked through the pages and saw Dan's photo. 'You wrote this book?'

'Yes.'

'One moment, Sir. I must speak to my senior officer.' The customs officer left him standing at the counter and walked into a corner office with frosted windows. A moment later, the officer returned with a serious looking, tall, balding man.

The tall man looked stern as he addressed Dan. 'Mr Scott, are you aware this is a banned book in Zimbabwe?'

'Erm, yes, I believe so.'

'It is a crime to smuggle banned books into the country.'

'Well, I'm not smuggling it. The government has invited me here to carry out work based on this book.'

'Oh! Who invited you?'

'David Jones. He works for the Zimbabwean government. He visited me in Melbourne and told me the highest authority has invited me to work here for the next six months.'

The tall man smirked. 'That might be six months of hard labour.' Before Dan could respond, the man continued. 'I don't know this man, David Jones. Who is he? How can a white speak for the Zimbabwe government?'

'He's not a white man. He's a black African. Like you.'

The officer nodded to someone over Dan's shoulder. As he glanced behind him, two police officers stepped forward and took him by his arms. 'You are under arrest, Mr Scott,' one of them said. 'You're booked into the Hotel Chikurubi.'

Dan's heart sank. Chikurubi was not a hotel but a notorious prison, nineteen kilometres outside the Harare CBD. 'I need my things,' said Dan.

'We'll keep your passport here, Mr Scott,' said the customs officer. 'The police will take your other belongings with you to Chikurubi.'

'David Jones said he'd meet me here at the airport. He's probably waiting for me in the terminal.'

'There's no one waiting outside, Mr Scott. Everyone from the flight has already left, and there's nobody waiting for you.'

The police officers marched Dan from the airport terminal into the back of a waiting police van. He sat on the hard bench seats in the caged canopy as the van bumped along the potholed roads to the prison.

At Chikurubi, a warder showed him to a bare room with a desk and two upright wooden chairs and instructed him to wait. Time passed, and he wondered if they'd forgotten him. The shadows lengthened as the sun sank lower on the horizon. After an interminable wait, a prison officer instructed Dan to follow him.

After a quick toilet break, they walked out of the building and across the yard towards an unlit, long, low building. In the darkness, Dan could make out rows of cells full of prisoners. The prison officer stopped at a cupboard and pulled out a blanket, which he handed to Dan. At the end of the corridor, the officer unlocked a cell and motioned him to enter.

The cell was full of Africans lying on the concrete floor, all holding on to their blankets wrapped around them. The crowded cell was packed to overflowing. Darkness made it hard to find a vacant spot. An African hissed to attract his attention and cocked his head to one side, indicating a small space next to him.

'Thanks,' Dan mumbled.

The African didn't respond.

What troubled Dan was the lack of formality when he entered the prison. They didn't ask his name or get him to sign any papers. What if they just left him there? How would anyone know where he was? With insufficient room to lie down, he sat against the wall and closed his eyes, trying to sleep. But there was little chance of that between his racing thoughts and the uncomfortable, cold concrete floor.

It was a chilly night with the single blanket. The only other source of warmth was the heavy breathing of the sleeping prisoners. As the first light of dawn invaded the cell, Dan felt tired and dirty. A 'million miles' separated this place from the luxury he experienced at the airport hotel in Johannesburg.

Soon a warder came along shouting something in Shona. Everyone stood up, so Dan followed. As the prisoners filed out, and Dan approached the cell door, the warder stopped him. 'Not you! You must stay here.'

'OK, so something was happening. Perhaps they were going to process his paperwork?'

Two hours later, Dan was still waiting. He'd not eaten or drunk anything since the flight from Johannesburg. It was fortunate the overnight toilet bucket was still there for his convenience.

Laughter and loud voices speaking in English sounded down the corridor. 'There's one male here that might interest you,' someone said. 'He's quite docile and vaccinated, but I'm not sure if he's been microchipped. If you want him de-sexed, you'll have to arrange it yourself. If you take him, it'll save us having to put him down.' More raucous laughter.

'Mr Scott, here you are! I've been looking everywhere for you.' It was David Jones. 'Sorry, I was late at the airport. When I arrived, there was no sign of you. Then someone said you'd come here. Unfortunately, they couldn't release you last night. There was no one on duty with the authority to discharge you. Apparently, they couldn't free you until they completed the paperwork to admit you.'

'Thank goodness you found me. I worried I might be stuck in here indefinitely.'

'Well, I've completed all the paperwork, so let's get going.'

As they walked out of the administration building at the front of the prison, the warder called out, 'We hope you enjoyed your stay with us, Mr Scott. We look forward to your next visit.'

In the car, driving away from the prison, David Jones said, 'For goodness' sake, Dan! Why on earth did you bring that banned book with you? I needed to call in a few favours to get your release. Not everyone is aware of your mission here. Can't you be more conscious of the local sensitivities?'

'If the "very top" approved my coming here, what's the problem?'

'The "very top" will deny any connection with your visit. They must keep up appearances. Any misstep by you will only embarrass them. This business today was awkward for me. You've drawn the attention of customs, the police, and the prison authorities. We may laugh and joke together, but it doesn't mean we're all friends or on the same side.'

'OK, well, sorry about that. I'll be more careful.'

'I hope so. Now let's get to the hotel. You can freshen up, and then we'll go for a decent lunch and discuss the details of your mission.'

* * *

David Jones drove Dan to the Meikles Hotel. 'When you're ready, meet me here in the lobby. I'll wait for you in the bar.'

After the previous night's experience, the comfortable, large room delighted Dan. The hotel was reputed the best in Harare. He stood under the warm spray of the shower, soaping himself. What a relief to get clean again! He dried himself and brushed his teeth, and afterwards, he looked through his carry bag. Everything was there except his passport and the book. To his relief, his wallet was untouched.

He was starving, and lunch preoccupied his thoughts. When he got downstairs, he found David Jones relaxing in the lobby bar with a cold beer. He smiled at Dan. 'You look a lot better now. Not so much of an embarrassment anymore.' He waved a waiter over and ordered two beers.

Later, in the restaurant, a waiter showed them to a table near a window and handed them a menu each. Dan ordered a steak, and the thought of it got his salivary juices flowing.

'Tomorrow,' said David Jones, 'I'll take you to the office. You'll meet John, the person you'll be working with in your time here.'

'So, he runs a government department, does he?'

'No, he does jobs for the government. Jobs the government would rather not do for themselves.'

'But he works for the government, right?'

'No, he's a private operator. He works for both the government and other parties.'

'And you work for the government's diplomatic service?'

'No, I'm a free agent, doing deals the government would rather not do for themselves.'

'You mean deals like recruiting me?'

'That's right.'

'So I don't have any official capacity here?'

'Important people are aware you're here, but they won't admit to that.'

'What if I need help?'

'I'm all the help you're going to get. That's why I told you to be careful. Your presence here is welcome, provided you keep a low profile. You don't want to frighten off your sponsors.'

'David, you told me my job was to streamline the administration. That's why I thought it was an official government job. What exactly does this private operation do?'

'You can ask John tomorrow. He might give you some answers, but he's very secretive. You won't be concerned with the day-to-day field operations, so I'd recommend you stick to the administration and not ask too many questions. When he does government work, it could fall under national security or the Official Secrets Act.'

'By the way, David, customs took my passport. I understand them confiscating the book, but I need my passport.'

'OK, I'll look into it. I don't know why they'd want to hold on to your passport. Maybe they just forgot to give it back to you.'

'No, they said they'd keep it there, at customs.'

CHAPTER 5

Dan looked down at the morning traffic. Despite all the shortages and problems in Zimbabwe, Harare looked busier than ever. He'd been up early for a seven o'clock breakfast in the hotel dining room. Why must everything start so early in Zimbabwe? Office hours were eight to five, compared to Australia's nine to five. He had become accustomed to the latter in his time in Melbourne.

David Jones would pick him up soon and take him to the office where he'd work for the next six months. Dan dressed in a navy-blue suit, white shirt, and yellow tie. Black leather shoes and matching belt put the finishing touch on his appearance. He wasn't sure what the others in the office would wear. He noticed David Jones always dressed in a smart business suit. A professional first impression would stand him in good stead for the rest of his stay.

'Good morning, Dan.' It was David Jones. 'The car's parked right outside. Are you ready to go?'

In the car, Dan remembered his passport. 'When will I get it back, David? Customs said they'd hold on to it.'

'Don't worry, I'll make enquiries when I go to the airport this afternoon to meet someone.'

It was a short drive down Jason Moyo Avenue (Stanley Avenue) to Rotten Row, where the office stood amongst scattered large trees. A guard saluted David Jones as he passed through the gate and parked the car in the shade of a tree. The office was a converted, large, old house on a sizeable block surrounded by a storm mesh fence. The building was well maintained, with a charming appearance. It looked a nice place to work.

David Jones led Dan through the hallway with its stained-glass windows, past the double doors bisecting the wide passage, and down to the end where the passage turned left. He stopped at the first door. It was open, so he knocked on the doorframe.

'David, come in.'

David Jones entered the room, motioning Dan to follow him. 'Captain John, I'd like you to meet Dan Scott.'

Captain John dressed in an elegant light grey suit with a white shirt and a light blue tie. He wore a trimmed, military style moustache, and looked to be in his late fifties. He shook hands with Dan, who was glad he'd dressed for the occasion.

After the pleasantries, David Jones excused himself. 'Well, I must be going. I'll leave you two to get acquainted. I'll call you later, Dan. Tonight or tomorrow.'

Captain John turned to Dan. Is Dan short for Daniel?

'Yes.'

'Well, welcome to the COU, Dan.'

'Thank you. What work do you do here? What exactly is the COU? David didn't tell me too much. I thought it was a government department, but he said it's your private business.'

John laughed. 'Once upon a time, I also thought of it as a government department. Someone high up decided the COU was surplus to their requirements and closed our operation. There was an obvious demand for our services, so I reopened it as a private enterprise.'

'David calls you *Captain John*; that suggests you're in the army.'

'I was a captain in the army. When I joined civilian life, people continued to call me by that name, so it stuck.'

A knock on the doorframe interrupted them. 'Ah, Eunice, come and meet our latest recruit. Dan is doing consulting work for us for an unspecified period, though it will be at least six months.'

Eunice was a pretty lady, with a hint of plumpness. She shook hands with Dan and welcomed him to the COU. She handed Captain John a slim manila folder. 'Here's the updated Honey File, Sir.'

'Thank you, Eunice, I'll check it later.'

After she left the room, John rose and walked to a four-drawer filing cabinet and put the folder in the front suspension file. 'Eunice is my second in command. A very ambitious lady. Her office is just beyond the strongroom next door. And your office is next door in the passageway leading to the entrance. Come, I'll show you!'

Dan's spacious office was a little smaller than Captain John's and well furnished, with a large wooden desk and high-backed leather chair on castors. Dan remained puzzled as to the exact nature of his role. Captain John hadn't answered his question about that.

'Now, Dan, make yourself at home. Familiarise yourself with everything in your office, and at five o'clock this evening come to my office, and we'll share a scotch or two. Ambrose, the tea boy, will make you tea or coffee and will also take your lunch order. I'll be out today, so if you have any questions, you can ask Eunice.'

After Captain John left him alone in his office, Dan sat down in his plush chair. So comfortable. The windows looked onto scattered, large shady trees and smooth earth, baked hard over the years. No other plants grew there. He opened the desk drawers, which were mostly empty other than the top right-hand drawer, which contained neatly laid out stationery, including ballpoint pens, pencils, erasers, and paper. There was no sign of any computer. Not even in Captain John's office. On the desk sat an old-fashioned dial phone. In a ring folder, he found a confusing organisation chart.

Dan's office door looked straight onto the side of a large, floor to ceiling, built-in cupboard, so even with his door open, it afforded him some privacy. From the passageway, no one could see his desk.

A knock on the doorframe introduced a smiling face. 'Tea, Sah?'

'Thank you. You must be Ambrose?'

'Yes, Sah.' Ambrose was a cheery faced, thin, elderly man with grey hair. 'Welcome to Harare, Sah.'

'Thank you.'

'May I suggest toasted cheese sandwich for lunch, Sah?'

'Yes, you may. Do you order lunch for everybody?'

'Just for the captain, his girlfriend and you, Sah.'

'The captain's girlfriend?'

'Miss Eunice, Sah.'

'Oh!'

As often happens, the first day dragged. There was no set task to keep him occupied. He was relieved when five o'clock came, and Captain John popped his head around the corner and invited him to his office. Dan had familiarised himself with everything in his office, but what was his role?

Captain John took two crystal tumblers from the bookcase and ice cubes from the minibar behind him. He poured scotch over the ice and handed one glass to Dan. John hadn't asked him if he drank scotch or how he took it. He just assumed Dan liked it the same way as he did. John was right.

'So, John, before we were interrupted this morning, you were telling me what we do here. What is the precise nature of your business?'

John looked at the ceiling and exhaled. 'We're a multifaceted business. Our two major endeavours are consultancy and cleaning.'

'That's an odd combination. How does that work?'

'Well, our consultancy relates to our cleaning. When a company requires our services, we recommend the best solution to resolve their problems. Once a client agrees to our fees and method, we step in and clean up the mess. Often, the client lets us choose the method. That gets the best result because we are then free to adapt our methods in the face of changed circumstances.'

'So, do you clean factories and offices, or domestic properties?'

'No, no, we clean organisation charts.'

'Oh, you mean you specialise in outplacements.'

'Yes, that's the word I wanted. We're outplacement specialists.'

'I suppose in the present economic climate, many companies would want to downsize?'

'That is true, though we're busy even in good times.'

'There are no computers here. How do you manage your business?'

'Paper, all on paper. Our clients are sensitive about their downsizing plans and don't want their competitors to find out about them.'

'How do you manage without email?'

'Eunice handles the customers these days. She believes in the personal touch.'

'Have you considered the internet to keep you up to date with what's happening?'

'We don't want our details on the net. Not even our phone number or address. Our clients value our discretion. That's why they come to us. Everything in our business is by word of mouth and private.'

'John, what is my role here? David Jones said the ideas in my first book impressed the highest authority. I assume that included you. I've reread my first book, and it's all about a clandestine secret police unit and the methods they used to catch and dispose of activists and others. How can that help your outplacement business?'

'Your first book? Perhaps David got that wrong. Maybe it was the second book. It's not so much about the ideas in your book, but more about your obvious problem-solving skills. Already you've suggested getting on the internet as a source of information. Why don't you organise that, but only for you, me, and Eunice? No one else. And only as a source of information.'

'OK. I haven't yet met the rest of the staff.'

'You've met Cherry, the receptionist, who also does our books. Then there's me, Eunice and Ambrose. All the others are field workers. They've nothing to do with admin. I can't hold your hand and tell you what to do. Investigate our procedures and tell us how to improve our administration. Remember, you must keep our confidentiality and clear anything with me if you're not sure.'

A knock on the doorframe interrupted them, and Eunice walked into the room. 'Is there anything else you need me for this evening, Sir?'

'No, thank you, Eunice. You can go. Dan and I have things to discuss. We'll see you tomorrow morning.'

'Yes, Sir.'

Dan thought he caught a flash of anger in Eunice's eyes. An uneasy feeling coursed through him. He sensed he'd already made an enemy there. As Captain John's second in command, she might have expected to be invited to join them, and not dismissed like a junior secretary. Perhaps there was truth in old Ambrose's comment about her being John's girlfriend.

'John, what do the letters COU stand for?'

'Oh, it's just a leftover from the old army-controlled business they closed down. I haven't bothered with a new name. COU stands for Covert Operations Unit, though these days, I like to think of it as Consultancy and Outplacement Undertakings.'

After a second round of scotch, John said he needed to go home. He dropped Dan at the Meikles Hotel but said nothing about a lift in the morning. Dan had already decided he would walk to work each day. It would keep him fit and in closer touch with the city streets, which somehow always contributed to his novels.

Dan returned to his hotel room, stripped off, and stepped into the shower. It was a warm day. How could the night he'd spent in Chikurubi be so chilly? That cold, concrete cell floor sent a chill right through him. Perhaps his tiredness and hunger also contributed.

It occurred to Dan he'd got no closer to understanding Captain John's business, or his role within it. He didn't buy John's roundabout explanation covering consultancy, cleaning and outplacement. He'd been deliberately vague. David Jones hadn't given him any answers, either. Dan was more confused than ever about his job with the COU. If ever he'd encountered an example of *bullshit baffles brains*, this was it.

Only his own reason for coming to Zimbabwe was clear. He hoped to get more material and inspiration for his next novel.

Time for dinner. Perhaps another steak would hit the spot. Dan dressed in slacks and a sports jacket and headed for the hotel's restaurant. A waiter showed him to a table and took his order. While he waited for his meal, he looked at his cell phone to check on any messages. There was one, which he opened and read, and reread. The message said, 'Be warned. Your new friends are not your friends.'

Back in his room, Dan puzzled over the mysterious message. This was not how he hoped to start his stint in Zimbabwe. The message meant someone not allied to David Jones, Captain John, or the COU knew of his mission. He didn't want to be caught in a dispute between rival groups. That would be dangerous.

Which group did his 'new friends' support? Dan was aware of the dispute between the rival factions in the governing ZANU-PF party. Loyalties in Zimbabwe were split three ways. Emmerson Mnangagwa led the Lacoste faction made up of the old guard. Generation 40 were the *Young Turks*, allegedly backing Grace Mugabe to succeed her husband as president. Morgan Tsvangirai led the MDC opposition party. It was a toxic mix.

Dan opened the minibar, grabbed a beer, and flipped off the cap. He took a swig and slumped into the armchair by the window. Outside, it was already dark. Nightfall came fast in these parts. After the long, muggy day, he needed an ice-cold beer. The two scotches didn't quench his thirst. He wondered how his employer could afford this luxurious suite in the best hotel in Harare. The country was bankrupt, so his secret employer must be the government.

A knock on the door! Who might that be? David Jones, perhaps?

CHAPTER 6

DAN frowned and eased himself from the armchair to answer the door. He stared in surprise at the attractive young African woman who stood there with one hand resting on the doorframe. She dressed in black high heel shoes and stockings, a bright red miniskirt and waistcoat over a shiny black, plunging, long-sleeve blouse, revealing a scarlet bra. A tangle of curls framed a pretty face. Her figure and dress didn't need any explanation.

'Mr Scott?'

'Yes, what can I do for you?'

'It's more about what I can do for you, Mr Scott.'

'Who are you? What do you want?'

'My name is Nikita. Cupid's Bow sent me.'

'There must be a mistake. I never ordered a girl from Cupid's—'

The young woman brushed past Dan into the room. 'There's no mistake, Mr Scott.'

'Listen, Nikita, leave now, before I call hotel security.'

'Close the door, Mr Scott, before people see the company you keep.'

'Well, I wouldn't have to worry about that if you dressed properly. Fancy coming here dressed like that!'

'Never mind my outfit, Mr Scott. I'm here to warn you, you're in grave danger.'

Dan closed the door. 'Did you send me an email, saying my new friends were not really friends?'

'No, though a colleague in my group may have.'

'What group is that: Lacoste, G4o, MDC?'

'None of those. We're just a group of Zimbabweans who are working for democracy, justice, and the end of corruption in Zimbabwe.'

'Good luck with that! What do you mean, I'm "in grave danger"?'

'The question is, what are you doing here, Mr Scott?'

'An agent for the government invited me here for a six-month consultancy to improve his client's administration. They provide services to the government.'

'On your last visit, you were lucky to escape Zimbabwe. Didn't you think it dangerous, coming back here?'

'Yes, but David Jones said he represented the "very top," and the invitation came with their full support. So I took the risk.'

'Who is David Jones?'

'I thought he worked for the government. It turns out he's an independent agent.'

'An agent for whom? Did he give you any names?'

'No, he just said he represented "the very top".'

'We were concerned for your safety and hoped you'd change your mind about coming back here.'

'Aren't you being overdramatic?'

'You realise your books have caused a stir and are banned here?'

'Yes.'

'Well, have you wondered why they invited you back to Zimbabwe?'

Dan laughed. 'I've already said. I worked in the corporate world before, and they wanted me to reorganise their administration.'

'Or, perhaps, to jail you.'

'No, no, no! They put me in Chikurubi upon arrival, but it was a misunderstanding. They set me free the next morning.'

'So, why do they want you here? If they didn't plan to jail you, there may be some other ulterior motive. You need to be careful.'

'All right. Well, thanks for the warning.' Dan opened the door for Nikita.

'Mr Scott, if I leave too soon, both our reputations will suffer. The hotel staff will say you must be impotent or gay, or that I'm inadequate.'

'So what!'

Nikita spotted Dan's half-drunk beer. 'Drinking alone! I'll join you. A beer will be fine. In a glass please.' She sat down in a chair at the table, to emphasise she wasn't leaving.

Dan opened the minibar and took out a Zambezi and a glass. He flipped off the cap, and held the beer and glass out to her. She raised her eyebrows. He got the message and poured the beer before handing the glass to her.

'Thanks.'

'A pleasure,' said Dan with a touch of sarcasm. He sat down in the chair opposite her. For the first time, he noticed the sweet smelling perfume she wore. In other circumstances, she'd have been an alluring companion.

'This evening, you shared a scotch with Captain John in his office.'

'How did you learn about that? How did you know I was coming to Zimbabwe?'

'We have our sources.'

'Apparently!'

'Did he tell you about the COU?'

'Well, he said they do outplacements for clients who want to downsize.'

Nikita laughed. 'And you believed him?'

'He was a little vague.'

'These are dangerous people, Mr Scott. It's rumoured they're involved in abductions and disappearances. They say Captain John works for the highest bidder. That's why we worried about you.'

'You said "it's rumoured," so you don't have any proof? It all sounds a little fanciful. David Jones seems a respectable person. I can't imagine him being mixed up in something like that.'

'Don't be naïve, Mr Scott. You must take this seriously!'

'If Captain John and the COU are involved in abductions and disappearances, why don't the authorities shut them down?'

'They won't do that. The COU is a useful resource.'

'So, based on rumours, you went to all this trouble to warn me?'

'Yes, though that's not all. We need your help to get some information from Captain John's office.'

'What information?'

'You said we "don't have any proof." So that's where you come in. We need to see the contents of one of his files. If we stole the file, it would alert Captain John that someone was on to him. So, we'd like you to take this cell phone and photograph the contents.' Nikita held out an old cell phone.

Dan sat back in his chair, holding up the palms of both hands. 'No way! How would I manage that? One minute you're worried about my safety and the next you're trying to get me killed. If the COU's business is disappearances, I won't risk something like that. Besides, there'd be no opportunity to photograph any file's contents. There are too many people around.'

Nikita put the phone on the table. 'It's called the Honey File, and they keep it right at the front of the top drawer in the four-drawer filing cabinet in Captain John's office.'

That caught Dan's attention. The Honey File was the file Eunice gave Captain John that morning, and he saw where she put it. 'Anyway, what's so important about that file?'

'We can answer that question once you've photographed the contents.'

'Impossible! I can't. What if someone saw me?'

'Mr Scott, if their business is murder, why do you imagine they got you back here? Whatever their reasons, I'm sure you won't like them.'

'I don't want to get involved.'

'Too late! You already are involved. I'll leave this cell phone for you to take the photos. When you've done the job, I'll pick up the phone. Simple as that!'

'Don't bother. I won't do it.'

'Well anyway, I'll leave it for when you change your mind.'

'I won't change my mind. What makes you think I'll change my mind?'

'Just a hunch.'

'If it's that simple, why don't you get your source to photograph the file?'

'Our source doesn't have the access that you will have when sharing Captain John's scotch.'

'That was probably just a welcome drink. He might not invite me again.'

'Oh, he will. Captain John loves a scotch after work, and he'll enjoy chatting with you for an end of day debrief. Perhaps not every day, but often enough. Captain John craves intelligent company. He doesn't get that from his team of thugs.'

'What about Eunice, his second in command?'

'She has her uses. Sharing his scotch and intelligent conversation are not amongst them. Beware of her. Eunice is ambitious and likely to resent any attention Captain John pays you. If you keep his interest, evening drinks should become more frequent, and you will get the chance to take the photos.'

'Don't hold your breath.'

'Do you need a charger?'

'No, my charger will fit that phone. Why can't I use my phone? Why this one?'

'If you take the photos and somehow the phone falls into the wrong hands, they won't be able to trace it back to anyone.'

'Can't I just send you the photos? Why must you pick up the phone?'

'If you send the photos, they might trace them to me.'

'What number should I call when the photos are ready?'

'Don't call any number. I'll come around and pick up the phone.'

'How will you know I've taken them? '

'From time to time, I'll check in with you, but don't delay, because lives may depend on it.'

'I'm not promising anything.'

'An hour already! Time to go.'

'What if someone sees you coming here? That could put me in danger.'

'That's true. The quicker you take those photos, the less often I'll need to visit.'

'Oh, thanks a lot!'

'Thanks for the beer.'

Nikita opened the door and disappeared down the corridor.

Dan pondered her request. She put him on the spot by saying not to delay, 'because lives may depend on it.' Then she said she'd keep visiting until he gave her the photos. They both understood that meant more risk. Who was she? How could he trust her? Who did she really represent?

What if she worked for a rival group, and they were using him to get some commercial advantage? What if David Jones or Captain John were testing him? Dan wasn't sure what to do. The six-month consultancy suddenly looked a lot more complicated than he'd imagined.

David Jones seemed trustworthy until now, but Nikita put doubts in his mind. Even Captain John seemed all right. Yes, he'd been vague in answering his questions, but David warned him John was secretive.

The suspicions and fears Dan held before this trip now came to the surface. The Central Intelligence Organisation's (CIO's) reputation was well known. It was Zimbabwe's secret police. He didn't imagine the COU was similar or even worse.

The phone rang, startling Dan, interrupting his thoughts around Nikita's visit. Only a few minutes passed since she'd left. Who would ring so late? Was someone watching him to see who visited his room? He hesitated before picking up the phone.

CHAPTER 7

AT breakfast, David Jones chatted away with no idea of the suspicions swirling in Dan's mind. His late-night phone call to arrange breakfast with Dan in the hotel coincided with Nikita's departure. Was it a chance happening? Might they be working together? How could he trust anyone?

It didn't help that David didn't recover Dan's passport from customs at the airport. 'The customs said they've handed it over to the police. Don't worry, I'll get on to them as soon as I can. My meeting this morning is at the Rainbow Towers Hotel. I'll give you a lift. The COU office is on my way.'

After breakfast, Dan returned to his room to brush his teeth and grab his jacket. He was torn between taking the cell phone Nikita gave him and leaving it in his locked travel bag in the cupboard. Dan stood over the travel bag, undecided, and then grabbed the phone and snapped shut the bag's lock. He made sure Nikita's phone was on silent, before he slipped it into his trouser pocket and put his own cell phone into his jacket side-pocket.

A smiling David Jones waited for him in the lobby. Dan tried to interpret that smile, but without success. As on the previous day, David parked his car in front of the hotel. The morning sun threatened a warm day, and David tossed his jacket onto the back seat. Another day with no defined task to complete was a daunting prospect.

'I'm not yet clear what I should do in the office. Captain John says I need to decide for myself.'

'Why don't you examine the accounts? That way, you'll soon understand the nature of the business, and how you can assist us. Cherry will help you with that.'

Go through the accounts? That didn't sound too interesting, but Dan kept those thoughts to himself.

'Oh, by the way!' said David Jones, 'I almost forgot to tell you. Weekend after next, we're invited to an American embassy barbecue and cocktail party. You'll need to dress for that. It's not what we'd call a braai. They have chefs and waiters and all the luxuries of a top-class restaurant.'

'We got an invitation?'

'Well, I did. I'm allowed a guest. That's you.'

'Isn't there a Mrs Jones?'

'Yes, but she's not interested in socialising and small talk. Besides, you can never tell who else you might meet there.'

David Jones dropped Dan at the office gate and sped off to his meeting. The security guard on the gate saluted as Dan passed. He walked up the short flight of steps to the veranda, through the impressive, carved front door set between the colourful leadlight windows, and past Cherry's reception desk in the entrance hall.

'Good morning, Mr Scott,' she said when she saw him.

'Dan, please call me Dan. Good morning, Cherry. I'd like to go through the accounts today if that's convenient.'

'Yes, Sir. No problem.'

Ambrose gave him a cheerful smile as they passed in the passage. 'I will bring your tea, Sah.'

'Thank you, Ambrose. Is Captain John in?'

'Yes, Sah. In his office.'

Dan walked to John's office to say good morning before returning to his own desk. A steaming cup of tea waited for him. Good old Ambrose! Cherry came in carrying a set of foolscap sized books of accounts. 'Everything is here, Sir. Except wages. You can see those later in my office.'

'Thanks Cherry. Remember, you can call me Dan.'

'Yes, Sir.'

Dan looked at the books. All the usual ones were there. He flipped open the debtors' ledger and smiled at what he saw. The accounts had no names, only code numbers. It was straight out of his first novel. Nobody could identify the clients in this ledger. Captain John would have a list of names with code numbers filed somewhere secure.

The size of the transactions astounded Dan. Invoices of ten, twenty and thirty thousand U.S. dollars. And some were only fifty percent deposits. The COU made a lot of money. What services could they offer to warrant such high fees? Perhaps Nikita was right about their true purpose.

The general ledger showed low expenses, with salaries and wages, and travel being the biggest costs. Captain John and Eunice's salaries probably accounted for most of the former, as the earnings of the remaining staff members would be low, if in line with Zimbabwe's wage levels.

Dan poured over the books, familiarising himself with the COU's structure and operations. A knock on his doorframe signalled Ambrose with morning tea and biscuits. As he enjoyed his tea, Dan swivelled his chair to stare through the window. Despite the bare earth, the canopy of trees gave the garden an attractive appearance.

Suddenly, he sensed a presence behind him. It was Eunice. 'Cherry tells me you have the books of accounts. Is Captain John aware you are looking through them?'

'Yes, he is.'

Eunice grunted her disapproval and stalked out of the office. It was the second time Dan had cause for concern about her apparent resentment of his presence in the COU. He'd seen enough of the financial books for now, and he returned them to Cherry at the front desk. Next, he wanted to examine the wages, and Cherry showed him into her office behind reception.

Once again, Dan noticed with satisfaction the use of codes, with no names to identify the staff members. That also came straight out of his first novel. There was an enormous difference between the total wages paid and the amounts shown as salaries and wages in the general ledger. It confirmed his suspicion the bulk of the money went as salaries to Captain John and Eunice.

The afternoon soon passed, and at a little past five, Captain John popped into Dan's office to invite him for a drink. Perhaps Nikita was right about Captain John wanting an end of day debrief and intelligent conversation. Dan patted his pocket that held Nikita's phone. He didn't expect there'd be an opportunity to take photos of the Honey File's contents. Even if there were, he wasn't sure he'd take it.

Captain John was ready with the glasses and ice cubes when Dan entered his office. He took out the bottle of Aberfeldy twenty-one-year-old single malt and explained its origins and the history of the distillery that produced it. He extolled its virtues and was effusive about its nose, palate, and finish. John's knowledge of scotch whisky impressed Dan, who thought one whisky was much like any other.

'It's good of you to share your scotch with me, John, but I feel guilty about draining your whisky supplies. I couldn't replace these fine scotches you offer me.'

John laughed. 'Don't worry about that. I've accumulated a huge stock of the finest scotches and can always replenish my stocks. Tell me, how are you settling in?'

'I'm slowly getting familiar with the business and its administration.'

'I'll introduce you to Jonas Nyandoro, one of my team leaders. He's one of our best men in the field. You'll improve your understanding of the COU if you spend time with him. Hang on, I'll check if he's still here.'

John left his desk and walked out the door. Dan listened to his steps on the wooden floor of the passage leading to the large, open-plan office the field operators shared. He'd not seen the office but could make out the laughter and chatter of several male voices.

Dan turned in his chair and looked at the filing cabinet. The key was in the lock. Unbelievable! Already an opportunity to take the photos! If he heard John's footsteps going down the passage, he should be able to hear them returning. Dan jumped up and hurried to the filing cabinet. He carefully slid open the top drawer to avoid making any noise. There it was! The Honey File!

But was there time to photograph it? He peered into the manilla folder without removing it from the suspension file. Only a single sheet of paper! This would be easier than he imagined.

In his excitement, Dan focussed on the file, forgetting for a moment to listen out for Captain John's footsteps. Now he strained his ears to make sure John wasn't yet returning to his office. He cocked his head to listen. The faintest of creaks in the passageway? He wasn't sure. Better not take a chance! He closed the drawer and moved away from the filing cabinet. Before he'd taken even three steps, a harsh voice behind him rang out.

'What are you doing?' Eunice stood there with her eyes blazing. Dan thought she'd already left for the day.

'Nothing! Just waiting for Captain John!'

'You're waiting by walking around his office?'

'I wanted to view those certificates he has displayed on the wall.'

Eunice gave him a cold, hard stare. No mistaking the animosity in those eyes. She didn't even try to disguise her hostility.

Captain John walked into the room. 'No luck, Dan. He's already gone home. Eunice! You're still here! I thought you left ages ago?'

'I came back to pick up my phone.'

'All right, see you tomorrow.'

As she left the room, Eunice flashed Dan a knowing look. What did it mean? A slight chill ran through him.

After another scotch, John dropped Dan back at the hotel. Dan watched the tail lights of the silver Mercedes disappear down the street into the distance. John and his associates certainly lived the good life!

After a shower and dinner in the restaurant, Dan returned to his room. There was a lot on his mind. He worried about Eunice. When did she enter the room? Had she seen him at the filing cabinet? Did she see him slide the top drawer closed? Or did she come in when he'd moved one, two or three steps from the filing cabinet, as he tried to distance himself from it? They were all troubling questions.

Dan realised he needed to be more careful. It seemed too easy. Too good to be true. He should have known taking the photos would not be straightforward. In his hurry to get the job done, he'd been careless. Perhaps, he should try to improve his relationship with John's unfriendly assistant. But if he tried to do that, would it make him look guilty and raise her suspicions further?

His thoughts swirled round and round and only stopped when the buzz of his own cell phone interrupted.

'Mr Scott, this is Inspector Michael Mzamane of the South African Police. I took your statement at the Intercontinental Airport Hotel in Johannesburg.'

'Oh, yes, Inspector.'

'We found the man the car hit when he and his accomplice tried to mug you. His body was in a culvert near the hotel. He must have crawled away and died, or perhaps his companion dragged him there.'

'Thank you for letting me know, Inspector.'

'The man was a Zimbabwean. He and his companion are known enforcers in the Zimbabwean diaspora. The second man has gone into hiding.'

'I see! Well, let's hope you find him, Inspector.'

'What's of concern, Mr Scott, is the dead man had a photograph of you in his pocket. It looks like a page torn out of a book.'

'Yes, all my books have photos of me.'

'That suggests to us the mugging was a professional hit.'

Dan was dumbfounded. 'A professional hit?'

'The question you must answer, Mr Scott, is who knew of your travel arrangements, the date and time of your arrival, and your hotel booking?'

'One or two, I'm aware of, but there could be others. I didn't make the bookings.'

'Sometimes, the criminals return to Zimbabwe to let things cool off. If we can't find the dead man's accomplice in Johannesburg, keep an eye out for him in Harare. I'll let you know of any developments.'

'Thank you, Inspector, and thanks for the warning.'

What a day! The brush with Eunice was bad enough. Now, he'd been warned of a price on his head. Dan considered the possibilities. David Jones knew his itinerary, and presumably, so did Captain John. Perhaps Eunice also knew, or even someone at the Zimbabwean embassy in Canberra?

CHAPTER 8

INSPECTOR Michael Mzamane's unwelcome phone call came late on Friday evening, so Dan had the weekend to consider his warning. Not the start he expected to his six-month stint in Zimbabwe. David Jones and Captain John had been most welcoming. That applied to everyone except Eunice. He couldn't imagine her setting up the Johannesburg hit without Captain John's knowledge.

Saturday dawned a beautiful morning. Sunny, though not too hot. Dan was at a loose end. Neither David Jones nor Captain John made any arrangement to see him, so he'd have to make his own entertainment. He set out for a morning walk and a coffee to reacquaint himself with Harare. What would he do in the afternoon?

After a light lunch in The Explorer's Bar, Dan worked on the outline of his next novel. It was the main reason he'd come to Zimbabwe. His deluxe room overlooking Africa Unity Square, once known as Cecil Square, included a workspace with internet access.

No good! With Inspector Mzamane's warning on his mind, he struggled to concentrate. Should he challenge David Jones about it, or would that be foolhardy? If David Jones or Captain John were behind the hit, it might encourage them to bring on another try, sooner rather than later. And besides, he still didn't have his passport. He'd not go anywhere without that.

A shower followed by an early dinner in the hotel's restaurant sounded like the best choice. Dan stood under the warm spray, letting the water flow over him. Heaven on earth, but the hotel sign requested guests to have regard for the water shortage. He'd feel guilty if he didn't comply.

How long would he be able to stay in this beautiful hotel? David Jones said nothing about it, and Dan assumed it to be a temporary arrangement until he found something else. A flat in the Avenues, perhaps.

Six o'clock. The restaurant would be open for dinner, and Dan was hungry. The smiling waiter showed him to a table by the window. Outside it was getting dusk, and people walked to their various Saturday night engagements. Others returned home after work or from a day at their vending stalls. Dan found it interesting to watch people. Where'd they been? Where were they going? Each person was on their own mission, and everyone else was oblivious to it.

Another steak. Was he eating too much red meat? In Zimbabwe, he found them hard to resist. It was the hotel's fault. Their chef did too good a job cooking them. Dan also enjoyed fish and seafood, though he wouldn't find anything to match the seafood in Melbourne. So, steak, it must be.

When eating alone, there's little else to do other than eat, and it meant the meal finished quicker than when eating in company. Now, even the passing crowd thinned out, so that distraction didn't much help. Still early evening, the restaurant was not yet busy.

A slim, young-looking African man ate alone at another table. Dan found it comforting he wasn't the only person in the restaurant eating alone. The young African man dressed in a light grey business suit, and Dan began his musings. Why was he here, alone? What did he do for a living?

The waiter brought the dinner invoice, and Dan signed it with his signature and room number as he finished his coffee. He left the restaurant and descended the stairs to the lobby and headed for The Explorer's Bar. In contrast to the quiet of the restaurant, here it was busy. Noisy, chatty groups occupied all the tables. Tall wicker chairs lined the bar, and three in the corner stood vacant.

Dan most often drank cold beer, but his after-work drinks with Captain John gave him a taste for scotch on the rocks. He looked at the selection on the shelf and ordered a fifteen-year-old Glenfiddich single malt.

'That one's on me,' said a voice over his shoulder.

It was the young man who'd been eating alone in the hotel restaurant.

'Thank you. To what do I owe the pleasure?'

'To being alone on a beautiful evening.'

'Yes, I also love these balmy evenings.'

'Daniel Moyo. Pleased to meet you Mr...?'

'Daniel Scott. My friends call me Dan.'

'Well, Dan it is, then.'

'Are you here on business, Daniel?'

'No, I live here. I have a legal practice here in Harare. My wife and son are visiting relatives, so I thought I'd treat myself to a dinner and a night out. I'm not good at cooking for myself. And what do you do?'

'I'm here on a six-month business consultancy, but most of the time I'm a novelist. Part of the reason behind my visit is to get inspiration for my next book.'

'That's an interesting coincidence. Are you familiar with Ian Sanders, the writer?'

'Of course. He's better known than I am.'

'He's a friend of mine. I met him in a bar at the Monomotapa Hotel a few years ago. He was also here to work on his novel. His first one, I believe.'

'Really? I've never met him.'

'He lives in Gaborone in Botswana. If you're heading down that way, I'll give you his phone number. Just tell him I suggested you meet him. He told me how you writers like to compare notes.'

'That'd be great! Thanks.'

'Are you married, Dan?'

'No, not yet.'

'Well, why don't I show you some of Harare's night life?'

* * *

Dan jumped into the passenger seat of Daniel's white Range Rover Evoque.

'A beautiful car, Daniel.'

'Yes, I did my training as a lawyer in the UK, and now I'm biased towards everything British.'

As they drove out of the city centre along the dimly lit streets of the suburbs, a worrying thought occurred to Dan. Daniel Moyo approached him in the bar at the hotel. Was it by chance, or a setup? He knew next to nothing about him. Inspector Mzamane warned him to be careful. Now here he accompanied a person he'd just met, heading to an unknown location.

Dan wasn't too familiar with many of the suburbs in Harare. Daniel might be driving him into a trap. Too late to back out now. He didn't have a plausible excuse, and if Daniel was genuine, he might end up looking foolish.

'You've gone quiet, Dan.'

'No, no. I'm trying to work out where we are.'

Daniel didn't respond, and it only made Dan more apprehensive. A short distance further on, Daniel turned the car into a property with a sizeable parking area for about twenty cars. Luxury vehicles of all makes and types occupied several of the spaces.

'Here we are, Dan. This is an exclusive nightspot where professional folk come for a quiet evening. You know, doctors, lawyers, accountants, etcetera.'

Judging from the thumping base of a live band, it didn't sound like the place for a quiet evening. Dan reasoned it to be an unlikely place for a professional hit. Daniel led him into the dim lounge with a small dance floor and a stage for the band. The room was busy, though not crowded.

'They only allow enough people to fill the lounge chairs. They don't want patrons to have to stand. As my guest, you cannot pay for anything, so this evening is on me.'

Dan surveyed the room. All the patrons were men, while several scantily clad young waitresses served the tables. One was already approaching to take their order.

As they enjoyed their scotches, Dan counted the guests and waitresses. 'There're about forty customers and fifteen waitresses.'

'They're not all waitresses, Dan. A few are dancers. Part of their job is to make the patrons comfortable. If one of them catches your eye, or you catch their eye, they'll join you for a chat and a drink.'

'Are they prostitutes?'

'Not officially, though I'm sure they'd consider a generous offer from an attractive male. I've never seen a white here before, so be prepared for extra attention.'

Once again, Dan's suspicions were raised. Might this be a honey trap? He didn't want to be paranoid, but he was on his guard. A further dimming of the lights interrupted his thoughts. A spotlight lit the centre of the dancefloor, and an attractive young African woman stepped into the beam.

The music started, and she gyrated with an energetic athleticism. Gradually, the music slowed, and her gyrations transformed into a seductive sway. She shed her clothing in an unhurried manner, focussing everyone's attention on the dance rather than the striptease. As her act approached its conclusion, she stood almost naked.

Her milk chocolate coloured body looked perfect. Like the bodies one sees in glossy fashion magazines. Dan realised he wasn't breathing. How long had he been holding his breath? He didn't even realise he was doing it. 'Wow, she's amazing! What a beautiful girl!'

'Would you like to meet her?'

'No, I don't think …'

Too late! Daniel had already beckoned her over. The girl wrapped a colourful sarong around herself as she approached.

'Rita, this handsome guy is my friend, Dan. He's a famous Australian writer.'

'Pleased to meet you, Dan,' said Rita, holding out her hand.

Dan stood up and took her cool hand to shake. Up close, her young skin looked as flawless as when she stood in the spotlight's beam on the dance floor. A young, natural beauty with no sign of makeup.

'Ah, a gentleman, Dan,' she said. 'Many men come here, but few gentlemen.'

'Thanks, won't you join us?'

Rita took an armchair at the low table, and Daniel ordered a soda water for her. Another dancer came onto the dance floor, and Daniel ordered another round of scotches for Dan and himself. Dan barely noticed the new dancer as he and Rita tried to assess one another.

'So, Dan, have you come here to meet girls?'

Rita's direct question surprised him. 'No, I came with Daniel. He didn't tell me where we were going.'

'Did you like my dance?'

'Yes, very much.'

'Would you like me to give you a private lap dance?'

As Dan scrambled for a response, a passing waitress spoke to Rita in Shona.

'I must get back to work,' said Rita. 'I finish at midnight. Will you wait for me?'

'I can't tonight,' said Dan. 'Perhaps, another time.'

'Yes, another time. Please don't forget.'

Dan watched the gorgeous young woman walk away. How could he forget someone like that? He wasn't naïve and knew clubs paid their hostesses to boost men's egos. That was their job. Relationships with bar or lounge hostesses seldom ended well.

After Rita departed, a steady stream of waitresses stopped for a brief chat, but Daniel soon waved them away. He looked at his watch. 'Time to go, my friend.'

Dan cast around for Rita as he left the lounge, but he couldn't see her.

'Did you have a fun time, Dan?'

'I did. Do you come here often?'

'Not often, though I've met most of the girls.'

'Has Rita worked here long?'

'A few months. She's got a three-year-old daughter. This job will pay for the child's upkeep and schooling.'

'Wow! With that figure, I'd never have imagined she'd borne a child.'

Daniel dropped Dan back at the hotel and gave him his business card. 'Call me if you want Ian Sanders' phone number.'

'I will, and thanks for the evening. It was great.'

Standing outside the hotel, Dan watched Daniel's Range Rover turn right and disappear around the corner into Second Street. He'd enjoyed the evening, but why did Daniel take it upon himself to entertain him? And what about Rita? Now, he'd have two more pieces in the equation to consider.

* * *

Sunday was a lazy day, with Dan again at a loose end. He walked in the city before lunch and again in the late afternoon. The city, busy with people everywhere. Everyone appeared to have somewhere to go.

Dan suddenly felt lonely, with no real friends and no one to call for company. After dinner, he retreated to The Explorer's Bar. Unlike Saturday night, no one approached him for a chat. Perhaps he should have shown more interest in Rita's offer. At least he wouldn't have been alone, though she'd most likely be working or looking after her child.

Between Inspector Mzamane's warning and the unexpected Saturday night with Daniel Moyo, he struggled to figure out what to believe. Somehow, he needed to check out Daniel's bona fides.

* * *

Monday morning, Dan's first chance to walk to the office. A bright morning, with the comfortable temperature so common at this time of year. Now, he'd familiarise himself with his route to work and see things he'd missed on his rides with David Jones. Several passers-by greeted him with cheerful smiles. This was the Zimbabwe he loved.

In the office, Cherry and Ambrose greeted him with broad smiles as he walked through the front door. Dan settled at his desk as Ambrose brought in the welcome morning cup of tea. With Captain John and

Eunice both out on COU business, he'd follow up on Daniel while he had the chance.

He took the business card out of his jacket's breast pocket and looked at it. There he saw the landline and cell phone numbers, and the business name. He'd already checked the business's landline number online, so that would be authentic, but there was no cell phone number online. Dan rang the landline. 'Good morning. Daniel Moyo and Associates.' The young woman's voice sounded professional.

'Good morning, may I please speak to Daniel Moyo?'

'I'm sorry, Sir. Mr Moyo is in Johannesburg on business.'

'Oh, when did he leave?'

'On Friday.'

'Are you sure? I thought I saw him here in Harare on Saturday night.'

'Well, he left here on Friday at lunchtime, saying he was going to Johannesburg. Perhaps he changed his mind and left on Sunday.'

'Could you please confirm his cell phone number?'

'I'm sorry, Sir, we can't give out his personal number.'

'I've got his business card with his cell phone number on it.'

'Well, ring him on that number, Sir.' The woman's voice sounded cool.

Dan guessed his questions made her uneasy, and he was unlikely to get any further information from her. 'All right, thank you. When is Mr Moyo due back?'

'At the end of the week, Sir.'

'OK. Thank you. Goodbye.' Dan ended the call. He cursed himself. He should have taken more time to prepare his questions. In retrospect, he saw how his line of questioning might have raised the young woman's suspicions. In Zimbabwe, the wrong alliances or political leaning could have dire consequences for certain people. Dan didn't know where Daniel stood on these matters.

Damn! All he wanted was to confirm Daniel's identity. If the Daniel Moyo he met was an impostor, he might have printed the business card with his own cell phone number, so phoning it would prove nothing.

Who were Daniel and Rita? What part might David Jones and Captain John have played in the 'professional hit,' as Inspector Mzamane described it? Dan was becoming paranoid after what had happened in Johannesburg.

CHAPTER 9

THE week passed quickly. Dan busied himself with setting up the COU's small computer network. Neither Captain John nor Eunice attended the office on Monday and Tuesday. John was out for the week, but Eunice returned on Wednesday. Her initial antagonism towards Dan mellowed a little when she discovered he was installing a computer for her.

Jonas Nyandoro was out of the office. Captain John suggested Dan should meet him. Although he would be back on Friday, Dan thought it best to wait for John to introduce them.

With all the senior staff members away, a relaxed atmosphere pervaded the office. In the passageway, Dan bumped into the operatives, who spent most of their time locked in the open plan office next door to Eunice. The men clearly relished their moment of freedom. They seemed as curious about Dan as he was about them. One of them warned him to say nothing about meeting them, because the boss, Captain John, wouldn't like it.

Dan was in and out of Captain John's office all week, setting up the computer. The locked four-drawer filing cabinet gave him no opportunity to photograph the Honey File. He tested Captain John's desk drawers, hoping to find the keys to the filing cabinet. They, too, were locked. Oh well! One less thing to worry about this week.

Late on Friday afternoon, Dan received a phone call from David Jones. 'Don't forget, we have the barbecue with the U.S. embassy people tomorrow night.'

'No, I hadn't forgotten, though when I didn't hear from you all week, I thought you may have.'

'I'll pick you up at a quarter to six tomorrow evening.'

After dinner in the hotel, Dan visited The Explorer's Bar. He kept a lookout for Daniel Moyo, but there was no sign of him. The visit to the live music lounge remained the highlight of his stay in Zimbabwe, and Dan hoped a repeat might be possible. First, he needed to check the man was genuine. He'd try to contact Daniel on Monday.

* * *

Dan spent most of Saturday working on his novel. During the week, he spent the evenings in the Explorers' Bar in the hotel's lobby. As a result, he'd not made much progress with his novel. Still, he told himself, he'd plenty of time for that.

At five, Dan took a shower and got ready for the evening. David said, "dress was smart casual," because the embassy barbecues resembled cocktail parties. Dan chose black trousers and shoes and an open-neck black shirt. They went well with his tan jacket. Satisfied with his image in the full-length mirror, he caught the lift down to the lobby.

The Explorer's Bar bustled with after-work drinkers, but he resisted the urge to join them. David Jones would be there soon, so Dan contented himself watching the patrons enjoying their end of week celebration.

'Ready?' It was David Jones.

'Yep.'

'I've double parked out front, so let's go before someone gets overexcited about being boxed-in.'

As they drove, Dan remembered his passport. 'Did you talk to your contact in the police about my passport?'

The question seemed to catch David by surprise. 'Ur, yes. The police say they haven't got your passport. The customs are mistaken.'

'I can't be without my passport. I need it.'

'Don't worry, I'll try customs again. I'll speak to the head guy at the airport. It must be in a drawer somewhere.'

'Jeez, I hope so.'

They passed through suburbs with elegant houses and large trees lining the road. After a fifteen-minute drive, David turned right onto a side-road. One block down, he turned right again, and then parked his car in the lane outside an extensive property with mid-sized trees and a sprawling bungalow.

Several other cars parked there, and Dan noted the trees full of twinkling lights, providing a fairy-tale atmosphere. As they entered the garden, he saw people standing amongst the trees. The women dressed in colourful evening dresses and the men in slacks, jackets, and open-neck shirts.

On one side, two Africans dressed in white uniforms with tall chef's hats prepared the barbecue fires. On the other side, a platform with musical instruments stood ready for the band. In between, a temporary wooden dance floor signalled the entertainment to come.

A waiter in a white uniform and gloves offered them drinks from a tray. Dan and David both chose beers. Speakers in the trees played music from an Eagles album Dan recognised.

'Come, I'll introduce you to the guys.' David led Dan to greet the senior embassy men and their wives. They were younger than he expected. Not like the tough, old characters depicted in many American movies.

More people arrived at the barbecue and soon, quite a crowd developed. The aroma of sizzling steaks, sausages, and onions wafted in the air. Soon, a queue of hungry guests lined up at the trellis tables, waiting to be served by the chefs.

Under the trees, beyond the dance floor, several small tables with chairs stood waiting for the diners to eat in comfort. Flickering candles in glass chimneys graced each table, adding to the atmosphere. David said it would be nothing like a traditional African braai.

For Dan, it was an eye-opener. 'This is the life!'

'The embassy holds these evenings two or three times a year. Isn't it wonderful?'

'How do you get invitations to these occasions, David?'

'I know lots of people and have done deals for them. It keeps me in touch with my clientele. In Zimbabwe, even the Americans sometimes struggle to get what they need. So, when that happens, I'm their man. If I can't help them, no one can.'

'How does your business tie in with the COU?'

'They're separate businesses. Occasionally they overlap, though not too often.'

'David, if you know everybody, can you tell me about that woman in the cream-coloured evening dress?'

David followed Dan's eyes. 'Oh! You have good taste. That's Eva Chirau, Colonel Victor Chirau's wife. She's a lovely lady, yes? Captain John has always lusted after her, but she's faithful to her husband.'

'Yes, she's a lovely lady. I wouldn't blame Captain John for fancying her.' Eva Chirau was tall and slim, and cut an eye-catching figure in any group.

'That's the husband there, the big guy in the cream jacket.' Victor Chirau towered over the other men. Even dressed in a suit, his athletic frame was apparent.

'They're a handsome couple.'

'Do you want to meet them?'

They strolled over to the couple. 'Victor, Eva, I'd like to introduce you to my friend, Dan Scott, the famous Australian novelist. You may have heard of him when our censors banned his books last year.'

'Hello, Isaac. Yes, I remember reading about it. Pleased to meet you, Mr Scott. This is my wife, Eva.' They all shook hands. Eva's eyes held Dan's for a moment too long. With her high cheekbones, slim nose and even features, she was quite beautiful. Her hair was pulled back tight in a neat bun.

'David exaggerates when he says I'm famous,' was all he mumbled. After that, he struggled to make further conversation, and seemed dumbstruck. Perfect timing! The live band came to the rescue. 'Dan, do you dance?' Victor enquired. 'Eva loves to ballroom. I'm not much good at it. Would you like to dance with her?'

'It would be my pleasure.' Dan and Eva moved to the dance floor to join the slow foxtrot to the strains of *Summer Wind*, one of his favourite songs. Dancing under the stars with the lovely Eva was heaven.

'Are you here on holiday, Mr Scott?'

'Please call me Dan. No, I'm here on a six-month management consultancy.'

'Will you visit the game reserves and the Victoria Falls while you are here?'

'Yes, if I get the chance.'

'And would you take photos?'

'I never brought a camera with me.'

'If you have a cell phone, you might use that.' Eva held his gaze until he blinked.

'Um, yes. I suppose so.'

After half a dozen tunes, the band took a rest, and Dan led Eva from the dance floor back to her husband.

Victor smiled as they approached. 'Enjoyed the dance, My Dear?'

'Yes, and Dan is an excellent dancer.'

'You two had a good understanding. It looked like you danced together before.'

'Yes, we danced together well.'

'We'll be saying goodnight,' said Victor, shaking hands with Dan and David. 'I've got an early start in the morning.'

Eva smiled. 'Thank you for the dance, Dan. I enjoyed it.'

Dan watched the couple walk over to the host and thank him for the evening, before walking away towards the gate. He couldn't help feeling disappointed as they left. Something about her made him want more. More of her and her company.

Around eleven, David and Dan thanked their host for the pleasant evening and headed back to the car. Dan looked at David. 'Isaac? Really?'

'When I was a kid, people called me Isaac. These days, people know me as David Jones. Strange though, Victor getting you to dance with his wife. He said he didn't dance well, but I've seen him dance. He's an excellent dancer. What did she say to you?'

'Nothing much. She asked if I'd visit the tourist spots and take photos.'

Back at the hotel, lying in bed, Dan couldn't sleep. He remembered the way Eva looked at him. Surely that look was a come-on? He didn't believe she fancied him; how could she? Her husband was a handsome man, tall and athletic, and admired by all.

Dan remembered his arm around Eva's waist, so firm and toned. He turned his pillow over and thumped it. He couldn't get her out of his mind. A restless night lay ahead.

Still awake at three in the morning. Apart from the lovely Rita, he'd not thought about women up till now. David said Captain John lusted after Eva. He wasn't the only one.

* * *

Dan woke early around seven, refreshed, with Eva, the first thing on his mind. She was like a dream. Now he felt motivated to progress his book. He'd have an early Sunday breakfast and a quick walk. Then he'd spend the day working on his novel.

As usual, things didn't go according to plan. He found it hard to concentrate and ended up going downstairs for a mid-morning coffee. There, he chatted to a South African tourist until lunch.

The afternoon was a little more successful as regards working on his book. In the evening, The Explorer's Bar exerted its magnetic pull. The bartender proved a pleasant companion for a chat. Dan thought of it as research for his book, but he was conscious he was drinking too much. He hardly touched a drop at home in Melbourne where he had friends and family to distract him. What he needed was company. Someone whose attractions proved stronger than those of the Explorers' Bar.

There were so many questions swirling in his mind, he was losing track. He needed to list them. Nikita's visit on his first night in the hotel. Inspector Mzamane's phone call and everything that entailed. The unexpected evening with Daniel Moyo, and now, the memorable encounter with the alluring Eva and Victor.

Something just didn't fit. He sensed the pressure building. He needed to be prepared for any eventuality. What might happen? Where would it occur? Where was his passport? Could he trust any of his newfound friends?

There were warning signs everywhere, but maybe he was making too much of them. It wasn't like him to be paranoid. He'd been in more threatening situations before, but the drip, drip of his present visit was unnerving. The twists and turns of the last couple of weeks were getting to him.

Somehow, he'd have to deal with his concerns. One at a time. Tomorrow, he'd make a start with Daniel Moyo. First cab off the rank.

CHAPTER 10

MONDAY morning. Everyone was back in the office, friendly and cheerful. To Dan's relief, even Eunice seemed friendlier. He wouldn't trust her, even though she appeared a little less intent on trapping him with something to report back to Captain John.

John and Eunice were both pleased with the office's computer network that Dan installed. After a quick chat with John, Dan returned to his office to contact Daniel Moyo. He picked up the phone and dialled the number just as a figure entered, giving him a little start. He relaxed when he saw it was Ambrose, with his morning cup of tea.

'Good morning. Daniel Moyo and Associates. How may I help you?'

Dan recognised the secretary's voice. 'May I please speak to Mr Moyo? My name is Dan Scott.'

'One moment, please.'

'Dan, how are you doing? I trust you had a pleasant weekend?'

'Yes, thanks, Daniel, a great weekend. I'm calling about Ian Sanders' phone number in Botswana.'

'Why don't I drop by for a drink at the hotel this evening, and I'll give you the number? Say around six?'

'Great! I'll look forward to it.' Dan put the phone back in its cradle. So, Daniel Moyo seemed genuine. That was a relief. It meant Rita was also genuine.

A knock on the door and Captain John entered. 'I've brought Jonas Nyandoro to meet you.'

Jonas shook Dan's hand in an energetic pumping motion. He was a tall wiry man with receding hair. His pleasant features boasted white, even teeth, and a smile that suggested a mischievous sense of humour. A friendly manner coupled with an enthusiastic mode of speech showed why he was a leader amongst Captain John's operatives.

'Dan,' said Captain John, 'I mentioned it would be useful for you to work with Jonas. On Wednesday, he's going to Johannesburg to meet one of our contacts. Go along and see how he operates. It will only be one night. Two at the most.'

'I've not yet got my passport back from customs. David Jones hasn't been able to find it.'

'Don't worry. We'll get you a Zimbabwean passport for the trip. You were born here, weren't you?'

'Yes, but I haven't kept up my citizenship.'

'That's OK. We'll handle it. See to that please, Jonas.'

'Yes, Sir.'

A few minutes after Captain John and Jonas left, Jonas returned with a camera to take Dan's photo for the passport. 'It'll be ready by tomorrow afternoon.'

Dan wondered about the Johannesburg trip. His last visit didn't encourage him to return. Not so soon, anyway. Could this be another setup? If David Jones or Captain John didn't arrange the failed hit, who might have? He believed one of them must have known something about it, yet they both seemed genuinely friendly towards him.

Dare he raise the issue with Daniel, but if he wasn't involved with the COU, how could he help? At five, Dan excused himself and walked back to the hotel to meet Daniel. He looked forward to seeing him again.

Dead on six, Daniel walked into The Explorer's Bar where Dan waited. 'When you phoned me this morning, I thought you were after Rita's number. If you want to see her again, we must return to the Lounge Club. Anyway, here's Ian Sanders' number. When are you going to Botswana?'

'I haven't any concrete plans at present, but once I get my passport back from customs, I'll be able to think about it.' Dan didn't say the real reason he contacted Daniel was to decide if he should keep him on his list of concerns.

'How'd your weekend go?'

'Great! I was invited to a barbecue at one of the American embassy houses.'

'How did you manage that?'

'Oh, you know, contacts! They introduced me to Colonel Victor Chirau and his wife Eva. Have you heard of him?'

'Yes, I have. The Americans like him, though it's rumoured he won't go any higher in the military.'

'Why not?'

'Chirau is not a ZANU man. He is anti-corruption and has a western view of democracy and is against Mugabe's patronage system of government.'

'I got my invitation to the barbecue through David Jones.'

'Is he with the American embassy?'

'No, he's an agent who does deals for the U.S. embassy, among others. Sometimes he goes by the name of Isaac. I'm not sure if he uses any other surname. He's the person who got me the job at the COU.'

'I've never heard of him. What is the COU?'

'It's an outplacement agency. You know, when companies want to downsize their senior employees.'

'They must have done well in Zimbabwe, with so many senior employees losing their jobs. The unemployment here is massive. I wouldn't have imagined outplacement services were still in demand?'

'Maybe turnover in senior roles keeps them busy.'

'You work there. Don't you know?'

'I've only been there a couple of weeks. And I'm not involved in their day-to-day operations.'

'Next time my wife visits her family, I'll call you. I'm sure Rita would like to catch up with you.'

'Yeh, sure.'

* * *

On Wednesday morning, Dan found himself with Jonas Nyandoro in the immigration queue at Harare International Airport. He was a little uneasy as he held his boarding pass and new Zimbabwe passport. The issue date in the passport was eighteen months earlier. An obvious fake, but to Dan, it looked genuine enough. What would Zimbabwe and South African immigration make of it?

Zimbabwe immigration must have thought it was fine because soon he and Jonas passed through to the boarding gate for the quarter to nine SA Airlink flight to Johannesburg. Within a few minutes, the loudspeaker announced the flight. They showed their passes and walked across the apron and up the stairs into the plane. After stowing their carry-on luggage in the overhead lockers, they settled back to watch the other passengers come on board.

Jonas kept up his enthusiastic, often humorous chatter. Dan found him good company as he teased and flirted with the air hostesses, but he remained someone to be taken seriously. One of those people everyone likes and follows. A natural leader.

Dan's last visit to Johannesburg's OR Tambo International Airport stuck in his mind.

'What are we doing in Johannesburg, Jonas?'

'We're meeting with Absalom Muzenda, the prominent economist. He's in the diaspora in Johannesburg. Zimbabwe needs people like him to help rebuild the economy, so our job is to convince him to return to Harare. We're meeting him for dinner tonight.'

'Why do we have to convince him?'

'He's got it into his head that he'd be in danger returning to Zimbabwe, so we need to reassure him he'd be most welcome and safe.'

'Why does he think he's in danger?'

'He criticised several economic measures in the country. The guys who make those economic decisions are sensitive. They take the criticism personally. One or two made threatening comments, so Absalom made a run for it. Really, there's no reason for him to worry.'

To Dan's relief, the South African immigration stamped his passport, and they soon passed through customs to the Gautrain. They took the airport train to Johannesburg, heading for Park Station at the end of the line. There they caught a taxi to Berea.

'What hotel are we staying in tonight, Jonas?'

'We're staying in an apartment in Berea, near to the restaurant where we are meeting Absalom this evening.'

The taxi made its way through Hillbrow, an ageing, high-rise suburb with neglected apartments and commercial properties at ground level. Soon they passed into neighbouring Berea, an area almost entirely composed of high-rise residential apartments. A few looked well maintained. Others were rundown. Rubbish accumulated in huge piles on several street corners. There was little sign of rubbish collection by the municipal authorities.

The taxi stopped on Lily Avenue, just around the corner from Abel Road.

'Here we are,' said Jonas.

Dan was aghast. 'We're staying in this wrecked building?'

'Don't worry, it's not as bad as it looks.' It was. The lift didn't work, so they took the stairs to the eighth floor.

Jonas took keys from his pocket and opened the door to the apartment. 'Ah, home sweet home.' A large bird took fright and flapped past a sheet stretched across the entire end of the room. Ropes nailed to the room's cornices and skirting boards secured the four corners of the sheet.

Dan took the sheet to be a makeshift curtain covering the floor to ceiling window. He walked across to peer out of the window and stepped back in alarm. 'There's no window! There's only a sheet between us and an eight-storey drop!'

'Yes, someone stole all the windows in this building. None of the apartments have windows. People use sheets, blankets, whatever to close off the flat from the elements.'

'I hope nobody in this building has toddlers.'

'Are you kidding? This is Africa. There're a lot of toddlers here.'

'Don't they fall over the edge?'

'Yes, sometimes.' Jonas shrugged as if to suggest Dan made an unnecessary fuss.

Dan was afraid of heights and stayed well away from the sheet. Only then did he notice the flat's filthy condition. A simple passage separated the bathroom from the kitchen. It led to a room with two single beds pushed against the walls. Marks on one wall suggested a built-in cupboard once stood there.

Dan tried the taps in the bathroom, and rust-coloured water trickled out before it spluttered and splashed and returned to a trickle once again. The toilet was unflushed, though the flush worked when he pulled the handle. A clear sign of an unreliable water supply. In the room, Dan noticed movement behind the sheet. Then, a man stepped around it.

'Jonas, man! How are you?'

'Dan, meet Francis. He lives next door.'

'He came from behind the curtain.'

'Yes, he climbed around from next door. There's only a wall between us.'

'Jonas, you and your friend must come and say hello to Sally.'

'That's Francis' wife,' said Jonas, as he walked to the edge of the sheet. 'Are you coming?'

'I'm not climbing around a wall on the eighth floor.'

'I'll tell them to open their front door for you.'

Francis and Sally, the neighbours, also covered the end of their flat with a sheet tied in all four corners to look like a sailboat's square sail. The way Jonas and Francis moved back and forth between their apartments turned Dan's stomach.

At a quarter to six, he and Jonas left for their meeting with Absalom Muzenda. The restaurant was only two blocks away. They strolled along, enjoying the last of the daylight. The towering apartments cut out most of the lowering sun's rays. They walked a block down Lily Avenue and turned onto Abel Road, which was busy with traffic and pedestrians, heading home for the day.

A block and a half farther on, they stood in front of the restaurant. Jonas entered to see if Absalom had arrived. 'He's not here yet. Let's grab one of these tables on the veranda where we can talk in private. Inside, there's a long communal table. No good for our discussion with Absalom.'

Dan preferred to sit on the front veranda overlooking the pavement. Inside, the restaurant looked dingy. It wasn't catering to the more monied classes. Jonas selected a table in the corner where their conversation wouldn't be overheard.

Moments later, a large, jovial looking man walked up the steps to the veranda. Jonas waved and a broad smile broke out on Absalom's face. He shook hands with Jonas and Dan as a waiter stood by to take their orders. Beers and chicken and chips for all.

With the usual pleasantries completed, it was straight down to business. Jonas wasted no time. 'Absalom, when are you coming back to Harare? You know we need your contribution to help solve our economic woes.'

'Hah, Jonas! My life would be in danger there. I had to flee Zimbabwe. Evil forces searched for me. If someone hadn't warned me, I'd be starving in Chikurubi by now. Jail can be a death sentence for the regime's critics.'

Jonas laughed. 'I understand you love your food, Absalom, but believe me, things have changed. Ask Dan here. He also needed to flee Zimbabwe, because of his books critical of the regime, but now he works for us, helping to improve our administration and accountability. Not so, Dan?'

'Uh, yes.'

'The regime may be less inclined to dispose of a white man, but I'm a black man. I doubt I could expect similar treatment.'

Jonas ordered another round of beer and more chicken and chips. Dan noted old Absalom could put the food away. No wonder he was so big.

'Absalom, please understand, I'm not here on a little errand for the CIO. I have support from the very top to enlist your help. They appreciate the country needs the economic expertise you have.'

'What about my fellow economists who have allowed the country to get into its existing mess? They will be after my blood.'

'That is why the country needs you. Your fellow economists have allowed politics to override economic sense. You're the only one who speaks the truth. The very top recognises that.'

Dan's ears pricked up at the repeated mention of the 'very top.' David Jones used those words to convince him to return to Zimbabwe. True, they'd released him from Chikurubi and welcomed him back to Harare, but he still had qualms.

'I'm happy here in Johannesburg,' said Absalom. 'If the regime needs my help, I'll give it from a distance. No piece of economic news in Zimbabwe escapes my attention, so I can draft a paper to give my views on what needs to be done. As things progress, I will update my advice. Then, the "very top" can accept or reject it.'

'What can I do to convince you, Absalom?'

'Nothing can convince me.'

Jonas ordered another round of beers, and Dan needed a pee. He excused himself from the table and walked inside the restaurant. 'Hold on, I'm also coming,' said Absalom.

A few minutes later, they returned from the toilet. Jonas sat there with three new beers.

Absalom took a gulp of his beer.

'I'm going out for a smoke,' said Jonas. 'I know Absalom doesn't like me smoking at the dinner table. He thinks it affects the flavour of the food.'

When Jonas left, Absalom turned to Dan. 'Is it true you're working with Jonas?'

'Like he said, I'm just doing administration and computers.'

Absalom took another gulp of his beer. Then he appeared to wobble and looked confused. 'Is something wrong, Absalom?'

'I feel dizzy and my head hurts. Perhaps I ate too much or too fast.'

'This is our fourth round of beer. Maybe you drank too much.'

'Yes, it's tasting bitter. It makes my tongue tingle.' Absalom seemed agitated, and his breathing laboured. Suddenly, he turned in his seat and vomited on the floor. He sat back in his chair, staring wide-eyed at Dan.

'Are you all right, Absalom?'

He tried to reply, but no words came out.

'Hang on, I'm going to get help.' Dan ran into the restaurant. 'Who's the boss here?' The waiter pointed to a tall man standing by the communal table. Dan hurried over to him. 'My friend is sick. Can you please call an ambulance? I don't know what's wrong. He might be having a seizure.'

The restaurant manager punched a number into his cell phone while Dan rushed back to the table to check on Absalom. The man gasped for breath and seemed unaware of his presence.

Where was Jonas? Dan rushed out of the restaurant onto the pavement. Jonas stood at the corner of the restaurant talking on his cell phone. Dan ran up to him. 'Something has happened to Absalom. The restaurant has called an ambulance. You better come and see.'

Jonas switched off his phone. 'If they've called an ambulance, that's fine. There's nothing we can do. We better get out of here fast.'

'What do you mean? We can't just leave him.'

'If the ambulance comes, the police may also arrive. Believe me, you don't want to be answering their questions. Especially when you're travelling on a fake passport. They'll jump to all the wrong conclusions.'

'But, but—'

'Come on! Let's go! You're not a doctor. What can you do?'

Dan had little choice but to follow Jonas. That damned passport! He knew it would bring problems. Jonas stepped out, and Dan struggled to keep up with him. He was puffing hard by the time they reached the block of flats. Now they had the sixteen flights of steps to contend with to reach the eighth floor.

Back in the flat, they slumped onto the beds. Dan's mind was in a whirl. What happened? The evening wasn't supposed to end this way. He tried to catch his breath. Then, a sharp rap on the door.

Jonas jumped up from his bed. 'Someone must have followed us. Quick, grab your bag and let's go next door.'

'What? How? I'm not crawling around that wall.'

'Dan, you've got no choice. Don't worry, I'll help you.' Jonas grabbed his bag and hurried to the end of the room and swung it around the corner into Francis' flat. Then he did the same with Dan's bag.

'Now I'm going next door. Stand in the corner next to the wall and put your hand around it? You'll see it's only two bricks thick. See this groove in the wall? Hang on to that. That's where the window was attached. There's one like it on Francis' side. Try to find it. Point your right foot to the wall and swing your left leg around the wall. When you put your hand around the wall, I'll grab your wrist. Remember, swing your left leg around the wall as you step off with your right. And don't hold the sheet. It won't take your weight. Got It?'

'Yes, no, I don't know!'

'Let's go!'

Jonas disappeared around the wall. Dan stepped up to the corner where the window once stood. His stomach twisted in a painful, icy knot. It twisted over and over, like an excruciating tickle. He did not dare look down. Eight storeys to the concrete below. No, he couldn't do it!

The banging got more urgent. Then, a loud crash with something heavy. They were trying to smash their way into the flat. Dan put his hand around the wall and felt Jonas grab his wrist. He swung his left leg around the wall as he pushed off with his right and stepped into space.

CHAPTER 11

DAN was off balance! He sensed he was falling backwards. But Jonas' powerful grip on his wrist held firm as he dragged him into Francis' flat. Dan's legs wobbled as his left leg shook and twitched. With a life of its own, the nerves tingled, and the muscles spasmed, making it impossible for him to stand. He flopped onto the floor.

The flat was in darkness, and Francis put his finger to his lips to keep everyone silent. They heard angry, shouted words next door, but after a few minutes, the voices faded away and silence returned.

'They must have followed us to the flat,' said Jonas.

'But why did they follow us?' said Dan, struggling to regain his composure.

'The way we left Absalom must have made them suspicious, or perhaps they chased us to pay the bill.'

'I wonder what happened to Absalom. He struggled to breathe or talk.'

'That Absalom was always a glutton. Did you notice how much he ate? So fast and so much. Perhaps he choked on the food.'

'No, it didn't start like that. He only choked later after he got dizzy. I thought it might have been food poisoning, though it didn't affect us.'

'Not yet.'

'We can't go back next door. Those people might return. How did they know which flat we occupied?'

'They must have watched us from Olivia Road and seen which flat we entered. That's why we didn't notice anyone following us.'

'So, what do we do now?'

'Our plane leaves at twenty-five minutes past six in the morning. Francis is taking us to the airport, so we'll leave here at four.'

'We won't get any sleep tonight.'

'You can rest on one of these beds. Francis won't mind.'

'I'm too wound up to sleep.'

'In that case, I'll use the bed to get a couple of hours.'

Jonas lay down and appeared to fall asleep in an instant. So many thoughts raced through Dan's mind. If he was the target of a hit, Jonas had the perfect opportunity to let him fall when he circumvented the wall. In the excitement and trauma, he didn't consider that possibility. Just as well! The crossing was enough on its own. He didn't need something else to worry about.

So, it looked like Jonas's instructions didn't include disposing of him. Did that mean Captain John wasn't behind the failed hit at the Intercontinental Airport Hotel? That left David Jones, though he couldn't imagine him getting involved in that sort of thing. What about Eunice or Nikita? He couldn't think clearly. His brain seemed sluggish.

Dan woke to Jonas shaking his shoulder. 'Wake up! We must go now.' He must have fallen asleep in a sitting position, leaning against the wall. He didn't remember sitting down on the floor. Tiredness and adrenalin combined to confuse him. Sally handed him a mug of hot tea to help him get going.

Ten to four in the morning, Francis was ready to go. 'I'll walk out ahead of you,' he said. 'You two keep below balcony level. If anyone is watching the passageway from Olivia Road, you don't want to alert them you're on the move. They'll know that somehow you gave them the slip, but you must leave the building at some point. When I bring my car to the front entrance, get in as fast as you can.'

Francis stepped out into the passageway. Jonas and Dan ran hunched over behind him. At the top of the stairs, Francis held up his hand to stop them. 'Keep a little distance behind me while I make sure each floor is clear.'

Flight by flight and floor by floor, they descended. On the fifth floor, Francis held up his hand. A group of noisy youths came down the passageway, talking and laughing. They ran down the stairs, jumping over the lower steps of each flight. Though they passed right in front of Francis, standing on the flight of steps above the fifth floor, none of them noticed him.

Francis was more cautious now. He didn't know if the youths ran to ground level and exited the building, or if they'd stopped partway for a smoke. Slowly, the three descended the flights of stairs until they reached the ground floor. Jonas and Dan stood back in the shadows under the steps while Francis hurried off to fetch his car.

Five minutes later, a car pulled up in front of the building, and Jonas strained his eyes to check if Francis drove it. 'I think that's him. Let's go!' They ran to the car and flung open the doors. They threw their bags onto the back seat, and Dan jumped in after them. Jonas sat in front with Francis. The streets were deserted at that early hour. Even the five youths had melted away.

Within two blocks, they exited Berea. The Ponte City Apartments loomed threateningly on their right. Dan had hoped to tour that notorious building, but there wasn't time. Perhaps on his next visit. For now, he was keen to return to Zimbabwe. Their trip descended into a chaotic mess, with them stealing away like thieves in the night. Their mission was a failure, though Jonas didn't seem too concerned about it.

Francis dropped them at the airport and sped away. They entered the terminal and headed for the check-in counter. With only carry-on luggage, the process was quick. The shops were already open, and Dan bought a bottle of Royal Salute scotch for Captain John. An expensive scotch in a purple velvet bag, making it look extra special. He'd drunk enough of John's scotch to feel obliged to return the compliment.

Dan remained a little concerned about passing through immigration with his fake passport. He needn't have worried, and he breathed easier when the immigration official stamped his passport with no greater inspection than usual.

At customs, he got a nasty shock. The bottle of scotch contained too much liquid to carry in his hand luggage. Customs gave him a choice. Either they would confiscate it, or he could return to the check-in counter to check-in his bag. Blast! It was the last thing he needed.

He passed back through immigration and walked back to the check-in counter. Now he faced a queue that had grown substantially since he and Jonas had passed through earlier. To his relief, the check-in lady passed his bag through without debate or delay.

Time was running short, and he needed to hurry back to immigration and customs. He didn't want to miss the flight and have to explain his way out of the mess Jonas created through their rapid, inexplicable exit from the restaurant.

Immigration recognised him and waved him through without delay. They didn't stamp his passport on the way out, or on his return. Without luggage, customs presented no difficulty, and he was in time to join Jonas at the departure gate.

Once on the plane, he relaxed. He was drained and worried the authorities might detain them in connection with Absalom Muzenda's unfortunate illness. Because of his false passport, they'd fled the restaurant without paying for their meals. It wasn't too serious a crime, but he didn't want to get tangled up in the South African legal system.

As he flicked through the flight magazine, he noticed a disturbance at the plane's entrance. Two burly police officers walked down the aisle, looking carefully at each passenger. Dan's heart sank as he tried to shrink into his seat. As the police officers came to their row, the leading one stared into his eyes. Could he see the guilt written there?

The officers stopped next to Jonas sitting on the aisle seat. Suddenly, a scuffle broke out next to them. Dan's heart jumped as he thought the officers struggled with Jonas. Then he realised they pulled the passenger from the seat behind him. The man shouted and demanded his release, but the police officers marched him down the aisle and off the plane.

Dan's heart thumped in his chest as the aircrew closed the plane's doors before it taxied out to the runway. He only felt safely on his way when the plane's wheels lifted off the tarmac.

'What about the flat's broken door? The place is wide open. Anyone might walk in and steal stuff.'

Jonas seemed completely relaxed. 'And steal what? Two broken down single beds and a rusty kettle. Francis will handle it. Sometimes he stays in one apartment, and at other times he moves next door. That keeps away squatters while we always have one flat available for our use.'

'Do you always stay in that building when you are in Joburg?'

'Yes, I like it there. There's no check-in or questions about the purpose of our visit. And there's no record of our visit.'

'Are all your trips as exhausting as this one?'

'Yeah. Captain John says you can go back to your hotel and recover. He'll debrief with you tomorrow.'

At Harare airport, the yawning immigration officer stamped their passports. Next, they headed to customs. Jonas mumbled something to the customs officer, and he waved them through. Just then, Dan remembered his Australian passport. 'Can I speak to your boss? Is he here?'

The customs officer looked irritated but walked to the small office that Dan remembered from his last arrival. A tall, balding man came out. The same senior officer who he met on his last passage through customs in Harare.

'I'd like to have my passport back, please.'

'What passport?'

'The one you confiscated the last time I was here, when you falsely had me arrested and sent to Chikurubi.'

The senior officer's face darkened. 'We don't keep confiscated passports here. We gave yours to the police who arrested you.'

'Can you please have another look in your desk drawers? The police say they haven't got it. They say you must still have it.'

'Go, or you'll return to Chikurubi! If we confiscated your passport, how did you fly in from Johannesburg? Are you travelling on false documents?'

Jonas jumped in and spoke to the officer in Shona. The man walked off in a huff.

'Come Dan! We won't solve your missing passport problem here. I'll talk to Captain John about it. I'm sure he'll find your passport for you.'

Dan was reluctant to leave without his passport, but he saw the two police officers at the exit, looking agitated. Perhaps *discretion was the greater part of valour.* Jonas and Dan exited the terminal and caught a taxi to the city.

'You know, Dan, in Zimbabwe, you shouldn't try to achieve two things in one go.'

'What do you mean?'

'You wanted to get through customs, and you also wanted your Australian passport back. If it were not for me, they would've arrested you on some pretext. Do one thing at a time. First, get through customs. Come back another day for your passport. One thing at a time.'

'I'll try to remember that.'

The taxi dropped Dan at his hotel, but Jonas stayed in the taxi as it drove off into the distance on the busy Harare streets.

First, Dan hopped into a hot shower. It was hotter than normal, as he felt he needed to melt the grime from the Joburg trip and wash it down the drain. He wondered what Captain John would say about their trip. He also wondered how Absalom Muzenda had fared. They'd failed in their task to persuade him to return to Zimbabwe. Perhaps there would be a next time, though he hoped Captain John wouldn't send him on that assignment.

John said he'd learn a lot from Jonas about how the COU operated. As far as Dan could tell, he'd learned nothing, other than his demise didn't seem to be on Captain John's agenda. That left David Jones as the remaining suspect behind the attempted hit at the Johannesburg airport's Intercontinental Hotel. Though even that seemed unlikely. The whole situation was a puzzle.

The cell phone rang, and Dan scrambled to answer it. It was Inspector Michael Mzamane of the South African Police. Dan's anxiety level rose.

Might the inspector's call concern his trip with Jonas? Of course not. How would anybody link him with the events at the restaurant in Berea? A senior officer like Inspector Mzamane wouldn't waste his time on a minor matter like an unpaid restaurant bill.

'Mr Scott, Inspector Mzamane here. I'm calling to let you know we have made no progress with finding the surviving man who confronted you at the airport's Intercontinental Hotel. So, I repeat my warning to be on the lookout for him in Harare.'

'Thank you, Inspector, I will stay alert.'

Dan took out his laptop and searched on Google for Johannesburg's Star newspaper. He found nothing about the incident at the Berea restaurant. Dan checked other news sites but again found nothing. He typed in Absalom Muzenda's name. There, he saw a post headed, *Celebrated Zimbabwean Economist Dies in Berea Restaurant*.

The police did not rule out foul play. The post stated, Mr Muzenda dined with two unidentified men: a black and a white. Both men disappeared after the latter alerted the restaurant to Mr Muzenda's condition. The police ask that both men come forward to help with their enquiries.

As the news sank in, Dan realised with alarm he was a wanted man. The South African Police were hunting him, although they didn't know his identity. Now what should he do? Should he turn himself in to the South African Police? If he didn't, and it came to light later, it would appear he had something to hide. It was a quandary. What if there was CCTV footage?

CHAPTER 12

DAN was glad to be back in the COU office the next morning. He was gone for a short time, though it seemed much longer. Cherry greeted him with her usual bright smile, which always made it a pleasant start to the day. Ambrose followed him into his office with a steaming cup of tea. 'Welcome back, Sah.'

Captain John also appeared pleased to see him. 'We'll debrief this evening over a couple of scotches. It's much better that way.'

The office's small computer network worked well, and everything looked in order. Jonas and Eunice were both absent. At morning tea, Dan engaged Ambrose in a chat.

'It's a quiet day here in the office, Ambrose.'

'Yes, Sah. It is much better since you arrived.'

'Really! In what way?'

'Oh, Sah, before you came, Captain John was always angry, shouting at everyone and making a big fuss. Now he looks calm and more like a gentleman. This only happened since you are here.'

'That's strange. I wonder why?'

'I think he must like you. That woman is no good for him.'

'You mean Eunice?'

'Yes, Sah. That one is hard. All the men are afraid of her. Before they would laugh and joke. Now she is second to the boss. They keep quiet and try to keep away from her.'

'Well, she's not here today.'

'Yes, Sah. It's peaceful today.'

'Where is Jonas?'

'He was here yesterday. He spoke with Captain John all afternoon, so today is his off day.'

So, Jonas debriefed with Captain John yesterday. It gave Captain John twenty-four hours to digest it. Dan wondered if and how it might affect his own debrief.

* * *

At five o'clock, Captain John came to Dan's office to invite him for drinks. Dan presented him with the Royal Salute scotch in its purple velvet bag, and John seemed touched by the gesture. He opened it at once, and they shared a toast to fine scotch.

'Jonas told me about your eventful trip.'

'Yes, it's a pity we failed in our mission. Absalom was adamant he wouldn't return to Zimbabwe. Then he suffered that awful choking fit and died.'

'Absalom ate too much, too fast.'

'Yes, that's what Jonas said. I saw it too.'

'Absalom was a glutton. People always joked he would die choking on his food.'

'It seems Zimbabwe has lost an asset with his passing.'

'Yes, though it's not a total loss. He was a respected economist who could have helped this country. His constant criticism of the regime and his accusations of corruption undermined the government's efforts to get on top of the economic situation. Many thought he did Zimbabwe a disservice.'

'He said he had many enemies in Zimbabwe.'

'That is true. The circumstances are sad, but his enemies will rejoice that his voice is still. You and Jonas did your best to convince him to come home, and I'm grateful for your efforts.'

* * *

Back in the hotel, Dan enjoyed a warm shower and dinner at the hotel's restaurant. The waiters got to know him and gave excellent service. They enjoyed stopping for a chat whenever the opportunity arose.

In his room, Dan took out his laptop and searched the South African sites for further news of Absalom Muzenda. Nothing, and no mention at all, on the Zimbabwean news sites.

The following evening, he again looked for news of Absalom. Nothing new on any of the websites. On the next night, Friday, the South African sites displayed Absalom's photo together with disturbing news. A chill ran through Dan as he read, Absalom Muzenda died from cyanide poisoning. The police sought the public's help to locate the two men who dined with him in the Berea restaurant. It was now a murder enquiry.

Dan couldn't believe his predicament. How did he get into this mess? Was it a setup? He thought back to his debrief. Captain John didn't seem the least bit disappointed at how things turned out in Johannesburg. Cyanide poisoning?

When he and Absalom returned from the toilet in the restaurant, Jonas sat at the table with three beers already set down at their places. Did he poison Absalom's beer in their absence? He must have. Then, he excused himself from the table to go outside for a smoke. Or perhaps, for a quick getaway? That was why he insisted they not return to help Absalom.

Now Dan was implicated in a political murder. He did not expect a sympathetic hearing from the South African Police. He'd run away from a murder scene, and the more he thought about it, the flimsier his excuse sounded.

Things were accumulating. First, the failed hit at the Intercontinental Airport Hotel in Johannesburg. Then customs confiscated his passport at Harare airport. Now, the South African Police wanted him on suspicion of murder. All he wanted was inspiration for his next novel and to organise the COU office. Events now ran out of control, sweeping him out of his depth, like a rip current in the ocean.

Dan realised he'd been complacent, off guard. He'd been too keen to imagine those around him were his friends and liked him. Perhaps they did, though he couldn't be sure. He needed to protect himself. Get a little insurance. It never goes astray to get some cover. *Better safe than sorry*, as the saying goes.

The situation brought his mind back to Nikita. She'd given him the cell phone to photograph the Honey File. He'd taken it with him to the COU office a few times, though lately he hadn't bothered. The near miss with Eunice, when she almost caught him looking in Captain John's four-drawer filing cabinet, discouraged him from taking the phone with him each day.

Dan didn't trust Nikita, but it wouldn't harm if he took the photo and held on to it as insurance against any other sticky situation. Yes, that's what he'd do. Recently, he'd not even checked if the four-drawer cabinet was unlocked or if the keys hung in the lock. From now on, he'd do that. And if the cabinet was open, well ….

* * *

Over the next couple of weeks, Dan made a point of checking if any opportunity arose to access the filing cabinet. He realised that sometimes the keys hung in the lock, though most times not. He also noted that the drawer was accessible more often during working hours than after hours, when he and Captain John enjoyed a scotch together.

Dan's role, looking after the office computers, gave him the perfect excuse to be in Captain John's office from time to time. Finding the opportunity to photograph the file required more patience than waiting for the stars to align. The filing cabinet needed to be open or the keys in easy reach. Dan needed to be alone and uninterrupted in Captain John's office. And Eunice's absence from the office would be a bonus.

He remembered the last time she almost caught him near the filing cabinet. To make his proximity to it less suspicious, he used the top of the filing cabinet to store his replacement printer cartridges, new USBs, backups, and other computer items. He kept it tidy, to not draw Captain John's attention and elicit an instruction to store them elsewhere.

The days passed, and Dan waited to photograph the Honey File. It seemed he'd never get the chance to take the photo. Then one evening, as he and Captain John settled down for a scotch, an operative knocked on the doorframe. He spoke to Captain John in Shona. John excused himself and accompanied the man to the open-plan office.

The keys hung in the lock of the filing cabinet. Dan switched on Nikita's phone and jumped up and hurried to the top drawer and slid it open. There at the front, as before, stood the suspension file marked Honey File. He opened it. Damn! The manilla folder was missing. Where the hell was it? Another setback.

Dan saw the next suspension file marked Domestic. Just a single sheet inside a manilla folder. He grabbed the sheet and took a photo. As he stuffed it back into the folder, he heard footsteps in the passage. He slid the drawer closed and stepped away from the cabinet, and sat down in his chair.

Captain John walked into the room. As Dan turned to see him enter, he noticed the keys in the filing cabinet swinging like a pendulum. In his haste to close the drawer, he knocked the keys, which now swung back and forth. When John sat down, he would face the filing cabinet.

Dan stood up and walked to the filing cabinet to block John's view. He turned and held up a USB. 'This is new, high-quality USB which we can rely on to store our files. The next time you're saving something important, try this one.' The few extra seconds gave the keys time to stop swinging, before he returned to his seat to enjoy the scotch with John.

'Is there a problem?' said Dan. 'You look pensive.'

'A minor revolt by the operatives. They find Eunice's management style overbearing. As I mentioned once before, she's too ambitious. She appears hard and threatening. The men feel insecure. While Jonas is here, it's easier, but he's away for the next two weeks.'

'Employees are always one of management's biggest problems, John.'

'Yes. Perhaps I was a little hasty in making her my 2IC, but she had some good ideas. Our income and profits have increased since her promotion, though the cost has been a little unrest amongst the operatives.'

Dan recognised his evening drinks with Captain John displayed an interesting pattern. They were almost always on Tuesday or Thursday evenings, with Eunice often on hand. On the few occasions John invited him for drinks on one of the other weekday evenings, Eunice wasn't there. So, his best opportunity to photograph the Honey File would be on a Monday, Wednesday, or Friday when Captain John invited him for a drink and Eunice was absent.

* * *

Almost three weeks since Dan's escapade in Johannesburg with Jonas. He relaxed and felt comfortable with Captain John and the COU. He'd not seen David Jones for quite a while. A month passed since their barbecue with the U.S. diplomats. Nor had he heard again from Nikita. Did she know he'd not yet photographed the Honey File? If so, how did she know that?

Dan found many puzzles and contradictions in Zimbabwe. Friday evening, and once again, he faced a weekend with nothing much to do. He hoped to catch up with Daniel Moyo, but he'd been busy and left it too late to make any arrangement. Not even Friday night drinks.

As Dan entered the foyer of the Meikles Hotel, he bumped into David Jones. 'What a coincidence! Only this afternoon, I was thinking I'd not seen you in a month, and here you are.'

'Yes, I've been otherwise engaged. I came on the off chance you'd be available for a drink.'

'Sure, let's go to The Explorer's Bar.'

'Have you made any social connections since I last saw you?'

'No, I've been busy with the COU and working on my book.'

'Every man needs social time to relax. Otherwise, you lose your edge.'

Was that a coded warning? Dan viewed everyone with suspicion these days, especially David Jones. 'I'll remember that. You're right, I must maintain my edge.'

'Before I forget, the Harare Writers' Club has asked me to see if you would consider giving them a talk on your writing and methods.'

'When?'

'Next Friday, late afternoon.'

'Where?'

'If you're agreeable, I'll find out and let you know.'

'Well, it could make for an interesting Friday evening.'

'I've already spoken to Captain John, and he's happy for you to do it.'

'Good, OK. Well then, yes, I'll do it. But why do they want me? I'm not as famous as you keep telling people.'

'In Harare you are. Zimbabwe has banned your books. That makes you famous over here.'

'Will you be at the talk?'

'No, I've got a prior engagement. It's a pity. Incidentally, Captain John told me about your heroics, climbing outside on the eighth floor of a building, like Spiderman.'

'Not exactly like Spiderman.'

'Your penchant for danger worries him. He's concerned you might have an accident.'

'I don't have a penchant for danger.' Something about David Jones' words troubled Dan.

He recalled reading about Itai Dzamara's abduction ten months earlier, on Monday 9th March 2015. The authorities claimed to know nothing about it. The government promised an urgent investigation into the matter, though few believed they'd do anything.

Dzamara was at a barber's shop when five men in a white twin-cab pickup van abducted him in broad daylight in front of witnesses.

He was a persistent critic of Mugabe and his regime. His friends and admirers feared for his safety, and many foresaw something bad would happen to him. It is a sad truth that brave men seeking change for the common good rarely live to enjoy the fruits of their sacrifice.

No one knew what happened to him, and many feared the worst. The Central Intelligence Organisation (CIO), the police, and the army all came under suspicion.

CHAPTER 13

FRIDAY started out bright and fresh. Another beautiful Harare morning. Dan reflected that nowhere had he experienced mornings like these with their comfortable temperatures. Arriving at work to be greeted by Cherry's cheerful smile, and Ambrose's steaming cup of tea always gave him a lift.

The morning soon passed, and as Dan finished his lunch at his desk, Captain John popped into the office. 'So, you're giving your talk to the writers' club this afternoon? David Jones says it will be at five o'clock at the National Art Gallery in Julius Nyerere Way (Kings Crescent).'

'Yes, I'm looking forward to it.'

'Dark clouds are building. Take the white Hyundai, or you might get caught in a downpour. You don't want to arrive at the gallery looking like a drowned rat. Ambrose cleaned the car this morning. Cherry has the keys.'

Dan didn't prepare for his talk. In his opinion, notes made presentations rigid. He preferred impromptu talks where the audience could take part in a discussion-like format. With so many approaches to writing, he'd simply tell the attendees how he did it.

At half past four, Dan said goodbye and walked out to the car. He hadn't driven in weeks, and never a Hyundai. The spotless car started without any problems. He put it into gear and eased out of the driveway onto the road. The guard on the gate saluted, as he always did when Dan passed.

At the edge of the road, he stopped for passing traffic, and the Hyundai stalled. Oh, yes! The Hyundai was a manual. He hadn't driven a manual for many years and was used to automatics. On his way, the presentation preoccupied him, and he stalled the car three times. He could drive a manual, and got his licence in one, but he needed to remember he wasn't driving an automatic.

Driving in Harare was no problem. No one was speeding, and he just needed to watch for pedestrians and bicycles.

Along Julius Nyerere Way, just past the Monomotapa Hotel, Dan parked in the first free space he saw. A few big drops of rain fell, leaving splashes on the pavement, so he took the umbrella someone thoughtfully left on the passenger seat. What would he do without the care Ambrose and Cherry gave him?

As he walked along the pavement, loud claps of thunder shook the ground, and flashes of lightning compensated for the darkening sky. He quickened his steps as the sound of approaching heavy rain reached him. The modern, two-storey building he approached looked like it needed a repaint.

At the entrance to the gallery, a staff member directed him to a ramp leading to the mezzanine floor. Rows of white plastic chairs and a dais for the speaker filled a large space overlooking the street. Dan was twenty minutes early, but already a smattering of club members occupied several of the chairs.

The rain held off, and more members arrived, thankful to have beaten the threatened downpour. Mrs Olonga, the club president, introduced herself to Dan. Then she introduced him to members who'd already published a book or two.

The gallery closed at five and was quiet apart from the club members' chatter. Around thirty people were present. Most were women. The club president clapped her hands to hush the group. She introduced Dan, embarrassing him with an exaggerated outline of his achievements.

'Thank you, Mrs Olonga, for your kind words. I'm not that famous, so it's an honour for me to speak to you this evening. If you have a question, please raise your hand. You needn't wait until the end of my talk.'

Dan glanced around the audience. Most looked like university students or young graduates. A few mature women were there, including one elegant looking lady in her late thirties or early forties. Dan went through the reason he started writing and his writing process.

One young woman in the third row put up her hand. 'Mr Scott, you suggest you should write about what you know.'

'Yes, because that helps to give your writing authenticity.'

'In your first two novels, your white protagonist enters a romantic relationship with an attractive black woman. My question is, have you experienced such a relationship?'

Dan laughed. A titter went around the room. Then, Dan realised the young woman was asking a serious question. Her earnest expression was unaffected by the amusement of the other attendees.

'No, I haven't had that pleasure, but I assume all women are alike, irrespective of their skin colour.'

The young woman nodded in response to his answer. It focussed his attention, and from then on, he was conscious of her sitting in the audience. She wore black-rimmed glasses, a white, long-sleeved blouse with a bow at the neck, and a black pencil skirt. From her prim appearance, he assumed she worked in a professional office or in some other formal role.

When Dan mentioned how important research was, even when writing fiction, the same young woman raised her hand. 'Mr Scott, do you agree it would give your writing even more authenticity if you had experienced a romantic relationship with a black woman?' Again, a snigger bounced around the audience. The young woman still held her earnest expression.

Dan was a little flustered as he saw the grinning faces of his audience. He wondered if the young woman was part of a student joke at his expense. 'In your research, you can't experience everything. Say you are writing a murder scene. You can't go out and murder someone to make your writing more authentic. For certain things, you must use your imagination.'

The young woman nodded, acknowledging his response.

After the presentation and questions, the attendees flocked around a long table for tea, coffee, biscuits, and muffins. Several of those present came to chat with Dan. Outside, heavy rain fell on the glistening street. As the rain eased, people drifted away, and the numbers thinned out.

Soon, Mrs Olonga and two art gallery staff members who attended the talk were the only ones remaining.

'Mr Scott, we're planning a writers' festival in Bulawayo later in the year. Would you be interested in doing a repeat of this evening?'

'Yes, that would be fine. I'm planning to get in touch with Ian Sanders, the writer living in Botswana. He might also be interested in speaking at a session.'

'That would be wonderful! I'll get in touch with you when we have a firm date.'

Mrs Olonga thanked him again before she left. The gallery staff members accompanied Dan to the exit, locking the door behind him.

He stood at the entrance watching the steady downpour. Then he noticed a young woman standing to one side on the gallery veranda, sheltering from the rain. It was the young woman who asked him the awkward questions during his talk. 'Oh, hello! I thought you left ages ago.'

'It's too wet. I'm waiting for the rain to stop.'

'This steady rain looks like it's set in. Where are you going?'

'I'm going home to my flat.'

'Is it far?'

'No, about six blocks.'

'You're walking? Can I give you a lift? If you wait here, I'll fetch my car. I'll only be a minute.'

'Thank you.'

Dan opened his umbrella and skipped down the half-dozen steps to the pavement, and strode to his car. The rain was heavier than he first imagined. He reversed out of the kerbside parking, put the car into gear, and headed to the art gallery steps. Already the windows were fogging up in the damp atmosphere.

At the steps, Dan leant across the passenger seat and unlocked the car door. The young woman hurried down the steps, opened the passenger door, and jumped in beside him. A mix of damp and faint perfume reached his nostrils. The earthy smell of summer rain in Zimbabwe always heightened his senses.

'Where to, er ..., sorry, what's your name?'

'Gloria. Just straight ahead for six blocks, please.'

'And what's your interest in writing, Gloria?'

'After I graduated from university with an arts degree last year, I got a job in a bookshop. I've always enjoyed reading and now I'm trying to write my first novel.'

'Oh yes, and what's it about?'

'It's about a visiting American professor who lectures at the university and has a relationship with one of his students.'

Dan smiled to himself and couldn't resist a sly dig at her. 'Oh! Have you had a relationship with a visiting American professor?'

Gloria laughed. 'No, like you, I've not yet experienced an interracial relationship.'

They both laughed together.

'My flat is in that corner block.'

Dan pulled the car off the road into a vacant spot underneath a large tree in front of the entrance. 'Well, good luck with your writing, Gloria.'

'Thank you. I wondered if you'd look at my manuscript and tell me what you think of my writing?'

'Um, well, yes, if you like. I'll give you my phone number. You can call me when you feel ready.' Dan wasn't keen to critique other people's writing, but it seemed rude to refuse.

'Would you like coffee? I'll show you the first few pages now.'

'Er! I must be getting back. Oh, all right, but I can't stay long.' Dan switched off the windscreen wipers and the car engine and followed Gloria into the apartment block. They walked up to the first floor and along the public corridor to the end flat. She opened the Yale lock on the door.

The flat was a typical studio apartment with a short passage separating the bathroom and kitchen. The passage led to a single large room serving as a bedroom, lounge, and dining room. A private balcony overlooking the street ran the width of the room. A large tree in front of the balcony afforded it a little extra privacy.

The neat room was furnished with a sofa, bookcase, drinks cabinet, dining table and a double bed with bedside tables. Warm lighting from an elegant standard lamp gave the room a cosy feeling. It didn't look like the flat of a recently graduated student.

Gloria noticed Dan's surprise. 'It's my sister's flat, though she's seldom in Harare, so I live here now.'

'Where is your sister?'

'She's in Cape Town with her new boyfriend. She returned from London last week, stayed one night, and left for Cape Town the next morning.'

'Does she travel with her boyfriend everywhere?'

'Oh no, the London trip was with another boyfriend.'

Dan watched, intrigued, as Gloria put a heaped teaspoon of instant coffee granules into a cup and added a few drops of water—less than half a teaspoon. With the spoon, she ground the coffee granules. Then she beat the mix, as if whipping an egg, until it became a white paste. Only then did she add the boiling water and milk.

She handed him the cup of coffee and her manuscript.

'I won't have time to read it properly now. Can I take it with me? I'll return it in a day or two.' Dan put the manuscript on the dining table with the car keys so he wouldn't forget it when he left.

The coffee was excellent. It looked and tasted like it was made in a professional coffee machine. Though it took a few minutes to prepare, the wait was worth it. Dan wondered how Gloria learned to make coffee like that.

'My sister used to go out with a Brazilian boyfriend, and he showed her how to do it. Would you like a drink? I've got a bottle of whisky here.'

'You drink scotch?'

'No, it's my sister's, but if you like whisky we can open it.'

'Your sister wouldn't approve of us drinking her scotch.'

'No, it's fine. She said I could drink it if I wanted. Because she can get more anytime.'

'Hmm! OK, just one glass. Have you poured scotch before? You pour a little. Only an inch.'

'No, I've never drunk whisky.'

'Well, you better sip it, or it will go to your head, and you won't be able to stand.' Gloria laughed. 'No, I'm serious. You must just take little sips.'

She poured the scotch into two tumblers and handed one to him. They chatted about Zimbabwe, and Harare in particular. Gloria had never been outside the country and not even visited Bulawayo. She'd visited Chinhoyi (Sinoia) once with her parents, to see the caves, when she was in her early teens.

Dan took off his suit jacket and hung it on a chair at the dining table as Gloria poured another two tots. The Glenfiddich was moreish, and when Dan visited the toilet, she poured a third round. He wondered how she could take so much if she'd never drunk scotch.

Their chatter got livelier with lots of laughter and giggling. When she moved to pour a fourth round, he resolved not to let a novice scotch drinker get the better of him, so he didn't object. His head was spinning a little. Or was it the room?

'What are you doing this weekend, Dan?'

'I don't know. Perhaps I'll do some research for my book, and I'll read your manuscript.'

'What sort of research?'

'Not the sort of research you were suggesting at the writers' club. But then, maybe ...,' they both laughed, 'we could both get our writing research done together.'

'You're not thinking what I think you're thinking, are you, Mr Scott?'

'That depends on what you think I'm thinking.' They both laughed again. This time, out loud. 'What a shame, Gloria, I don't have a condom with me.'

'That's OK, my sister has left condoms in the bedside table drawer.'

'Jeez! This sister of yours sounds like quite a girl.'

'Oh, she is! I'm very proud of her.'

'I wouldn't mind meeting your sister.'

Gloria jumped onto the double bed and reaching across to the far bedside table, opened the drawer and took out a condom in a shiny red, sealed foil packet. 'Do you prefer the red or the blue packets?' Dan grabbed his scotch and walked to the bed. Four scotches never affected him like this before, but Gloria showed no signs of it affecting her.

CHAPTER 14

THE sun crept over the horizon, lighting the room. Dan stirred and tried to focus his thoughts. At first, the unfamiliar surroundings puzzled him. As he tried to reboot his mind, he realised he was not in his hotel room. Oh yes! That girl. He struggled to remember her name. It began with a *G*. Oh, yes, Gloria. That's it. Dan checked behind him, and there she lay, sleeping peacefully.

He'd not seen her without her glasses before now. She had a pretty face, and he wondered if she needed glasses. Many ambitious young students and graduates liked to wear glasses because they imagined it made them appear more intelligent and mature. Almost a fashion statement. Often the glasses were weak and unnecessary, though what struggling optician would try to talk their customers out of it?

Dan needed a pee. That's when he realised he was naked. He peeped under the sheet and saw that Gloria also wore nothing. Yes, now he remembered her selecting a condom from the bedside table drawer. He noticed the damp patch between them when he propped himself up to slip out to the toilet. How would there be a wet spot if they'd used a condom? Then he saw the unopened packet on the bedside table.

Oh, no! Damn! How could he have been so stupid? In the heat of the moment, they forgot to use the condom. With HIV rife in Zimbabwe, Dan cursed himself. Was Gloria on the pill? Somehow, he doubted it. Another problem he didn't need!

Dan got out of bed, taking care not to make any noise or disturbance. He dressed quickly and picked up the car keys and manuscript, forgetting about the toilet. The well-oiled Yale lock in the door shut with a soft click. He hurried to his car, ignoring the suspicious glare he got from a lady on the stairs.

His bladder was bursting, and every robot (traffic light) seemed set against him. Dan saw it as his punishment for sneaking off the way he did. The events of the previous evening didn't work out as he planned. In fact, he'd planned nothing beyond the talk at the writers' club. Somehow, Gloria, with her easy charm, swept him along into this difficult situation.

Dan wasn't proud of the way he sneaked off. He needed to think, and the wet spot and the unopened condom gave him plenty to think about. Until now, he hadn't noticed the splitting headache or the slight sensation of nausea. The urge to puke was almost irresistible when he reached the Meikles Hotel and parked the car. He rushed to his room to bring up in the toilet bowl.

The awful experience made it hard for him to focus, and Dan slumped onto the bed. When he opened his eyes, the room swayed, and the ceiling spun. He needed to vomit again. Another dash to the bathroom to repeat the experience.

Each time he vomited, he felt worse. Any sign of improvement seemed a vain hope. He placed the Do Not Disturb sign on his door. His head throbbed, and in mid-afternoon he brought up bitter bile. How long would this last? He couldn't remember the last time he'd been sick from drinking alcohol. How often he'd vowed never to touch another drop again.

By five-thirty in the evening, Dan felt drained. Then, his nausea and headache vanished over the next thirty minutes. He needed strong flavoured food to remove the awful taste of bile in his mouth. Brushing his teeth didn't quite do the trick. He remembered the convenience store around the corner that sold ice lollies.

Dan selected an orange ice lolly as he recalled its extra strong flavour. Now he needed solid food. At the hotel restaurant, the chef agreed to prepare a hot curry for him. It wasn't on the menu, but he'd been a hotel guest for weeks and became a favourite with the waiters. After the curry dinner, his mouth seemed back to normal. Thank heavens for that!

He wondered how Gloria fared with all those scotches. If they'd floored him, what might they have done to her? Tomorrow he'd check on her. In the meantime, he'd read her manuscript.

Later, in bed, Dan tried to remember what happened the previous night. He remembered walking to the bed when Gloria pulled out different coloured condom packets from the bedside table. After that, things got a little hazy.

He had a vague picture of wrestling on the bed with Gloria. They laughed and giggled as he put his hand up her skirt and tried to pull down her panties. Did it happen, or did he dream it in his sleep? Damned if he remembered anything else! He couldn't remember them having sex, though the wet spot suggested otherwise.

* * *

Dan awoke refreshed, Saturday's nightmare almost forgotten. After breakfast, he settled down to read the manuscript. Although it was better than he expected, he found it difficult to concentrate. His mind kept returning to Gloria.

Her demure exterior cloaked a fun-loving young woman. Dan looked forward to seeing her again. A charge of excitement coursed through him as he recalled the evening. Where did their relationship stand? How far did they go? With no memory of events past a certain point, it would be awkward. A sunny Sunday afternoon might provide a different view of things from the intoxicating rain and darkness of a cosy Friday night. And of course, the alcohol played a part.

The day passed slowly, and as mid-afternoon approached, Dan had second thoughts about returning to see Gloria. Would he look too eager to be visiting her so soon after leaving her apartment? He'd only read half a dozen pages of her manuscript, so he didn't even have that excuse for the visit.

At ten minutes to four, he plucked up the courage to visit her. He jumped into the Hyundai and headed for her apartment on Central Avenue. He parked the car near the building entrance and walked up to the first floor. At the end of the public corridor, Gloria sat on a chair in her doorway. Propped against the corridor wall next to her was her mattress.

'Dan, what a nice surprise! After you disappeared on Saturday morning, I wasn't sure if or when I'd see you again.'

'Well, I would need to return your manuscript, but I haven't finished reading it. What's the story with your mattress?'

'I'm trying to dry it and get rid of the whisky smell.'

'Oh!'

'You spilled your whisky on the bed on Friday night. It left a big wet patch in the middle. The dull day yesterday didn't help, so today I sunned the mattress on my balcony this morning and brought it here to sun this afternoon.'

'Sorry, I never realised.'

'Now that you're here, please help me get it back on the bed?'

'Is it OK now?'

'Well, it's better. Last night's strong whisky odour is just a faint whiff now.'

'I noticed the wet patch yesterday morning, but I didn't realise it was whisky. I thought it was … well, you know.'

'Mr Scott, do you imagine I'd sleep with a man on a first date?'

'If Friday was our first date, can we count this as our second?'

'You said you'd do research for your book this weekend.'

'Yes, and here I am. Tell me, what happened on Friday evening?'

'When you came over to the bed, I showed you my sister's condoms. The next minute, you sat down and toppled over, fast asleep. That's when you spilled your whisky.'

'Is that all? Nothing happened?'

'No, nothing.'

'Did you get sick yesterday after all that scotch? I spent the entire day vomiting, and I worried about how you might be coping.'

'No, I was fine.'

'If you've never drunk scotch, how did you drink such a lot on Friday?'

'I didn't drink as much as you. I only drank about one glass.'

'You poured yourself a tot each time you poured me one.'

'When you weren't looking, I topped up your glass from mine. Sorry if it made you sick, but I didn't like it.'

'It's a relief to hear you say that, because I worried there was something wrong with me. No wonder I can't remember anything beyond you rummaging through the condoms in the drawer.'

'Did we wrestle on the bed for a while, or did I dream it? I seem to remember you laughing and giggling.'

'You must have dreamed it.'

'How come we both end up naked in bed?'

'Would you have preferred to sleep in your clothes? So, I had to remove them.'

'And what about you? You were also naked.'

'I always sleep in the nude.'

'Anyway, I've given up drinking alcohol, so how about one of your coffees? Perhaps you can show me your condoms again? The last time, I found it difficult to concentrate.'

Dan and Gloria carried the heavy mattress back to the bed. He wondered how she lugged it onto the balcony and, later, to the public corridor by herself. She was shapely but slender, so it must have been quite a struggle.

* * *

Later, back at the hotel, Dan's mind filled with thoughts of Gloria. Ten-thirty, and he realised he'd forgotten all about dinner. Gloria was a big distraction. He looked through the room service menu and ordered a hamburger and chips.

The best weekend yet, despite the awful Saturday, languishing in his room. He chuckled when he pictured himself telling Daniel to forget about a return to the Lounge Club. At least he wouldn't need to worry about being alone on the weekends. But a worry niggled at his mind. He wondered why he'd not considered the possibility earlier.

Gloria's cosy apartment, the drinks cabinet, the condoms in the bedside table drawer, the double bed. Did all that belong to her sister? Or was it possible Gloria might be a sophisticated young prostitute? She'd not attempted to charge him anything for her company and hospitality. Though, if she was the ambitious young writer she professed to be, she'd got him, a known novelist, to review her manuscript. The services he provided for free would cost her a lot of money if she paid for it. Perhaps that's how he paid for her hospitality. A quid pro quo, so to speak.

When Captain John gave him the car to go to the art gallery, he said Dan should hang on to it. He also mentioned his contacts looked for a suitable furnished apartment for Dan. That presented him with a problem. How would Nikita find him if he photographed the Honey File after he left the hotel? Though still unsure if he wanted her to find him, he thought it wise to keep his options open.

The way Nikita foisted a problem on to him irritated Dan. Zimbabwean politics was not his concern, so why should he get involved? But when he remembered the dinner with the unfortunate Absalom Muzenda and the way they implicated him in his murder, he knew he needed to do something. Also, the problem of his missing passport remained unresolved. Perhaps he'd need Nikita and her colleagues to help him out of this mess.

What if Captain John told him tomorrow they'd found him an apartment? With all John's contacts, finding a suitable apartment wouldn't take too long. Dan didn't need to give the hotel notice of his intention to leave. He could move in an instant.

The perfect opportunity to photograph the file might come too late. Only one thing for it. He must create the opportunity. He knew the enormous risk, but he'd have to take a chance. How often there'd been the opportunity, but caution held him back. Now, time was slipping away. He'd take the photo this coming week, and the sooner the better.

Dan passed a restless night. He'd resolved one concern but gained two more. Not the odds he favoured. This week, perhaps even tomorrow, he'd roll the dice and hold his breath.

CHAPTER 15

MONDAY morning. Another bright day to start the week. Dan drove to work in the Hyundai, though he preferred to walk. He didn't want to assume the car was for his permanent use until Captain John confirmed it. He parked it under the trees where he found it on Friday afternoon and skipped up the steps onto the wide veranda. Through the entrance, Cherry's beaming smile greeted him; the perfect tonic to start his working day.

Dan popped into Captain John's office to say good morning.

'How did the talk go?'

'Yeah, not bad, thanks. Mrs Olonga, the writers' club president, has asked me if I'd like to do a repeat at the Bulawayo writers' festival.'

'Yes, why not?'

'I was thinking of getting in touch with Ian Sanders, the writer in Botswana, and asking him if he'd also like to speak at the festival.'

'That's a good idea. Yes, do that.'

Captain John smiled, and Dan wondered about his obvious interest in his talk. To his relief, John said nothing about the search for a suitable apartment. The longer it took, the better. The search was underway, and every extra day before he needed to move counted as a precious opportunity to photograph the Honey File.

Even Gloria was forgotten as he pondered how to create the opportunity. The computer network would give him the perfect excuse to be in and out of Captain John's office without raising undue suspicion. A computer problem, perhaps? That wasn't so easy when everything worked well.

John's office was spacious; equivalent to two large offices. Dan's frequent presence didn't seem to disturb John, as they weren't on top of each other in the room. On a couple of rare occasions, John asked him to leave the office when he wanted to make private phone calls.

Through the day, no obvious opportunity arose, and true to the pattern Dan discerned, Captain John didn't invite him for drinks after work. He seldom did on a Monday. Tomorrow, Tuesday, John probably would invite him for drinks, so perhaps there'd be a chance then.

Back in the hotel, Dan wondered how he could warn Nikita he would soon be moving. If he had the means of initiating contact with her, it would be easy, but she didn't want any phone communication. She didn't give him her number, and she said she wouldn't phone him. Nikita said she'd know when he took the photo. That meant she had a source within the COU.

Perhaps the source would tell her when and where he moved. What if the source wasn't aware of his move? If he told everybody his new address, that might cover it, but he didn't want everyone to know where he lived. If he told everyone he would soon move, it might prompt Nikita to contact him and arrange a secure means of ongoing communication.

Dan realised all his thoughts were a way of trying to delay the inevitable. No, he needed to act before Captain John found him an apartment.

Tuesday's drinks did not present him with the opportunity to take the photo. The keys weren't hanging in the filing cabinet lock. John was about to pour his second scotch when he noticed Dan had hardly touched his first.

'Drink up Dan. You're slow tonight. Is something wrong?'

'Oh, I just feel a little off tonight. I should be fine in the next couple of days.'

On Wednesday, as usual, it was Eunice's turn to meet with John. Dan wondered why Captain John never invited him and Eunice for drinks on the same evening. Perhaps because their roles didn't overlap, or maybe he meant to keep them apart.

When Dan returned to the hotel, he found a message waiting for him. Daniel Moyo would pass by the hotel at six. If Dan was available, they could meet for a drink at the Explorer's Bar. Dan looked at his watch. Five minutes to six. He hurried to catch the lift down to the lobby.

Usually, they sat on the tall stools in the bar's corner, where they could talk in private. Sure enough, Daniel was already waiting there. He was the one male with no connection to the COU and David Jones, and Dan thought he could trust him. 'Daniel, have you heard of Cupid's Bow? I think it's an escort service or brothel.'

'Yeah, sure. Cupid's Bow is a high-class service; very expensive.'

'Are you familiar with the girls there?'

'A few. I've needed to make social arrangements for visiting clients from time to time.'

'Are you familiar with a girl called Nikita?'

'No, why do you ask? Do you want me to introduce you to one of the girls?'

'No, no, I'm just curious. Someone mentioned if I ever dealt with Cupid's Bow, I should ask for Nikita.'

'Sorry, I can't help you there. Perhaps she's new. Why don't you try your luck with Rita? She seemed interested in you when we were at the Lounge Club.'

'Thanks Daniel, I'm OK in that department.'

'Oh! Who's the lucky lady?'

'An aspiring writer, so we have a lot in common.'

'And in the important areas?' said Daniel with a mischievous grin.

'She's great. Young, attractive, and playful.'

'Is it serious?'

'I only met her last weekend.'

'So, why all these questions about Nikita?'

'No reason. Just curious.'

'It's best not to be greedy. Rita, Nikita, your writing friend, who is next?' They both laughed. 'What's your secret, Dan?'

'Novelty, I guess. There aren't many whites around here. Anyway, Nikita hasn't expressed an interest in me.'

'Oh! So you've met her?'

'No, I've just heard about her.'

'Are you sure? She seems to be occupying a lot of our conversation, considering you've never met her.'

'Yes, and how're your wife and kids?'

'Fine thanks, Dan. How about another scotch? Perhaps it might loosen your tongue a little more.'

'No, I'll have a beer, thanks. One scotch is enough for tonight.'

'OK! How come you're suddenly off scotch?'

'Oh, that's a long story.'

* * *

Later, in his room, Dan realised there might be another way to contact Nikita. He looked up Cupid's Bow on the net and dialled their number. A sultry voice answered. 'Cupid's Bow, your route to happiness.'

'Good evening, I'd be interested in meeting one of your girls.'

'Yes, Sir. If you tell me your preferences, I'll be able to recommend one that suits you.'

'There's a specific girl I'd like. Her name is Nikita.'

'Nikita? There's no one by that name at this service, Sir. Mandy and Sasha are on duty tonight. I can call in one of the others if you like, but there's no one called Nikita. Can you describe this girl?'

Dan did his best to describe Nikita, though he'd only met her once. He described what she wore and her long black curly hair, which was probably a wig. In describing her, all Dan could add was her approximate height and the fact she was shapely with a pretty face. He couldn't recall her features and wouldn't recognise her if she wore different clothing.

The sultry voice on the phone laughed. 'I know who you mean. Anita, not Nikita. I can call her in, but if she's the wrong girl, or you don't like her, you must still pay the callout fee of fifty U.S. dollars. Do you want me to send her to you?'

Dan hesitated, but had little choice. This might be his only chance to warn her about his impending move from the hotel. He gave the lady on the phone his room number.

'She'll be with you in one hour, Sir.'

Dan put down the phone. At least seeing Nikita again would give him a second chance to assess her bona fides. If he photographed the Honey File and put it in the wrong hands, he might create a major problem for himself. He realised the COU had already caught him in its net, but at least he seemed to be in favour. If Nikita or Anita, whatever her name, misused the photo, all that might soon change. And Heaven forbid if Nikita was a trap Captain John set for him.

The hour passed, and there was a gentle tap on Dan's door. He hurried to open it. The shy young girl who stood there wasn't Nikita. She wasn't the confident woman who brushed past him, ignoring his protests, when she entered his room. He couldn't picture Nikita's face, but he knew this was not it. 'I'm sorry, you are not whom I expected.'

'Oh, sorry, Sir. Did the lady say you must pay a fifty-dollar callout fee?'

'Yes, come in. I'll get it for you.'

'If you want me to stay, the fifty dollars will go against the one-hundred-and-fifty-dollar cost.'

'No, thank you. I wasn't looking for that service.'

'You can change your mind, Sir.'

'You are pretty, and in other circumstances I'd be happy for you to stay, but not tonight, thank you.'

Dan gave the young woman the fifty dollars, content he'd tempered her disappointment with his gentle dismissal. These poor girls had no other means of making a living and needed to take advantage of youth's bloom while it lasted. He appreciated he shouldn't feel bad about rejecting her services, though somehow, he did.

Tomorrow was Thursday, which usually meant drinks with Captain John. Dan drifted off to a restless sleep with mixed thoughts.

* * *

Thursday. Dan fiddled around with the computer network all day. Captain John worked at his desk and wasn't going anywhere. At five o'clock, John took out two tumblers and a bottle of scotch. A new one Dan didn't recognise. Eunice had already left, and the keys hung in the filing cabinet, teasing and tempting. John was settling in for a drink with his feet on his desk. He looked more relaxed than ever.

'Good news, Dan. We've found you a nice flat. We can't quite match the Meikles Hotel, I'm afraid, though it's a lot more spacious and very comfortable. You can move in on Monday. The apartment is well located, close to Harare Gardens. Cherry tells me it has a nice, treed aspect and is private. She'll give you the details tomorrow.'

For Dan, it wasn't good news. He feared this would happen. John rarely invited him for drinks on a Friday, so today was his last chance. And even if he photographed the file, Nikita may not hear about it until after he moved.

'John, the network is becoming a little slow. I need to do a couple of minor fixes before it all freezes.'

'I haven't noticed it being slow.'

'Perhaps not, but I've seen the warning signs. It's better to get in early before the sluggishness affects the entire network.'

'I need to make the adjustments from your computer. If you wouldn't mind, please go to Eunice's computer, switch it on, and login. You have her password. I'll jump on your computer for the fix. When you login, please note the exact time in the bottom righthand corner of the screen. I'll send you an email on her computer, and I need the exact time you get it. Sometimes, it takes a minute or two.'

'OK, let's give it a go.'

John walked out, heading to Eunice's office just past the strongroom. Dan sat down in John's chair and logged in as the network administrator. As he stood to move to the filing cabinet, John walked back through the doorway. Dan caught his breath. If John had returned only seconds later, he would have found him at the filing cabinet.

'I forgot to take her password.' John walked to his desk drawer and took out a piece of paper. This time, before moving, Dan listened to John's steps retreating down the corridor.

Now it was time to act. Dan jumped up and hurried to the filing cabinet, and opened the top drawer. He looked in the suspension file marked *Honey File*, and inside found the manilla folder. He pulled out the sheet of paper, and with Nikita's cell phone, photographed the page. The back was blank, so he stuffed the sheet back in the manilla folder.

'I'm going now, Sir, I'll see you tomorrow.'

The words sent a shock through Dan's body. On his inside, it was like an electric jolt. He hoped he showed no external reflex to Cherry's polite interruption. 'Goodnight, Cherry,' said Dan, sliding closed the cabinet drawer as if it was routine for him to be there.

He hurried back to the computer and sent a 'fix completed' email to Eunice's computer, where John waited.

Moments later, John walked into the room. 'Everything OK?'

'All fixed,' said Dan, thankful John wasn't too computer literate. His ruse to get Captain John out of his office seemed to have worked.

'Great! Time for another scotch then.'

Dan needed it. His spine still tingled from the chill Cherry's unexpected interruption gave him.

* * *

Later, back at the hotel, Dan worried whether Cherry would tell anyone about him being at the filing cabinet. She'd likely not seen him photograph the Honey File, though she may have seen him putting the sheet back in the folder. Though even if she had, it might not have raised her suspicions. As far as he was aware, Captain John alone knew the nature of his role at the COU. Hell! Even he barely understood what it was. To Cherry, it all might appear quite innocent.

The problem with Nikita remained. Now he'd taken the photo, he'd no means of delivering it. Thursday night to Monday morning, when he'd check out of the hotel, didn't give Nikita much time to react.

CHAPTER 16

Friday morning, and Dan faced the day with a little trepidation. He worried what Cherry may have seen last night, and what she might do. She gave him the same cheery greeting as always. Captain John seemed no different to normal, and no sooner Dan settled in at his desk, Ambrose appeared with one of his steaming cups of tea.

Moments later, Cherry popped into Dan's office. 'Here's the address of your new flat, Sir. It's a very nice flat. I hope you like it.'

'Thank you, Cherry. Who selected the flat? Do you know?'

'Ambrose and I chose it, Sir.'

'Oh!' Dan wondered about Cherry's tastes. What Cherry may have considered nice might not appeal to him.

'These are the flat keys, Sir. We have connected the electricity and water, but sometimes the authorities switch them off to make savings.'

'Thank you, Cherry.'

'And Captain John said you must keep the car. It's too far to walk from the flat.'

'OK, thanks.'

'The flat is furnished and there're towels and sheets in the laundry cupboard. Ambrose and I made up the bed, so everything is ready for you. There's bread and milk and other food, Sir.'

'You and Ambrose spoil me, Cherry.'

'That is our job, Sir.'

The day passed without incident. Cherry couldn't have mentioned anything to Captain John about Dan being in the filing cabinet. Either that, or John waited for his moment to act. John was as friendly as ever. If he had any issue with him, he hid it well.

Since the earlier weeks in the COU, Dan saw little of Eunice. It was obvious she resented his arrival, and initially, she hovered around, looking for any excuse to discredit him. Since he installed her computer, she seemed to have mellowed, and their paths seldom crossed. Dan wasn't unhappy about that.

At five o'clock, he retrieved the car keys from Cherry and headed back to the hotel. He thought about passing his new flat but decided against it. He wasn't due to check out of the Meikles Hotel until Monday morning and didn't want to spend the weekend worrying about the flat. It might not be so bad, though he wasn't too hopeful.

After the luxury of the Meikles Hotel, the inevitable drop in the standard of his accommodation concerned him. What worried him most was luxury hotels like Meikles had means of finding their way around the problems the city faced. This might include generators to ensure electricity supply, or water tanks to cover the periodic water shortages. Either way, at the hotel, he'd avoided such issues. In the apartment, it might be a different story. Was there television and an internet connection?

* * *

Saturday morning in Harare was always busy. After breakfast, Dan planned to visit Gloria in the bookshop where she worked. He made no concrete plan about when he'd next see her, so he thought he'd give her a surprise by popping into the shop. As he entered, he saw her talking to someone at the other end of the store.

He waited while she dealt with the person who looked like a potential customer. When Gloria saw Dan, she smiled before walking over to greet him. Once more, she looked like the demure young woman he'd met at the writers' club. But behind those black-rimmed glasses, he caught a twinkle in her eye.

'What time do you finish work today?'

'Lunchtime. One o'clock.'

'Did you work last Saturday?'

'Yes, of course. I work every Saturday.'

'Can I see you later this afternoon?'

'Yes, come at four. I'll make dinner this evening, and we can drink one of my sister's wines.'

Dan left the bookshop and walked around the city centre. On each of his city walks, he discovered fresh places of interest. Harare boasted many attractive buildings, but the condition of the pavements and roads let it down. The city needed better maintenance. Once a glorious centre, it could be again, with capable political and civil leadership.

After a light lunch, Dan read more of Gloria's manuscript. Then he enjoyed a refreshing shower and got ready for the evening. At a quarter to four, he caught the lift to the lobby and walked to the hotel carpark to collect the Hyundai.

Dark clouds gathered, suggesting another storm was on its way. Dan never minded the downpours as they cooled the hot days and freshened the air. The days with the storms that rolled in at regular intervals were his favourite. Brilliant sunshine followed by ominous dark clouds, leading to a torrential downpour, followed once again by brilliant sunshine. And so the pattern repeated.

On his way, Dan stopped to buy a bunch of colourful daisies from a street vendor. He parked the car outside the front entrance to the two-storey block of flats and skipped up the stairs to the first floor. At the corridor's end, he knocked on the door. Gloria opened it.

Dan gasped in surprise. This was the first time he'd seen her dressed for a date, albeit one at her flat. She wore a deep red, tight-fitting dress with matching stud earrings and open-toed, strappy shoes. Missing were her black-rimmed spectacles. Red lipstick set off her coffee brown skin. The image took Dan's breath away. 'You look gorgeous.'

'Thank you. Are those flowers for me?'

'Yes. Perhaps I should have worn a suit. I'm under-dressed.'

'Come in. I've had electricity all day, so the champagne is chilled.'

'Champagne? What are we celebrating?'

'I'll think of something.'

'Us together on a Saturday night? That saves me wondering what I'm going to do with myself.'

'That applies to me too.'

'Do you stay home on Saturday nights?'

'Yes, often.'

'Don't you have a lot of men chasing after you?'

'Not the right men. And besides, many men fear girls who wear business suits and glasses.'

'Well, you certainly scared me with your questions at the writers' club last Friday.'

'I didn't mean to scare you. My questions were only to get your attention.'

'They did that all right. So, you planned the whole thing?'

'I didn't plan the rain.'

'Hmm!'

'Is that my manuscript you've brought with you?'

'Yes.'

'And?'

'I like it. You must keep your writing style because it's your voice. There may be one or two tips on story structure I can give you, but overall, your story and writing are great.'

'You must be honest with your criticism.'

'Of course.'

'Can you please open the champagne?'

'Is this your sister's champagne?'

'Of course.'

Her reply amused Dan. 'And the dinner?'

Gloria laughed. 'No, that's mine.'

After they'd eaten and drunk a cup of her special coffee, she washed the dishes, and Dan did the drying, feeling at home.

Suddenly, the lights went out. 'Another outage. At least they waited for us to finish dinner,' said Gloria.

Only then, they noticed the flashes of lightning and the distant rumble of thunder. Gloria moved around the room, turning off the light switches.

'What are you doing?'

'Switching off the lights. The power often comes back on at four in the morning.'

Dan thought about his new flat. 'Do these outages happen often?'

'Yes, often.'

'What do you do then?'

'Sometimes I light a candle. When there's thunder and lightning, or a big storm, I love to lie in bed and watch it.'

'Oh, I like that idea!'

The lightning flashes were more frequent, and the thunder louder. 'The storm is coming our way,' said Dan.

'Would you like to lie in bed and watch it?'

'Yes, I would.'

Without another word, Gloria slipped off her shoes, unzipped her dress, and let it fall to the floor before hanging it over the back of a chair. Dan caught his breath as a flash of lightning silhouetted her slim, youthful body. She wore no underwear. Gloria jumped into bed, covering herself with the blanket, and turning onto her side to view the lightning. Each flash of lightning and thunderclap was more spectacular.

Dan watched Gloria undress, spellbound. Now he hurried to remove his clothes. He slipped under the blanket and drew himself up close behind her. Blinding flashes of lightning forked through the sky, with claps of thunder that rattled the apartment windows.

Gloria snuggled her back into Dan, and he put his hand around her waist, holding her tight. His right hand moved up and cupped her breast, so warm and firm. This was the first time he'd touched her. The previous Sunday, he'd joked about taking another look at the condoms, but she didn't take the bait, and they spent the evening chatting.

Now she moulded herself into him as the lightning flashed and the thunder crashed, and with his hands, Dan explored her body. The hiss of the rain grew to a roar as it drummed on the apartment roof. When the storm at last eased, Gloria turned towards Dan. She must have had the condom under her pillow. She took it from the packet and carefully rolled it onto his erection. He was so hard he felt he might burst.

Gloria was wet, and Dan entered her with a single, smooth stroke. He'd waited a frustrating week for this moment. Only now did he realise how much he needed her. They made love twice more, before falling asleep to the drip, drip of the raindrops falling from the trees.

* * *

In the morning, they again made love before Gloria prepared a breakfast of soft-boiled eggs and toast. It was all unhurried, and when Dan returned to the hotel, it was close to midday.

He was in a good mood. The morning seemed brighter, the air fresher and the people friendlier. He parked the car and skipped up the steps to the hotel lobby. After a light lunch, he planned to spend the afternoon working on his novel. Dan felt motivated and ready to make progress after a longish period of procrastination.

Throughout the afternoon, he thought a lot about Gloria. Meeting her made all the difference to his stay in Zimbabwe. Despite his misgivings about several issues, he was more than pleased he'd accepted David Jones's invitation to return to the country.

As evening closed in, Dan showered, and then caught the lift to the lobby for a beer at The Explorer's Bar. Perhaps one last steak in the hotel restaurant, before he found himself consigned to the tribulations of a bachelor's life in his new apartment. The waiters were a little downcast when they heard the news of Dan's pending departure, but a generous tip helped to lift their spirits.

Dan was sorry to be leaving his luxurious room at the Meikles Hotel. Just as his relationship with Gloria advanced, he was moving to more modest accommodation. He would have liked to show her the hotel and his luxurious room, but he'd missed the opportunity. It was a luxury beyond anything she would have experienced.

He'd not heard from Nikita; perhaps it was just as well. If he didn't give her the photos, she couldn't use them in any way that might lead back to him. It was best not to get involved in whatever Nikita and her colleagues planned. It wasn't his business or his fight.

Dan took a beer from the minibar and pulled up a chair to the window overlooking Africa Unity Square and the buildings beyond. Just a few blocks ahead lay Gloria's flat. He wondered what she was doing this evening. Almost ten o'clock. After last night, she'd probably be in bed, catching up on her sleep. Yes, and he should do the same.

A knock at the door. Perhaps it was the hotel's final account for his stay. Dan eased himself from the chair and walked to the door. He opened it, and there stood Nikita, dressed as she was the first time he met her. She didn't wait for his invitation to enter the room as she brushed past him. He closed the door and turned towards her. 'Nikita, I've been trying to get in touch with you.'

'A beer would be fine, thanks.'

Dan opened the minibar, grabbed a beer, and flipped off the cap. He was about to hand it to her, when he remembered she liked to drink from a glass. He opened the minibar again and took out a tumbler, still sealed in its paper cover declaring its sanitary condition.

'Did you get the photo?'

'Yes. In fact, I got two photos. On my first attempt, I got a photo of a file marked Domestic. Then on Thursday, I photographed the Honey File. How did you know I'd taken the photo?'

'I didn't. I just came to hurry you along. Lives may depend on us getting those photos. Have you looked at them?'

'Yes, I had a quick look. Both photos just contain a list of African names. They meant nothing to me.'

'Well, they mean everything to us, so thank you.'

'My pleasure. Actually, it wasn't. It was quite stressful. I hope it's the end of it and you don't expect me to get anything else for you.'

'I can't promise that.'

'You know I'm moving, don't you?'

'No, when?'

'Tomorrow. That's why I thought you came tonight.'

'What's your new address?'

'If I don't give it to you, you won't be able to give me any more dangerous tasks.'

'Don't be silly. You can't hide from me in a city as small as Harare. Not for long, anyway.'

After Nikita left, Dan puzzled over the situation. She must have known he was leaving the hotel the next day. Was her last-minute visit a coincidence? Cherry must have seen him replacing the sheet of paper into the filing cabinet. But if Cherry was her contact, why didn't Nikita know his new address?

It was obvious she was an intelligent woman. To throw him off the scent, she pretended not to know he was moving. Yes, that must be it!

CHAPTER 17

MONDAY morning. Dan ate breakfast in the hotel, and it gave him the opportunity to tip the waiters he'd not seen at dinner the previous evening. Afterwards, he returned to his room to brush his teeth and check he'd not forgotten anything. He surveyed the view from his window before grabbing his bag and heading for the door. One more glance at the room, and he pulled the door closed behind him.

Time to check out. The hotel was sorry to see him leave. He'd become a regular around the restaurant and The Explorers' Bar. The staff would miss him. The inevitable invitation to come back soon accompanied all the usual farewell pleasantries.

Dan wasn't due in the office until after lunch, so he would spend the morning settling into his new apartment. He collected his car from the hotel parking and drove through the morning rush hour traffic, heading for The Avenues, a suburb close to Harare Gardens.

He found the address and viewed the north facing, white, two-storey block with interest. The exterior didn't look too bad. The apartments looked onto the avenue, with private, black, wrought-iron balconies running the width of the building. Established wisterias entwined themselves through the wrought iron, reminiscent of New Orleans. There appeared to be four apartments on each floor, eight in all.

It was an old-fashioned exterior, but the interior would be telling. Dan parked the car and ascended the stairs at the end of the building. The public corridor looked clean and well maintained. His apartment was number seven, upstairs, second from the end. Dan swung open the door and was struck by the clean, modern appearance of the open-plan room's antique-white walls and black vertical blinds.

Left of the front door stood the kitchen area, beyond which the dining area and lounge led onto the balcony overlooking the avenue. To the right stood the bedroom door. The ensuite bathroom and toilet backed on to the public corridor. Like the lounge, the bedroom also boasted floor to ceiling windows with black vertical blinds and sliding doors onto the private balcony which ran the full width of the apartment.

In the bright interior, the modern kitchen gleamed with a black fridge and oven, and stainless-steel appliances, while the lounge boasted a large flat-screen TV and an internet connection and modem. The bedroom contained a queen-size bed with tasteful furnishings and built-in cupboards.

Overall, the apartment was a pleasant surprise, and he would never doubt Cherry's tastes or judgement again. With modern lighting and plumbing, it was obvious the old building had been renovated. Water tanks collected rainwater from the roof, and Dan would later discover the caretaker operated a generator during lengthy electricity outages. Only air-conditioning was missing.

In the fridge, Dan found half a dozen beers, a bottle of white wine, long-life milk, eggs, tomato sauce, and vegetables. In the kitchen cupboards, he found a bottle of red wine, tea bags, coffee, salt, and pepper. He walked through to the bedroom and hung up his clothes. In the corner of the built-in cupboard stood a mini-safe big enough to hold his laptop. Also, there was an iron and ironing board. In the enormous bathroom stood a washing machine, washing powder, and other cleaning chemicals.

He couldn't believe the amount of thought Cherry and Ambrose had put into making his apartment ready for his arrival. The apartment was setup for visitors who needed more spacious accommodation than a hotel could offer. Perfect!

Dan's broad smile as he entered the COU offices told Cherry and Ambrose everything they wanted to know. They'd done a good job that delighted him. Ambrose brought in Dan's steaming cup of tea and quizzed him about the apartment. He wasn't as perceptive as Cherry about reading everything from Dan's demeanour. Even Captain John didn't need to ask him how he found the apartment.

Before Cherry left work at five, she came into Dan's office with sausages for his evening meal. It suited him fine. He was not a gourmet chef, so sausages, mashed potatoes and tinned green peas would be his dinner tonight; all courtesy of Cherry and Ambrose, though no doubt funded by the COU. A cold beer while he tested his culinary skills should help him through the process.

* * *

Dan took out two sizeable potatoes from the rack in the kitchen. He peeled them, cut them into quarters, and put them in a pan of water on the stove to boil. Next, he opened a tin of peas and poured them into a pan on low heat. He heated oil in a frying pan, and when it was ready, he put in two sausages, which crackled and spat. Dan looked in the fridge for butter for the potatoes he was mashing.

This would be an interesting dinner. Back in Melbourne, he always bought packaged meals from the supermarket. He'd not cooked for himself but simply put the packaged meal in the microwave, following the instructions on the packet.

The dinner worked out well, but Dan wondered what he'd do tomorrow night. There was no meat in the fridge. It would soon spoil with the frequent electricity outages if the caretaker didn't start the generator. Breakfast wouldn't be a problem. He'd seen packets of cereals in the kitchen cupboard, and the bread and milk Cherry put in the fridge still seemed fresh.

Dan sat on a chair on the veranda. The street wasn't too busy, so he enjoyed a beer in the gathering gloom as evening set-in. There was nothing of interest on the television, but the internet connection worked fine. Somebody left written instructions on how to connect to the Wi-Fi.

Well, this was different! No convenient Explorers' Bar downstairs, and no hotel staff to engage in a chat. The environment was peaceful;

too quiet. Dan was unaccustomed to being so isolated in Harare. At least, at the hotel, he could walk, though he seldom did at night. In The Avenues, there seemed little point in walking the quiet streets. So, it was back to his novel.

Ho-hum! Time for another beer. As he opened the fridge, he heard a knock on the door. Ah! Who could that be? Perhaps it was someone from the office. Dan walked to the door and opened it. A woman with long, dark, curly hair and dressed in conservative clothing stood there.

'Hello Dan.'

Dan hesitated; he wasn't sure, but he thought he recognised the voice. 'Nikita? Is that you?'

'I didn't recognise you dressed like that.'

'Now that you're not in the hotel, I don't need to pretend I'm a visiting prostitute, so my disguise is not as elaborate.'

'Your disguise?'

'You don't think this is my real hair, do you? Without a disguise, I'm too recognisable in Harare. Being linked with me could make trouble for you, so I disguised myself.'

'But why as a prostitute?'

'Who else would visit a single man in his hotel room late at night?'

'The hotel warned me about undesirable female visitors.'

'Sorry about that, but it was important.'

'You're just in time to join me for a beer.'

'Thank you. Tell me, how carefully did you read the list of names on the Honey File?'

'I just flicked through them. Why?'

'I printed the Honey File for you to read. Here! Take a closer look.'

Dan took the A4 sheet of paper Nikita handed him. The top three names were crossed out, though they were still legible. At the top of the list was Dr Abel Sibanda, and in the column next to his name was the word *family*. The second name was Professor Gideon Ncube, and the third was Absalom Muzenda. Both had gluttony written in the column next to their names. Ncube's name also had the word *whisky* next to it, and Muzenda's was marked *food*. Dan paused. He hadn't noticed Absalom's name on the list when he saw it on the cell phone. 'Why are the first three deleted?'

'Because they're all dead. That's a list of people marked for elimination.'

'Why is it called the Honey File?'

'It lists people in the diaspora who needed to be enticed back to Zimbabwe. The second column lists their individual weaknesses, and that suggests the honey that might entice them back. And the third column looks like the code numbers for each contract. The Domestic File you photographed is a list of local people they're targeting. Anyone opposed to the regime must be careful. You never know who's got you in their sights.'

'Is Itai Dzamara, the political activist, on the domestic list?'

'No, he's not on the current list, perhaps on an earlier one. Though his case doesn't have the hallmarks of a COU operation. They are much more subtle and wouldn't have sent five men in broad daylight to abduct someone in front of witnesses. The abductors claimed they were detaining him for stealing cattle. A clumsy abduction like that was more likely the army, police, or CIO.'

'What happened to him?'

'Dzamara was at a barber's shop, having his beard trimmed, when five men abducted him in a white, twin-cab pickup van. No one has seen him since then. Examine the list carefully and tell me what else you see.'

Dan looked at the sheet of paper. 'They're all African names. I don't know any of them.' Then he saw it; eight or nine names down from the top, *Dan Scott*, and in the second column, *pride/ego*. His blood ran cold. 'My name is on here!'

'Don't worry, they follow the order of the list, so you'll be fine for now. That's the way it's worked in the past. Captain John is very methodical, so you should be safe until he gets down to your name.'

'But if he goes in order, why did they try to get me at Johannesburg airport?'

'He's methodical, but not inflexible. Why wouldn't he get rid of you outside the country and blame it on Johannesburg's dangerous criminal element?'

'I've twice been to Joburg with Jonas Nyandoro. Why didn't they get rid of me then?'

'Captain John is playing with you. You don't have your passport. They've involved you in a murder, and now you're a fugitive from South African justice, though the authorities haven't yet identified you. I tried to tell you the first time we met, the COU is an assassination unit, not an outplacement business. And be careful of Jonas Nyandoro. He's charming, but he's a ruthless killer. If Captain John gives the word, that's it for you.'

'I need another beer. Would you like one?' Dan opened two beers. He'd have to buy more tomorrow.

'Anyway, enough of this gloomy talk. This is a nice apartment.'

'Yes, courtesy of Captain John and the COU. They found it for me.'

'Oh! Have you met your neighbours? I noticed it would be easy for someone to climb across to your balcony from next door.'

'No, not yet.'

'Perhaps you should keep your balcony doors locked when you go to bed.'

'Yes, it would be easy for someone to climb up those wisterias.'

'Your apartment is nice and spacious, but security is a little weak here. There's plenty of room to practise your ballroom dancing.'

'Ballroom dancing? What do you mean?'

'You don't recognise me, do you?'

'Have we met?'

'More than that. We've danced together.'

Dan's jaw dropped. 'Eva! Colonel Chirau's wife? I wouldn't have recognised you in a million years. At the barbeque, you combed your hair back in a bun.'

'Well, that was my real hair. What you see now is a wig. I suppose we Africans all look the same to you whites.'

'No, not at all. But hair, makeup, and clothing make such a difference. You disguised yourself well.'

'That's true. Not even an African would have recognised me in Nikita's disguise.'

'So, what do I call you now? Nikita or Eva?'

'That depends on my hair. If it's long and curly, I'm Nikita. If it's brushed back into a bun, I'm Eva.'

'What does your husband say about your clandestine activities?'

'We are together in the cause. Victor knows what I'm doing.'

'What's David Jones' involvement in all this?'

'David Jones?'

'Yes, your friend Isaac.'

'Oh, so that's who David Jones is! Isaac is an old acquaintance of Victor. I think he is harmless. He's only interested in doing deals and making money. He knows everyone and everyone's business. The biggest risk with him is what he might let slip when he's talking to others. I don't think he'd deliberately put you in danger, though it's always best to assume he might be a double agent. He's not part of our movement, so he knows nothing about what we do, or your connection with us. And don't forget, he is a friend of Captain John.'

'And Eunice?'

'She's an evil woman. Worse than Captain John. Since she became his second in command, she's proven herself to be a ruthless operator. Stay away from her. Eunice is not methodical like Captain John, and she would make you disappear in an instant if the opportunity presented itself.'

'Don't worry, I will stay away from her.'

'I don't think Captain John knows what she does behind his back. Even powerful men fear her. Captain John has some principles. For example, he won't go after the wives and children of his targets unless they are the targets themselves. Eunice has no such qualms. She will use a man's wife or children to get to him. They say she'll even double-cross Captain John and take over the COU one day.'

'I know she doesn't like me. She's made that clear from the start.'

'Because I'm involved with Victor's movement, I would also be a target, even for Captain John. That is why our connection must stay a secret. If it came out, it would put us both in greater danger. You'll only hear from me if it's essential. Remember to keep an eye on the Honey File, so you know when your name nears the top.'

After Nikita left, Dan's mind buzzed with everything she'd told him. He must be under no illusion about Captain John's friendship. His missing passport now seemed more important than ever. He'd try to get David Jones on to it once more. It struck him he'd not seen David for quite a long time. Where was he? Why hadn't he been in touch? Dan's venture was feeling more and more like being caught is a sticky spider's web.

CHAPTER 18

D AN settled in at the apartment. The neighbours on both sides were elderly white women who owned their apartments and appeared well-off. A distinguished looking black man occupied apartment five at the top of the stairs. Downstairs, the friendly, black female caretaker occupied one apartment, and young black couples occupied the other three.

The polite occupants got on well together. Aside from Dan, everyone else owned their apartment. Gloria visited often and spent each Saturday and Sunday night with Dan. They both enjoyed the huge shower in the bathroom and the large, deep bath, though because of the ongoing water shortage, they seldom used the latter.

Dan entered the relationship with Gloria with little forethought. At first, she was a delicious distraction and company on the weekends. Slowly, he became more attached to her. He didn't like attachments because they restricted his free-wheeling lifestyle and hampered his research. Common interests and a mutual attraction were moulding them into a couple. Dan hated it when she returned to her own apartment, and he toyed with asking her to move in with him. He was conflicted.

At the COU, things moved along smoothly, and Dan relaxed into his role, though he worried about his name on the Honey File. It turned out he wasn't the only white on the list.

The bottom two names, Sarah Kagonye and Ian Sanders, stood bracketed together, with blank rows between them and the rest of the list. Dan recognised the latter as the well-known author living in Botswana. Why was he on the list? He hadn't been too critical of the regime. Nikita pointed out, a lot more than activists and government critics populated the list. Anyone who could afford it could put a contract out on someone. And it might include anyone in the diaspora. Once listed, they'd be lured back to Zimbabwe or dealt with in situ if necessary.

Much to his relief, Dan remained well down the list, with less than three months left on his six-month contract with the COU. Captain John seldom visited his office, but one morning, he knocked on the door and entered. 'Dan, we're pleased with your contribution here and would like to add another six months to your contract, if you're willing.'

'Er, yes, that would be fine.' Dan welcomed John's offer. The six-month project was passing quicker than he expected, and he worried his time in Zimbabwe would be over before he'd made any significant progress with his novel. Then there was Gloria to consider. He wasn't ready to part from her so soon in their relationship. The added six months also appeared to confirm Captain John had no imminent plan for his demise. His missing passport remained a big concern and barrier to his exit from the country whenever that might be. 'John, is there any progress with locating my passport?'

'Regrettably, no. I'm sure it will turn up somewhere. An incompetent police officer or customs official will have mislaid it or left it in a drawer. Don't worry, you will get it back. In the meantime, there's a little job for you and Jonas in Johannesburg. This time you'll be staying in a decent hotel.'

Since Nikita's last visit, Dan thought long and hard about his situation. The Johannesburg trip was another opportunity to escape the COU's tentacles, though several obstacles stood in his way. If he visited the Australian Embassy in Pretoria, he could claim he'd lost his passport. Did they have any means of checking with South African immigration the date of its last use? He wasn't sure. If they did, they'd discover he flew to Zimbabwe on that passport, so what explanation might he give for being back in South Africa?

Although they might not link him to Absalom Muzenda's death, that remained an added complication. And once again, the question of Gloria. He wasn't yet ready to leave her, nor ready to take her with him. The dilemma troubled him often.

Later at the apartment, as he prepared his evening meal, a ping on his cell phone alerted him to a message. Most likely it would be Gloria, but when he checked his phone, he didn't recognise the number.

When he opened the message, he found it was from Jonas. The message read, *Hi Dan, we're off to Joburg again soon. Attached is a souvenir from our last trip. Cheers.* The souvenir was a photo of Dan and Absalom Muzenda on the Berea restaurant's veranda. Judging from the angle, Jonas took it from the pavement outside the restaurant.

The message was a friendly but unsubtle reminder that the COU was one step ahead of him. He realised they would betray him to the South African authorities if he absconded. The COU's evidence of his involvement in Absalom Muzenda's murder would include his fake passport and the photograph. So it would be difficult to use the upcoming Johannesburg trip to escape his situation. When his name neared the top of the Honey File, he'd have no such qualms.

In the meantime, this clear warning pushed him into a decision he'd been avoiding. The Honey File provided him names of people in the diaspora marked for elimination. It also gave him an approximate timetable for their demise. If possible, he'd use this valuable information to help those individuals on the list. At first, he thought their predicament wasn't his problem. Now that he'd joined them on the list, he saw it was.

The next name on the list was Jacob Nkala. If he and Jonas were going to Johannesburg soon, it suggested that's where they'd find him. Dan carried out a Google search for Nkala's name, using Chrome incognito mode. Nothing came up.

It puzzled Dan why Captain John sent him with Jonas on these trips. Didn't they have enough on him already? What else did they hope to achieve by sending him on another mission? His name in the Honey File forewarned and forearmed him. Now, he would be extra careful to avoid any further entanglement in the COU's web.

On his way out of the apartment the next morning, Dan noticed a butterfly struggling to extricate itself from a spider's web. This little drama held extra meaning for him as it reflected his own situation. From experience, he knew any attempt on his part to free the butterfly would only entangle it further. He could only watch the little creature wait for its inevitable doom.

* * *

Gloria arrived at the apartment at lunchtime on Saturday to spend the weekend. She unknowingly played a part in Dan's thinking about using Johannesburg to escape from the COU's net. That option evaporated when he received Jonas's email, and paradoxically, he was grateful for that. The warning relieved him of a difficult decision.

Dan couldn't abandon Gloria in Zimbabwe when she was such an important part of his life. He hadn't intended for it to be so, but his relationship with her created its own sticky web. It appeared life wasn't simple, and what may seem like small decisions can have life-changing consequences. Most important right now was she'd relieve him from having to prepare lunch.

Gloria always came prepared for any eventuality. Tonight, Dan planned to surprise her with dinner at the Meikles Hotel. But the biggest surprise was for him. She emerged from the bedroom in a royal blue, textured, tight-fitting dress complemented by black strappy shoes and orange, daisy-shaped earrings. Somehow, she always took his breath away. He wondered if she was going commando again. He'd find the answer to that later.

'I expect that's your sister's dress,' said Dan with a grin.

'Almost all my dresses once belonged to my sister, but they're a little tight for her now.'

'I hope you don't outgrow them because they look lovely on you.'

At the hotel, the waiters were pleased to see Dan and his 'beautiful' girlfriend and fussed around, giving them VIP treatment. After dinner, they had a drink at the Explorers' Bar. The staff there welcomed him like an old friend.

'You're popular here, aren't you?'

'Well, I stayed here for several weeks. I didn't want to leave the hotel, but I'm happy at the apartment now. Have you visited this hotel before tonight?'

'No, not even in the lobby.'

'Next week, I have to go to Johannesburg for a couple of days.'

'Well, hurry back. I hate you being so far away.'

'It's not so far. Your sister is in Cape Town.'

'That's different.'

'In what way?'

'I need you more. A few blocks between us are all I can bear.'

'Yes, I know what you mean. It's the same with me.'

Their sticky web just got a little stickier.

Suddenly, Dan glimpsed Captain John sitting at a table at the far end of the bar. He leant to one side to see who accompanied him. An attractive white woman, not his wife, whom Dan knew to be black. The woman sitting with John had short auburn hair and wore a smart, light green dress. She looked to be in her fifties, and it was obvious she kept herself in great shape.

'Come on,' said Dan, 'Let's go.'

His rush to leave the hotel surprised Gloria. 'So soon?'

'Don't worry, we'll come again before long.'

'What's the hurry?'

'I can't wait to get you into bed.'

'Oh! OK. That's all right then. Race you to the car!'

Dan didn't want Captain John to see him with Gloria. Nothing good would come from introducing her to anyone in the COU. He now understood how that unit operated. If they thought she meant anything to him, it would only give them an extra hold over him.

Lying naked in bed, cuddled up under the sheets, Dan and Gloria listened to the inner suburb's night sounds: a dog barking in the distance, the occasional scrunch of a passing car's tyres, muffled voices of the few passers-by.

'Who was that man in the hotel?' asked Gloria.

'What man?'

'The one you saw just before you said we must leave.'

'Oh, him! I work with him.'

'Why didn't you say hello?'

'Never mix business with pleasure.'

'So, you'll never introduce me to any of your friends?'

'My work colleagues aren't friends. Some of them aren't very nice.'

'What do you mean?'

'They're dangerous people.'

'Then why do you work there?'

'I only found out after I joined the business. Anyway, it's not for long. I came to Zimbabwe to find inspiration for my novel. When it's finished, I'll leave the organisation.'

'And what happens then?'

'That's not for ages.'

'You said, "it's not for long."'

'I meant it's temporary. I won't work with them for too long.'

After they made love, Dan fell asleep, but Gloria lay awake, thinking. She wondered about their future together. Until now, she'd not considered what might happen when Dan finished his novel and completed the contract with his employer. He never spoke about his work, only saying it was top secret. Now, their brief chat made her feel a little insecure in her relationship with him. When she suggested she hated being away from him, she meant it. Was he serious when he said that? She wasn't sure.

CHAPTER 19

TUESDAY morning, beautiful with clear blue skies. Johannesburg looked fresh in the sparkling light. Dan's fake passport worked well. The accumulating immigration stamps gave it an air of legitimacy. Francis waited in the arrivals hall to meet Jonas and Dan. He was disappointed they'd not stay at the flat, though he appreciated it was too close to their last visit to risk returning there. Someone might recognise them so soon after the Absalom Muzenda incident.

Francis confirmed he'd organised the repair of the flat's door, and it was now liveable. Dan questioned that description. Stretched sheets and blankets would still cover the missing floor to ceiling windows and give little protection against a cooling April breeze.

'We'll go to Nkala's shop this afternoon,' said Jonas, as Francis dropped them off at the Crowne Plaza Hotel in Rosebank. 'Pick us up at two.'

After Francis left, they checked in to the hotel and rode the lift together. Their rooms were on different floors, and as Jonas exited the lift, he said, 'Meet me in the lobby in half an hour for lunch.' Dan had a comfortable room with views across the tree canopy into the distance. A significant upgrade from Francis's flat.

Following a light lunch in the hotel, they drank coffee in the spacious lounge area. 'I noticed you checked in under a false name,' said Dan.

'Yes, your fake passport worked so well, we decided I should do the same. No point in leaving a trail for the authorities to follow.'

'My fake passport is in my real name.'

'Yes, we won't make that mistake again.'

'That means I'm leaving a trail for the authorities to follow.'

'Perhaps, but I'm down here so often it's a bigger problem for me. You should be OK.'

* * *

Right on two, Francis arrived, and they bundled into his old car and headed off to meet Jacob Nkala in his cell phone shop on the old eastern edge of the city. This was a neglected area in Johannesburg with rubbish piled against shop windows and on the street corners. The elegant northern suburbs and the run down southern and eastern parts of the city were worlds apart.

No matter how lowly paid or unemployed, people still somehow afforded cell phones, and Nkala did well in financial terms. His reputation for laziness and greed preceded him, and someone wanted him gone.

Francis parked in a side street near Nkala's shop. He stayed to guard the car while Jonas and Dan walked to meet Nkala. Several Africans loitered in shop doorways or dawdled on the pavement. Many spent their day watching others walk past, heading nowhere in particular.

Nkala, a large slovenly looking man, sported heavy rings on four of his fingers. It was surprising how well he stocked the shop. While Jonas spoke to Nkala, Dan looked at the phones on display.

Jonas hadn't even bothered to introduce him to Nkala, and Dan wondered what the hell he was doing there. Why couldn't he have stayed in the car and Francis visit the shop with Jonas?

Dan picked up a business card from a holder on the counter and listened in to Jonas's conversation. Nkala looked agitated. 'Listen Jonas, I'm not stupid. If I returned, it would be the end of me. People are jealous of my success.'

'It's not your success that puts you in danger, Jacob. It's your constant criticism of the regime, and the people you rub up the wrong way.'

'Can you imagine me running a business like this in Zimbabwe? Some ZANU bigwigs would muscle in and push me out. And then, to avoid repercussions, they'd make me disappear.'

'Jacob, you're not safe here either. Don't you understand South Africans want foreign blacks out of the country? Look at today's unrest.'

'I keep quiet about my origins. Many people take me for a Zulu.'

'You're crazy if you think you can get away with that.'

'I'll take my chances.'

Dan had heard enough. He stepped out of the shop and viewed the phones in the window. A few minutes later, Jonas joined him. 'That stubborn old fool will be sorry. Just wait and see.'

When they returned to the car, they found a nervous Francis ready to leave. 'I've had people tap on the window and ask me what I'm doing here. I used my best Joburg accent to brush them off, but they're suspicious. See, they're hanging around here. It would be the end for me if they discovered I'm from Maputo.'

'Agh man,' said Jonas, 'you grew up here. How would they guess you're from Mozambique?'

'Man, you can't hide your tribe. They'd soon find out I'm not South African.'

As they pulled out of the parking spot, someone threw a bottle at the car. Francis sped down the road and around the corner. Jonas spoke to him in a low, whispered voice. 'We'll fix that bugger tomorrow, when the trouble starts.' He thought Dan sitting in the back seat wouldn't hear him, but Dan's acute hearing caught the mumbled comments in the front.

At dinner in the hotel, he asked Jonas the purpose of their visit.

'That fool, Nkala, is in danger with all these demonstrations against foreign blacks. Didn't you see how nervous Francis was? I'm trying to encourage Nkala to leave South Africa and return to Zimbabwe. Tomorrow, they think the demonstrations will be even bigger.'

'Then aren't you also in danger?'

'I'll be careful, in and out, in a couple of minutes. You should stay here in Rosebank tomorrow. You're not black, but you never know what may happen when a crowd gets worked up and violent.'

'What about Francis?'

'He'll drop me at the shop and pick me up when I call him. Francis doesn't want to wait in the car like he did today.'

Back in his room after dinner, Dan watched the television. All the news featured angry South African blacks claiming criminal foreign blacks took their jobs. The xenophobic mob that afternoon was threatening, and the demonstrators promised worse for the following day.

* * *

In the morning, at breakfast, Jonas encouraged Dan to look around the shopping centre. 'Rosebank has some of the best shops in Joburg.'

'All right., what time will you be back?'

'I don't know. I'll call you when I'm back in the hotel.'

As they finished their coffee, Francis arrived, and Jonas jumped up to go off with him. Dan returned to his room and took out the card he picked up at Jacob Nkala's shop and called the number.

'Hello.'

'Mr Nkala?' said Dan in his best imitation South African accent.

'Yes.'

'You are in great danger. Lock up your shop and go home.'

'Who is this? Who are you?'

'It doesn't matter. Your safety does. Lock up and go home.'

'You can't scare me.'

'I'm not trying to scare you. I'm trying to save your life. Big trouble is coming your way. Please listen to me.'

Nkala put the phone down. Dan called him again. There was no answer. What more could he do? Pictures on television showed an angry mob threatening to damage shops and beat foreigners. He hoped Nkala took his advice and left.

Dan strolled through the nearby Firs Shopping Centre with its glamorous stores. By late morning, he was over window shopping and looked for a cafe to buy coffee. Just then, his phone rang. It was Jonas. 'Come back to the hotel. We're checking out.'

Dan hurried back to the hotel where Jonas and Francis waited for him. He rushed up to his room to get his things while Jonas checked out and settled their bill. Francis raced them to the airport, just in time to catch the three-forty afternoon flight to Harare. They needed to run to the departure lounge. At least they'd be back home nice and early, at a quarter past five.

'Why the rush?' Dan enquired.

'I finished my business early, so we might as well get back.'

'So, what happened to Nkala?'

'The fool refused to leave. I couldn't stick around with those demonstrators looking for foreigners. So, I left him in his shop.'

Dan imagined every trip with Jonas would end in a mad rush. That night, in his apartment, he checked the internet for news about South African xenophobic violence. He read, a small, angry crowd killed a Zimbabwean shopkeeper and looted thousands of dollars of cell phones. The police speculated it might have been a targeted hit, as certain criminal elements incited the mob to attack the shop. They attacked no other businesses, which reinforced the police's view it was an isolated incident and not xenophobic violence on the scale of the previous year.

CCTV footage of visitors to Nkala's shop the previous afternoon supported the theory. The pictures showed Jonas and Nkala in animated disagreement. Dan spent his time in the shop looking at the cell phones under the glass countertop. From the camera's angle, only the top of his head was visible. And there was nothing distinctive about his clothing. The South African Police said the African and the white may be the same two individuals wanted in connection with Absalom Muzenda's murder. Both victims were Zimbabweans, and it appeared the same two suspects spoke to them shortly before their murders., though the police conceded the xenophobic mob inflicted most of the violence.

There was also CCTV footage of looters inside Nkala's shop. Dan leant forward in his chair as one man in the crowd caught his attention. He wore a black T-shirt and a baseball cap. Yes, that's the big man who confronted him when he walked to the Intercontinental Hotel at

Johannesburg airport. The South African Police were right. Someone used the cover of the riots to settle scores. Dan was certain Jonas played a part in Nkala's demise.

Should he tell Inspector Michael Mzamane of the South African Police? Then he thought better of it. Perhaps it wasn't wise to get involved when he didn't have his genuine passport, and the South African Police looked for him, even though they didn't know his identity.

Earlier, Dan pondered the reason Captain John had sent him on this trip with Jonas. Now, he believed he had the answer. It was an attempt to further implicate him in the COU's activities. He felt their vice-like grip constricting him. To survive the unit's hold over him, he'd have to be a lot smarter in the future.

* * *

Dan was proficient in accounts and administration, and Cherry was an eager student with a voracious appetite for learning. At first, he wondered how he would keep himself busy at the COU. Accounts and administration alone wouldn't suffice, but the IT role complemented his other duties.

Since he set up the computer network, there was plenty for him to do. Dan wasn't an IT specialist. The job wouldn't have kept him occupied if he was. He needed to learn about computers and networks along the way, so it took him much longer, and it had given him six more months in Harare. Fortunately, Captain John and Eunice were computer dinosaurs and didn't question his slow progress.

Dan's thoughts returned to the Honey File. Nkala's name would be crossed off by now. He'd tried to help the man, but he wouldn't listen. Who was next in line? With his own name climbing the list, he was on a mission to save those who preceded him. He couldn't do it alone. He needed Nikita's help.

CHAPTER 20

DAN took out the A4 sheet of paper Nikita gave him. It was the COU's death list, code-named the Honey File. He crossed out Jacob Nkala's name and looked at the next one. Dr David Tawanda. Professional titles such as Dr or Professor, and a smattering of military ranks such as Colonel or Major, preceded many names on the list. Dan felt like an underachiever. It listed him as Dan Scott.

The last time Nikita visited him, they agreed if he needed to see her, he would place three marble-sized pebbles, close together in a row, on top of the post boxes at the entrance to the apartment block. When she saw them, she'd try to visit him on the next weekday.

It wasn't scientific, and not much use in an emergency, but it kept their communication discrete and anonymous. There were no addresses or phone numbers involved and no calls to trace. If she maintained her disguise, there was a negligible risk of anyone linking them.

On Friday evening, Dan placed the pebbles in the agreed location.

He was sorry for the names following him on the list. In theory, he'd not be around once the COU passed his name. He'd either be dead or out of Zimbabwe. Of course, Nikita and Victor's colleagues would also try to help those on the list, but as he, Dan, shared the list with those other names, he felt compelled to play his part.

* * *

Saturday came, and at a quarter past one, as usual, Gloria arrived with her overnight bag. She and Dan were working their way through her sister's supply of condoms at an alarming rate. On the weekends, Gloria would bring condoms with her. If Dan visited her flat during the week, the magic bedside-table drawer was an endless source of supply.

But it wasn't a bottomless drawer, and the stockpile of condoms of all varieties and brands in their colourful packets was running low. These were the ones her sister brought from overseas. Now, Gloria sourced a supply of condoms in plain wrapping and of questionable quality. 'Damn!' said Dan. 'If I'd thought of it, I would have bought some in Joburg while I wandered around the Rosebank shops.'

'Ah well, next time.'

'I hope there won't be a next time. Perhaps you should go on birth control pills.'

'In Zimbabwe? We don't even have essential medicines or antibiotics here.'

'How reliable are these condoms?'

'I don't know. Perhaps we should start thinking about boy's and girl's names, just in case.'

Dan guffawed. 'Seriously?'

'What if I fell pregnant?'

'Let's cross that bridge if we come to it.'

'No, we must think of these things.'

'Goodness! Is it that time already? We're going to have a late lunch.'

The topic would arise periodically. As always, Dan prevaricated. He wasn't sure what he'd do or how he would react if Gloria fell pregnant. In the meantime, their lovemaking continued with abandon.

* * *

Monday night brought the tap on the door Dan expected. Sure enough, it was Nikita, conservatively dressed, apart from her long, black, curly hair.

'Hello, Dan. Is there a problem?'

He explained what had happened on the trip to Johannesburg and how he'd failed to help Jacob Nkala.

'Well, you can't help people who won't listen. They always said he was a stubborn old fool, but that doesn't mean he deserved to die. He was irascible and made many enemies. I doubt he had enough influence for the government to bother with him, so it's likely a business rival put out a contract.'

'What about this next one, David Tawanda?'

'He's already back in Zimbabwe, so he's in the same position as you. We have teams keeping a watch on his house, but our people worry that the CIO, police, or someone is monitoring them. If the authorities use force to take Tawanda, what can we do? Though the adverse publicity may prevent them from making any such move.'

'Why would he be on the list?'

'He's not aligned to the opposition, though he's a major regime critic and well regarded. His concern for his safety is justified, and there're rumours he may try to leave the country. The government has confiscated his passport. If he can reach Botswana or Zambia, they might give him sanctuary. Many people hope he will escape.'

Dan looked at David Tawanda's entry. The second column displayed the word *jealousy*. 'How did they lure Tawanda back to Zimbabwe?'

'It was easy. They started a rumour that Tawanda's younger brother was having an affair with his wife. Tawanda rushed back to Harare to pick up his wife and intended to take her with him to Zambia. The authorities confiscated his passport on arrival, and he's been here ever since then. His response has been to be more vocal in his criticism of the regime. That's why there's concern for his safety.'

'If I hear anything at the COU, I'll tell you. He's on the list, so the COU is tasked with dealing with him. What about the Domestic File?'

'Many of those are private contracts put out by business rivals, personal enemies, or family members. You can put out a contract on anyone if you can afford it. Sometimes, there're government contracts on the list, especially in Matabeleland. Often, the government doesn't want to waste their time chasing someone down there, so they give the job to the COU, or some similar organisation.'

'Are there many domestic contracts put out?'

'Quite a lot. Remember, the Domestic File is only showing the contracts the COU gets. The most recent one that looks like a government-connected contract was a compounding chemist by the name of Paul Tinashe. People said he prepared the white powder someone sprinkled on Emmerson Mnangagwa's desk.'

'What happened to him?'

'He drowned in the swimming pool of his father's property in Lupane.'

'Could it have been an accident?'

'I doubt it. They said he was an excellent swimmer, but they found him floating fully clothed in the pool. Apparently, he was trying to leave the country because they blamed him for the white powder not working.'

'Yes, I remember reading something about that. So, who blamed him?'

Nikita shrugged. 'Someone blamed him.'

'That third column looks like code numbers for clients who put out the contracts. I recognise some of them from the COU's debtors' ledger. There must be a list somewhere that matches code numbers to clients' names.'

'It would be useful to know who's requesting each hit. Could you get that list?'

'I'm not sure. I'd love to find out the person with the code number next to my name.'

'That can be your next task!'

'Who's watching over the Domestic File people? Do any of their code numbers match those on the Honey File?'

'The code letters next to Paul Tinashe's name appears in the Honey File twice, and one of them, HMV 17, is the code next to your name. Tinashe was HMV 16. So, HMV must be the client, and the number is the client's contract. If you're in Tinashe's league, you must be important to that client. My guess is you're a government contract.'

'You're full of good news.'

'Perhaps that's how we can find out which domestic contracts the government connections sanctioned. Look! There are a couple of HMV contracts on the domestic list.'

'Do you watch the people on the domestic list?'

'We have limited resources. Those near the top of the list in the Honey File are our priority. They are the important ones who could help this country. The people on the Domestic File need to lie low and hope their enemies forget about them. We warn people on either list, though our focus remains those at the top of the Honey File list. It helps that Captain John likes to follow the order of the lists. Otherwise, we wouldn't know where he may strike next.'

'I saw him on Saturday night in the Explorer's Bar at the Meikles Hotel. He was with an attractive European woman with short auburn hair. He never saw me.'

'That woman was probably Ruth Bernstein. She's from Johannesburg and had long blond hair when I first saw her. The rumours are they're in business together, smuggling illegal Marange diamonds out of Zimbabwe. For many years, she bought diamonds from illegal miners and smuggled out small quantities in the heels of her shoes.'

'Would that be profitable?'

'Only if they're of gem quality. Then, they can be worth between five hundred and a thousand U.S. dollars per carat. On average, Marange diamonds are worth less than fifty U.S. dollars per carat.'

'So, someone was feeding her gem-quality diamonds?'

'Yes. Captain John found out and threatened to expose them unless they made him a partner. He has contacts in customs, so now they never question her, and she takes out larger quantities. The rumour is she's also taking out rhino horns.'

'How does she smuggle them through South African customs?'

'Ah! That's the thing. Ever since Captain John got involved, she gets a light plane to Beira in Mozambique and flies from there to Johannesburg on a commercial flight. So, it's likely the diamonds don't even reach South Africa. Mozambique is a well-known smuggling route for Marange diamonds and rhino horns.'

'If Captain John has contacts in customs, why can't he get my passport back?'

'If he wanted to, I'm sure he could. It's possible they confiscated your passport on his orders. The gossip is he and Mrs Bernstein are having an affair. I'm not sure if it's true, but people like to talk.'

'What about his wife? Wouldn't she object?'

'I think she's used to him having affairs with lots of different women.'

Nikita and Dan agreed to keep in touch regarding David Tawanda and to report any moves against him. They'd need to stay alert and keep their eyes and ears open. As she left, Dan called out with a grin, 'Give my regards to Eva.' Nikita smiled back.

Dan examined the lists with a little more care than usual. Any code on the domestic list that also appeared in the Honey File, he highlighted with a yellow marker. As Nikita suggested, there weren't many. He was getting a deeper understanding of the way the COU operated. And despite Captain John's charm, it wasn't a pretty picture.

Dan hoped his colleagues at the COU didn't work through the list too fast. Twice now, they'd implicated him in the murders of Zimbabweans in the diaspora. Did they need him to accompany Jonas on any more escapades? If they didn't, he might not hear when they planned to move on David Tawanda. And anyway, as Tawanda was already in the country, they may not use him on that job.

Dan worried about the striking similarity between his and Tawanda's return to Zimbabwe. Both had their passports confiscated on arrival. It reinforced his determination to save the old man.

CHAPTER 21

TUESDAY morning, and Dan drove to work with a lot on his mind. Nikita's visit gave him much to ponder. The advantage he held over others on the list was he knew his position on it. By keeping track of the names at the top of the list, he'd have a rough idea of when his enemies might move against him. It also helped that the COU were unaware of his knowledge of the Honey File.

Dan wondered how he might get hold of the list that matched the client names with the codes in the Honey File. Photographing the Honey File was not too difficult because he saw where Captain John kept it. But where was the list of codes? Perhaps they'd be in one of Captain John's desk drawers. Only he had access to their contents. Eunice might also need the codes, in which case, they would be in the four-drawer filing cabinet. But in which one?

At five, Captain John summoned Dan for their regular Tuesday evening drinks. John poured the scotch over the ice cubes. 'Some pundits say ice spoils a good scotch, but I like the chill it gives it. In our warm climate, we need that. Scotch with water or soda is popular, but I don't like to water down scotch. Of course, if you allow scotch on the rocks to stand too long, it becomes scotch and water. Here you are, drink up. Cheers!'

'How are you finding the computer, John? Is it useful for you?'

'Yes, it keeps me up to date with the outside world.'

'Did you see the news about the xenophobic riots in Johannesburg? They showed footage inside Jacob Nkala's mobile phone shop. The South

African Police suspect people are using the riots and violence in South Africa to settle old scores. They believe Absalom Muzenda and Nkala's cases may be linked. There was CCTV footage of Jonas in Nkala's shop. Perhaps he shouldn't go Down South for a while.'

'He must go down there. He's in charge of our entire external operations.'

'Couldn't Eunice do that?'

'No, they are all Jonas's team. Eunice has no connection with them. She's in charge of domestic operations.' Captain John laughed. 'If I didn't send Jonas on the external jobs, you'd need to do them.'

Dan smiled at John's little joke. 'I'm not sure how successful I'd be, getting people in the diaspora to return to Zimbabwe. What if they said no? I mean, if your best man failed twice, what chance of success would I have?'

'Those two trips weren't an entire failure. They just didn't achieve our preferred result. If you couldn't persuade them to return to Zimbabwe, you'd just need to tell Francis.'

'Does Jonas have anyone on his team inside Zimbabwe?'

'Only you from time to time.'

'I thought he ran a team?'

'Not anymore. He did when he reported to Eunice. That changed when he took over external operations.'

'So, Eunice runs all the teams inside the country?'

'Yes, all the field operatives, other than Jonas, report to her. She, Jonas, and the admin staff all report to me.'

'And I report to …?'

'Me, unless I lend you to Jonas.'

'I'm not sure how much help I am to him. I just seem to tag along doing nothing.'

'Eunice would love to control both the external and domestic operations. If I allowed that to happen, all I will have achieved is to put someone between me and the entire field operation. I will then have made myself purely administration. That's the perfect scenario for a coup, don't you think? Eunice is ambitious and envious of my position. The COU is my company, but if I give her all the troops, what power will I hold?'

'So …?'

'So, I cannot give her, or anyone reporting to her, control of external operations. It's ironic, you are the only person I can trust to help Jonas on his missions.'

'Help in what way?'

'What if something happened to him? We'd have to start over again. I don't know too much about his external team. I'd like you to draw a plan of his operation, so we're not caught out if he gets arrested or worse. Call it an organisation chart if you will. So far, you've only met Francis and his wife Sally, and you have been to their flat and seen where they live. In time, you'll meet others.'

'Can't you just ask Jonas for the information?'

'In this business, your secrets are your security. He has given me a little information, but I suspect it's only the tip of the iceberg. That's where you come in. Your covert task is to give me the full picture. This is just between you and me, you understand?'

'Yes, of course.'

'I've made your role here financially rewarding. The accounts and the computer network won't keep you busy. Your missions with Jonas will be intermittent. So, I don't mind if you spend the rest of your work hours on your novels, as long as you build that picture of external operations.'

'This doesn't sound like something I'll complete within the six-month extension of my contract.'

'Perhaps another year or two. You must gain Jonas's trust, as well as that of his team. How does that sound to you?'

'Another year or two sounds fine. And I would also be able to further improve your computer systems. For example, I wondered if you'd like me to computerise your filing cabinet?'

'No, it would be too risky. Someone might hack into it.'

'A pity. It would work well. I presume you've categorised your files.'

'Yes, of course. The top drawer is for outstanding jobs and the bottom one for completed jobs. The second drawer is for potential jobs, and the third is for jobs we reject.'

* * *

Later, in his apartment, Dan thought about his discussion with Captain John. Their chat about the filing cabinet didn't give him any clue where he might find the list of codes. They might be in either the jobs pending, or jobs completed drawer, or as he first suspected, in one of Captain John's desk drawers.

The questions around his new role in the COU occupied Dan's mind. It would give him time to decide about Gloria. He'd yet to commit to their relationship, though he realised he was not ready for it to end.

The prospect of more missions with Jonas was daunting. They were nothing more than planned assassinations. If he didn't go with Jonas, the target was almost certainly doomed. If he did, perhaps he'd be able to warn the target and save their life. And if he met more of Jonas's team, did that include the big man who tried to mug him at Johannesburg airport? The same man he saw in the CCTV footage looting Jacob Nkala's mobile phone shop?

Dan was making a lot of money through the COU, and Captain John's permission to write his novel in his ample free time in the office was another irresistible bonus. And, if Captain John was considering another year or two, it was unlikely his name would soon reach the top of the Honey File.

He realised Captain John was putting a lot of trust in him. A relaxed familiarity was growing between them, a friendship of sorts. Perhaps his name might even be removed from the list, rather than struck out. Yes, things were looking up. Though he still didn't have his passport back.

Dan couldn't wait to tell Gloria his business in Zimbabwe would extend for another year or two. It might even relieve the gentle pressure she put on him, to be honest about his intentions.

* * *

A fortnight later, Nikita dropped in unexpectedly to Dan's apartment. She was a little more circumspect than Dan about the news he gave her. 'It's possible Captain John meant every word he said, though like you, we've wondered about your role at the COU. John is no fool. He would have foreseen your questions about your role there. So, it's possible he's just keeping you off guard by giving you a plausible explanation for why he needs you.'

Dan was reluctant to have his cosy, new sense of security disturbed. 'Yes, I suppose you could be right.'

'Tell me, did you feel a lot more comfortable after your discussion with him?'

'Yes, of course I did.'

'So, my alternative explanation of his motives is a realistic possibility?'

This wasn't the explanation Dan wanted to hear, though he agreed it was a distinct possibility. 'Don't worry. I'll be careful. I will stay alert to all possibilities.'

'All I'm saying is let's watch the Honey File. If you get near the top of the list, we'll need to consider your options.'

'Yes, I understand.'

'Is there any news regarding David Tawanda?'

'No, nothing. Eunice oversees domestic contracts, so maybe she's planning something.'

'Tawanda was Jonas's responsibility. He's the one who got Tawanda back to Zimbabwe.'

'Yes, and now he's here, they might classify Tawanda as a domestic issue. I'm uncertain how that works. I sense a rivalry between Eunice and Jonas, at least on her part. Captain John said she wanted to take control of external operations. Some of Jonas's former team still regard him as their team leader, and it creates a lot of friction. Officially, they all report to Eunice, but from what I hear, she's not popular. There's always shouting going on in the open plan office. Her style is management by intimidation.'

'She must have learned that from Captain John.'

'Well, he's not like that anymore. Now he can see that behaviour from someone else, he must realise it's no way to gain loyalty or manage people. There's always tension around Eunice. At first, I thought it was just me, though I'm sure others feel it too. For Captain John to speak to me about her, suggests something's got to give.'

'Dan, in a secretive organisation like the COU, it may be dangerous to be privy to sensitive information. They can always resolve any potential problem by silencing the holder of that information. I mean, what if Eunice comes back into favour? If Captain John has told you anything negative about her, he might see you as an inconvenient, loose end.'

CHAPTER 22

DAN thought the new understanding with Captain John worked well. The small computer network ran smoothly, and Cherry did much of the financial accounts. It allowed him time to work on his novel, and he made genuine progress.

Gloria spent every weekend with him at his apartment, and he often spent Wednesday nights at her place. On the occasional Monday or Friday evening, he would meet Daniel Moyo for a drink at the Explorer's Bar. Everything settled into a comfortable routine.

In the office, Eunice left Dan alone, which suited him fine. He'd almost forgotten about his added responsibilities, though he sometimes wondered what Jonas did in-between his visits to Johannesburg.

A loud banging at the apartment door woke Dan from his sleep. He glanced at the alarm clock, four am. Who'd bash on his door at this hour? It was lucky he got an early night. He put on his tracksuit and picked up the heavy torch he kept beside his bed. It served its purpose during electricity outages but would also make a handy weapon.

As he approached the door, he called out. 'Who's there?'

'It's me Jonas. C'mon, open the door. We've got work to do.'

Dan swung the door open. 'Work? It's four in the morning. What work?'

'We're catching the six o'clock flight to Bulawayo. Pack for overnight. Hurry, we must get to the airport.'

While Jonas waited in the car downstairs, Dan dashed to the bathroom for a quick shower and brushed his teeth. He was used to overnight stays with Gloria, so it only took him a couple of minutes to pack his carry bag. The nights were getting chilly, so he put on a warm coat.

'Why this rush to Bulawayo?'

'I don't know. Captain John said he'd tell me later. I've got to call him at six this evening. Have you got your passport?'

'Yep, everything I might need.'

The early hour with deserted streets made for an easy run to the airport. Their tickets waited for them at the information desk. A few other bleary-eyed passengers also waited in the departure lounge. The airport was quiet, and the plane departed on schedule for the fifty-minute flight to Bulawayo.

Khumalo, the COU's Bulawayo man, met them at the airport and drove them into the city centre. It was a little past seven thirty, and Dan was eager to get a decent breakfast somewhere. Khumalo suggested the Bulawayo Rainbow or the Holiday Inn.

'Let's stay central,' said Jonas. 'Take us to the Bulawayo Rainbow.'

Khumalo parked the car, and the three men trooped into the Bulawayo Rainbow Hotel. In the breakfast room, they ordered tea and ate cereals before selecting a cooked breakfast of fried eggs, bacon, and grilled tomatoes.

'This tea's not bad, but couldn't compete with Ambrose's tea in the office,' said Dan.

'You're lucky. We must make our own tea in the open plan office,' said Jonas.

'You're both lucky.' said Khumalo. 'My wife makes me tea in the morning, and my next cup is when I get home at night.'

The three men laughed at the comparisons of their morning tea.

'So what now?' said Khumalo.

'We wait until six this evening. That's when Captain John will give me instructions about our trip.'

'Oh, I almost forgot,' said Khumalo. 'This is for you.' He handed Jonas an envelope. Jonas looked inside and grunted with satisfaction.

It was a long day as the trio explored Bulawayo on foot. Khumalo pointed out several places of interest, including the city hall, the high court, the police station, and other buildings of lesser significance.

For lunch they ate hamburgers and chips, followed by milk shakes. At six in the evening, they returned to the Bulawayo Rainbow for dinner. While Dan and Khumalo ordered their meals, Jonas excused himself and walked out to the pavement to make the call to Captain John. He came back in a few minutes to join them for dinner.

'Well, what's the story?' asked Dan.

'We're catching the train to Victoria Falls. And guess what? First-class!'

It was already pitch black by seven o'clock when Khumalo dropped Jonas and Dan at the station. He didn't wait to see them off. After spending all day with them, he was keen to get home. Dan grabbed his carry bag and stood with Jonas, watching Khumalo drive out of the station parking area.

'Jonas, where's your bag?'

'I didn't bring one. We're away for only one night. My toothbrush is in my jacket pocket, and I can use your toothpaste.'

'Didn't you want a change of clothes for tomorrow?'

'You know, there's no bedding on this train. We'll sleep in our clothes and fly back to Harare tomorrow, just after lunch. There's nowhere for us to shower, so I doubt you'll change your clothes, either.'

'Before you spoke to Captain John, how did you know it'd only be one night?'

'Lucky guess, I suppose. Haven't you noticed we're always away for only one night?'

'For all you know, we might have stayed in a hotel overnight.'

Jonas shrugged, and Dan wondered if he already knew the details of the trip before his phone call to Captain John.

A gust of chilly wind made Dan shiver. He zipped up his coat and followed Jonas through the station entrance onto Platform One. Bulawayo was Zimbabwe's railway hub. The station once boasted one of the longest platforms in the world. The dim lighting gave the platforms a ghostly, abandoned appearance.

But overall, the platforms looked in reasonable condition, unlike the trashed commuter stations in Johannesburg. There, those once attractive suburban stations now looked like war zones.

'We're leaving from Platform Four,' said Jonas.

They walked to the end of the platform where the buffer stops stood. Here, passengers could access the other platforms. Platform Four stood empty. The train was yet to arrive, though it was only twenty minutes to departure.

Jonas read Dan's thoughts. 'They're often late. Nothing to worry about.'

'What's this trip about, Jonas?'

Jonas looked around before lowering his voice. 'The carriage has toilets at both ends. Next to each is a coupé—that's a two-berth compartment. The four-berth compartments are between the coupés. David Tawanda and his wife are on this train in the four-berth compartment next to our coupé.'

'And?'

'We must keep an eye on him.'

'And then what?'

'Nothing. If you spot him on the train, you just need to tell me.'

'Where will you be?'

'I might be sleeping. I'll take the first watch from ten to twelve. You take twelve to two, and I'll do two to four. If I'm asleep, make sure you wake me when we get to Dete.'

'You think we'll see him in the middle of the night?'

'He's an old man, so he'll need the toilet. He'll go to the nearest one next to us. We'll leave our door a little open. Wake me if he passes.'

Dan didn't like the sound of it. What did Jonas intend to do? It wasn't too hard to guess. If he saw Tawanda pass by on his watch and Jonas was asleep, he'd tell him the old man never passed their coupé. But what if he passed by on Jonas's watch? Dan saw the pattern in Jonas's missions and feared for the old man's safety.

A deep, approaching rumble interrupted Dan's thoughts. The huge Garrett locomotive, with its distinctive water tank preceding it, rolled into Platform Four. Hissing steam and the smell of burning coal pervaded the area. The locomotive hauled several passenger coaches, with the single first-class coach quite close to the engine. A crowd of Africans stood farther down the platform where they expected to find the economy coaches.

Jonas elbowed Dan. 'There he is. That's Tawanda with his wife.'

Dr David Tawanda was a short, balding, overweight man with spectacles and a lived-in face. His wife was a tall, well-built woman with jet black hair and glasses. If Tawanda passed their coupé at night, there'd be no mistaking his profile.

Roofs covered the open-sided platforms. The chilly night breezes swirled around the waiting people, and Dan pulled up the collar of his coat to protect his neck.

He followed Jonas into the carriage. The first compartment was theirs. It was narrow, with two bunks, one above the other. 'Mine is the lower bunk,' said Jonas. 'I'll be up more than you.'

The compartment was a mess, with torn vinyl bunks. It needed a thorough clean to get rid of a quarter of a century of grime. Filthy windows obscured the view, and the cover of the dim fluorescent tube in the ceiling was missing. The door slid closed, but the latch was missing, and the washbasin lacked water.

Dan viewed the upper bunk with scepticism. Its fragile state gave him no confidence it would hold his six-foot athletic frame. He wondered who would be at greater risk of injury; himself or Jonas lying on the bottom bunk.

'Hey, Jonas, I thought you said we were travelling first-class?'

'If you saw standard or economy, you'd soon see this was first class.'

On schedule, the carriage jerked as the locomotive took up the slack. Jonas sat on his bunk, but Dan was standing and needed to grab hold of the upper bunk to keep his balance. He stepped into the corridor to view the platform slide past as the train pulled out of the station.

The train moved at a leisurely pace, leaving behind the dim platform lights of Bulawayo Station. But soon after it cleared the station, it squealed to a halt. 'Stopping already?' said Dan.

'Yeah, the engine is changing ends. First-class goes near the back of the train and economy at the front.'

After a ten-minute stop, the train gave a sudden violent jerk as it lurched forward to resume its journey. Once more, Dan hung on to the upper bunk to stay on his feet. Now the train moved a little faster, as Bulawayo's outer suburbs passed by in the middle-distance. The dim lights of isolated properties soon took over, before disappearing just as fast.

Once the lights passed, there was nothing to see outside the window. In the dim compartment light, all Dan saw was his reflection in the glass.

Soon, the conductor came to check their tickets. 'Is first-class full tonight?' Jonas asked.

'No, just four compartments.'

Jonas nodded, looking pleased with the response.

'How long have you worked for Captain John and the COU?' asked Dan.

'Six years.'

'And when did you become a team leader?'

'Three years. I only became the senior team leader when Hilton Nyoka, Captain John's last senior team leader, died a year ago. That's when he made Eunice his 2IC. Then Captain John changed things and put me in charge of external operations and made Eunice responsible for domestic.'

'Is this operation external or domestic?'

'It's my operation.'

The response didn't answer Dan's question, but he already knew its implication.

Jonas got up from his bunk. 'I'm going to the toilet.'

When Jonas left, Dan stood in the corridor outside the compartment. The train was going fast, and the sway and loud rattle were quite overwhelming. It didn't seem the train was fully under control and travelling at a safe speed. The doors at each end of the carriage swung open and closed, adding to the cacophony of rattles, squeaks, squeals, and thumps.

The door of the neighbouring compartment slid open, and Tawanda's tubby figure appeared. With the sway of the train, he staggered towards Dan, heading for the toilet. Dan turned to check if Jonas had emerged from the toilet. He hadn't.

'This toilet is broken,' said Dan. 'You'll have to use the other end.'

'Thank you,' Tawanda mumbled, before staggering to the toilet at the other end of the carriage.

Dan prayed Jonas wouldn't emerge while Tawanda shuffled down the corridor. Just as he reached the far end and entered the toilet, Jonas reappeared. Dan exhaled. How long before Jonas realised Tawanda used the carriage's other toilet? At least Tawanda wouldn't pass their open doorway during the night.

Jonas lay down on the lower bunk and Dan climbed onto the upper bunk. The sliding door stood open about ten inches for them to catch sight of Tawanda when he passed. Dan soon dozed off with the soporific effect of the train's sway and rattle. It made frequent stops at small sidings without platforms. Shouts, laughter and banging doors accompanied each stop, and Dan stirred, but soon fell asleep again.

A gentle shake of his shoulder woke him. 'Your turn to keep watch,' said Jonas.

Dan got out of his bunk and walked to the toilet next door. He'd slept since nine o'clock. It was just three hours, but he felt quite rested.

'I can't understand it,' said Jonas. 'Tawanda hasn't been to the toilet once. He'll pass by on your watch for sure, so wake me when he does.'

'Are you sure you didn't fall asleep?'

'Of course not.'

It worked, thought Dan. Tawanda must've gone to the other end of the carriage. With all the noise on the train, Jonas wouldn't have heard him sliding open his compartment door.

Dan's shift passed at a crawl. He couldn't risk falling asleep, to be woken by an irate Jonas, blaming him for missing the old man passing by their compartment. He listened to the sounds of the train, sometimes slowing down and at others increasing its speed. The long, lonely whistle of the steam engine was the romance of overnight train travel in Africa. Sometimes he heard the chuff, chuff of the locomotive, and at others, only the carriage's rattle and the bogie's steel wheels grind on the track. Now and then, his nostrils caught the smell of burning coal in the locomotive's firebox.

Jonas kept the torch, and in the darkness, Dan couldn't see his wristwatch's hands, and his cell phone was in his carry bag. It was no big deal. He'd wake Jonas when they reached Dete, close to two in the morning.

At last, the train slowed, and the orange platform lights of Dete Station slid into view. A crowd of Africans waited to board the train or meet arriving passengers. Dan jumped down from the upper bunk and shook Jonas awake. 'Jonas, wake up. We're at Dete.'

Jonas woke with a start. 'Didn't Tawanda pass during your shift?'

'Not once.'

'I can't believe it. Maybe he's peeing in the washbasin.'

The stop at Dete lasted around ten minutes. Once again, laughter and loud shouts and slamming doors signalled the late-night exchange of passengers getting off and on the train. Bundled possessions passed through the windows and doors of the carriages, with some unceremoniously tossed out onto the platform. Dan's writer's brain wondered about all the stories they might tell. What was the purpose of their individual journeys? Most were likely simple and innocent, but others, darker and disturbing. His imagination ran wild.

The train pulled out of Dete, heading for the Falls. 'I'm going to stay in the corridor,' said Jonas.

Dan worried about what might happen. Tawanda would emerge from his compartment at some point, following the stop at Dete. How might he save him? There was little he could do.

* * *

Jonas leant against the corridor window outside the compartment. He was glad to be out of the claustrophobic, narrow **coupé**. If Tawanda didn't emerge from his compartment soon, he'd go in and drag him out. The wife was a problem, but he couldn't do the job in daylight. If she gave too much trouble, she may also have to go.

Only ten minutes passed when the sound of Tawanda's door sliding open caught Jonas's attention. Just then, the train slowed, and the squeal of brakes pierced the night air. The train jolted to a stop. Tawanda's door slammed shut. The train's rattle, squeaks, and bangs were stilled, but the hiss of the stationary locomotive was clear.

Jonas stuck his head out of the open window. This wasn't a siding or routine stop. Perhaps something blocked the line. Voices approached from his right. Two men in khaki overalls passed, heading for the rear of the train.

Ah well! Time for a smoke. Jonas tapped out a cigarette from the packet of twenty he kept in his breast pocket. He found the box of matches in his trouser pocket and struck one. It flared brightly in the darkness, and he lit his cigarette. He walked to the open carriage door and descended to the bottom step to enjoy his cigarette in the fresh night air. With each draw, the end of his cigarette glowed a bright orange red.

The two railwaymen stood at the end of the train talking. Jonas thought of joining them, but they turned and walked back in his direction. As they passed, he enquired, 'Any problem?'

'No, it's all fine,' one man answered, as they walked on back towards the steam engine.

Jonas watched them until they disappeared into the darkness, and their voices faded in the distance. He took one last draw on the cigarette and flicked it away. It hit the ground, sending a brief shower of sparks into the blackness. Jonas took one last deep breath of the fresh winter air and turned to haul himself up the steps into the carriage.

CHAPTER 23

THE early morning light came into the compartment, and Dan stirred. Despite the lack of bedding and the shake, rattle and roll of the carriage, he'd slept well. He'd woken at each stop, yet he felt refreshed. He stretched and rose onto one elbow. There was nothing quite like dawn in the African bush. He checked his watch. Six o'clock, still three hours to the Falls. Without water in the hand-basin, he couldn't wash. At least he'd brought his battery shaver.

Dan looked over the edge of his bunk to check if Jonas was awake. He couldn't see him, so he slipped on his shoes and jumped down onto the floor. Jonas wasn't in his bunk. Perhaps he was in the toilet next door. Dan unzipped his carry bag and took out his shaver. He stood looking through the window at the passing bush as he shaved.

Trees adorned with weaver bird nests, looking like baubles on a Christmas tree, drifted past the compartment window. Dan put away his shaver. He checked the corridor. There was no sign of Jonas. The toilet door swung open and closed with the sway of the carriage. Jonas wasn't in there. Perhaps he walked through the train in search of a kiosk selling cool drinks or cigarettes.

As he stood in the corridor, viewing the passing bush, the door of the next compartment slid open. Tawanda emerged and greeted Dan with a smile. So Jonas hadn't dealt with Tawanda during the night. A pleasant surprise; but where was Jonas? Did he have some other strategy if Tawanda didn't emerge from his compartment? So, it might be an external operation if he planned to follow Tawanda over the border.

Seven o'clock and no sign of Jonas. If he met an acquaintance in another carriage, he might catch up on news of mutual interest. Though that seemed unlikely.

Victoria Falls was close, and he still hadn't appeared. Something must be wrong. The surrounding vegetation became greener and the morning air warmer. The train slowed as the squealing brakes protested and brought it to a stop. Dan grabbed his carry bag and checked the compartment to make sure he'd not forgotten anything. He walked down the corridor to the open carriage door and descended the steps to the low platform.

The economy carriages disgorged their crowded passengers with their assorted bags and bundles. Soon, the baboons leapt on the carriage roofs and jumped through the open windows in search of any delicacies left by the departing passengers. The railway staff did their best to shoo them off, but the agile baboons found other means of access to the carriages.

Dr Tawanda and his wife passed their luggage to a man on the platform before risking the three-step descent. Dan watched the Tawandas and their welcomer walk out of the station entrance and step into a black Mercedes saloon.

Everyone disembarked, but there was no sign of Jonas. Dan waited another fifteen minutes before ringing Captain John. 'Jonas has disappeared and the Tawandas have left the station in a black Mercedes.'

'Did Tawanda have a bodyguard with him?'

'No, none that I saw.'

'When did you last see him?'

'The train stopped ten minutes out of Dete. He said he'd wait out in the corridor for a while. I think he hoped to catch Tawanda when he left his compartment to go to the toilet. Tawanda couldn't have done anything to Jonas.'

'Perhaps he got off the train and missed it when it moved off again.'

'Who knows! I'll have a word with the engine driver and ask if he saw him.'

'OK, if you can't find him, you better come back to Harare.'

'Jonas has the airline tickets.'

'All right, call Cherry and ask her to arrange something.'

Dan walked to the locomotive to find the driver and the stoker.

'My colleague in first-class is missing from the train. I haven't seen him since we stopped outside Dete. He's a tall African with thinning hair in the front, and he wore a blue shirt with black trousers.'

'Yah, we saw him last night. When we passed the first-class carriage, he stood on the steps smoking a cigarette.'

'That would be him, but I've not seen him since then.'

'Phone Dete railway station or the Dete police. They will look for him.'

Dan held little hope it would do much good. But he needed to do something. He made the calls and found the Dete station master and police most cooperative. 'Yes Sir, we'll phone you if we find anything.'

As he ended the call with the police, Dan's phone rang. Cherry told him there was a problem with his return flight. He'd have to stay in Victoria Falls overnight and catch the eleven o'clock flight to Harare the next morning.

Now mid-morning, Dan was hungry. He picked up his bag and walked from the station across the lawn to the Kingdom Hotel over the road. He crossed the bridge to the hotel's reception counter. 'I don't have a reservation. Do you have a room for tonight?'

'No problem, Sir,' said the pretty receptionist. 'Please fill out this form.'

Dan carried his Visa credit card, and check-in was a smooth process. He followed the porter past the huge, open dining room with its soaring ceilings and down two long corridors. In the third corridor, the porter stopped and opened a door. The room looked comfortable with a green canopy blocking the view and giving it privacy.

Dan explored the room before taking a quick shower. After the dirty train, this was heaven. A shower and change of clothes made all the difference and energised him. He headed for the dining hall for an early lunch, but it would only open in half an hour.

Thirty minutes to kill, so Dan explored the hotel. The central court-yard boasted an elegant swimming pool, though at this time of year no one swam. The shop sold typical hotel-shop items, such as seasonal clothing and cosmetics. As his stay was only one night, he ignored the tour desk. Soon, the dining room opened, and he ordered a light lunch.

Dan didn't dawdle over lunch as he wanted to visit the Falls. After a cold beer, he stepped out to walk to the Victoria Falls Bridge. He'd done the walk many times before, though never alone. This time it seemed a lot longer in the humid early afternoon sun. Vendors pestered him to buy Zimbabwean notes of huge denominations of billions, if not trillions, of dollars. Others tried to tempt him with tourist trinkets and carvings. He was not on holiday and was a poor target for the eager vendors.

At the border post, Dan got a re-entry permit to go onto the bridge. He walked towards the Zambian side, and as the Falls came into view, a cooling spray on the breeze greeted him, reminding him what a warm day it was. The refreshing, moist air and earthy rainforest smell filled his lungs. Although the views were distant and the Falls only partly visible, this was one of his favourite spots. It's where he'd seen the Falls for the first time from the train, crossing the Victoria Falls Bridge. Like each of his other visits, he felt it was a glimpse into paradise. Here, the spray was cooling, not soaking, like on the Rainforest Walk.

Dan walked back past the bungee jump, through the border post, and on to the drenching Rain Forest Walk. He paid the entrance fee but declined to hire a raincoat. Part of the fun was getting wet, and in the warm, humid atmosphere, he knew he would soon dry. Dan didn't intend to go up to Danger Point, where the heaviest spray occurred. He walked along the path towards the Falls, and as he neared, the distant hiss grew louder, sounding like rolling thunder and then a continuous mighty roar.

As Dan walked all the way from the Livingstone Statue to the Bridge View, he passed several bedraggled individuals who looked like they braved the view from Danger Point. There, the heavy spray obscured the view, while most other views were clearer. The thrill of Danger Point was the heavy spray and the slippery rocks close to the edge of the Falls. The river's high flow, and the roar of the Falls complimenting the spray, emphasised the power of nature. He'd visited this glorious spectacle often, yet each occasion took his breath away.

Dan left the Rainforest Walk at five o'clock and headed back towards the hotel. After the last few traumatic months, he enjoyed being a carefree tourist. When he reached the hotel, instead of turning left towards the entrance, he walked on to Victoria Falls village. He found a corner restaurant where he enjoyed a steak and salad and a couple of Lion Lagers. This, the life of his dreams, inspired him—somewhere he should write. Gloria hadn't seen the Falls, so next time, he'd bring her for a leisurely visit.

He walked back to the hotel in the darkness, and after watching African dancers entertain the dinner guests, he returned to his room for an early night. Tonight, he'd make up for his interrupted and uncomfortable sleep on the train.

* * *

The flight to Harare was at a little past eleven the next morning. The taxi dropped him at the airport. Next door to the old terminal, the Chinese built terminal would soon be opening. It looked like the modern gateway to one of the world's natural wonders.

Dan found his window seat near the front of the plane, with no wings to interrupt his view. It was a little over an hour's flight to Harare. He wasn't in the mood for chatting. The woman seated next to him was breathless with excitement. A man on the Bulawayo to Victoria Falls train went missing after an unscheduled stop, ten minutes out of Dete.

'It was on the news this morning. Perhaps he got off the train, and it left without him. A man who travelled with him is helping the police with their enquiries.'

'Is that so!'

'Yes. The police haven't ruled out foul play. They're keeping an open mind about the man's disappearance.'

By the time they landed in Harare, Dan was glad to be saying good-bye to his travelling companion. She spent the flight suggesting various scenarios and surmises, none of which he wanted to hear.

He caught a taxi from the airport and went straight to the office. Cherry greeted him with her usual cheerful smile, and Ambrose brought him a steaming cup of tea. He gulped it down and walked to Captain John's office and knocked on the doorframe.

'Come in, Dan.'

'Hi John. Any news from Jonas?'

'No, nothing. The police are coming up from Bulawayo tomorrow to interview us.'

'Interview us? I was the only one with Jonas, and I've already told them all I know.'

'We better get our stories straight.'

'What stories?'

'Well, they're bound to ask why you two were on the train.'

'Why were we on the train?'

'It's best to say you and Jonas were the best of friends and headed for the Falls on a quick sightseeing visit.'

* * *

Soon after lunch the next day, the police arrived. They introduced themselves as Detective Inspector Tshuma from the Bulawayo police station and Sergeant Khuphe from Dete. The first interview was with Captain John.

'How would you describe the relationship between Mr Scott and Nyandoro?' the inspector asked.

'Excellent,' said Captain John. 'They were the best of friends and always stuck together. They applied for a couple of days off to visit the Falls.'

'So, you've no reason to believe Mr Scott would wish to harm Nyandoro?'

'No, none.'

'What was their work connection?'

'Mr Scott assisted Nyandoro.'

When the inspector asked Eunice the same questions, her answers differed.

'I think Mr Scott resented being bossed by Nyandoro. He's an ambitious man and felt he should be Nyandoro's equal or perhaps even his superior.'

'So, with Nyandoro out of the way, he might assume his position?'

'Yes, that might be a motive.'

'Thank you. We'll make up our own minds about that.'

Next, the inspector and Sergeant Khuphe spoke to Cherry. 'So, you booked the return flight to Harare?'

'Yes.'

'If they arrived in Victoria Falls at nine in the morning, and booked to return to Harare on the lunch time flight, when would they do their sightseeing?'

'There was an error in the booking. They were supposed to return the following day.'

'So, the airline got it wrong?'

'Yes.'

'After you discovered Mr Nyandoro was missing, wouldn't you want Mr Scott back in the office ASAP? Why then did you put Mr Scott's flight back a day?'

'That was another mistake by the airline. We would have preferred Mr Scott's instant return. They should have only cancelled Mr Nyandoro's ticket. In error, they cancelled both, so Mr Scott had to stay overnight in Victoria Falls.'

The inspector spoke to Dan last. 'Mr Scott, we've considered several possibilities for why Mr Nyandoro might have got off the train. Perhaps for a smoke, or to use the bushes as a toilet. We understand you cannot use the toilet while the train is stationary. Either way, the train may have left without him. The train driver and stoker confirm they saw Nyandoro standing on the steps of the carriage smoking a cigarette.'

'Yes, Jonas was always thoughtful towards others. He knew not everyone appreciated someone smoking near them.'

'We cannot rule out the possibility he met an unfortunate end. We hold grave fears for his safety. From our discussions with senior staff members here, we believe you stand to gain from his disappearance and may fill his position.'

'I could never fill his position. Did Captain John tell you that?'

'Let me finish, Mr Scott. We are not accusing you of being responsible for his disappearance, but you must appreciate our position. You are a person of interest in our investigation, so I must instruct you not to leave Zimbabwe without informing me first. Do you understand?'

'Yes, but you don't understand. I could never fill Nyandoro's position. It requires an African to do his job. I'm just in charge of administration over here. I couldn't do a field operatives job.'

'Mr Scott, your boss, Captain John, tells me you are well-qualified with good corporate experience. He spoke highly of you, so we must consider the possibility that ambition motivated you to remove an obstacle to your advancement.'

'I'm in Zimbabwe to write my novel. I've no interest in a long-term position here. Writing is my business, that's all I want to do.'

'There's no point in us debating it, Mr Scott. We will continue our investigation and be back in touch when we've made more progress. Remember, don't leave Zimbabwe without first telling me.'

By the time the police officers left, it was close to six o'clock, and Captain John had gone home. Dan didn't have the chance to discuss the police officers' visit with him. That meant he'd have plenty of time to stew over its implications. It was Wednesday, and he was due to spend the night with Gloria at her flat.

CHAPTER 24

Dan knocked on the door, and Gloria opened it. She was as radiant as ever. Every time he saw her, it reminded him of what was important in life. She was young, beautiful, and his. It helped him forget his worries. Though tonight, the police officers' visit hung heavy on his mind.

Dinner was less chatty than usual as Dan's thoughts slipped back to the events of the last three days. Might Jonas's disappearance be a Machiavellian plot to entrap him? Was the plan to get him arrested for Jonas's murder? Meanwhile, Jonas might sun himself on a Zanzibar beach until the fuss abated. Why did Captain John send him on the train with Jonas? John must have realised he'd do nothing to aid the mission and might even try to sabotage it.

It was all too neat. Captain John joked about Dan taking over Jonas's role if anything happened to him. Now, only days later, something had happened. Did Captain John and Jonas cook this up between them? How could they foresee the train would stop ten minutes out of Dete? Was it a spontaneous decision? Maybe he planned to disappear somewhere further down the line but left during the unscheduled stop. Did Jonas bribe the driver to stop at that point on the track? Did a car wait for him there?

From what the inspector said, it sounded like Captain John suggested he would be a capable replacement for Jonas. That was ridiculous. He and John both knew Jonas was a trained killer. Not in his wildest imaginings could John believe he'd get involved in any such activity. Did John give the police officers the impression he would promote him to Jonas's position? It might look like he had a motive for getting rid of Jonas.

'What's on your mind?' said Gloria.

'Oh, nothing much.'

'You're quiet tonight. Is there a problem?'

'No, not really. Work is stressful right now.'

'You never talk to me about your work. What's troubling you?'

'It's nothing for you to worry about.'

'If it worries you, it worries me. Sometimes, I feel you don't include me in your life.'

'Drop it, Gloria, I don't want to talk about it.'

'OK, OK! No need to bite my head off.'

'I'm sorry. It's not something you can help me with.'

'Why don't you try me?'

'What if I told you I'm suspected of murdering a colleague?'

Gloria laughed. 'Don't be silly. Be serious. What's the problem?'

'I phoned you from Bulawayo to tell you I'd be away for a couple of days.'

'Yes?'

'I was on the Bulawayo to Victoria Falls train when my colleague disappeared.'

'I heard about that on the news.'

'Well, the police have the silly idea I may have murdered him to get his job.'

'That's ridiculous!'

'Yes, that's what I said. The media puts the police under pressure to solve the case, so they come up with crazy, desperate ideas. I was with him on the train, so I suppose it makes me the logical suspect.'

'The papers said the train may have left him behind when it departed.'

'That's the only other explanation. They say they've found no trace of him. If the train left him behind, you'd expect him to turn up after a couple of days.'

* * *

In bed with Gloria, Dan soon fell asleep. He didn't have the restless night he imagined. But when he awoke in the morning, the police interview was on his mind. After a quick cereal breakfast, he kissed Gloria goodbye and returned to his apartment to shower and change into fresh clothes. He was keen to discuss the matter with Captain John.

Cherry and Ambrose greeted Dan with their cheery smiles and a steaming cup of tea. How wonderful to be untroubled by the machinations of the senior managers. He knocked on Captain John's doorframe. 'Can we have a chat, John?'

'Let's leave it until drinks this evening, Dan. That will give us plenty of time and privacy.'

'Yes, OK.'

For Dan, it was the longest day. Every minute dragged. At last, lunchtime arrived, and Ambrose entered with a bag of sausage and chips and a steaming cup of tea. Dan always enjoyed those cups of tea. They remained consistently good, just as Ambrose was consistently cheerful.

'Ambrose, tell me something about yourself. Are you married?'

'I was married, Sir, but my wife was killed in the 2008 election violence.'

'Was she involved in politics?'

'No, Sir. She was coming home from work when the crazy mob looked for opposition supporters. They saw her and chopped her.'

'That's terrible! Unbelievable!'

'Yes, Sir.'

'Have you married again?'

'No, Sir. I couldn't find another woman like my wife. Ah, that one was so special.'

Ambrose's story surprised Dan. The tragedy of losing his wife did not destroy his natural cheerfulness and positive attitude. It occurred to him he'd asked little about the lives of his colleagues. Was Cherry married?

Did she have children? He'd only ever spoken to her about work. Following the chat with Ambrose, his afternoon went by much faster than the morning. He focussed on his work, and soon, Captain John knocked on his door to invite him for their Thursday evening scotches.

Dan put away the loose items on his desk and followed Captain John back to his office. John took two crystal tumblers from the bookcase behind his desk. He opened the built-in bar fridge and grabbed the ice tray and put two cubes in each glass. Next, he took out an unopened bottle of Lagavulin sixteen-year-old single malt scotch. 'Tell me how you like this one,' he said, handing Dan a glass.

'John, did you tell the police you planned to give me Jonas's position?'

'No, of course not. The police suspect you might have had something to do with Jonas's disappearance. If I said that, they'd be even more suspicious of you. They're casting around for a motive.'

'Did they tell you they suspected me?'

'No, Eunice told me.'

'Eunice? Did they interview her?'

'Yes. Her and Cherry.'

'If Eunice told you they suspected me, what did she tell them?'

'Dan, just answer this one question, please. Did you and Jonas fall out and fight, and he fell from the train? Accidents happen.'

'No, we got on well. I liked him. What reason would I have to fight with him?'

'You must excuse me for asking, but it's hard to trust anyone these days. Anyway, how's the scotch?'

'Beautiful! Nice and smoky.'

* * *

Later, back in his apartment, Dan mulled over his chat with Captain John. While he spent the previous evening worrying about what part John may have played in Jonas's supposed disappearance, it appeared John spent the evening wondering if he was behind it. It would be a mystery if Jonas was genuinely missing.

Now that he knew the police officers interviewed Eunice, he was sure she'd pointed them in his direction. She was jealous of his dealings with Captain John right from the start. The situation gave her the perfect opportunity to be rid of him.

It was not surprising that he, Captain John, and Eunice all distrusted one another. In the COU's murky world, trust was in short supply. Anyone might spy, betray, or inform on anyone else. He got the distinct impression Captain John felt the same insecurity as he about the loyalty of his work colleagues.

Dan recalled his discussion with Ambrose that afternoon. He knew little about him and Cherry, his favourite people in the COU. Though he wouldn't trust them any more than the others in the unit. He needed to be wary. Like himself, Ambrose and Cherry worked for Captain John. How foolish it would be for him to imagine they'd throw their support behind him, rather than their employer.

And what about the mysterious David Jones? He must be more involved than Nikita suggested. Common sense told Dan that only David Jones and Captain John held the knowledge and authority to arrange his attempted mugging at the airport in Johannesburg. Either of them, or both, must have arranged it.

So, who to trust? Only Nikita, Daniel Moyo and Gloria. On reflection, they'd all inserted themselves into his life. He didn't approach them. They all found him. Each had been assertive in befriending him.

Nikita virtually forced her way into his hotel room. She said her clandestine group was aware of his planned return to Zimbabwe, but hoped he wouldn't come. How did she learn of his intentions? She suggested she had a source in the COU. So, perhaps, not only Captain John and David Jones were privy to his plans.

Daniel Moyo bought him a scotch even before introducing himself. Earlier that evening, he'd seen Daniel sitting alone at a table in the hotel dining room. Moyo followed him to the Explorers' Bar. His story about being alone for the weekend with his wife visiting relatives seemed plausible enough, and he'd been generous with his money and his time.

The irresistible Gloria admitted she'd planned on getting his attention and meeting him face to face. Her plan worked well. He'd toyed with the idea of a long-term, even permanent relationship. The idea scared him because he'd always worked hard to resist any such encumbrance.

How he met his trusted friends now put doubt in his mind. Should he trust them? Any of them? He was getting paranoid.

* * *

Days passed, and Dan heard nothing more from the police. All remained quiet in the COU offices, and he relaxed. Captain John said nothing about filling Jonas's role, and Dan hoped he wouldn't pass the responsibility on to Eunice. There must be someone else in the team capable of filling it.

Captain John held a high opinion of Khumalo, the Ndebele, based in Bulawayo. If the role focused on external operations, what would his tribal roots matter? Perhaps Khumalo's persuasiveness wouldn't work on Shonas in the diaspora. Then again, the Honey File held many Ndebele names.

When absorbed in his writing or the admin work, Dan found it quite easy to forget the dark nature of the COU's operations. But incidents like Absalom Muzenda's poisoning and Jacob Nkala's murder dragged him back to reality.

It was a surprise then, when Captain John knocked on the doorframe and walked into his office.

'Dan, you remember I said I joked when I suggested you might need to take over the external operations. There's no one else I can trust with the job.'

John's words stunned him. He'd never be able to fill Jonas's role.

'You said yourself the police would be more suspicious of me if I took Jonas's job.'

'Don't worry! If they say anything, I'll explain it's only a temporary measure.'

'What about Khumalo in Bulawayo? He could do it.'

'Khumalo wouldn't have the stomach for the job.'

'And I do?'

'It would just be a caretaker role. You'd need to manage the communications with Francis and his Johannesburg network once you've established contact with them. I don't want the entire group to disintegrate through inactivity. They've got to believe we're operating as normal, but don't worry, you wouldn't need to get your hands dirty. There'll be no significant external jobs for now. For you, it will be an admin position, no different from your present role. Someone must look after the team.'

The two locked eyes. John suspected Dan understood the true nature of the COU's business, while Dan realised John was aware he'd guessed its real purpose. Somehow, that mutual recognition increased the level of trust between them. It seemed Jonas wasn't as discreet as John might have hoped, and Dan worked out the COU's role. They wouldn't speak of their mutual understanding. There was no need.

In his apartment, later that evening, Dan reviewed his conversation with Captain John. If he was to oversee external operations, did that mean he'd come off the Honey File list? How might he raise that issue with Captain John if they'd not discussed the COU's true purpose? Besides, John was unaware he knew about the Honey File and its contents, and it was better if it stayed that way.

Dan grabbed a beer from the refrigerator. What an unbelievable situation! In effect, John asked him to act as one of his two lieutenants. From what John said, it sounded like the external operations would be on hold. Well, that suited him fine. The entire situation was like a charade. Might it be yet another ruse to entrap him further in the COU's web?

The COU's business was assassination for hire. It wouldn't be legal, even if the government used their services. So, it must be a criminal organisation. How would he explain away his senior operational role in the business? Admin was one thing, but running external operations, quite another, even if nothing much happened during his tenure.

Did Captain John imagine he'd be OK with murder and assassination? True, in one sense, he'd ignored what went on. But what could he do about it? Who'd listen to him, anyway? His best course was to sabotage or undermine any jobs that came his way.

CHAPTER 25

Eva sat on the edge of the bed, watching her husband knot his tie. She noted yet again how handsome he was. With his rugged good looks and muscular frame, she was proud to be married to him. Her only unspoken complaint was he spent more time with his army colleagues and supporters than he did with her. The army and their cause ruled both their lives.

'What is the occasion tonight, Victor?'

'We're celebrating promotions for three of my officers.'

'No promotion for you?'

'That will never happen. Not in the present situation.'

'Yes, only the obsequious and fawning ones get recognised.'

'Not my men! I only put the deserving ones forward for promotion.'

'The promotions board doesn't endorse all your recommendations. Those who are most loyal to you seem to progress the slowest.'

'That is true, though the ones they promote are also good men. I can't afford to have any favourites. If I did, I'd lose the support I now enjoy.'

'Are you sure they are good men? If the promotions board rejects your known supporters, how do you explain those that are successful?'

'They can't reject everyone I recommend for promotion, so some advance. For the others, their time will come.'

'Are you sure someone hasn't turned some of the successful ones? The army might have promised them promotion for switching their allegiance.'

'True, but I can't suspect everyone who rises through the ranks. No one has told me that someone has made them an offer. One or two may be open to a proposal. Though I'm sure someone would have warned me.'

'Well, if they've taken the bait, they wouldn't, would they?'

'You're too wary, my dear. Sometimes you need to trust people. I didn't reach the rank of colonel by distrusting everyone.'

'I would be most careful about whom I trusted. Politics and the army are a dangerous mix in Zimbabwe. Look how many have fallen foul of the government and met an unhappy end.'

'Everyone knows my views. My men can't say anything that would surprise my superiors.'

'Superiors in name only! There's nothing superior about that lot. What if they spread rumours about you? Even though untrue, they could use it as an excuse to move against you. You wouldn't be the first person to suffer the consequences of a lie.'

'You worry too much, my dear.'

'I worry about your safety.'

'And that's why I love you.'

'What time will you be home?'

'About eleven or half-past.'

'Be careful!'

'I will.' Victor kissed Eva, grabbed his car keys, and walked to his car on the gravel drive.

Eva watched as her husband got into the car and started the engine. He blew her a kiss as he eased the big saloon through the garden gate. The tyres' scrunch on the gravel was the sound she looked forward to hearing later that evening. That would signal he was home. She couldn't help worrying whenever he attended army social functions. Too many senior officers ran into trouble in the competitive and conspiratorial ranks of the army hierarchy.

* * *

Victor's new Mercedes delighted him as it glided down the road. He avoided the worst potholes, and the car's suspension took care of the rest. A smooth, comfortable ride, much like his army career to this point. But there were gathering clouds ahead. His pro-democratic views gained supporters and detractors alike.

He was a brilliant soldier, though in military circles the rumour was he would advance no higher through the ranks. While he didn't directly criticise the dictatorial regime, his advocacy for Westminster-style government was more than enough criticism for the leadership to swallow. Someone high up saw him as a potential threat and blocked his promotion. Victor didn't care, believing truth and justice would prevail in time. Modern history provided little evidence, giving credence to this view.

Victor turned into a parking space close to the hotel's entrance. He switched off the engine and jumped out. The car door closed with a satisfying thud. It was a beautiful Harare evening with clear skies in the cool, dry winter air. Victor was content with his lot. Three of his officers got promoted, and although his views restricted his own rise through the ranks, he was proud of his men and happy for their success.

At the hotel entrance, he strode past the two gigantic vases underneath the sign proclaiming *The Rainbow Towers*. The concierge directed him to the private function room, where his men already waited. When he entered the room, the officers snapped to attention and then clapped him. There was no doubting his popularity amongst the men who idolised him.

Soon, waiters entered the room with finger food and trays of drinks. The views of Harare at night added to the celebratory atmosphere. Victor spoke a few words to each officer, so none of them felt neglected. He made a brief speech congratulating the three promoted men, wishing them long and successful careers in the army.

The merry group enjoyed the informal gathering. They all dressed in civilian clothes, which helped to keep military protocols to a minimum. The celebration was like a gathering of friends, rather than an official army function. The party would continue until Victor, the senior officer present, made moves to leave.

'Just one more beer, Sir! One for the road!'

Victor drunk two beers during the evening, not that anyone else noticed as they took full advantage of the free liquor. He accepted a third drink, but after a few sips, he made his excuses and left. That last beer put a sour taste in his mouth. He learned from experience it was a sure sign he'd drunk enough. He'd eaten no dinner, and although the finger food kept coming, it didn't make up for his smaller than usual intake.

As he exited the lift on the ground floor, he felt a little light-headed. Drinking was part of army life. He'd cut back in recent times, being conscious of setting a good example for his men. It was just as well he'd not gulped down that third beer because he was unsteady on his feet. At his car, he searched for the car keys in his pocket and fumbled as he tried to open the car door.

'Here, Colonel. Let us help you, Sir.'

Two men approached him. Were they two of his officers? He got the impression they were, though he wasn't sure. Victor shook his head to clear it, but it made no difference. He'd not before experienced this sensation after only two beers. There was always a first time. Perhaps he should have eaten a proper dinner before attending the function. Everyone understood you shouldn't drink on an empty stomach.

'You don't look well enough to drive, Sir. Get into the passenger seat, and I'll drive you home.'

'Home? Do you know where I live?'

'Yes, Sir.'

Victor always kept his personal life separate from his role in the army and didn't think anyone knew about his domestic arrangements, least of all his own men. One's juniors are often curious about their superiors, and someone may have followed him to see where he lived.

'And how will you get home?'

'My colleague will follow us in his car, Sir. When I drop you off, he'll take me.'

Victor settled into the passenger seat, and a wave of tiredness washed over him. He closed his eyes and almost at once fell into a deep sleep.

CHAPTER 26

A knock on the door. Ten-thirty! Who might that be at this hour? Dan wasn't expecting anyone. Gloria never came on a Friday night because she worked on Saturday mornings. Tomorrow lunchtime was when she'd arrive.

With the security chain latched, the door only opened three inches. A woman stood there. She dressed in a black, three-quarter length coat and wore her hair pulled back in a bun.

Dan hesitated. 'Nikita? Eva?'

'Yes, Dan.'

Dan opened the door. 'Come in, Eva. What brings you here? What a surprise!'

Nikita once told him, if her hair was pulled back in a bun, she was Eva. Before now, she'd always come as Nikita, wearing a long, curly, black wig. As she passed through the doorway, Dan saw her face streaked with tears.

'What's the matter? What's wrong?'

'They've killed Victor. Someone has killed Victor.'

The news shocked Dan. 'Who? How? When?'

'This evening he attended an army function to celebrate three of his officers getting their promotions. I was always worried when he attended those army socials, but somehow, I had a bad feeling about this one. I told him to be careful, and he promised he would.'

'At eleven o'clock, I heard someone walking up the gravel driveway. Victor would drive in, so I knew it wasn't him. It was the police. They said he'd drunk too much and crossed the railway line in front of a train.

Victor never drank a lot. Not enough to affect his driving. I'm sure someone staged the accident.'

'But Victor wasn't on the domestic list.'

'Eunice doesn't always follow the list, or they may have updated it. Though the CIO, army or police could be responsible.'

Eva's face crumpled, and Dan put his arms around her. She sobbed into his shoulder, taking deep shuddering breaths. He held her tight, waiting for her tears to subside. Nothing he might say would ease her pain.

Eva finally stopped crying and raised her head. 'Sorry, I've made your shirt soaking wet.'

'It's nothing. Don't worry about that.'

Dan fetched a bottle of Cognac and poured a glass for Eva. 'So, what now?'

'The police say they'll investigate the accident, but these investigations never lead to a proper result. They've already made up their minds it was an accident. The news will devastate and frighten the rest of the group. If this happened to Victor, it could happen to any of us. He held the group together.'

'Have you seen Victor?'

'No, they wouldn't let me see him. They said it's up to the coroner to decide whether I can view the body.'

'Eva, I'm so sorry this happened. I get no news about the domestic operations of the COU. Even if Eunice organised it, there's no way they'd tell me.'

'In the army, Victor's views went against the flow. He said, with the top brass against him, he'd never get another promotion. But neither of us expected this to happen. Victor said if he was open in his views, it would be a shield to protect him from his enemies. Someone must have given the word to kill him. I wonder if it was because we watched over Dr Tawanda until he could leave Zimbabwe. You know he escaped to Botswana?'

'Yes.'

'The authorities must be furious. Perhaps they decided Victor and the group had become too much of a nuisance.'

'Have you spoken to anyone who attended the function this evening? Perhaps they can tell you if he drank too much.'

'I doubt anyone at the function would yet have learned of Victor's death. Three of his officers are in our group. They will tell me if they saw anything suspicious. It will devastate the others in our group when they discover what's happened. I can't believe it! I just can't believe it! Everything was normal this morning, and now, a few hours later, this!'

Dan and Eva talked until the early hours. Eva needed to talk and talk. It helped her in her hour of grief. Around three in the morning, she glanced at her watch. 'Look at the time! I'm sorry. I've kept you up so late with my problems.'

'No need to apologise, Eva. That's what friends are for, isn't it? I'm here for you. Remember that.'

'Thank you, Dan.'

After Eva left, Dan deliberated over their talk. Was Victor's death payback for the protection his group offered Tawanda during his stay in Harare? Did his own intervention, to protect Tawanda on the train, lead to Victor's death? He hated the idea he might have inadvertently contributed to his fate.

It seemed too much of a coincidence that he died so soon after Tawanda's escape to Botswana. Eva mentioned once before, Victor's followers suspected someone watched them guarding Tawanda's house, and they feared for their own safety. It meant the authorities were aware of the group's existence. Might others be in danger? How about Eva? Would they go after her next?

CHAPTER 27

THE phone rang, and at first, Dan didn't recognise the voice. 'Oh! Mrs Olonga, how are you?'

'Well, thank you. Mr Scott, I'm phoning to confirm the dates of the Bulawayo Writers' Festival. The committee has selected the last weekend in September. The opening cocktail party is on Friday evening. Most of our presentations will be on Saturday, and the readings on Sunday morning. The festival will wrap up at lunchtime on Sunday. You offered to invite Ian Sanders to present the keynote address. Have you spoken to him yet?'

'No, now that I have the dates, I'll call him and let you know if he's available.'

Dan said he would invite Ian Sanders to speak at the writers' festival. How could he invite him, now he'd found out the novelist's name was in the Honey File? He didn't want to be party to the author's demise. He would wait a few days and then tell Mrs Olonga that Ian Sanders wasn't available.

It was Tuesday, and as usual, Captain John came to Dan's office at the day's end to invite him for drinks. As John poured the scotch over the ice in the tumblers, he said, 'My wife tells me the writers' club has set a date for the Bulawayo Writers' Festival.'

'Yes, that's right. Mrs Olonga, the president of the Harare Writers' Club, phoned me this morning to confirm it.'

'You said you would try to get Ian Sanders to speak at the festival.'

'Yes, but he's a busy man. I don't think there'd be much chance of getting him.'

'It's all about how you approach someone. Don't phone him. Fly to Gaborone and meet him face to face.'

'Shouldn't I call him to make sure he'll see me? I don't want to turn up and find he's not available. It would be a waste of money.'

'OK, phone him and introduce yourself, and say you'd like to meet him. Don't mention the festival until you're sitting in front of him. It's harder for people to refuse such requests face to face. Over the phone, it's easy to say no. On your way back, you can stop in Joburg and see Francis. Tell him about Jonas, and that you're now in charge of external COU operations.'

'He won't believe me.'

'I'll give you his next salary envelope to make it more convincing.'

John dismissed every obstacle Dan put forward about why Ian Sanders might not agree to speak at the festival. He seemed determined that Dan should try his best to convince Ian Sanders to attend, and Dan guessed why John was so set on the novelist being there.

'Are you thinking of attending the festival?'

'My wife would love to hear him speak.'

'Your wife enjoys reading?'

'Yes, very much.'

Later, back in the apartment, Dan took out the piece of paper with Ian Sanders' telephone number, which Daniel Moyo gave him. He tapped out the number on his cell phone.

To Dan's surprise, Ian Sanders was keen to meet him. 'Yes, I'm familiar with your work. I've read your books.'

* * *

The following Monday, Dan left Harare at one o'clock on the four and a half hour SA Airlink flight to Gaborone. The stopover in Johannesburg added to the length of the journey. A direct flight would have taken less than half the time.

Dan's first impression from the plane was of a dry country, flat to the horizons. The Gaborone skyline suggested a small, developing city, full of promise. Sir Seretse Khama International Airport was modern and clean, signalling Botswana was a country on the rise. Immigration and customs were quick and efficient, reinforcing that impression.

Dan picked up his small hire-car and studied the map to find the route to the Peermont Mondior Gaborone Hotel. It looked simple enough. He drove out along Airport Road, crossed the Francistown Road onto Nelson Mandela Drive, and headed south to the CBD. It was rush hour, a quarter to six in the evening, though the traffic wasn't too bad compared to Johannesburg or Harare.

The hotel was on Maratadiba Road, and Dan soon found it. He parked the car in the hotel parking and grabbed his overnight bag and walked into the building. A young woman at the reception desk welcomed him with a cheerful smile, handing him a check-in form to complete.

A porter led Dan to the lift past the African décor mounted on the walls. He pressed the button for the first floor, where yet more African artefacts decorated the walls. The porter led Dan down a passage to an attractive central atrium filled with palms. He stopped at one of the heavy looking wooden doors and opened it.

The ensuite room was spacious with dark wooden furnishings and heavy curtains. African prints above the bed headboard and raffia mats and bowls on the opposite wall added to the ambience. Dan's choice of hotel pleased him. He was due at Ian Sanders' house for dinner, so he needed to move fast. He took a quick shower and dressed for the evening.

Dan studied the map to find Ian Sanders' house. It wasn't far out of town. The size of Gaborone meant nowhere was far out of town. He picked up the bottle of wine he'd bought and headed for the door. In the car, he checked the map again before setting off in the darkness.

With the clear directions, Dan had no difficulty in finding the address. He stopped in front of the enormous iron gates set into a towering wall. As instructed by Ian Sanders over the phone, he gave a toot, toot, toot on the car horn. A moment later, the gates slid open, and Dan drove through, stopping in the driveway. The scrunch of tyres on the firm, sandy surface was a familiar sound in this part of Africa. The heavy iron gates clanged shut behind him.

Dan opened the car door and hopped out, just as Ian Sanders descended the steps leading to his front door. They introduced themselves and shook hands. 'Welcome to Gaborone, Dan.'

'Thank you. Here's a bottle of red wine I bought at the airport in Joburg.'

'Thanks. Come in and meet my family.'

Dan followed Ian into the spacious house. Large rooms led into each other—almost open plan, with a clever layout and arches separating the lounge, dining area, kitchen and what looked like an enormous study with bookshelves to the ceiling. The bare red brick walls and mood lighting gave the entire place a cosy atmosphere.

'My, you've lots of room here.'

'Well, there's six of us. Michael, my youngest, is a year old already, and soon he'll be running around, making the place feel a lot smaller.'

Dan was about to reply when two African women entered the room.

'This is Sarah and her mother, Esther, our cook extraordinaire.'

Both women were tall and slender. Esther wore a cream, mid-calf tight dress, while Sarah wore a bottle-green caftan with delicate gold leaf patterns. Sarah looked most glamorous, and Dan noted Ian was a lucky man.

After introductions, Sarah said, 'What can I get you to drink, Dan? Ian likes scotch on the rocks.'

'Yes, me too. Thank you.'

Sarah walked to the study to pour the drinks, and Esther excused herself to go check on the dinner.

Suddenly, two children ran into the room. 'Daddy,' said the boy, fidgeting shyly, 'Grandma said we must say hello.'

'This is Sam and Kemi.'

'Ah, twins! Your glamourous wife doesn't look like a mother of three.'

Ian laughed. 'Almost twins. Sam is Jemma's boy and Kemi is Sarah's daughter.'

'And Michael?'

'Jemma is Michael's mother.'

'Oh, I'm sorry. I thought Sarah was your wife.'

'Well, they both are, so to speak. Sarah and Jemma are sisters, and we make up one family. Ah, here she is. Jemma, come and meet Dan Scott.' Jemma looked serene in a long white dress set off by a colourful string of African beads. She wore a broad gold comb to hold back her longish hair. Dan remained undecided which of Ian Sanders' two wives looked the most striking.

Sarah brought in the scotches, and Jemma took the children off to bed. Soon after Jemma returned, Esther announced dinner was ready, and they all sat down at the huge carved dining table to eat. The weather was turning chilly, but an enormous open fireplace heated the entire area. The cosy atmosphere, red wine, and Esther's traditional roast beef dinner made for a grand feast with lots of laughter and chatter.

After the coffee and port, Jemma and Esther bid goodnight and left Ian and Sarah to chat with Dan.

'Daniel Moyo sends his regards,' said Dan. 'My visit here is a little awkward. A few months ago, I gave a talk to the Harare Writers' Club. I mentioned to the club president, Mrs Olonga, that I'd get in touch with you to see if you'd be interested in giving the keynote address at the Bulawayo Writers' Festival. Last week she phoned me and said they scheduled the festival for the last weekend in September and reminded me of my promise to see if you'd be interested.'

'I'm not sure that would be wise, Dan. You realise we needed to escape from Zimbabwe? Forces there were out to get us. Heaven knows what would have happened if they'd caught us. If you've read my first book, you'll get the idea.'

'I have read your first book, but I never realised you based it on your own experiences. I do management consulting work for a business in Harare. The owner was keen for me to invite you to speak at the festival because his wife is an avid reader and a member of the writers' club. On second thoughts, I agree with you. It would be unwise for you to accept the invitation.'

'What makes you say that?'

'Politics is unpredictable in Zimbabwe. Now that I understand your first book is about your experiences in the country, I feel you would tempt fate if you returned, even for a visit. There are dangerous people there, and it's rumoured they're looking to settle old scores. I'm told the CIO is active in the diaspora in Johannesburg. Did you hear about the suspicious deaths of Absalom Muzenda and Jacob Nkala?'

'Yes, we did. You must have noticed our heavy sheet metal gates when you drove in.'

Dan nodded.

'Wrought-iron gates once stood there. There was a full-length mirror in the entrance hall. Someone must have seen our reflection and thought it was Sarah and me and shot at it. So, we put up the sheet metal gates to prevent anyone looking into our property.'

'Who runs this business you're working with in Harare?' said Sarah.

'He calls himself Captain John.'

'John Ziyambi, or Jedson Ziyambi, as I knew him. Also known as The Leopard.'

'Yes, that's right.'

'Will he be at the festival?'

'He seems to be interested in books, but he's said nothing about attending. He said his wife would probably go.'

'Tell him Ian might be interested.'

'Sarah, what are you saying?' said Ian.

'If I were you, I'd think twice about that,' said Dan.

'Say, there's a good chance Ian will speak at the festival. If we change our minds, we'll let you know.'

'OK, though please consider what I've said. I must also be careful because my writing isn't too popular with the regime. They've banned my books.'

'Then why are you still in Zimbabwe?'

'It's a complicated story. I'm stuck there for now, but I'll leave as soon as I can.'

A little past eleven, Dan waved goodbye to Ian and Sarah and drove back to the hotel. He would not have much time to appreciate his comfortable room as he was flying out on SA Airlink at ten thirty-five the next morning.

CHAPTER 28

IT was a beautiful morning, and Dan relaxed on the one hour and forty-five-minute flight to Johannesburg. He had no way of contacting Francis beforehand, as he didn't have his phone number. Apart from finding out who made up Jonas's Johannesburg team, he'd need to set up a means of communication with him. He was sure he would find Francis's flat again, but he'd not bothered to note his address when he and Jonas stayed there.

Immigration and customs presented no problem, and Dan soon walked out of arrivals and headed to the car rentals area. He made his way to the Europcar counter and selected a compact car for his overnight stay. The desk called a man to lead him to the car, where they checked for existing damage and scratches. Dan signed off on the damage summary before setting off for the city.

Driving in Gaborone was a breeze, but here in Johannesburg, he needed to concentrate on the heavy traffic. He studied the map before leaving the airport carpark and tried to memorise the route. To be on the safe side, he kept the map open on the passenger seat beside him. He didn't want to look like he'd lost his way. Joburg's notorious criminals would soon spot a dithering driver, and that might make him a target for a mugging.

There was nothing wrong with his memory, and it proved a straightforward drive towards the city, using the unmistakable Ponte City Apartments as a beacon. Despite a few wrong turns, he soon found himself in Berea. He recognised the area now and drove straight to the corner of

Lily and Olivia. He turned right into the quiet dead end of Olivia Road and parked.

Dan locked the car and strode to the high-rise apartment block where Francis and his wife Sally lived. He hurried because he wasn't confident about either his own safety or that of the car. On this visit, Jonas wasn't on hand to extricate him from any scrapes.

Now what was Francis's floor? For a moment, he worried he'd forgotten. Then he remembered his hair-raising crossing from Jonas's flat to Francis's. Eight floors to the concrete below—how could he ever forget that? Dan didn't wait for the slow lift, a perfect spot for a mugging. At least on the stairs, he could make a getaway if confronted.

Eight floors didn't sound like much, but by the time he reached the eighth floor, he was puffing, and his legs ached. He resolved to keep more fit in the future. Dan walked down the public corridor and knocked on Francis's door, which was next to the one he and Jonas used on their brief visit. He knocked again, a little harder, and waited. No reply. What if he couldn't contact Francis? He didn't want to come back later if he could avoid it.

Dan knocked once more. Still no reply. He remembered Jonas saying Francis and Sally often moved between the two apartments. He knocked on the door of the apartment he and Jonas had used. Within moments, it opened.

'Hello Sally, I'm Dan. I came here before with Jonas. Do you remember me?'

'Yes, of course, come in.'

'Is Francis here?'

'Yes, yes, come in.'

Francis came forward to greet him. 'How are you, my friend? Where's Jonas? He didn't tell me you two would be coming.'

'I've got bad news, Francis.'

While Sally made tea, Dan and Francis talked.

'How can it be? Jonas disappeared?'

'We'd all like an answer to that question.'

'So, you are taking charge?'

'For now. Before I forget, here are your wages.' Dan handed Francis the envelope Captain John gave him.

'Ah, thank you.'

'Now, what I need is your cell phone number and the details of your team here in Joburg.'

'The cell phone number is easy, but the team in Joburg is just Sally and me. When Jonas wanted a job done, he'd either do it himself or ask me to find one or two people to handle it. I'd visit the shebeens and see who was available.'

'So there's no fixed team?'

'That's right.'

'Did you see the CCTV footage of the people looting Jacob Nkala's shop?'

'Yes.'

'And the big man with a black T-shirt and baseball cap? Did Jonas use him before on some jobs?'

'Yes, people call him Gustave. I don't know his real name. Jonas used him when I wasn't available. I don't like that man. He's a killer and doesn't have much brain. That makes him extra dangerous.'

'You accompanied Jonas the day Jacob Nkala was killed. Did you see Gustave on that occasion?'

'Yes, we parked around the corner near the shop. Gustave was waiting there, and Jonas got out and spoke with him. I didn't hear what they said.'

'So you didn't enter the shop?'

'No, I'm from Mozambique and Jonas is a Zimbabwean. It was dangerous for us foreigners to be there.'

'Have you ever met Captain John?'

'No, and I've never even spoken to him.'

'What about David Jones?'

'No, I've never met him. Who is he?'

'Before Jacob Nkala, when did Jonas last use Gustave?'

'Maybe eight or nine months ago. I was sick, so I couldn't help him find two men for a special job. If he was desperate, he might have gone to Gustave for that one.'

'Eight or nine months ago? That's when I arrived here. Do you remember what the job involved?'

'No, he didn't say.'

'All right. Well, I'd better be going.'

'When will you be back?'

'I'm not sure. You will either hear from me or Captain John.'

Dan thanked Sally for the tea and said goodbye to her and Francis. He hurried down the flights of stairs to the ground floor and walked to the corner before crossing Lily Avenue onto Olivia Road. To his relief, the rental car looked undisturbed. There was no prospect of him catching the SA Airlink three-forty flight to Harare, so he drove to the Crowne Plaza Hotel in Rosebank where he and Jonas stayed on their last visit. He hadn't booked, but it didn't present any problems.

In Rosebank, Dan bought a few packets of condoms, so he and Gloria wouldn't need to worry about the quality of their existing supply.

At six o'clock, he walked to The Grillhouse (Rosebank) restaurant, only two blocks from the hotel. Well known for its steaks, it was an irresistible draw for him. The cosy atmosphere and melt-in-the-mouth fillet steak provided the perfect answer to the chilly evening outdoors.

Later, back in his hotel, Dan ordered a coffee in the lounge before returning to his room. The trip had gone well so far. He hoped he'd dissuaded Ian Sanders and Sarah from risking a return visit to Zimbabwe. Why did she insist Ian would consider going? It made little sense.

Tomorrow he'd catch the ten-forty SA Airlink flight. It took an hour and thirty-five minutes, which meant he should be back in Harare at a quarter past midday. It would be Wednesday, so he'd spend the night at Gloria's flat. He always looked forward to that. In the meantime, all alone in Johannesburg, he'd get an early night.

Dan lay in bed, looking at the hotel room's ceiling. An early night didn't always lead to an early sleep. His mind went back over his visit to Francis and Sally. Jonas visited them around the time he arrived in Johannesburg. He needed two men for a job. What Job? Might it have been his attempted mugging at the airport? Then why hadn't he seen Jonas that night?

Where was David Jones these days? He hadn't seen him for ages. Nikita thought him harmless, though Dan wasn't so sure. Jonas may have put a team together, but it didn't mean David Jones was involved, though he'd recommended Dan should book in at the Intercontinental Hotel at Johannesburg airport. Who else might have known where he planned to stay?

* * *

Meanwhile, in Gaborone, Ian and Sarah chatted about Dan's visit.

'Sarah, why did you say I might be interested in speaking at the Bulawayo Writers' Festival? I can't go back there. Not under the present circumstances.'

'It's me they want. So, if you returned to Zimbabwe and they detained you, what might they expect to happen next?'

'That you would try to rescue me?'

'That's right. Captain John is laying a trap for us.'

'Why then, did you suggest I might speak at the festival?'

'It will buy us time. If he thinks you'll be at the festival, he's unlikely to bother us before then.'

'That's only three months away. What then?'

'I'm not sure, but I'm working on it.'

Ian laughed. 'Now don't go getting any crazy ideas.'

'It's been a long time since my stint with the COU. All my survival skills are getting rusty. If I leave it much longer, I won't be capable of making him pay for what he's done.'

'What we have is more important than getting revenge on Captain John. Can't you just forget about him?'

'He murdered my father and Joseph, my fiancé. Then he tried to get us. What do you think would have happened if he'd been successful? So yes, I would forget about him if he forgot about us. Remember, someone tried to shoot us here, in this house? I got the feeling Dan Scott was trying to warn us, though I don't believe he gave us the full story. If we don't finish Captain John first, it will never end. He'll always be hunting us.'

CHAPTER 29

DAN sat at his desk, enjoying one of Ambrose's steaming cups of tea. It was a crisp, chilly winter morning. Soon, the sun would warm the air. The phone on his desk rang, and he picked up the receiver. Cherry was on the line. 'Sir, Detective Inspector Tshuma from the Bulawayo police station wants to speak to you. Shall I tell him you're not available?'

'No, Cherry, I better talk to him.'

'Putting you through now, Sir.'

'Good morning, Inspector.'

'Mr Scott, how are you?'

'Fine thanks. And you?'

Tshuma got straight to the point. 'Mr Scott, I understand you visited Gaborone and Johannesburg recently.'

'Yes, that's right.'

'Do you remember I told you not to leave Harare without advising me first?'

'Oh, yes. Sorry. I forgot. I'm back now, so I've not absconded or done anything illegal.'

'If you don't treat this matter seriously, Mr Scott, I'll have to take you into custody. My friends in Harare would be happy to accommodate you in Chikurubi until we've sorted out this business with Jonas Nyandoro.'

'No need, Inspector. I take your instructions seriously, but it slipped my mind when I left at short notice. My apologies. How did you discover I was away?'

'Let's just say not everyone is your friend.'

'Sorry, Inspector. It won't happen again.'

'It better not, Mr Scott.'

Dan put down the phone. Who tipped off Inspector Tshuma? Someone tried to compromise him. Who would be aware he needed to ask the police for permission to leave Harare? Captain John, Eunice, Cherry, or Ambrose? He dismissed the prospect of the last two reporting him to the police. So, Captain John or Eunice? Which one? He knew who he suspected.

Over a glass of scotch in Captain John's office that evening, Dan mentioned the inspector's phone call. At first, John offered no comment and looked thoughtful. Were they both thinking the same thing?

After a long silence, John said, 'If someone is trying to bring you down, they're working against me. As you will appreciate, we need to show that our external operations are ongoing and unaffected by Jonas's disappearance. When I find someone suitable, I'll appoint them to run things, but in the meantime, I need you to make it look like everything is normal and under control. If you run into problems, our whole external operation will be at risk. We must be alert if we want to find this mischief-maker.'

'There's not a long list of suspects, John.'

John looked at Dan. 'No, not a long list. Tell me, what was Ian Sanders' response to your invitation to be the keynote speaker at the Bulawayo Writers' Festival?'

'He said he was interested.'

'Oh, good! Alice, my wife, will be pleased to hear that.'

'Will you both be attending?'

'Perhaps. It depends what else I've got on.'

'I didn't realise you were interested in books and reading.'

'Oh, yes, I am. That's how I met my wife; through the Writers' Club.'

* * *

It was a week since the terrible news about Eva's husband, Colonel Victor Chirau. Dan was not surprised when Nikita dropped by unexpectedly.

'You've gone back to your long curly wig.'

'Yes, I shouldn't have come as Eva the last time I visited you. I was upset about Victor and wasn't thinking straight. It would put you in danger if anyone found out we worked together, so I must keep up my Nikita disguise.'

'That's no problem. I understand how bad it must have been for you.'

'Members of our group spoke to two men who witnessed the train accident. They said Victor looked unconscious, lying in the passenger seat. The driver stopped the car on the track in front of the oncoming train. The witnesses couldn't help Victor because the car doors were locked.'

'So, it looks like a targeted assassination?'

'Yes. He might already have been dead before the train crash.'

'Did they recognise the driver?'

'No, when he ran off, they only viewed him from behind. They never saw his face. I'm sure it would have been the COU. The government wouldn't entrust an important target like Victor to any of the other incompetent operations, and I doubt they would risk involving their official security services on such a job.'

'What makes you think the government was behind it?'

'Victor was a threat to them. He was popular with the people. Many in the army also supported him, so he was a potential rival in the longer term. Eunice may have organised the hit, though I'm sure Captain John sanctioned it, or at least knew about it.'

'What are you going to do?'

'I'll wait until an opportunity arises to get my revenge.'

'Is there anyone in your group who could replace Victor?'

'The group wants me to lead them.'

'And?'

'I've not yet decided, but I'll need the group's support to avenge Victor. Then after that, who knows? Victor was like the puff adder, lying in plain sight for everyone to spot the danger he presented. We'll be like the spitting cobra. They'll not see us until we strike, and then they won't see at all.'

CHAPTER 30

Now, in mid-winter, Harare was going through a chilly spell. The usual sunny winter days gave way to leaden grey skies with nippy gusts of wind blowing dust in the faces of pedestrians bowing their heads to protect against the unwelcome cold.

Dan's apartment had no air-conditioning or built-in heating, though the frequent power outages would have reduced their usefulness. On cold, miserable days, the solution lay in wearing warm clothes. On weekends, he and Gloria cuddled up under a blanket on the bed. She was his live hot-water bottle, though she saw herself as much more than that.

The supply of condoms he bought in Johannesburg ran out, and Gloria once again worried about the risk of falling pregnant. The cheap Chinese condoms didn't give her much confidence, and he'd made no firm commitment to her.

'What if I fall pregnant?'

'Well, what if you don't? We'll worry about that if it happens.'

'I often tell you I love you, but you never say that to me.'

'You know I do.'

'Well, why don't you say it?'

'OK, I love you. Happy now?'

'No, I shouldn't have to ask you. You should say it of your own free will.'

'I did.'

'You only say it when I raise the issue.'

'You worry too much. Do you think I'd tie myself to seeing you every weekend and Wednesday night if I didn't love you?'

'You love having sex with me. That's what you love.'

Dan gave little thought to what he'd do if Gloria became pregnant. In Zimbabwe, there was no one with whom he'd rather spend his time. Neither was there anyone at home in Melbourne? He'd always planned to travel the world and broaden his horizons. Gloria's world was Harare, and even there, she led a narrow life. He hadn't planned to tie himself down with anyone, let alone an unworldly twenty something.

His feelings for her were genuine. She was the most important person in his present circumstances, but he was careful to avoid saying anything she might interpret as a long-term commitment. He relished his single status. When he completed his novel, he intended to return to Australia and publish it. Then what would he do? Perhaps write a book in another exotic location. How might Gloria fit into all that?

In the meantime, their weekend finished with unanswered questions and frustration on Gloria's part, though he sweetened it with an idea that popped into his head.

'On the last weekend of September, I'm going to the Bulawayo Writers' Festival. If you take Friday and Saturday off, you can come with me.'

'I'd love to go. I'll clear it with my boss tomorrow.'

'Good, and I'll see you on Wednesday evening.'

Dan thought it was an effective way of appeasing Gloria. In the unlikely event Captain John attended the writers' festival, he needed an alternative plan. He feared the COU finding out about their relationship. A visit to Victoria Falls with Gloria would be nice, but he wouldn't mention it just yet. He'd save it for the next time she pressured him about their relationship.

* * *

Monday morning. The start of a new week. Things were going well in the office. Everything was getting organised and efficient. Dan was sure Captain John and everyone else could see the improvements he'd made.

No longer did he sit around, wondering how to keep himself busy. If there was no obvious outstanding task to tackle, he could always fall back to writing his novel. And as Captain John promised, there were no confronting external missions to challenge him.

Dan sipped his hot cup of tea. He needed it on this wintry morning. He switched on his computer and surveyed the completed chapters of his novel. Just then, the phone rang. He picked up the receiver.

It was Mrs Olonga. 'Mr Scott, did you speak with Ian Sanders?'

'Yes, I did, and he says he's interested.'

'Oh, dear! Bad news, I'm afraid, Mr Scott. We must postpone the Bulawayo Writers' Festival. We left it too late to get the venue we wanted. There're also a few other difficulties with September, so we've moved it to June next year. September is a busy time in Bulawayo. The writers' festival would have clashed with several other functions and festivals.'

'No worries, Mrs Olonga, I'll let Ian Sanders know.'

After he put the phone down, he felt relieved Ian Sanders wouldn't be coming to Bulawayo for several months yet. Then he remembered Gloria. Darn! She looked forward to accompanying him to the festival. Now he'd have to think of something else to distract her from her concerns about their relationship. There was a four-day weekend coming up in early August—the Heroes and Defence Forces Day weekend. The water level at Victoria Falls would be low. That trip would keep for another occasion. A drive to Nyanga and Vumba might be a pleasant alternative.

* * *

On Tuesday evening, as usual, Dan joined Captain John in his office for drinks. John seemed annoyed when he told him the writers' club postponed the Bulawayo Writers' Festival.

'Those damn people! Can't they get anything right? They're always changing their arrangements!' John's reaction puzzled Dan. Why was he irritated by such a minor matter? There must be deeper currents flowing under the surface. Might John's eagerness for Ian Sanders to give the keynote address have something to do with the latter's place on the Honey File list?

Later that evening at the apartment, his thoughts returned to the coded client list. Who put out the contract on him? Where would he start his search? He'd no idea where the coded client list might be filed.

Perhaps Captain John's desk drawers would be a good place to look, but he seldom left his drawers unlocked. And Eunice always skulked in the corridor. Every time he found himself alone in Captain John's office, she would appear. She watched him, even if John did not.

From tomorrow, he'd be on the lookout for an opportunity to search John's desk drawers. It was risky, but what alternative did he have? He wanted to learn who marked him for elimination.

The other nagging concern on his mind was his position on the Honey File list. Who was next in line? He took out the list and scanned it more closely than ever. Three names preceded him. Next in line was Evan Garanganga. Who was he? Why was he on the list? He'd ask Nikita next time she visited.

* * *

The opportunity to search Captain John's desk drawer came sooner than he expected. Eunice was out of the office, and Dan stood at John's shoulder in his office, looking at the computer screen. John was explaining a problem with his computer when an operative knocked on the door frame. 'Sir, there's an issue we need you to resolve.'

'Not again! What is it?'

'Sir, there's a disagreement between Benjamin and Tony about our new operation.'

'Can't Eunice resolve it?'

'She's not here, Sir, and she wanted it done before lunch.'

John exhaled in exasperation. 'OK, I'll handle it.'

He walked out of the office, leaving Dan at the computer. Dan listened to John's footsteps recede down the corridor. He could hear excited, raised voices. John's appearance in the open-plan office didn't immediately quell the disturbance.

Dan looked down to see the keys hanging in the desk drawer's lock. If not now, when? He slid open the draw to inspect the contents and quickly flicked through the papers. Nothing of interest to him. He slid the draw closed and reached for the second draw, which boasted no lock.

'Found what you're looking for?'

He jumped as his heart seemed to miss a beat. Eunice stood in the doorway.

'No, Captain John has a problem with his computer. I'm trying to find what's wrong.'

'Hmm!' Eunice smirked and walked on to her office.

What had she seen? How long had she stood there? Her response to his explanation worried him. She plainly doubted it. What would happen now? Would she tell Captain John? Did she have anything to tell him? All these thoughts raced through his mind.

He returned to his own office, just as Ambrose brought in his morning tea. He sat down and picked up the cup. That's when he realised his hand shook. That damn woman always turned up when John left him alone in his office. She'd almost caught him when he searched for the Honey File. Now, she must have seen him looking through the papers in John's drawer. Dan carried on working, waiting for any repercussions. In the meantime, he needed to review the accounts with Cherry.

As they checked the receipts from clients, Cherry sighed. 'This one, I must contact. Their payment is overdue.'

'Do you ever have any bad debts? You know, people who don't pay us what they owe?'

'Not bad debts, though sometimes late payments.'

'How do you handle those?'

'I call them and remind them their payment is due. If we don't receive the money within fourteen days, I tell Captain John. Then, the payments soon arrive.'

'You say you phone them?'

'Yes, that's the first step.'

'How do you know who to phone? The debtors are all coded.'

'Captain John gave me the list of names and codes.'

'Can I look at it?'

'Yes, Sir, of course.'

Cherry pulled open the draw to her desk and took out a slim manilla folder. A single sheet of paper listed the codes and names of the clients. Dan scanned the list, looking for a particular client.

'This one here, HMV, doesn't have the client's name next to it.'

'No, Sir, I don't have that name, but they always pay on time, and I've never needed to phone them. It reminds me of the record label, His Master's Voice. They must be someone extra important.'

Disappointed, Dan waited for an opportunity to photograph the list with his cell phone. When Cherry left the office for a moment, he got his chance. Nikita would appreciate the information. Now, his only worry was how much Eunice saw when he rifled through Captain John's drawers.

CHAPTER 31

THE Heroes and Defence Forces Day weekend in August replaced the old Rhodes and Founders' weekend, which used to take place in early July in Rhodesia. Dan made the hotel bookings for the long weekend. In planning the road trip, he hadn't counted on the police roadblocks dotted along the highway, sometimes within ten kilometres of each other.

Police officers often needed to wait for lengthy periods to get their wages, sometimes even months. The roadblocks raised cash through on-the-spot fines for a variety of questionable transgressions by the motorists and their vehicles.

The economic conditions in Zimbabwe played havoc with the hotels, and most needed renovation. Dan booked the most expensive rooms, which he hoped might be better maintained and have superior views of the surroundings.

Gloria didn't work that Saturday, so spent Friday night at his apartment. They packed their things and left Harare at nine in the morning. There was no hurry to reach their destination, so between the roadblocks and lunch in Rusape, they arrived at the Troutbeck Resort in the early afternoon.

The area differed from anything Gloria had ever seen. Evergreen forests made it look like another country. The weather remained cool in early August, and she was glad Dan insisted she bring warm clothing, including her winter jacket.

The hotel looked inviting. A crackling fire in reception and in other lounge areas created a cosy atmosphere. Gloria wanted to stay inside the building, but after dumping their things in their spacious room, Dan suggested a walk around the lake.

'We can see the lake from here. Why must we walk around it?'

'Because it's different. You need to breathe the fresh air and enjoy the cool environment.'

The temperature dipped mid-afternoon, and Gloria was relieved when Dan agreed to return to the hotel.

He was impressed that the Troutbeck Resort, formerly known as the Troutbeck Inn, kept its old world, colonial charm, with the staff proving attentive and most helpful. This was despite additions to the hotel since his last visit.

Before dinner, Dan and Gloria strolled into the Hare and Hound bar, where he ordered a Scotch on the rocks for himself and a glass of white wine for her. They sat in the armchairs by the cosy log fire, sipping their drinks.

After dinner in the cosy dining room, they drank coffee by the fire in the lounge. An elderly gentleman with white hair and a sun-dried ruddy complexion engaged them in conversation. 'How are you and your niece enjoying your stay?' Dan laughed, but Gloria didn't get the joke.

The elderly man had farmed in the local area until the farm occupations began. His farm was one of the first to go, and he believed he was lucky to escape unharmed. He regaled Dan and Gloria with his stories of yesteryear when he migrated from England sixty years earlier. He proved to be most entertaining, and the evening soon passed.

Later, back in their room, Dan and Gloria enjoyed a cup of tea and appreciated the king-size bed and satellite television. The electric blanket kept them cosy, and soon they fell fast asleep. In the morning, they planned to drive to the Leopard Rock Hotel in Vumba, where they would spend two nights.

They enjoyed their breakfast, and by ten o'clock, they were ready to go. They said goodbye to the cheerful staff and set off towards Mutare, formerly Umtali.

Gloria enjoyed touring the country in Dan's car. She'd never ventured this far from Harare, and it thrilled her to see the Eastern Districts. Scenic Mutare fascinated her. It was Zimbabwe's third largest city, though much smaller than Harare. After morning tea at a café, they pressed on to the Leopard Rock Hotel in Vumba. The good road and lack of police roadblocks made for a pleasant drive.

Soon, guti (light drizzle) closed in, obscuring the spectacular scenery. The Leopard Rock Hotel stunned Gloria when she spotted the pink edifice. It stood out against the green backdrop of the mountain, like a pink diamond in a green velvet case. The welcoming receptionist called a porter to carry their cases up to their large room with its spectacular views to the east.

After a quick inspection of the room, they walked downstairs in search of a light lunch. As the afternoon progressed, the weather became gloomier, so they relaxed in the bar lounge in front of the fireplace. Dan sipped on a Zambezi beer and Gloria settled for a glass of white wine.

Exploring the hotel was great fun, though the casino downstairs was closed. Photographs of famous hotel guests, including the Queen Mother and Princess Margaret, adorned the walls. The hotel's British colonial ambience was so relaxing. There were fewer guests than Dan expected, but the hotel maintained its excellent service.

The hotel room boasted an ensuite bathroom, with no television to detract from the peaceful atmosphere. Views of the mountains rolling into the distance kept drawing them back to the windows to stare out at the magnificent scenery. The delicate pastel hues of pink and grey stretched into the far distance.

The mists cleared, allowing them to take a short walk in the rainforest behind the hotel. Exotic ferns and other tropical plants filled a small valley along the path. They returned for sundowners and snacks served on the roof of the old castle, where they admired the views of the Burma Valley leading to Mozambique. The guti returned, and they headed back to their hotel room to get ready for dinner.

An excellent dinner proved the chef knew his stuff. Dan enjoyed a medium-rare steak with chips and salad, and Gloria ate a delicious chicken curry. After a nightcap by the cosy fireplace in the bar, they returned to their room to luxuriate in a bath, followed by the warm, king-size bed with its goose-down duvet. It was so comfortable they fell asleep in minutes.

After their sumptuous dinner the night before, breakfast didn't disappoint. Fruit and cereals, followed by creamy scrambled eggs, crispy bacon, and grilled tomato accompanied by lashings of hot tea; a great way to start the day.

The morning began with a game drive. Zebra, wildebeest, and several varieties of buck predominated. Giraffe and ostrich also inhabited the park. The small predatory jackals and civets remained hidden.

A walk around the golf course in the afternoon emphasised the beauty of their surroundings, with sweeping views of valleys and mountains extending to the horizon. Once again, the fifteen-minute walk to the old castle for sundowners and snacks welcomed their evening.

Their stay was too short to let them do everything they would have liked, but their visit to Leopard Rock oozed relaxation, which was the purpose of their trip. The fresh Eastern Highlands air braced them, and they regretted having to leave the next morning. After a wonderful long weekend, both felt reluctant to return to their separate daily routines.

* * *

The lead into Christmas was quiet for Dan. He'd finished the first draft of his novel, and despite his intention to edit it back in Melbourne, he began the process in Harare. His work at the COU was undemanding, and he'd no plans to leave Gloria too soon, so staying put made sense.

Christmas Eve was a Saturday, and Gloria worked until noon. Soon after she arrived at the apartment, angry dark clouds gathered. After lunch, she set about preparing a roast chicken for Christmas dinner. Dan loved her cooking. The smell of the roast chicken, roast potatoes, carrots, and peas filled the apartment. They'd celebrate Christmas Eve and

Christmas night with her roast chicken and the traditional Christmas pudding he bought.

In the late afternoon, the rain set in with thunderclaps rattling the apartment windows. Flashes of lightning lit the room. The rain on the corrugated iron roof built to a crescendo so loud they couldn't hear each other speak. They laughed. Neither could remember when they'd been so happy.

The romantic candlelight at dinner was a common occurrence thanks to the frequent electricity outages. This was their first Christmas together, and they both recognised its significance.

After their meal, cosy and contented, they jumped into bed and made love before falling asleep.

Christmas Day dawned cloudy and grey. After a light breakfast of fruit and cereal, they took their tea to the Christmas tree to give each other their presents. Dan gave Gloria an attractive gold bracelet he bought in Johannesburg. She gave him a wool jumper she knitted herself. Once again, she surprised him with her endless talents.

Outside, the streets were quiet. Families got together to celebrate Christmas. Overall, fewer people milled around the city and inner suburbs than on a normal Sunday. They went for a walk, but otherwise spent a lazy day. In the evening, the thunderstorms returned as they prepared the table for dinner. Dan reflected on how Christmas and eating always go together, no matter where you lived.

Dan and Gloria celebrated New Year's Eve on their own in the apartment. They were growing closer, and although neither of them raised the subject, Dan wondered how he could ever face life without her.

CHAPTER 32

CAPTAIN John was as good as his word, and Dan, in his caretaker capacity as head of external operations, didn't face any tasks that might challenge his principles. In February, John asked him to pay a quick visit to Johannesburg to keep Francis 'warm' and pay him his wages. It was important for Francis to believe the COU's external operations were ongoing, and another operation would soon follow.

Captain John also asked him to find out from Francis about Evan Garanganga's whereabouts and situation. That name again! Garanganga was the next name on the Honey File list. He'd been meaning to talk to Nikita about him, but somehow, he'd always forgotten.

It would be the first thing he'd ask her the next time he saw her. Dan wouldn't have to wait long, as Nikita dropped by every few weeks. Her official mourning period still had three months to run, though she was back to her old self nine months after Victor's death.

In the evenings, when he wasn't with Gloria, Dan would sit on his balcony and enjoy a beer in the cool night air. Rain after a thunderstorm was even better. The thunderclaps and lightning flashes provided a dramatic introduction to the downpour that reinvigorated him with its intensity. The deafening roar of the rain on the balcony's corrugated iron roof added to the spectacle.

After the rain, small rivulets ran on both sides of the road, carrying fallen leaves and twigs to a nearby storm water drain or creek. The road would glisten, and the sound of car tyres amplified. The drip, drip of the drops falling from the tree leaves would continue until the early hours, long after Dan fell asleep. He often left the bedroom sliding doors open, listening to the soporific sound. On dry evenings, the crunch of some-one's footsteps on the patch of gravel on the roadside, or the voices of occasional passers-by, fading into the distance, also worked well.

Dan made good progress on his novel and with his work at the COU. He loved his beautiful apartment, and Gloria even more. His friendship with Nikita and Daniel Moyo grew stronger. Life was just great.

The one exception was the COU's true purpose, which niggled in his mind. Dan justified his work for the unit as an opportunity to frustrate its aims by helping the targets evade their planned demise. He'd failed in his attempt to help Jacob Nkala, but was proud of how he'd succeeded with David Tawanda.

* * *

Nikita leant against the kitchen counter, sipping the cold beer from the glass Dan handed her. 'Evan Garanganga is an activist critical of the regime. After what happened to some others, Garanganga left Harare in a hurry.'

'That makes sense.'

'He went down to Joburg, and after a while, we lost track of him. Obviously, he wants to stay invisible.'

'Well, now Captain John is trying to find him.'

'Keep an eye on the Honey File list. Only three names are ahead of yours. And that includes David Tawanda. Can you get an updated version of the list to see where you stand?'

'No, since I got you the coded list of clients, it's too dangerous. I'm sure Eunice saw me looking through Captain John's drawer. She has said nothing, though she keeps a close eye on me. I'm not sure if it's connected, but these days, Captain John keeps the keys to the filing cab-inet in his pocket. If she hasn't told him about me, she at least may have suggested he do that.'

'If Captain John is looking for Garanganga, it means the list is active again, and don't forget you're getting close to the top.'

'Captain John told me, while I'm in charge, he's suspending external operations. He said he wants to find Garanganga to make Francis think he's planning an operation. It's just to keep things together in the external operations team.'

'Don't be so sure. Captain John might go around you and deal directly with Francis? You mustn't get complacent. Don't forget, these people you're dealing with are paid killers.'

'Yes, you're right, I suppose. Though Captain John seems such a gentleman and too educated to fit that mould.'

As usual, Nikita had a way of disturbing Dan's rosy view of his comfortable little world. Whenever he imagined he lived in paradise, she'd come along and fill him with doubt. But then, she'd seen more of the COU's handiwork in the past and suffered its consequences.

'Do you have any news about David Jones? I haven't seen him for ages.'

'No, Dan, though he's like that. Suddenly, he'll turn up as if nothing has happened since you last met.'

'I'm sure he was behind that attempted mugging on me at Johannesburg airport. He made my travel arrangements. Few people would have known about them.'

'If he did, he would have been acting on someone's instructions. The HMV code in the Honey File is against a couple of big names that wouldn't have concerned him. That you have an HMV code next to your name is a worry. Captain John may hold back from moving against you for now. Perhaps he's having a bit of fun, or he may need your services for the time being, but he won't hold back forever. The HMV suggests someone high up put a contract on you.'

'I'm small fry in the scheme of things.'

'Dan Scott's books are distributed worldwide, so your revelations and stance against the regime would reach many. Someone doesn't see you as small fry. Leave Zimbabwe while you still can.'

'Thanks, Nikita. I was happy and settled until you pointed out all these things. Would you like another beer? It may help you see a better future for me.'

Nikita laughed. 'I'm only trying to look after you.'

'Oh, yes, I forgot you look after everyone on the Honey File list.'

'Well, just the ones near the top. In your case, you are also a close friend.'

'That makes me feel much better.' This time, they both laughed.

'And don't sleep at night with your balcony doors open. You're only on the first floor, so you'd be an easy target.'

Dan lay in bed, reflecting on his chat with Nikita. He enjoyed her visits because she was intelligent and good company. But she always left him with concerns and doubts. It was good advice, though how could he follow it? It would be difficult for him to leave Zimbabwe. The false passport worked well in Southern Africa, though Australian immigration may not be fooled so easily. How would he explain it away to the Australian authorities? Once back in Australia, he could claim he lost his passport, though he needed to get there first.

The real problem was, how could he leave Gloria? If he took her with him, it would be a significant commitment. Dan wasn't quite ready for that and was still mulling over it. He realised he had limited time to decide, though the more he pondered on it, the more it felt like he was trapped in a spider's web. He'd worry about it in the morning.

In a strange way, Dan enjoyed the uncertainty and the sense of danger. If he didn't, he'd be gone like a scalded cat. From the beginning, he found excuses to stay a little longer; even before the threads of the web started forming around him.

Ah well! He fluffed up his pillow and closed his eyes to sleep. The balcony's sliding doors stood wide open. Mosquitoes were becoming an increasing problem in Harare, though the fresh white net around his bed took care of that problem.

* * *

Dan sat chatting with Daniel Moyo in the corner of The Explorer's Bar in the Meikles Hotel.

'So, you had a successful trip to Gaborone? Ian Sanders enjoyed your visit. I understand you invited him to be the keynote speaker at the Bulawayo Writers' Festival.'

'Yes, that's right.'

'Though you recommended he not accept the invitation?'

'Confidentially, yes.'

'I don't get it. Why invite him, and then recommend he not come?'

'No one must learn of the details of my discussion with him. If anyone found out about it, I'd be in grave danger.'

'I understand he'd be crazy to return. He was lucky to escape Zimbabwe the last time. And don't forget the shooting at his house. They're lucky to be alive.'

'So I believe.'

'You surprised him with the news about Victor Chirau. Perhaps it didn't make the news in Botswana. Either that or they missed it.'

'Did he know Victor Chirau?'

'No, though everybody's heard of him. Many hoped Victor might improve the situation here.'

'Too bad, then.'

'Ian's partner, Sarah, is going to call Eva Chirau to offer their condolences.'

'Are they acquainted?'

'No, but she asked me for her phone number.'

'How come you have her phone number?'

'Well, they were clients of mine. Eva still is, I suppose.'

'Ian wants to know who's attending this festival of yours. He wondered if your boss was going?'

'I won't know that till nearer the time. And it's not my festival. I'm just helping the Harare Writers' Club with one or two things. If you have any influence over him, try to dissuade Ian Sanders from coming.'

'Funny how life balances out, isn't it?'

'What do you mean?'

'Well, Ian, the lucky bugger, runs off with two of Zimbabwe's best-looking women but must live with this threat hanging over him.'

'Yes, I met both his gorgeous wives.'

'Technically, they're not his wives. He can't marry both. If he marries one, it might upset the other, so they have this informal arrangement whereby they both regard themselves as his wife.'

'I wouldn't like that set-up.'

'He was reluctant to enter the arrangement, though now he says it was a great idea.'

'So why risk everything by returning for the festival?'

'Yes, why?'

CHAPTER 33

THURSDAY evening. Dan sat in Captain John's office, tumbler in hand, savouring the Glenfiddich 18-year-old single malt scotch. John certainly lived the good life.

'How's the planning for the writers' festival going?' Captain John asked.

'Not bad. Only a couple of weeks away now.'

'I'm looking forward to it.'

'Will Mrs Ziyambi be coming with you? You said she looked forward to hearing Ian Sanders speak.'

'Unfortunately, she can't attend, so I'm taking her place.'

'That's a shame. I hope she's not too disappointed.'

'Oh! I almost forgot. David Jones also wants to attend.'

'Good! The more the better. Mrs Olonga says fifty people have registered so far. And there's bound to be more registrations and casual drop-ins. We've got the downstairs function room at the Bulawayo Rainbow Hotel, so there'll be plenty of space.'

John rested his feet on the corner of his desk. 'David Jones tells me Eva Chirau is also going to the festival. It's a year since her husband's unfortunate accident with the train, so I suppose she will rejoin society now.'

'Oh! I didn't know she'd registered for the festival. The list of attendees changes so fast.' Dan recalled David Jones's comment about Captain John lusting after Eva Chirau. So that's why he's going to the festival without his wife.

John swirled the scotch in his glass. 'Are you acquainted with her?'

'Yes, David Jones introduced us at the American embassy barbecue.'

'An attractive woman, that.'

'Hmm, yes.' Dan didn't understand the pang of irritation that flowed through him when he heard Captain John speak about Eva Chirau. In her disguise as Nikita, she was his friend, so he supposed he was a little possessive about her, particularly as they worked together against John's interests. Why hadn't she told him she planned to go to the festival? How did David Jones and Captain John learn about it before him?

* * *

Dan looked forward to The Bulawayo Writers' Festival. Aside from the welcome trip to Bulawayo with Gloria, he was caught up in the festival's organisation, helping Mrs Olonga and the committee get ready for their showcase event.

Next to Saturday, Wednesday evening was Dan's favourite night of the week because he spent it with Gloria. They sat at the dinner table, each with their own thoughts, until he broke the silence.

'We'll drive to Bulawayo and see the countryside on the way. You're a member of the writers' club, so we can pretend we've just met at the festival. I don't want Captain John or David Jones to find out about us, so I'll book a second room in your name. When we are near the hotel in Bulawayo, I'll drop you off a block or two away, so they don't see us arrive together. Of course, we'll both stay in my room, but nobody will notice. If anyone does, bang goes your reputation, I'm afraid. They'll think I've picked you up at the festival. It happens.'

'Dan, I can't go with you.'

'What do you mean? Why not?'

'Remember, I told you they're selling our company to new owners. Well, there's a big stock take that weekend, and my boss won't give me time off on the Friday or Saturday. The shop is closed that weekend, and there'll also be the warehouse stock to count.'

'Oh, no! I looked forward to us going away together again. Can't you get out of it?'

'Not if I want to keep my job.'

'Well, that's life, I suppose. Full of minor obstacles and irritations. There'll be another time for us.'

'Don't go looking at other women while you're there alone in Bulawayo.'

'As if I would.'

'The members of the writers' club are mostly women, and many are pretty. What if one of them wants to get friendly with you?'

'I'll tell them to leave me alone. My heart belongs to another.'

'I hope that's me you're referring to, my love.'

'Of course. Who else?'

* * *

On Thursday, in the office, Dan received an email with the latest registrations for the festival. David Jones, Captain John, and Eva Chirau were all on the list. So John was right; she was going. Dan imagined David Jones and John as two predators planning a trap for their female prey. David Jones might not challenge John for Eva's attention, but he might act as an enabler on his friend's behalf. The thought plagued Dan all day.

After the usual Thursday evening drinks with Captain John, Dan returned to the apartment. On his way home, he bought a bag of fish and chips. He was in no mood for cooking as he pondered the upcoming festival, and Eva's attendance. Following his meal, he grabbed a beer from the fridge and sat on the balcony watching the occasional car pass.

That unmistakable knock! Nikita! Dan opened the door to find her leaning against the door frame. She looked sexy, no matter how she dressed. He'd always recognised she was a good-looking woman, and tonight, he found her so damned attractive.

He still smarted over how he learned she planned to go to the writers' festival. 'You didn't tell me you were going to the festival. Since when have you been interested in books?' Even to Dan, his tone sounded a little churlish, but he couldn't help it.

'I'm sorry. I thought you'd be pleased.'

'Captain John told me you were going.'

'Ah! Yes. I bumped into David Jones in town, and I mentioned I might go. He must have told Captain John.'

'Did you know David Jones and Captain John are also both going?'

'Really! Now that's interesting! No, I didn't know. David Jones said nothing about going.'

Dan wanted to tell Nikita of his suspicions about why Captain John planned to attend, but he couldn't find the words. He didn't want to appear jealous or that he thought she might be silly enough to fall into John's trap. She was a mature adult and would surely handle the situation appropriately.

'Anyway, how about a beer?' Dan took another beer from the fridge for himself and one for Nikita. 'Did David Jones say where he's been these past few months?'

'No, he claims he's been busy here in Harare.'

'Do you still hold Captain John and the COU responsible for Victor's accident?'

The minute he spoke those words, he regretted it. He saw the flash of pain in Nikita's eyes. Now he felt like a teenager, trying to undermine his rival for the girl he wanted to impress.

'I do,' said Nikita.

The silence that followed churned within Dan's stomach. Why was he behaving in such a clumsy manner? He loved Gloria, and Nikita was only a friend. He had few friends in Zimbabwe, and perhaps he was just afraid of alienating one of his closest. The funny way Nikita looked at him added to his discomfort. What was she thinking? Best to change the subject.

'Any news about Evan Garanganga?'

'Bad news, I'm afraid. He got into a fight in a Joburg shebeen. A drunk seemed set on picking a fight with him. They're not sure if it was personal or a xenophobic attack. The man stabbed Garanganga. The rumour is he died in hospital soon after they got him there.'

'That's terrible! It can't be the COU's doing. I should have known about it if it was.'

'I don't know if anyone's behind it, but it means you've likely moved up to second or third on the Honey list.'

'Please! Not now! One thing at a time. My focus is on the writers' festival. Besides, you said it was a rumour, so you're not sure he's dead.'

'No, we're not certain. My concern is for your welfare, and you're getting close to the top of the list.'

'If he's dead, it might just be a coincidence. It may have nothing to do with the list. So far, Captain John has stuck to his promise to suspend external operations while I'm babysitting the department. So it doesn't mean they've activated the external list again. If Garanganga is dead, it would be the first incident in months. It might be months again before anything else happens.'

'Maybe, but we must keep a close watch on that list. If anything happens to the next name on the list, you must leave Zimbabwe fast. I don't suppose Captain John will give you a month's notice when he replaces you as head of external operations.'

Dan gave a wry smile. Nikita was right. 'I used to look forward to your visits, though every time you come here these days, you leave me with a bunch of worries.'

'We must stay one step ahead of Captain John and the COU. And as you say, we can't dismiss the possibility of David Jones being involved with them.'

'OK, OK, you're right.'

'Tell me, how are you travelling to the festival in Bulawayo?'

'I planned to drive with Gloria, but because of her work, she can't go, so I suppose I might fly.'

'Well, I wouldn't mind a drive to Bulawayo. Can I come with you?'

'What about Captain John and the COU? Didn't you say it would be dangerous for me if they discovered our association?'

'Yes, of course. Sorry, it was a silly idea.'

'We could do what Gloria and I planned. I'd drop you a couple of blocks from the hotel so that no one would see us arrive together.'

'Let's make it three blocks, shall we?'

'OK, but if you're walking three blocks, you better pack a light travel bag.'

'I always travel light.'

'On the drive, you should be Nikita, and at the hotel, you can revert to Eva. You'd wear normal clothes, of course. So your only disguise would be your long, black, curly wig. That would fool most people.'

'It's a good idea, but you must still drop me three blocks from the hotel.'

Dan was relieved he'd steered their conversation away from their awkward opening exchange. So, he'd be driving to Bulawayo with Nikita, not Gloria. When she left, Dan was confident that the earlier tense situation between them was resolved and everything returned to normal. But she hadn't forgotten his petulant welcome that evening. It was not like him. He'd not behaved like that before tonight. She smiled as she recalled it.

CHAPTER 34

FRIDAY evening. Peals of laughter, excited chatter, and the clinking of glasses signalled the pre-conference cocktail party was well underway. Waiters in white uniforms hurried about with plates of finger food, while others carried trays of drinks, including South African wines, Zimbabwean beer, and cordials.

Dan stood chatting with Mrs Olonga and other members of the writing club committee when he spotted Captain John, David Jones, Eva Chirau, and a couple he didn't recognise, sitting at a corner table in the large function room on the seventh floor of the Bulawayo Rainbow Hotel. He excused himself from the committee ladies and walked over to the corner table to say hello.

'Dan, you remember Eva Chirau from the U.S. embassy barbecue?' said David Jones.

'Yes, how are you, Mrs Chirau?'

'Please, call me Eva.'

'I was sorry to hear about your husband. Please accept my condolences.'

'Thank you.'

Dan hated to raise the subject of Victor Chirau's death once again, but it was necessary if he and Eva were to pretend they'd not seen each other since the barbecue.

Captain John introduced the unfamiliar couple as Eric and Sylvia.

Soon, the talk moved on to the hotel accommodation.

'I've got a spacious room on the third floor,' said Eva. 'It's a little dark with wood panelling all round, and there's not much of a view as it looks onto a block of flats. I think it must be due for refurbishment.'

'Mine's the same, on the fourth floor,' said David Jones. 'I'm two rooms from the corner.'

'Yes, me too, said Eva.'

'So I'm right above you.'

'Yes, it looks like it.'

Everyone talked about the pros and cons of their respective guest rooms before the conversation moved on to the festival's schedule for Saturday.

'When is the keynote address?' asked Captain John.

'Tomorrow evening at six-thirty,' said Dan. 'It will lead on to dinner at eight for the attendees who bought VIP tickets.'

'Ian Sanders is the keynote speaker, I believe?' said David Jones.

'Yes, he confirmed yesterday.'

'Ah, good!' said John. 'We'll look forward to that.'

But Dan wasn't looking forward to it. He'd tried again to dissuade Ian Sanders from coming to Bulawayo, but the man seemed determined. He thought it was suicidal for Ian Sanders to return to Zimbabwe. His efforts to discourage him may have sounded a little desperate over the phone, but they were to no avail. Nothing he said made any difference.

At eleven o'clock, the party broke up and everybody went their separate ways. Dan stood on the balcony of his fifth-floor room, looking towards the Ascot Centre. Tomorrow was the new moon, and tonight, the faintest sliver was overhead and not visible from his vantage point. In the distance, the nineteen storey Kenilworth Towers (Ascot Centre) stood out on the eastern horizon. Captain John was staying at the Holiday Inn near the foot of the tall residential apartment block.

The evening was pleasant enough, though Dan struggled to understand how Eva could chat away in a friendly manner with Captain John and David Jones when she suspected the former had arranged her husband's death. John's effortless charm belied his vicious reputation, though Dan had seen no evidence to support the latter.

Eva appeared relaxed and looked gorgeous. She laughed at John's jokes and Dan caught her holding eye contact with John a little longer than he thought proper. That night, he struggled to sleep. No, he wasn't jealous, but he worried his friend Eva might be taken-in by John's charm.

People knew about Victor Chirau's views, though few would have known whether his wife also held them. Captain John and David Jones may not know her views or what part she may have played in Victor's group of supporters. But Dan believed she was taking a risk by socialising with those two.

* * *

Dan rose early after a restless night. He had tossed and turned, and although he tried to turn his mind to other things, Eva kept popping back into his thoughts. He didn't like her being in the company of Captain John and David Jones.

Following a quick breakfast in the downstairs restaurant, he headed to the ground-floor function room where the festival's proceedings would take place. A few early arrivals had already selected their seats, and soon others arrived. Among them was Captain John, who'd driven from the Holiday Inn. When Eva and David Jones walked in, John waved them over, pointing to the two seats he'd reserved for them. Though Dan sat at the front with the members of the committee, John's gestures didn't escape his attention.

Mrs Olonga welcomed the attendees to the festival. It was an ambitious venture, and the committee members had feared low attendance. But the room soon filled with book lovers, novice writers, and a few established names. Zimbabwean authors made most of the presentations, talking about their latest books. Interspersed between the authors' presentations, various committee members led discussions relating to the future of Zimbabwe literature. A few presenters gave the attendees writing tips and advice about getting their work published.

The programme was full; too busy, with several interesting presentations cut short to keep up with the schedule. The morning passed quickly, and the lunch break was reduced from one hour to thirty minutes to give the presentations more time. Dan noticed there was no sign of Captain John or David Jones after lunch. His own presentation was scheduled for five-thirty. He aimed to finish just after six, which would give him time to welcome Ian Sanders and introduce him to the festival attendees.

* * *

The silver Mercedes turned off the Bulawayo Road onto a dirt track, fifteen minutes north of Francistown. Ten minutes down the dusty track, it arrived at a ranch-style gate topped with a small sign saying Francistown Aerial Services. 'They're in the middle of nowhere,' said the driver. 'They can't get much business hidden out here in the bush.'

Despite its remote location and dusty unkempt yard, the hangar building looked solid and well maintained. A man in khaki overalls approached the car to greet the arrivals. 'Gooday! Call me Jim. I'm your pilot this evening.'

The driver recognised the Australian accent. He nodded in acknowledgement but didn't introduce himself. The female in the passenger seat next to him said, 'Hi Jim, I won't be a minute.'

Jim nodded and walked back to the hangar.

'I'll wait for your call at the motel in town,' said the driver.'

'OK, my love, I'll ring you as soon as we are on our way back.'

'Where is the satellite phone?'

'All tucked away in my overnight bag.'

The couple kissed, and the female passenger stepped out of the car. In the late afternoon winter sun, she picked her way over the rough ground to the hangar. The driver reversed the car onto the dirt road, waved, and drove back towards town, sending a cloud of dust over the area. The woman opened the door Jim used to enter the building.

It was a remarkable transition from the African bush to a modern aviation enterprise. In front of her, two helicopters occupied a significant part of the floor space. Towards the back of the hangar stood rows of pallet racks holding spares and other equipment, all stored in boxes and canvas wrapping. The bright interior belied the dark exterior of the building. The throb of a generator somewhere also operated the air-conditioning. This was a sophisticated set-up and no rough country operation that the dusty exterior suggested

'Do you attract much business here in the bush?' the woman enquired. 'How do your customers find you?'

'On the internet, like you did. It's most unusual for customers to come to our premises. You requested to come here, but in most cases, we fly to our customers and pick them up at their location. Tell me, why did you choose our service?'

'A friend of my husband has done work for your organisation. I think he supplied some of the material for this building. He said you might provide the discreet service I need.'

'I understand. My boss told me you'd be paying in cash and hinted I didn't need to get names. That's OK. We've done hush hush work before now. Well, I'm ready when you are.'

'OK, let's go.'

Jim opened the enormous sliding doors at the end of the hangar. He used a small tractor to tow one helicopter into the open, where he disconnected it before driving the tractor back into the building. The solid-looking doors slid closed with little effort, and he took care to lock them behind him. He jumped into the helicopter and signalled the woman to do likewise.

Two African guards, armed with large knobkerries and dressed in long khaki great coats, stood by the locked gate. They weren't noticeable before the late afternoon sun illuminated them. The engine started, and the rotors began their slow turn. Soon they spun at considerable speed before the helicopter lifted off the ground with the ease and grace of a bee leaving a flower.

'We'll fly low and fast, to minimise the possibility of inquisitive or hostile reaction from the ground. Our man in Bulawayo will meet you and drive you to your destination. When you're ready, call him, and he'll bring you back to the drop-off point, where I'll be waiting.'

'When will we get to Bulawayo?'

'In about forty-five minutes.'

'If we fly low, might we hit something, a hill, or a high tree?'

Jim laughed. 'We're not flying that low.'

Below, there was nothing to see other than the dry, featureless bush. In the distance, they saw an occasional dull light or flicker of a village fire. It wasn't a scenic flight. Then, out of nowhere, the distant lights of Bulawayo appeared on the horizon.

Darkness was falling, and before too long, Jim slowed the helicopter. A few moments later, three quick flashes from car headlights guided him in towards a dark, isolated patch of ground.

The landing was gentle. As the rotor blades slowed to a stop, a man dressed in khaki longs and shirt stepped from the gloom.

'Hi, Jim. An easy flight?'

'Yep, no problems.'

Jim turned to the woman. 'Meet Alan Drake. He'll take you to wherever you're headed.'

The woman smiled in acknowledgement. Alan put his arm out to help the female passenger alight from the helicopter, but instead of taking his hand, she jumped down, landing lightly on her feet.

'Well, that's my old Land Rover there. Sorry it couldn't have been something more comfortable, but it's all my father-in-law's business allows for in these economic times.'

The woman gave a tinkling laugh. 'I don't mind. I'm not here on holiday.'

'Where are we going?'

'The Bulawayo Rainbow Hotel.'

'I hear the hotel is full. There's a writers' festival going on at present.'

'It's OK, I've got a booking for one night.'

'Here's the number to call when you want me to collect you.'

'I expect it to be later tonight.'

'That's OK. Any time, any hour.'

Fifteen minutes later, the Land Rover pulled up in the dimly lit Samuel Parirenyatwa Street—formerly Borrow Street. 'The hotel is a block that way.'

'I know my way, thanks.'

'I'll come right here when you want me to pick you up.'

The woman thanked Alan and walked along 10th Avenue towards the hotel. He watched her until she reached the front of the hotel. He wondered what the attractive woman in the smart business suit was doing in Bulawayo, and what was in her small overnight carry bag. Ah well! He'd go home and enjoy a cup of tea with his wife, Avril, and wait for the woman's call. If he hurried, he might be home in time to read Donna a bedtime story before Avril switched off her light. At least his wait would be more comfortable than Jim's, sitting alone in the cold helicopter in the darkness, in the middle of nowhere.

CHAPTER 35

DAN was about to wrap-up his presentation when someone handed him a note. He glanced at it and then read it more carefully. 'Ladies and gentlemen, I'm sorry to have to tell you that Ian Sanders is ill and cannot attend this evening. He sends his sincere apologies.' Dan caught the frown on Captain John's face. It was not the news he wanted to hear.

Mrs Olonga came to the microphone. 'Well, everybody, thank you for attending today. That concludes our Saturday schedule. Tomorrow morning, we will recommence at ten o'clock. If you've booked for the festival dinner, please go up to the seventh floor. Pre-dinner drinks will be available from seven, and dinner from eight.'

The festival attendees filed out of the function room. A few attendees left the hotel straight away, while others chatted in small clusters. Those staying in the hotel returned to their rooms to freshen up before catching the lift to the seventh floor. Dan walked up the four flights of stairs that led up from the fifth floor. Captain John and David Jones were already there.

'Well, that's a disappointment,' said John. 'I looked forward to hearing Ian Sanders speak. We're here, so we might as well enjoy the party.'

David Jones looked quiet. While John appeared ready to make the best of it, David seemed irritated. Dan hadn't before seen this side of him.

Dan ordered a beer just as Eva walked into the room. 'Make it two beers,' he said, turning to the waiter.

The four, plus Eric and Sylvia, sat at the round table. Now it occurred to Dan, Eric was an operative he'd seen in his early days at the COU. He looked so different dressed up for the festival. Dan imagined Sylvia to be his wife. But it turned out she was a doctor, specialising in anaesthetics. Captain John's plan for Ian Sanders was coming clear. A chill ran down Dan's spine as he pictured the welcome John intended for the author.

The dinner was typical conference fare; satisfactory, but nothing special. When was a conference meal ever delicious? Dan had bigger worries than the quality of the meal. Eva was her usual vivacious self, and she was flirting with Captain John. She wore a tight, red cocktail dress that took her appearance up a notch. No wonder John desired her.

In other circumstances, Dan might have enjoyed the evening, but Eva's behaviour preoccupied him. He realised they needed to pretend to be barely acquainted, though for her to pay so much attention to John was galling. Where was the Nikita he knew? His friend and confidant appeared to have melted away, to be replaced by a frivolous woman, flaunting her feminine charms and alluring good looks.

John focussed all his attention on Eva, leaving the others to chat amongst themselves. For Dan, it was hard going.

At ten o'clock, Eva suddenly announced to the table she was going to her room.

'Catching up on beauty sleep?' said David Jones.

'No, there's a new moon tonight. It's so dark and romantic. I must try to find it.' She bid goodnight to the party and walked to the lift. Everyone at the table watched her in silence until the lift doors opened and she disappeared from view.

* * *

Eva pressed the G button for the ground floor, and the arthritic lift crawled to the foyer. When the doors opened, she stepped out and walked to the reception counter. The hotel foyer was now deserted, apart from a woman in a dark business suit sitting in the brown armchair in the alcove opposite the reception. A broad pillar that helped support the mezzanine floor partially shielded her from view.

At reception, Eva enquired about moving to another room. 'There's no view from my window. I can only see the block of flats opposite.'

'I'm sorry, Mrs Chirau, the hotel is full, and we don't have a better room available.'

'Let her have my room if she wants.' Eva turned to see who spoke.

'I'm here for one night, and I'm not fussed about the view. I'm on the fifth floor, and my room has a balcony.'

'Are you sure?' asked Eva.

'Of course.'

'It's fine if you and Mrs Chimedza wish to swap rooms,' said the receptionist. 'They're both the same price. I'll just have to adjust the records.'

'You are too kind, Mrs Chimedza. I'm Eva Chirau.'

'Please, Eva, call me Sarah.'

The two women went up to Eva's room, where they swapped keys. The room was tidy, and Eva appeared to be living out of her travel bag, and already packed. In minutes, she was off to the fifth floor. In her new room, she dumped her travel bag on the bed and opened the balcony door. A gentle winter breeze brushed her cheeks as she searched the night sky for the new moon.

* * *

Up on the seventh floor, the festival party was in full swing. A band appeared from nowhere and loud music filled the room. A few couples danced on the small dance floor.

'What a pity Mrs Chirau left so early,' said David Jones. 'Dan here could have shown us his ballroom steps. At the American embassy barbecue, he impressed us with his moves.'

Dan could only muster a weak smile in response to the comment.

'Perhaps I could impress her with my moves,' said John, giving David a wink. He rose from the table. 'Well, it's time I also looked for the new moon. I'll see you all tomorrow.'

Dan noted the look John gave David. Not for one second did he believe John was returning to the Holiday Inn for a good night's rest.

* * *

Sarah jumped at the loud rap on her hotel room door, though she'd been expecting it. She'd waited years for this moment, and now her nerves were stretched to breaking point. 'Who is it she called?'

'It's me, Captain John.'

'Just a moment.' Sarah unlocked the door and slipped into the bathroom before he could enter. She closed the bathroom door behind her and put her ear to it. She heard him enter the room and close the door behind him. 'Help yourself to a drink from the minibar,' she called. The clink of bottles, as John pulled open the minibar, told her where he stood in the room.

John looked at the choice of beers. 'I'll have a Zambezi Lager. Shall I pour one for you?'

'Yes, thanks.'

Sarah took a deep breath and felt the Glock 19's weight in her hand. She attached the silencer and stepped into the room.

The smile on John's face froze. 'S-Sarah, it's you?' His eyes fell on the silenced barrel of the handgun Sarah held.

'Hello, Jedson, or John, or whatever the hell you call yourself these days.'

'Where's Eva?'

'Who's Eva?'

'This is her room.'

'Not anymore.'

'It's good to see you, Sarah.'

'Don't bullshit me, Jedson. You had my father and Joseph, my fiancé, killed. Then you tried to get rid of me. Believe me, there's nothing good about you seeing me again.'

'Sarah, all of that is long forgotten. It's water under the bridge.'

'It's not forgotten, Jedson. I've been dreaming of this moment.' Sarah raised the Glock to take aim. 'Where would you like the first bullet?'

'Sarah, please, we can talk about it. There's no need for this.'

Unexpectedly, Sarah's hand shook. It wouldn't stop, and she tried to steady her aim by using both hands, but it made no difference. She couldn't understand it. John deserved to die. She'd killed before, though not someone she knew or once respected. He took a step towards her.

'Stop there! One more step and you're dead.'

'That's enough, Sarah! Let's sit down and talk like adults.'

John took another step forward. In that instant, Sarah's hand stopped shaking, and she squeezed the trigger.

In the confined space of the hotel room, the single shot was louder than she'd expected. It was a loud bang, not the quiet zip, zip seen in the movies. John stood there, staring at her in disbelief. He looked down and clutched at his chest and sank to his knees. His arms fell to his side, and he toppled onto his back.

Sarah stared in fascination at the red dot on his chest. It grew on his white shirt like a red rose blossoming in a time-lapsed video. His eyes seemed to pierce hers. She'd not before hung around to watch her quarry's life drain away. She felt an odd mixture of horror at the pleasure it gave her, and disappointment at how her time away from the COU made her soft.

John made a fatal mistake. The men Sarah confronted before posed an imminent threat to her. When John moved closer, her COU training kicked in, and her shaking hand steadied.

Sarah picked up the spent shell and put it in her bag. She'd taken care not to touch anything except the door handles, bathroom taps, and one or two other surfaces. She wiped those down with a cloth from her travel bag and replaced the Glock in its oiled linen wrapping in a concealed corner of the bag. At reception, she'd used her own pen and made sure not to touch the registration form, which she completed with false information.

Despite the loud bang, no one came to investigate the sound. Sarah dialled Alan's number on her satellite phone to tell him she was ready. She put her ear to the door for any sound of footsteps or voices. All quiet. She opened the door with her cloth and stepped into the corridor.

Rather than risk bumping into someone in the lift, she used the stairs down to the first floor. There, she used her elbow to press the button for the lift because if she used the stairs, it would take her past the reception desk. The lift doors opened. There was no one inside, so she entered and pressed the *G* button with her elbow. On the ground floor, she hurried to the hotel entrance. The two receptionists were busy calming an agitated man and didn't notice her leave.

Sarah paid cash on arrival, so she'd already settled her bill, except for the beers John opened. She walked the single block to the corner where Alan said he'd wait. As she reached it, Alan's Land Rover pulled up beside her.

'Can I give you a lift, Madam?'

Sarah jumped into the old Land Rover, and Alan sped away. There was little late-night traffic, and in less than half an hour, they neared the location the helicopter waited. Alan switched off the headlights as the Land Rover trundled to the rendezvous. Jim waved to them, confirming all was well. Alan didn't waste any time. As soon as Sarah got out of the Land Rover, he bid her farewell and drove off in a cloud of dust. He wasn't speeding, for fear of drawing unwelcome attention, but the winter dry on a dirt road always was a dusty affair.

'In time for breakfast,' said Jim. He produced a large flask and poured two cups of hot coffee. Next, he unwrapped a wax paper parcel and offered a generous-sized sandwich to Sarah. 'Delicious ham sandwiches with the compliments of Francistown Aerial Services. We always look after our passengers with our first-class catering service.'

'Breakfast! It's only just on midnight. Shouldn't we get going before someone notices us?'

'I doubt anyone is in miles of this spot. We'll leave at the first glimpse of daylight on the horizon.'

'Didn't you say this helicopter could fly at night using navigational instruments?'

'Yes, but it's better to fly when there's vision, even if it's minimal. As soon as we see the first hint of light, we'll go. It'll still be dark, but within a quarter of an hour it will be daylight and we'll be halfway to the Botswana border.'

CHAPTER 36

David Jones, Eva, and Dan sat at breakfast chatting about the festival dinner. Captain John said he'd join them for coffee at breakfast, but he didn't show.

'Perhaps he's overslept,' said David. 'Did you see him again after you left us last night, Eva?'

'No, I stayed in my new room once I'd settled in.'

'New room?' Dan enquired.

'Yes, I asked reception to change my room for one with a view. There were none available, but a lady waiting at reception offered to swap with me. She said she wasn't concerned about a view.'

Dan smiled at the thought Captain John didn't find Eva after he left the dinner. Perhaps he returned to his hotel for an early night.

After breakfast, the trio made their way to the festival function room. As soon as she saw Dan, an anxious Mrs Olonga hurried across to him. 'Have you heard the news? A terrible thing has happened. Last night, someone shot John Ziyambi. His wife, Alice, is one of our members.'

The news stunned the group. 'How horrible,' said Eva.

'You three sat at his table for dinner last night. The police want to talk to you.'

'Is he OK?' asked David.

Mrs Olonga shrugged. 'The ambulance took him late last night. The police aren't saying anything.'

Sure enough, the police soon came to interview them. David Jones couldn't say much about what happened. He was still at the festival dinner when the incident occurred. Eva was a person of interest because she'd swapped rooms with the mysterious woman suspected of shooting Captain John. But neither she nor the hotel receptionists could throw any light on the woman's identity, beyond the details on her check-in form.

When Dan walked into the room where the police conducted their interviews, it surprised him to see Detective Inspector Tshuma. 'Ah, Mr Scott! We meet again. Who else amongst your work colleagues is at risk? At this rate, you'll soon run the business.'

'Really, Inspector Tshuma! You must be joking.'

'No, Mr Scott, I'd be worried if I worked with you. I've met ambitious men before, but none as ambitious as you.'

The rueful smile on Inspector Tshuma's face told Dan the man enjoyed his own little joke. 'Tell me, Inspector, is there any progress with the Jonas Nyandoro investigation'

'Now you sound like my chief, Mr Scott. Please tell me you will not apply for a job in the police force.'

'I'll leave police work to you, Inspector.'

'Good! Well, I planned to phone you to say we'd made no progress with the case, and we no longer regarded you as a prime suspect. That meant you would have been free to leave Zimbabwe. Now this has happened, we'll reserve our judgement on that. I don't suppose you'd know anything about this mysterious woman who swapped rooms with Mrs Chirau?'

'No, nothing.'

'Of course not. Could it have been a tryst?'

'Yes, Captain John was a ladies' man.'

'Yes, most crimes involve sex or money.'

'Well, that alone should prove I had nothing to do with Jonas Nyandoro's disappearance.'

'Didn't your promotion to his role get you a higher salary?'

'No, I don't receive a salary. I get a consultancy fee fixed by contract. You can ask Captain John.'

'If only I could!'

'How is he? How is Captain John? Is he dead?'

'You must ask the hospital that question.'

'So he's in hospital? Not in the morgue?'

'As far as I'm aware, but don't hold out too much hope.'

'Who found him?'

'A hotel guest complained about the noise, demanding reception go up to check.'

'Inspector, you imply anyone working with me is in danger. Instead of focussing on me, have you considered it might be anyone working for the company who's in danger?'

'Be assured we've considered all possibilities, Mr Scott.'

* * *

For Dan, Eva, and David Jones, the writers' festival was over. Mrs Olonga and the committee carried on the rest of the programme until its conclusion at lunch. David Jones left at eleven to catch the lunchtime flight to Harare. The police said they'd take care of Captain John's possessions at the Holiday Inn. Dan and Eva checked out of the Bulawayo Rainbow and walked to the hotel parking at the rear. The guard gave them a smart salute as they drove out of the hotel parking, appreciative of the two U.S. dollar tip.

Dan's mind was racing. Eva didn't seem to be the least bit perturbed by what had happened to John. She said she thought John may have arranged a romantic meeting which went wrong. The shooting occurred in her former room. A coincidence? It all seemed too neat. It was possible, but improbable.

And then there was her flirting with Captain John. What was that about? Was that a ploy? Had he been worrying about her welfare for nothing? 'Daniel Moyo told me Ian Sander's partner, Sarah, planned to phone you and offer her condolences for your loss. Did she call you?'

'Yes, she did. What a kind woman!'

'Anything else?'

'No, what do you mean?'

'Have you ever met her?'

'No. What's she like?'

'So you wouldn't recognise her if you saw her?'

'No, how would I?'

'It's odd. I can understand why Captain John visited your old room. He wouldn't have known you moved. But why was the mysterious woman armed? And why did she shoot him?'

'Maybe she planned to rob him. Or if she was a prostitute, she may have needed the gun to protect herself. Perhaps he tried to force himself upon her.'

'He'd been drinking, but I can't imagine him doing something like that. I wondered if this was your spitting cobra's work.'

'No, my group had nothing to do with it. Someone else got there before us.'

'You were most friendly towards him. Almost like you led him on.'

'I thought if I gained his confidence, it might lead to an opportunity for my revenge, but now that chance has gone.'

* * *

In the office on Monday morning, the news of Captain John's shooting spread fast. When Dan arrived at work, everyone was talking about it. Eunice strutted around the office, barking out her orders, while Cherry and Ambrose both looked downcast.

Ambrose brought Dan his morning cup of tea. 'Good morning Sah. If Eunice is in charge, we'll all suffer.'

'Good morning, Ambrose. What is everyone saying?'

'They've taken the Captain to Johannesburg.'

'Ambrose, get back to work!' Eunice's shrill voice gave both men a start. They hadn't seen her come through the office door. Captain John always knocked on the door frame, but Eunice didn't bother with such niceties. Ambrose hurried from the room as Eunice turned her attention to Dan. 'I'm in charge of the COU now. I'll decide what changes we need down the line, but for now we'll carry on as normal.'

'Fine.'

'We'll debrief in my office every Tuesday and Thursday, as you did with Captain John.' Eunice turned on her heels and walked off without another word.

Carry on as normal! That wouldn't last too long. Eunice's demeanour showed she intended to run things her way. She was the boss, and she was letting everyone know it. He already missed Captain John. It was day one, and they hadn't yet drunk morning tea. It promised to be a long day.

Ambrose appeared anxious, and when he brought Dan's tea, he spoke in a whispered voice and didn't hang around for their usual chat. Cherry also suppressed her natural cheerfulness and kept her head buried in the books of accounts. A sombre atmosphere pervaded the office, which now seemed as quiet as a library.

'You can talk to me, Cherry. We work together,' said Dan.

'Yes, Sir, but we must be careful. Eunice doesn't like us chatting in the office.'

'We must discuss our work, otherwise we can't do our jobs. She won't know that we're just chatting.'

Cherry gave an uncertain smile. It was clear his argument didn't convince her.

CHAPTER 37

TUESDAY. Two long working days before he would see Gloria on Wednesday night. To Dan, it seemed a long wait. He spoke to her on the phone on Monday. But it wasn't the same as seeing her in person. Last weekend, she worked on her employer's stock take, and he was at the Bulawayo Writers' Festival. Wednesday would make a whole week without seeing her. It felt like forever.

Work was a lot less fun with Eunice prowling the corridors, and Dan contemplated ways to get out of his arrangement with the COU. He still didn't have his passport. He'd given up hope of David Jones getting it back for him. The man was full of promises and reassurance, but nothing ever happened. Captain John told him immigration would soon return his passport. Now that John lay in a Johannesburg hospital, fighting for his life, the prospect dimmed.

Dan kept busy with admin work, and despite the less congenial atmosphere, the day soon passed. An operative surprised him with a knock on his door. 'Miss Eunice wants to see you in her office.' Dan looked at his watch. Five o'clock already! He tidied his desk and packed up his things before making his way to the Tuesday night debrief.

He walked down the corridor, and as he passed Captain John's office, a sharp voice called out. 'Here!'

Dan turned to see Eunice sitting at John's desk. 'Oh! I was on my way to your office.'

'This is my office now.'

'What about Captain John?'

'Don't worry about him. He won't be coming back.'

'Has he died?'

'Not yet, though he most likely will. Either way, even if he lives, he'll be an invalid needing care at home. Anyway, come in and sit down.'

Dan entered the office and sat in the chair he'd occupied so often when sharing a scotch with Captain John. Now, it was different, and he wasn't comfortable.

'Scotch?' Eunice already set two tumblers filled with ice cubes on the desk. She held up the bottle to show him the label of the expensive scotch.

'That's one of John's favourites. I'm not sure he'd appreciate us polishing it off.'

'I told you, forget about him. We're moving on. You need to decide if you are going to support me.'

'Yes, of course I'll support you.' Dan almost choked on the words as they stumbled out and needed to clear his throat before completing the sentence. The situation was deteriorating. How could he support this power-hungry psychopath?

'I plan to stick to Captain John's external schedule, said Eunice. He put it on hold, but I'm restarting it. That means we are looking for Evan Garanganga.'

'Looking for him?'

'Yes, we want him back in Harare, so you and I are going to Johannesburg, where you'll introduce me to Francis and your other contacts.'

'There's only Francis and his wife, Sally.'

'Well, we're going to motivate them. We have paid them for doing nothing for months now. If they can't prove their worth, we'll get rid of them.'

'You're thinking of firing them?'

'Yes, something like that.'

'Francis is our only contact down there.'

'David Jones tells me different. Francis is too soft and doesn't fit an organisation like this. And don't pretend you're unaware of what the COU does. We are assassins for hire, and you are one of us.'

'Captain John told me it was an outplacement business. I didn't sign up to be part of a hit squad.'

'Long ago, you worked out the true purpose of the COU. No, you're one of us now, Mr Scott, and you can't wriggle out of it. We have proof of your involvement. Remember, you've been complicit in the murders of Absalom Muzenda, Jacob Nkala and Jonas Nyandoro. Detective Inspector Tshuma in Bulawayo and the South African police would be most interested in hearing about it. Captain John pussy-footed around you, but you'll find me a little more direct.'

Dan was stunned. After everything Eunice said, he didn't know how to respond. He took a sip of the scotch and waited for her to continue.

'Get Cherry to arrange our bookings for Johannesburg,' said Eunice.

'When will that be?'

'Next Monday, early morning flight.'

* * *

Wednesday night with Gloria brought calm to the madness of the last few days. Dan sighed with relief to find normality still existed. 'How will I tolerate that woman?'

'What will you do?'

'I haven't decided yet. I suppose I'll wait to find out what's happening with Captain John. Eunice says he's never coming back, but where does she get her information?'

'Ask her.'

'Good idea! I will ask her. If John dies or is disabled, she'll stage a coup. Although it's his company, I'm not sure to what extent his wife is involved. He never mentions her, so she may be unaware of what goes on. If Eunice takes over, John's wife might not even realise it.'

'Why don't you contact her?'

'I have no means of contacting her, though Ambrose or Cherry may have her phone number or address. Or Mrs Olonga may help. But I'll wait for more news of Captain John's condition.'

'Don't wait long. Or you might be too late.'

'No, I won't. I'll keep my eyes and ears open.'

Dan appreciated Gloria's no nonsense direct approach to things. It helped him make up his mind when he mulled over a hard decision.

'And don't forget to tell Inspector Tshuma about your trip to Joburg next Monday.'

'I've already done that.'

'And?'

'He said it was fine as long as I keep him informed.'

* * *

On Thursday morning, Cherry told Dan Eunice was away for the day. That was good news. It meant he wouldn't have to face the five o'clock debrief with her. While he enjoyed the scotch, he was uncomfortable with the manipulative Eunice. She was up to something. How might it affect him? Her absence was the perfect opportunity to call Francis and inform him of what happened to Captain John.

'Oh, no!' said Francis. 'Jonas told me that woman was trouble. Why is she coming here when I've told you everything I can?'

'Perhaps she wants you to understand she's the boss.'

'But you'll still run external operations, right?'

'She has said nothing to the contrary. No doubt she'll soon tell me where I stand.'

It occurred to Dan that Eunice's absence would also give him the chance to take a more leisurely look around her office. He needed the latest version of the Honey File, which Eunice updated from time to time. As manager of the computer network, he had the excuse to linger there if anyone questioned his presence. Though it would be best if no one noticed him there.

First, he tried the filing cabinet and desk drawers. They were all locked. A glass ashtray served as a holder for paperclips, a rubber, a small pencil sharpener, and a silver key. Dan tried every lock in the office, but the key fitted none. As he went to replace it in the ashtray, it slipped from his hand and fell on the wooden floor.

He bent to retrieve it and noticed an envelope taped to the underside of the desk. What might that be? It must be important for someone to hide it there. The envelope wasn't sealed, so Dan carefully removed the contents. He was disappointed to find it was only the desk's delivery note. Next, he looked under the desk's blotting pad. Again, nothing there.

Then another thought crossed his mind. He took the key to the front desk and tried it in Cherry's cash box. It opened. There was nothing special about the key. Cherry possessed a copy, and so did Captain John and Eunice. Though it was surprising someone left theirs in the ashtray. Dan's search was a disappointment, coming up with nothing. At least it appeared no one saw him checking the drawers and filing cabinet.

* * *

After another wonderful weekend with Gloria, Dan woke at five thirty on Monday. The early morning flight turned out to be the SA Airlink eight forty-five, arriving in Johannesburg at ten forty. Eunice took the window seat, and Dan got the impression she'd not flown too often.

'Any news about Captain John's condition?' he asked.

'No.'

'Are you sure he won't be coming back?'

'Yes.'

'How do you know that?'

'If I shot you in the spine and you were fighting for your life in hospital, what chance of you coming back?'

'Shot in the spine?'

'That's the rumour.'

'Where did you hear that rumour?'

'David Jones attended the festival in Bulawayo with you. He told me.'

'Are you in touch with him?'

'When necessary.'

'Did he get that information from Mrs Ziyambi?'

'Why so many questions, Mr Scott?'

'I just wondered.'

They spent the rest of the flight in an awkward silence. Eunice wouldn't tell him any more than what she considered necessary. Dan wondered if he should talk to David Jones. Eunice wouldn't give him his contact details. Perhaps Cherry or Ambrose could help.

Johannesburg airport was a crush. At first, they couldn't see Francis. Then Dan spotted him in the throng. He introduced Eunice, who barely acknowledged their man in Johannesburg. Francis flashed Dan a worried look, which Dan pretended to not notice. If their actions gave her any cause to suspect they'd formed a relationship that excluded her, the consequences would not be pretty.

Francis drove them straight to his flat where his wife, Sally, greeted them enthusiastically and made them a cup of tea. Eunice did not hide her disdain for the couple. 'Do you live here in this hovel?' She didn't touch the tea Sally gave her. 'Is this cup clean?'

'Now to business,' said Eunice, fixing Francis with her glare. 'Dan is my second in command, for now. Whether he stays in that position depends on his performance, and the same goes for you. Think about that! These flats belong to the COU. If I replace you, you'll have to look for somewhere else to live. Do you understand?'

Francis could only nod, while Sally looked anxious.

Eunice continued. 'Captain John once told me Jonas used someone else for extra dirty jobs.'

'That must be Gustave,' said Francis.

'Bring him here tomorrow morning to meet me.'

'I'm not sure if I can find him so fast.'

'Eleven o'clock, tomorrow. If you can't find him, Sally can pack your things.'

Francis didn't want the murderous Gustave coming to their flat, but what choice did he have? 'I'll do my best, Madam.' The man looked miserable.

'Right, now you can take us to our hotel.'

Francis drove them to the Crowne Plaza Hotel in Rosebank. As she got out of the car Eunice said, 'Pick us up at ten tomorrow morning.' The words, *please* and *thank you,* seemed foreign to her. As Dan thanked Francis for the lift, he glimpsed Eunice's scowl. His politeness, it seemed, undermined the firm approach she took with her underlings.

After they checked in, they had a light lunch before Eunice headed into the shopping centre. A little later, Dan also made for the shops. He needed a fresh supply of condoms and headed for the same place he bought them on his last visit. As he paid for them at the till, Eunice appeared over his shoulder. 'Planning a party, I see.' Dan responded with a weak smile.

'Come, let's have afternoon tea,' she said. 'Where do you recommend for dinner tonight?' Her light, friendly manner was a sudden switch from the stern, demanding woman she presented to Francis. Over coffee, she confessed she enjoyed putting fear into her employees. 'It's the only way to get their respect. I needn't treat you like that because you're a senior manager, but for those lower down, it's the right approach.'

Dan didn't believe it was the right moment to admit her hovering presence in the office also worried him.

In the early evening, just before sunset, Dan and Eunice walked to the Grillhouse Restaurant, a short three to four blocks from the hotel. From the exterior, the restaurant looked modern, but inside, a cosy atmosphere prevailed. The candlelit tables and the deep orange horizon set a romantic scene. Dan thought it incongruous he was there with Eunice. It should have been Gloria.

Both ordered rib eye steak and accepted the waiter's recommendation from the wine list, a deep red, mellow shiraz. Eunice was charming as she chatted on about how the COU would blossom under her control. Then she turned the conversation to personal matters. Was he married?

Did he have a girlfriend in Harare or Melbourne? Dan was on his guard. If he revealed Gloria's existence, it might expose her to danger and give the COU a hold over him.

'Well, you didn't buy those condoms for nothing. Don't tell me you're using the ladies of the night?'

Eunice didn't wait for his answer before continuing. 'You appreciate things needn't be so formal between us? If I could rely on your support, we'd make a good team. Makes sense, don't you think?'

It shocked Dan she imagined he'd fit into an assassination squad that worked outside the law. Even if the authorities ignored the COU's activities for now, they could close them down and imprison them on any pretext. When things got hot, governments were quick to shift the blame. He wondered if Eunice was serious or if it was the alcohol talking.

On the walk to the hotel after dinner, Eunice put her arm through Dan's and chatted away. They looked like a close couple on their way home. But inside, Dan's alarm bells sounded. The direction the evening was going disturbed him, and he needed to be on high alert.

In the hotel lobby, Eunice suggested they go to the bar for a nightcap. 'Let's have one more drink before bed.'

'My parents in Melbourne expect my call every Monday. Right now, it's seven in the morning there. If I don't phone them, they might go out, and then they'll worry all day about missing my call.'

'OK, but hurry back. I'll be in the bar.'

'I'll try, if they don't keep me talking too long.'

Dan hurried up to his room and got ready for bed. He switched the lights off and lay there, pondering the awkward situation with Eunice. As he got drowsy, a knock on his door focussed his senses. Who could that be? He hadn't ordered room service. Another knock on the door, and he held his breath. Might it be Eunice? Who else? After a third tap, tap, tap on the door, there was silence. Dan breathed again. Tomorrow morning might be difficult. He needed an excuse for not returning to the bar.

CHAPTER 38

WHEN Dan walked into the breakfast room, Eunice was already there. He walked over to her table, hoping his cheery *good morning* might brush over his clumsy non-appearance in the hotel's bar last night. Her response was cool.

'What happened to you last night? I waited in the bar for ages.'

'Sorry about that. My mother kept me talking on the phone, and I fell asleep. You know how your parents have a thousand questions when they haven't heard from you?'

'I thought you said you phoned them every Monday?'

'Yes, but last week my phone battery was low, and it cut off after five minutes.'

It was a poor excuse, but better than nothing. Eunice didn't appear convinced. After several minutes of sullen silence, she spoke again. 'Have you met Gustave?'

'Er, no. Not yet.' Dan said nothing about the attempted mugging at Johannesburg airport's Intercontinental Hotel. He didn't relish the prospect of meeting the big African again. It would be a relief if Francis couldn't find him, though Eunice's threat to evict Francis and Sally remained a concern. And to make matters worse, she seemed in a bad mood this morning. He hoped his no-show at the bar wasn't the reason for it. He liked the hospitable couple, and he would hate it if his actions contributed to problems for them.

With breakfast over, they returned to their respective rooms to pack their things before checking out. When Dan arrived at the hotel check-out, Eunice had already settled the bill for both their rooms. He only needed to hand in his key card and confirm he'd not used anything from the minibar.

A few minutes later, at ten o'clock, Francis's car pulled up in front of the hotel entrance. They walked down the short flight of steps and got into the back seat. Eunice ignored Francis's greeting and left it to Dan to respond.

'Have you set up our meeting with Gustave?' Eunice enquired.

'Yes, he's due at eleven.'

'So, it wasn't too difficult to find him?'

'I was lucky. I checked all the shebeens I thought he might frequent, and I found him in the last one. It's always the last one,' Francis chuckled. Dan realised he was trying to lighten the atmosphere and chuckled along with him. Eunice's stony silence made both men uncomfortable.

At the flat, Sally was waiting for them. As the kettle boiled, she proudly told Eunice she'd bought a nice new mug for her exclusive use. Eunice ignored Sally's attempt to please her. Francis and his wife now occupied the flat they used when Dan first met them. They would meet Gustave in the flat next door, where he and Jonas had planned to stay, following the Absalom Muzenda poisoning.

Sally remained in her flat, while Francis and his two visitors opened the neighbouring apartment in readiness for Gustave's arrival. A loud knock signalled eleven o'clock, and Francis hurried to open the door. There he stood, even bigger and uglier than Dan remembered. There was no mistaking him. Dan unconsciously moved his position, from near the stretched sheet covering the missing windows, to the solid wall on the opposite side of the room.

Eunice introduced herself. 'Dan here is my assistant, and that's Francis from Mozambique.' She never even bothered to say what part he played in the organisation.

Gustave showed no flicker of recognition, and Dan wondered if he even remembered the failed mugging at the airport.

'Francis says he found you in a shebeen. If you want to work for me, you'll need to cut out your heavy drinking. I want reliable people, not drunkards.'

'Yes, Madam.' The monstrous killer's meek response to the overbearing Eunice astounded the two men.

'I want details of every man you've used in operations for Jonas Nyandoro. Do you understand?'

'Yes, Madam.'

'Eunice turned to Dan and Francis. You two can go back next door while I speak to Gustave.'

The men got up and left. Both shared the same concerns. Things didn't look promising. Why did she exclude them from the meeting?

'Is his real name Gustave?' Dan asked.

'No, it's his nickname. No one knows his real name. They named him after the giant crocodile in Burundi because he's killed so many people.'

'I don't like it, Francis. Please be careful to not upset her.'

'Jonas said she'd be big trouble.'

'I'm afraid he was right. All the signs of trouble are there.'

Sally made Francis and Dan tea while they waited for Eunice to return. 'What's happening?' she asked.

'Sally, we don't know. But if Francis can't become a vicious killer doing her bidding, look for a different job and accommodation. That's what I would do.'

Dan was concerned for the couple. Both approached middle age, and Francis didn't have the nature or physique to satisfy the ruthless Eunice. But then, neither did he.

One hour later, Eunice returned, looking satisfied with her meeting's outcome. 'Where did Jonas find that brainless thug?'

Dan gave an internal sigh of relief. She wasn't happy with Gustave. 'So you won't use him then?'

'Oh, yes. He's just the person we need down here. He's embedded in the diaspora. If anyone can find Evan Garanganga, it's him. And he's given me the names and contact details of the half-a-dozen people he's used in his work with Jonas.' Eunice turned to Francis. 'If Jonas gave you the idea that you were his main man in Johannesburg, he misled you.'

In her stride now, she continued. 'In every job you took part, you left Jonas to do the dirty work. You operate more like a *mujibha* (informer) than a COU operative. When Jonas used Gustave, he could leave it to him to do the job. Jonas didn't need to be present. Do you even know what jobs Gustave has done for Jonas? That man will do what he's told and won't question his instructions.'

Poor Francis and his wife, Sally, looked miserable, and Dan felt sorry for them. But what could he do? Eunice seemed set on belittling Francis's work for the COU. Perhaps he might have a word with her later.

'Time for the airport,' Eunice announced, suddenly standing up. She grabbed her bag and walked to the front door. There was no thank you to Sally for her hospitality. She left that to Dan. They drove to the airport in silence. Under the circumstances, chatting didn't seem appropriate. At the airport, Dan took their bags out of the car boot and thanked Francis. 'I'll call you in a day or two, and we can talk then,' he said, speaking in a lowered voice that he hoped wouldn't get Eunice's attention.

On the three forty SA Airlink flight to Harare, Dan felt drained and drowsy. Eunice also didn't seem in the mood for talking. Dan closed his eyes, listening to the hum of the plane's engines, and dozed off. The next thing he heard was the *fasten seatbelts* announcement before landing. It was a quarter past five in the evening. After passing through Harare's immigration and customs, they made their way to the airport carpark where they'd left their cars on Monday morning.

Driving home alone in his car was a welcome relief as his thoughts turned to calling Gloria for a dose of normality. He accepted the role with the COU to collect ideas and motivation for his novel, but the last few days with Eunice in charge delivered more than he'd bargained for.

The road into the city bustled with pedestrians and traffic. Dan never expected the African man to run onto the road in front of him. He slammed on his brakes and stopped only inches from the startled man. A host of problems preoccupied Dan's mind, and he realised he needed to concentrate harder on his driving.

How ironic, he'd left his Melbourne problems behind, only for new ones to replace them in Africa. A classic case of being able to run, but not hide. And when he thought about it, compared to Zimbabwe, his Melbourne problems weren't really problems after all.

CHAPTER 39

For Dan, the screws were turning. Gloria was once again raising questions about their future together. It was time for him to make his intentions towards her clear. In the office, Eunice appeared to have recovered from her sullen spell that prevailed on the second day of the Johannesburg trip. Now, once again, she acted sweet and friendly towards him, and it made him nervous. On Thursday morning, she reminded him of their five o'clock debrief that evening.

Ambrose and Cherry worried about Eunice's change of attitude towards Dan and were both a little less chatty than usual. When Ambrose brought in morning tea, Dan asked him if something was wrong. It was in Ambrose's nature to be candid, and he didn't hold back. 'Now you and Miss Eunice are friends. We must be careful what we say. The others are saying you have taken Captain John's place with Miss Eunice.'

Dan laughed. 'No, Ambrose, I've not taken his place. I too am wondering why she's being so nice.'

'She is only nice to you, Sir. Not to everyone else.'

'Don't worry, Ambrose. You and Cherry are still my best friends here.'

The reassurance seemed to cheer up Ambrose, but his words set Dan thinking. Ambrose and Cherry reported to Captain John, who treated them with respect. Eunice did not seem to respect anyone and treated the staff more like servants. This particularly applied to Ambrose, who ran errands and made tea for the managers.

At five o'clock, an operative knocked on Dan's door frame to deliver Eunice's summons for the Thursday evening debrief. It annoyed him that Eunice always sent an operative to call him. Captain John used to invite him in person. Dan put his things away and headed for her office. She'd got the tumblers and ice blocks ready and was about to pour the first round when he entered.

'So, Dan, what are your thoughts about the Joburg trip?'

'Well, I wanted to talk to you about Francis. I understand he's not a man for violence, but he's reliable and sets things up for us. Jonas found him invaluable. He carries out many essential tasks Gustave could never manage.'

'Such as?'

'He's our taxi in Johannesburg and keeps his ears open and warns us about any issues that might affect our operation.'

'Is that all?'

'No, there're lots of things he does for us, and he keeps his mouth shut. At least give him time to show you his value down there.'

'You like him, don't you?'

'Yes, he's a good man, and his wife, Sally, is an asset too.'

'Well, I'll consider it, but I won't wait long. If he can't prove his worth soon, he'll be out. Francis has had four months to find Evan Garanganga, and so far, nothing. Let's see what Gustave can do.'

'To be honest, I didn't push Francis to find Garanganga because we heard rumours he was dead.'

'There is no positive proof. If he's dead, where is his body? Is there a death certificate? Someone must know something concrete.'

'Eunice, all the criticisms you make of Francis could also apply to me.'

'That's true, and as you must be aware, I wasn't in favour of bringing you into the COU. Captain John wanted you here.'

'But why?'

'He felt a well-known white novelist would lend an air of legitimacy to the unit.'

'How?'

'Would anyone imagine Dan Scott joined an unofficial hit squad?'

'Doesn't your work for the government give you all the legitimacy you need?'

'If it suited the government, they'd disown the COU in a flash. What legitimacy would we have then? They'd simply label us a criminal gang.'

'So, did Captain John get David Jones to contact me in Melbourne?'

'No, I don't think so. David Jones probably mentioned your expected arrival to Captain John, and that's when John would have requested you come to the COU.'

'Who then asked David Jones to invite me back to Zimbabwe?'

'Ask David Jones.'

'He told me the invitation came from the top.'

'Perhaps it did.'

The conversation was going round in circles, and Dan was no wiser. He'd given up hope of ever finding out who put his name on the list in the Honey File.

Eunice leant forward in her chair. 'Have you thought about our discussion after dinner in Joburg? About us making a great team. First, you'd need to pledge your full support for me.'

'No, I thought you were joking.'

'I never joke. As my two IC you'd have a lot more influence and money.'

'So you want me to join a criminal hit squad?'

'You wouldn't need to get your hands dirty. Not when you're second in command to me. Do you imagine I carry out the hits?'

'The authorities wouldn't distinguish between the leaders and the perpetrators in the unit. They'd make no special allowance for us if it suited them to shut down the COU.'

'No need to be squeamish, Dan. I am sure you've got it in you. Look how neatly you got rid of Jonas.'

'Please, now you must be joking! You know I didn't get rid of him. I don't know what happened to him.'

'Are you in or out? What's your answer?' Eunice poured another two scotches and pushed one towards Dan.

'If I'm in, what exactly does that entail?'

Eunice smiled, rose from the chair, and walked around the desk. 'Hang on while I check everyone has locked up and left. I'll be back in a minute.'

As Dan waited, he took a gulp of the scotch. Was this the second or third? His mind felt fuzzy, and he'd lost count.

Eunice returned and kicked off her shoes. She leaned against the edge of the desk in front of Dan before raising herself to sit on its polished wooden top. Her short navy-blue dress allowed him a flash of her snow-white knickers. Dan was conscious of her unblemished, coffee-coloured skin, and understood why John was in a relationship with the attractive woman. Her mid-length hair framed an angelic face.

'You'd continue with your present duties and any other responsibilities I give you from time to time. All the operatives and admin staff would know your new role, so when I'm away, you'd be in total control. And there'd also be other privileges.'

Dan was stuck for a response. If he said yes, he'd be putting his head in a noose. Someone wanted him dead. That's why he was on the Honey File list. Involvement in a criminal assassination squad would be the perfect excuse for his elimination or indefinite incarceration. If he declined, he'd stay on the list until his turn for elimination came.

'Well, what do you say?' As she uttered those words, Eunice put her right foot on the edge of Dan's chair, resting it lightly against his crotch.

Dan shoved his chair back as if he'd received an electric shock and jumped to his feet. His reaction must have looked more dramatic than he'd intended.

'What's the matter?' Eunice asked.

'I've got to go. It's getting late.'

'Aren't I pretty enough for you? Don't you find me attractive?'

'Yes, but we're very different people, Eunice. There can be nothing between us.'

'Are you gay?'

'No, of course not.'

'Then I don't understand.'

'I must go, Eunice. Good night.' As he turned to leave, Dan saw the flash of anger on her face.

* * *

Eunice sat down in her chair, staring at the empty office doorway through which Dan exited moments earlier. The shock of rejection simmered until it reached boiling point. No one ever treated her like that. She always got what she wanted. Wasn't she a desirable woman, whose favours men sought? Since high school, men fought over her and strove for her attention. Few women could ensnare the likes of Captain John, but she'd managed it with ease.

She told herself she didn't fancy Dan Scott, but imagined he might have been an amusing distraction for a short while. He was nearing the top of the Honey File list, which meant he wouldn't be around much longer. If the fool imagined there'd be no price to pay for his behaviour, he was mistaken.

Eunice picked up her cell phone and punched in a number.

'Hello,' the gruff male voice answered.

'This is Eunice. You can go ahead.'

CHAPTER 40

IN Johannesburg, Francis and Sally worried about their situation. Eunice threatened their home and livelihood. True, there'd been no operations in recent times, but Dan said they would come in due course. Earlier, Dan asked him to find the elusive Evan Garanganga. There'd been rumours of his death, though others claimed to have seen him. Now, he needed to ramp up the search.

Francis planned to spend the entire week going over all the places he imagined Garanganga might frequent. He'd done this before without success, but now he'd give it another try. Johannesburg, a perfect place for someone to hide. Xenophobia remained the major problem which all foreign Africans faced. As a foreign African looking for another foreign African, Francis needed to be careful. Trouble could arise from any direction.

Seen from the expanding white dominated suburbs, the sprawling Alexandra township had long been a distant grey-brown smudge on the horizon. In the 1980s and 90s, Sandton grew into Johannesburg's second business centre, and soon building construction in the two suburbs stood less than a kilometre apart. The exclusive Sandton City shopping and business precinct, where many of the township's residents worked, was one of the richest areas in South Africa, while Alexandra was one of the poorest and most dangerous.

* * *

In the Workers' Bar, the owner provided a little information. 'Yes, it was here where the drunk tried to stab the Zimbabwean. For no reason, man. Though he inflicted only minor wounds. An ambulance took the Zimbabwean to hospital, with cuts on his hands and arms.'

'Where does he drink now?'

'Who knows? He hasn't been back since then. Try the Wrecker's Bar, three blocks further down this road. Turn right at the end of the third block, and you'll see it opposite.'

'Why would I find him there?'

'He must live somewhere in this area. The Wrecker's Bar doesn't live up to its name because they kick out anyone who drinks too much. It's a quiet place, good for someone who doesn't want trouble. That guy you're looking for never spoke, except to order his beer. He'd sit in the corner all by himself. Drunks often pick on people who are alone.'

'OK, thanks.'

Francis walked three blocks in the direction the bar owner indicated and turned right. He spotted the Wrecker's Bar half a block down, on the far side. As he approached the bar, he thought it looked rather exclusive in the run-down area. The sign on the window said Wrecker's Bar Lounge. Inside the front window, a row of large brass pots containing ferns gave the customers a little privacy from passers-by on the pavement.

The ferns blocked the natural light from the pavement and made the dimly lit interior even darker. How would he recognise anyone in there? Francis bought a beer as an excuse to take a leisurely inspection of the other customers, paying particular attention to anyone sitting alone. A long-haired, bearded drinker sat in an armchair at a corner coffee table. The soft cloth cap and glasses he wore made it difficult to get a clear impression of his face. The man looked nothing like the clean-shaven person in the photo Dan gave him.

Could this be the man he sought? Francis struggled to decide. Any resemblance? No, perhaps not. The man wore a long sleeve jacket covering his arms. Any sign of scars on his hands? It was too difficult to tell from the distance that separated them. He tried to be discreet, but the man caught him staring, so Francis raised his glass.

'How are you?'

The man looked startled. 'Er, fine, thank you.'

'Do you come to this bar often?'

'Yes, quite often.'

Francis recognised the man's accent, which sounded a lot like Jonas Nyandoro, so he guessed he was a Zimbabwean. 'Have the cuts to your arms healed?'

'How did you know I had cuts on my arms?'

'I saw you a few times at the Workers' Bar. The barman told me a drunk attacked you.'

'Yes, that's right.'

So, it was Garanganga. If it hadn't been him, his response would have been different. Francis's fifty-fifty guess paid off.

'This bar is nicer than the Workers' Bar. No drunks in here.'

'Yes.'

Francis didn't want to risk scaring Garanganga from returning to the Wrecker's Bar, so he downed the remnants of his beer and nodded to him as he left. Dan would be pleased to hear he'd found him. His detective work should even impress Eunice.

Back home, an excited Francis told Sally about finding Garanganga. 'This might solve our problems with that terrible woman. I'll phone Dan tonight and tell him.'

'Are you going to kill Garanganga?'

'No, I expect Dan will arrange something.'

'Dan is no more a killer than you, my love. Eunice will get Gustave to do it.'

'I want nothing to do with those evil ones.'

'Then we still have a problem.'

'Yes, but now they'll see how useful I am to them.'

* * *

Dan never answered Eunice's question. Where did he stand? He assumed, following his rejection of her advances, his position as 2IC was in jeopardy and would likely not eventuate. He didn't intend to offend her, but his automatic reaction to her bold approach was unfortunate. Her absence from work on Friday was a lucky break, as it meant he wouldn't have to face her until the following week, when she may have cooled down somewhat.

On Saturday lunchtime, Gloria arrived with a couple of items for the grocery cupboard. She was a capable cook, so they seldom ate out at restaurants. And they didn't need a restaurant to provide a romantic atmosphere. They had plenty of that at home in the comfortable apartment.

When Dan told Gloria about the events of Thursday evening, she remained thoughtful before responding. 'Well, your time in Zimbabwe might soon end. What are you going to do?'

'I haven't decided yet. I'm pondering over it.'

Gloria remained quieter than usual over the rest of the weekend, and Dan guessed it was because he'd not mentioned her part in any decision he might make.

He loved the weekends with Gloria, but they were never long enough. Saturday lunchtime to Sunday evening was all the time they had, apart from Wednesday night at Gloria's flat. She needed to rise early for work on Thursday mornings, so that made Wednesday evenings short. When they were together, Dan's work issues took up more than their fair share of the discussion.

On Sunday evening, Gloria declined Dan's offer to drive her back to her apartment, saying she preferred to walk. Soon after she left, Dan hurried to answer the knock on the door that he half expected. He felt relieved she'd come back. It might be an opportunity to settle things between them. He knew she was worried about where their relationship stood. Dan swung the door open. 'Nikita!'

'Yes, is that so surprising? You look disappointed.'

'No, no, come on in. I thought Gloria had come back. She only left a few minutes ago. We needed to sort something out.'

'Oh! I can leave if you want to catch up with her.'

'No, it can wait. I'll see her again on Wednesday.'

For the second time that weekend, Dan related the happenings of Thursday evening. This time, he gave a more detailed account because Nikita knew about the COU's activities.

'What did you do to give Eunice the impression you might be interested?'

'Nothing, absolutely nothing. She probably sees the role of the 2IC as including sexual favours for the boss. That's what she did for Captain John.'

'Your problem, Dan, is you're irresistible to women.' They both laughed.

'Though not irresistible to you. At the writers' festival, you only had eyes for Captain John.'

'Don't tell me you're jealous?'

'No, I realised you just strung him along.'

'Why would I do that?'

'That's a good question.'

'Is there any news about Captain John?'

'No, last I heard, he was fighting for his life in a Joburg hospital. Eunice has written him off. She says he won't be back and has taken over control of the COU. With Captain John out of the way, have you decided on your plans?'

'Well, I don't want to lead the group, if that's what you're asking. I'm happy to help where I can, but one of Victor's loyal officers should take over.'

'So, what are your plans?'

'Like you, I'm still working on that. Unlike you, I don't need to rush into any decision. You should leave the COU and take Gloria with you back to Melbourne.'

Dan handed Nikita a beer. 'I'll give it some serious thought.'

No sooner had Nikita left when Dan's cell phone rang. It was Francis. The news both pleased and troubled him. It was a good example of his value to the COU's Johannesburg operations. Even Eunice would have to acknowledge that.

But it wasn't good news for Garanganga or himself. Eunice would get Gustave to deal with the activist. And following that, Dan would advance one place on the Honey list. His other concern was Eunice may not even follow the Honey list, now that she was in charge, and it made his situation a lot more precarious.

'Thank you, Francis. Well done! I'll pass the information on to Eunice tomorrow.'

Dan ended the call and switched off his phone. He now had a problem, a moral dilemma. If he told Eunice, he would pass a death sentence on Garanganga. Could he live with the guilt? If he didn't tell her, he would consign Francis and Sally to homelessness and unemployment. Eunice made clear the need for Francis to prove his worth, or she would dismiss him.

There was a simple answer to resolving the situation. He could submit to Eunice's bold advances and use whatever influence that gave him to protect Francis from her volatile moods. But then, what about Gloria? He couldn't betray her love just to resolve the COU quagmire.

What to do, what to do? He'd sleep on it. Tomorrow was Monday, and if he didn't speak to Eunice about the matter then, perhaps he'd bring it up at the Tuesday evening debrief. Assuming there would be a Tuesday evening debrief after the unfortunate events of Thursday evening.

CHAPTER 41

MONDAY morning found Dan wondering how Eunice would react to him after Thursday night's fiasco. How would she behave, and what might the next few days entail?

Good news! Cherry told him Eunice phoned in sick. She'd be back tomorrow. Before the debrief on Tuesday evening, he'd have to decide what he'd do about Francis's news that he'd tracked down Garanganga.

A day and a half's breathing space didn't seem like much as the question hung heavy on Dan's mind. Perhaps he should just tell Eunice what Francis said. She seemed determined to eliminate Garanganga, but why should that concern him? He would only be the messenger. But then, he'd move up a position on the Honey list. Aside from Garanganga, only one name, possibly two, preceded him on his copy of the list.

Dan assumed David Tawanda, who'd escaped to Botswana, would slot back on the list in front of him, though he couldn't be sure, with the unpredictable Eunice running the show.

And he also needed to consider Francis and Sally and Eunice's threats against them. The conundrum spun in his head. The day dragged, yet it didn't give him time to reach any conclusion. Dan needed to return to the apartment. A relaxing beer on the balcony might help him focus on a solution.

But it made no difference, and the single beer only made his head fuzzy, and his thinking muddled. He wondered what was wrong with him. One beer shouldn't affect him like this, but it wasn't the beer causing the problem. Whichever path he chose would end up hurting someone, and that troubled him.

Dan realised he was hungry. He made himself fried eggs and chips, reminding him of his university days. His only problem then was a lack of discipline needed for study.

The phone rang as he sipped from a cup of hot tea, which failed to meet the standard Ambrose set in the office. Dan welcomed the phone's interruption, as he needed a break from worrying about what he should do.

An excitable voice, sounding like a child, greeted him. He couldn't catch what the person said. 'Please, please slow down so I can understand what you're saying.' Then he realised it was a hysterical woman, crying.

'It's me, Sir. Sally.'

'Sally! What's wrong? Where's Francis?'

* * *

When Sally rang off, Dan sat in shocked silence. After Francis phoned on Sunday night, he and Sally lay in bed, when they heard a sudden tapping on their door. They didn't answer the quiet knock late at night because they almost never received visitors at the flat. Only Dan visited unannounced, but he knew Dan was in Harare, as he'd spoken to him only two hours earlier. Something about the knock made them hesitate. The soft tap, tap, seemed designed to avoid alerting the neighbours.

Again, the quiet knock, and the couple held their breath. After the third knock, Francis slipped out of bed and climbed onto the kitchen counter to peek out of the long, narrow window that ran next to the ceiling. He saw a figure disappearing down the public corridor, but in the darkness, he didn't see any identifiable detail. All the bulbs in the building's public areas were stolen or burnt out. Francis wondered if the bulky figure might have been Gustave.

They didn't sleep well after the unnerving experience. If it was Gustave, what was the reason for his late visit? Francis had no direct dealings with him and didn't plan to start now. Nor did he want to talk to Eunice after her rudeness during her visit. He opted to wait and ask Dan if he knew anything. Might it be because he'd located the whereabouts of Garanganga, though that didn't seem likely? Dan would have said something during the phone call if he expected an immediate response.

The next morning, Sally walked out on one of her infrequent trips to buy groceries. Only half an hour later, when she returned from her shopping, a crowd gathered at the foot of her building. She enquired from a bystander what happened.

'There's been a suicide. A man jumped from one of the upper floors.'

The crowd hid the man's body from Sally's view, but she recognised a chair lying on the ground. She looked up to her flat on the eighth floor and noticed the sheet flapping in the breeze. An icy chill swept over her as she fought her way through the crowd. There he lay, Francis, in a spreading pool of blood. The police and an ambulance soon arrived on the scene. The paramedics tried to calm the hysterical Sally, while the police demanded she go with them to inspect her flat.

Upstairs, the front door to the flat hung lopsided from its hinges, with splintered wood lying in the entrance passage. 'Forced entry,' the police said.

Inside, the flat was a mess, with obvious signs of a struggle. A corner of the sheet that covered the missing window had pulled loose from its rope tie. The evidence suggested someone threw Francis against the sheet, and it gave way. Did Francis try to use the chair to protect himself against the intruder?

Sally remained in no doubt Gustave was the culprit, and Dan shared that view. That bitch, Eunice, must have organised the hit. But why? Dan paced the apartment in a rage. He'd confront her in the morning. She would not get away with this. But what could he do? Eunice held all the advantages.

* * *

Tuesday morning, Dan arrived in the office early. He was beyond caring and intended to challenge Eunice about Francis's death. She wasn't in the office. Cherry took a message she'd be in after lunch. Dan couldn't concentrate on work as he sat at his desk, fuming.

Lunchtime passed, as did afternoon tea. Just as he'd given up hope of seeing her that day, Eunice passed his office and called out in the sweetest voice, 'Don't forget our five o'clock debrief.'

Dan looked at his watch. A quarter to five. Bugger it! He wouldn't wait any longer. He packed up his desk and walked to Eunice's office. Without knocking, he entered the room and sat down in the chair opposite her.

'Is something the matter, Dan? You look flustered.' There was no sign of the awkwardness that ended their last debrief. Eunice looked relaxed, and her face held an innocent expression.

Dan's voice shook with anger. 'You know what's wrong!'

'No, I don't. What are you saying?'

'Francis! I'm talking about Francis.'

Eunice looked surprised. 'Has something happened to him?'

'Let's not play games, Eunice. You know damn well your man Gustave threw him off the eighth floor of his building.'

'No, I wasn't aware of that. Thank you for telling me. At least now I won't have to carry out my threat to dismiss him.'

'Well, I don't believe you. Captain John won't be pleased to learn you've killed his Joburg operative.'

'Captain John is irrelevant now. And while we're being frank, let me say, as my 2IC, you need to show me more respect. A glass of scotch?'

'No, I feel sick. I have to go.'

'Oh, not again! Get over it, Dan. I don't expect sulking from my head of external operations. Make sure you're back to normal by our Thursday evening debrief. This time, I'll overlook your behaviour because I realise you must be in shock over the death of your friend, but don't let it happen again.'

Dan stormed from Eunice's office and out the front door of the COU. He jumped into the car and sped from the drive onto the road. He wasn't sure of his next move.

The only positive to emerge from the tragedy was it resolved his moral dilemma, though he hated to view it in that light. Poor Sally would need to move elsewhere. There was nothing further Eunice could do to harm Francis. That meant there was now no need for him to disclose Francis's information about Garanganga's whereabouts. At least, he would benefit from the sad event.

* * *

Dan thought it unlikely he'd had his last discussion with Eunice about Francis's unfortunate end. He'd come off the boil since first hearing the news, though still his anger simmered. Already he'd been thinking about how and when to leave Zimbabwe.

On Thursday, when his five o'clock summons to Eunice's office came, he was ready for further confrontation. He sat opposite her, waiting for her to speak.

Eunice poured scotch over the ice cubes in the two crystal glasses in front of her and slid one glass across to Dan. 'Well, I was right about Gustave. He's already tracked down Garanganga in just over a week.'

'Gustave didn't track down Garanganga. He got that information from Francis before he murdered him. Francis told me on Sunday night he'd found Garanganga.'

'Oh! Then why didn't you tell me?'

'You weren't here on Monday. And on Tuesday evening, Garanganga's whereabouts were the last thing on my mind.'

'Funny how quickly Francis found Garanganga after I threatened him.'

'Yes, funny, isn't it?'

'I get the impression you and Francis didn't want us to find Garanganga.'

Dan didn't respond to Eunice's comment.

She continued. 'To work with me, Dan, you'll need a stronger commitment to the COU. How can I have a half-hearted 2IC who's too soft to carry out our essential work?'

'I was here to improve the administration, not to arrange people's murders.'

'Well, you're part of the COU now, like it or not. Toughen up and get with the programme. There's no easy way out for you, Dan. With a little guidance from me, you'll fit in nicely over here. Oh, and don't try to skip the country. We've cancelled your Zimbabwean passport. Try to make the most of it here, unless you want to risk joining our citizens crossing the Limpopo and feeding the crocodiles.'

CHAPTER 42

SATURDAY with Gloria was Dan's favourite day of the week. All would be fine till Sunday afternoon, which almost always ended with him complaining about Eunice. Concerns about work consumed him now. 'She cancelled my Zimbabwean passport to prevent me from leaving the country.'

'So what now?'

'Perhaps I'll wait a little longer to see the situation with Captain John.'

'And then?'

'Well, if he doesn't return to the COU, I'll leave Zimbabwe.'

'Even if he survives the shooting, it might be months before his situation is clear.'

'True, but I'll still wait to find out about his condition. Though not for too long.'

'If you leave, can I come with you?'

With everything going on at the COU, Dan found it difficult to concentrate his mind on his future with Gloria. He wasn't in the mood to debate the matter right now. 'One thing at a time, Gloria. When I've decided what to do, we can talk about us.'

'Shouldn't we decide about us, so we can make plans together?'

'No, I need to think about it.'

'You need to think about us?'

'No, but it's a distraction. First, I must decide about work.'

'If I'm a distraction, perhaps we should go our separate ways.'

'No, I don't mean it like that. I've got lots of troublesome work issues to worry about at present. Leave things for now, and we'll talk later. That's a promise.'

'I love you, and you claim to love me, so what's the problem?'

Dan didn't respond to Gloria's question, and she left the apartment that Sunday evening insecure and unhappy. She was not his focus, and if he loved her, she should be.

He wasn't insensitive to Gloria's point of view, but he recognised the danger he faced. He'd never explained to her the precise nature of his work at the COU, so she wouldn't be able to appreciate the seriousness of the situation. How could he focus on their relationship when his position on the Honey File list dominated his thoughts?

* * *

In the office, Eunice acted as if nothing much had changed. At Tuesday's debrief, Dan once again challenged her. 'How am I supposed to head external operations if you've cancelled my Zimbabwean passport?'

'We both know you heading external operations is nonsense. It was Captain John's way of keeping external operations warm until he found a suitable replacement for Jonas. Now that Francis and Sally have gone, there's no need to involve you. For now, I'll run all operations, and you can focus on admin.'

* * *

Dan spent Wednesday nights at Gloria's flat, but this week she worked late on a recount of stock in the bookshop's warehouse. At a loose end, he met Daniel Moyo for drinks at the Explorer's Bar in the Meikles Hotel. They sat on the stools at the corner of the bar, where they carried on their confidential chatter. Dan waved the barman over and ordered two scotches.

'What an exciting life you lead! I read about the shooting at the writers' festival.'

'Yes, someone shot an attendee. No one knows the motive, or the identity of the shooter.'

'Not any old attendee, Dan. The victim owns the business where you work. Who would imagine outplacement was so dangerous?'

'Yes, that's why I must leave the job and Zimbabwe.'

'Have you got your passport back?'

'No, and they've cancelled the Zimbabwean passport I've been using.'

'How can they do that?'

'Because the passport was likely a fake. They must have bribed someone working in the passport office to get a blank copy and enter my photo and details.'

'So what's the plan?'

'I'll try to get the Australian Embassy here to give me a replacement passport.'

'Why didn't you do it long ago?'

'How could I tell them I'd lost my passport when I know the Zimbabwean authorities have it?'

'The Australian Embassy might have got your passport back for you.'

'Yes, but first, I'll wait to find out the news about Captain John.'

'What about Gloria?'

'I haven't told her yet that I'll take her with me. Maybe she'll go on ahead and set things up for us. Ian Sanders did something similar. We may go to Botswana first, and later on to Melbourne.'

'Why the delay in deciding about Gloria?'

'I wanted to take it slowly, but circumstances have changed. Eunice, the second in command, has taken control of the business and claims the boss won't be back. I don't trust her, and I know she doesn't have my best interests at heart. That woman has plans for me, and I'm sure they're not good. Funny how I always viewed Captain John as the enemy, but now I'd love to see him back.'

'It doesn't sound too good.'

'No, and the only reason she hasn't yet moved against me is that she needs both our signatures to use the bank account.'

* * *

At Thursday's debrief, Dan asked Eunice if she'd heard any news of Captain John. Her response was chilling.

'Forget about Captain John. Don't imagine he'll return to put things back the way they were. Only by working with me can you make things easier for yourself, Dan. Even if Captain John wanted to return to the COU, do you imagine I'd let him?'

'It's his business, isn't it? The building and contents belong to him, and the bank account is in his name.'

'We're joint signatories to the bank account, so together, we don't need him. As for this building, well! I've made powerful friends in this job. They'll help me get the title in my name and the bank account too. I've not been sitting around doing nothing all this time.'

'How can that be legal?'

'My powerful friends will make it legal. If Captain John makes any trouble, I can deal with him. And if I take over the bank account, I won't need you as a co-signatory.'

'Are you so sure Captain John won't recover?'

Eunice didn't respond, but Dan noted her half-smile and the glint in her eye.

When the debrief finished and he left, Eunice picked up the phone and dialled a number. 'Hello Alice, it's Eunice speaking. How are you? And how is John? Everyone here at the COU misses him. We'd like to send a bunch of flowers to cheer him up. Would that be OK? Where should we send them? Can he appreciate what's going on around him?'

* * *

Dan realised Gloria was right. She was perfect for him. Now that he'd decided to commit to her, it was a load off his mind. He couldn't understand why he'd been so tardy in putting her mind at rest. He'd been selfish and allowed the situation with the COU to preoccupy him. Now he realised it was only his desire to be with her that kept him in Zimbabwe. He knew now he would never leave her. His missing passport was a problem, but like Gloria said, they'd sort things out together.

Dan felt a sense of elation and was excited about giving Gloria the news. They would get married in Melbourne, and wherever his research and writing took him, she'd be there. He remembered his promise to read and edit her manuscript. While he'd focussed on issues at the COU, the completed first draft lay gathering dust on a shelf in his bedroom cupboard in the apartment. Both Daniel Moyo and Nikita encouraged Dan to settle things with Gloria, but he'd been slow to act.

On Friday, Dan bought a bottle of Champagne to celebrate at dinner on Saturday night. Buoyed by his decision to commit to Gloria, like magic, his COU worries seemed secondary. He could hardly wait for Saturday to tell her.

CHAPTER 43

IT was one of those blustery winter days in Joburg when it paid to keep your eyes half-closed to avoid the dust. The wind buffeted the tidy upmarket northern suburb, blowing the loose sheets of a discarded newspaper along the road. This was a stamping ground of Johannesburg's wealthy citizens, but the wind didn't discriminate. The townships, with their uncollected rubbish and dirt verges, would have been much worse.

The big African was unfamiliar with the area, so he walked it to get his bearings and familiarise himself with the roads in the immediate surrounds. He pulled up the collar of his khaki, army-surplus, winter coat. It was late afternoon, and within an hour, it would be dark. He recognised the attractive, single-storey corner building in front of him and grunted with satisfaction. It was just like the image on Google Street View, except it was now grey in place of its former cream colour. Then he turned and walked in the opposite direction. One block back, he'd seen a florist, and that's where he now headed.

In the shop, the pretty young assistant was packing up in readiness to close, when the large black man pushed open the door, letting in the winter blast. Her initial alarm eased when he picked up a bunch of flowers and walked to the counter, opening a wallet stuffed with banknotes. He paid the three hundred rand without blinking. He didn't look like he could afford to spend that amount of money on flowers, though appearances can deceive. The assistant placed the flowers in a cellophane wrap with damp greenery at their base. Next, she wrapped the bunch in a large sheet of dark green crepe paper and secured it with an orange ribbon.

The big man thanked the assistant and exited the shop, taking care to shield the flowers from the powerful gusts of wind. Next door in the row of four shops was a food takeaway. He bought a hamburger and a packet of chips and walked past the last shop in the row. A park bench overlooking a small-treed area backed onto the side wall of that shop and gave him a little shelter from the wind. He made himself comfortable, as he was in for a lengthy wait.

From where he sat, he could see who entered and exited the grey building's corner entrance. He checked the time on his cell phone. Only six-thirty. Another two hours to wait.

A trickle of people came and went. Passing cars turned left at the grey building. Visitors to the building, parked along that stretch of road. The headlights of one car that drove straight on without turning illuminated a sign reading, Doctors' Parking Only. The darkness obscured the Medical Clinic sign above the entrance.

As time passed, the trickle of visitors grew less until they stopped around eight-thirty. The big African man picked up the bunch of flowers next to him on the park bench and made his way across the road to the private clinic's entrance. He stepped through the automatic doors, which closed with a loud click behind him.

The African nurse at the reception counter looked up in surprise. 'Oh! I just locked the doors. Visiting hours have ended.'

'Can I deliver these flowers to one of your patients?'

'Are you a relative?'

'I'm his nephew.'

'Sorry, only immediate relatives have access after visiting hours.'

'It'll only take a minute.'

'What's the patient's name?'

'John Ziyambi.'

'Only his wife can visit Mr Ziyambi.'

'Just give me a minute with him.'

'I can't go against the rules.'

'Don't worry, I won't tell anyone. Which is his room? I'll drop the flowers on his table.'

'No! No visitors for Mr Ziyambi. Those are strict instructions.'

'Sister, I'll be quick.' The big man hurried along the passage to his right and opened a door. A little old lady lay there asleep. He moved to the second door and opened it. The room stood empty. A thin elderly man occupied the third room.

'Stop!' the nurse shouted. 'You can't do that.'

She pressed the alarm, and within thirty seconds, two burly guards came racing down the opposite corridor towards reception. 'Quick, that man is checking all the rooms for a special patient. Don't let him get into R4. Hurry!'

The guards raced down the corridor, catching up with the intruder in room seven. He eyed their truncheons. 'OK, I'm leaving.' As he passed the reception counter, he hurled the bunch of flowers at the nurse. 'Give those to him.' At the automatic doors, he noticed the fire-safety map on the wall next to the green button he needed to press to leave the building. He'd heard the nurse shout about room R4, and he noted the room lay in the opposite wing to the one he entered. Four rooms from the end of the corridor and facing the road. That gave him all the information he required. Now he needed to wait until things quietened down.

One o'clock in the morning on a moonless night. Dim street lighting cast a faint shadow on the exterior wall under the fourth window from the end of the building. The shadow darkened as the figure got nearer. Carelessly closed curtains left a small gap. It was just enough to peer through. Despite the dark interior, there was enough ambient light to reveal a sleeping figure in the bed.

A tap on the window glass told the man it would break with a sharp blow from the concrete paver he'd prised from the driveway of a nearby house. He took off his scarf, folded it, and placed it over the end of the paver to deaden the sound. With the two guards on duty, he'd have to move fast. That meant a change of plan. He abandoned his original idea to smother the occupant. He checked the slim pocket on his lower trouser leg to make sure the screwdriver was in place.

The scarf did the trick, and the sound of breaking glass was softer than he expected. He worked fast to pull out any shards that might injure him. The figure on the bed stirred as the big African jumped into the room. In a flash, he grabbed the screwdriver, and struck the patient in the chest with several savage blows, before jumping out the window and hurrying from the scene.

Less than a minute. That's how long the incident lasted. Meanwhile, at the reception desk, the nurse played her radio and laughed with the two security guards, oblivious to both the sound of breaking glass and the impatient buzzing of Mrs Goldberg in room S7. The two other nurses on duty ate their dinner in the staff room, some distance from the stricken patient's suite.

* * *

Six a.m. Saturday, the morning shift arrived to relieve the night shift at the clinic. A nurse opened the dispensary to prepare the patients' medications. She was shocked when in room R5 she found the occupant lying in a blood-soaked bed. 'Quick! We must call Doctor Patel. It looks like the patient's stitches have opened.'

The clinic staff and Doctor Patel were in a panic before they noticed the broken window and the tiny stab wounds in the patient's chest. Doctor Patel felt relieved his stitches were not responsible for his patient bleeding to death. 'Oh, thank goodness for that!' He instructed a nurse to call the police, and another to call a window repairer. 'We can't use that room until it's fixed.'

In the boutique medical clinic, the news spread fast, and everyone was on edge. Soon, the police arrived. Inspector Michael Mzamane of the South African Police studied the scene. The clinic recalled the night shift nurse and security guards for questioning by the police. How could they have heard nothing? Who occupied R5 last night?

The night nurse remembered the persistent man. 'He insisted on delivering flowers to the patient in R4.' Who occupies that room? Inspector Mzamane asked to see the CCTV footage of the incident. Slowly, things came together in his mind. A big African, a murder with a slim blade, possibly a screwdriver, and a Zimbabwean patient in R4. It reminded him of something. Yes, the attempted mugging of Dan Scott at OR Tambo International Airport! Might there be a connection?

Did the killer know his quarry occupied R4? Why did he murder the patient in R5? How did he identify the room his victim occupied? The inspector walked down the passage to the rooms in question. R4 was the fourth from the end. He walked out of the building to view the crime scene from the road. Room R5's smashed window was the fourth window from the end.

The inspector noticed a section of wall ran between the last window and the end of the building. He turned to the nurse in charge, 'Let's check room R1.'

'Why do you want to see R1? It's only our dispensary.'

When they opened the door to R1, the inspector smiled. 'Just as I thought. R1 doesn't have a window. The killer thought the fourth window from the end was R4, occupied by his intended target. The intruder killed the patient in R5 by mistake. We better keep quiet about this, so the killer doesn't realise he's made a mistake. Otherwise, he may try again.'

Later that morning, when the police informed Alice Ziyambi about the incident, she organised for her husband to move to another private clinic. The police kept details of the transfer quiet, and even the doctors in the first clinic didn't know where they'd taken him.

CHAPTER 44

SATURDAY morning in Harare, and Dan looked forward to Gloria's arrival at lunchtime. The champagne cooled in the fridge. There'd been no power outage, and the fridge kept up a reassuring hum. Dan took that as a good omen. A power cut now wouldn't affect the champagne, which would stay chilled way beyond lunch.

The table, set with a white tablecloth and champagne glasses, would surprise Gloria. She would guess something special was afoot because Dan always left the table setting to her. Saturday lunch was always an informal affair. Perhaps it would have been better to leave the champagne for dinner to drink with one of Gloria's tasty meals. But he was too impatient to wait to give her the news. Besides, there'd be enough champagne for both lunch and dinner.

Dan hadn't yet bought an engagement ring, though now he'd made up his mind, his commitment to her would be no less binding. He'd find a beautiful ring on his next visit to Johannesburg. Everything stood ready and waiting by eleven-thirty. Gloria only finished work at one o'clock, so she wouldn't arrive until a quarter or half-past the hour.

With two hours to spare, Dan paced up and down like a caged animal. He stepped onto the balcony to see who passed. It wasn't a busy road, not even on a Saturday. He walked through the lounge to the bedroom. A sudden idea came to him. Now was the perfect time to resume editing Gloria's manuscript, which lay gathering dust on an upper shelf in his bedroom cupboard. Months ago, he'd given her general comments, but now he'd do a proper read-through and edit.

Dan's decision to make his life with Gloria gave him a rush of energy that he'd lacked in recent times. He sat on the balcony and read her work. After a while, he checked his watch. Twelve noon! Only half an hour had passed, though it seemed much longer. Up to another ninety minutes to wait.

As Dan read on, he realised the manuscript was better than he'd expected. The writing held an innocent quirkiness that gave it a charm of its own. The story and the characters drew him in, and he next looked at his watch at one o'clock, before returning his attention to the manuscript.

When he looked again, his Rolex showed a quarter to two. The manuscript absorbed him, and he'd not noticed the time passing. But where was Gloria? Work may have delayed her. Dan put away the manuscript and walked out onto the balcony. Although bare in winter, the row of jacarandas prevented him from seeing who approached from down the block.

Now, time dragged. After an eternity, two-thirty rolled around. Dan checked the time on his watch and his cell phone before calling Gloria. No answer. Two more unsuccessful attempts, and Dan jumped into his car and drove to her flat. He ran up the steps of her apartment block and hurried along the corridor and knocked on her door. He waited, but she didn't answer his knock. Usually, Gloria expected him and opened the door within a few seconds. He knocked again, but still nothing.

By now, she may be at his apartment, knocking on his door and wondering why he didn't answer. Dan hurried down the stairs and raced back to his apartment, driving a little too fast, while keeping an eye on the side of the road, in case he spied her walking.

There was no sign of Gloria at his apartment. Dan was now becoming anxious as he remembered her comment about going their separate ways. Had she decided on that course of action, or was she just trying to teach him a lesson to force a response from him?

The rest of the afternoon and evening passed more slowly than Dan could remember. He called Gloria's cell phone several times without success. In the evening, he drove to her apartment block. Gloria's flat was in darkness. Back in his apartment, he tried to read more of her manuscript but couldn't concentrate. For dinner, he ate cold baked beans on toast, not bothering to make fried eggs, his usual accompaniment for that meal.

A sleepless night would be an understatement. Dan tossed and turned and rose several times to break the monotony of lying in bed, with sleep a distant prospect. On one occasion, he drank a glass of water, and on another, he drank a cup of tea. Sometimes he just sat in the lounge staring at the opposite wall.

Dan was drained of energy, and dawn came as a relief. He'd wait until mid-morning and then drive around to her place and knock again. Where else might she be besides her apartment? He showered and dressed quickly to not miss her call if she phoned. He realised he was hungry. Cereal, toast, and tea were better than nothing, and helped the time pass.

Ten-thirty on Sunday morning, and Dan wouldn't wait any longer, so he jumped in his car and drove at a crawl to Gloria's flat. Now he feared she might have moved somewhere he'd not find her. Would she do that? At the block of flats, he trudged up the stairs, his nerves tugging at his stomach. What would he do if she didn't answer his knock? How might he find her? At work perhaps? An entire week passed since he saw her last Sunday, which gave her the time and opportunity to move elsewhere.

Dan paused at Gloria's door, took a deep breath, and knocked. Ah! He heard a noise inside the flat. Someone was coming. That must be her. He heard the Yale lock turn and relief flooded over him. She'd given him a nasty fright, but he'd forgive her anything right now. Dan recognised his prevarication contributed to the situation. Gloria suffered from his lack of commitment for weeks, if not months. He'd suffered from her ruse for less than a day, so she'd not come close to balancing the ledger.

The door opened. It wasn't Gloria. A striking-looking woman stood there. Dan was taken aback. 'Er, good morning, I'm looking for Gloria.'

'I'm Estelle, Gloria's sister.'

'Is she here?'

'Who are you?'

'I'm Dan Scott, Gloria's boyfriend.'

'Oh, yes! Gloria said she'd found someone special.'

'Where is she?'

'I'm sorry, Dan. Gloria was run over on Wednesday night. It was a hit and run. She's dead.'

'She's …?' The words stuck in Dan's throat. He tried to speak, but the words came out in a hoarse whisper. 'How? Where?'

'Right here on the corner. She came home late from work on Wednesday night. As she crossed the road, a car came racing around the corner and hit her. The car didn't stop. Witnesses didn't get the car's registration number or make. They said it was a dark colour. Gloria's employer had my details as her next of kin, so they called me in Cape Town on Friday, and I arrived on a flight this morning.'

'Where is she now?'

'Her employer identified her, so the authorities released her body to our relatives. They took her back to our home village yesterday. I'm following on later today.'

'Did she, did she…?'

'Did she suffer? No, she died instantly.'

Dan struggled to speak. A cold crawling sensation swept over him, making his chest feel hollow. 'Gloria always came to my apartment on Saturday at lunchtime. Yesterday, I planned to ask her to marry me.'

'Gloria was so excited about meeting you. She loved you very much and hoped to have a future together with you.'

'Yes, yesterday, I was going to ask her to marry me,' Dan said again, with his voice quivering and cracking.

'She was my precious little sister, so naughty and full of spirit. You and I will forever be connected, as we will both mourn her.'

'Yes,' was all Dan managed in response.

There was nothing more to say. They swapped cell phone numbers and said goodbye. In a daze, Dan almost tripped as he descended the stairs of the building. He jumped into his car and drove back to his apartment. Only when he closed the door behind him did the tears flow.

Dan sat slumped in one of the lounge chairs. He felt sick and thought he would vomit. He took out Gloria's manuscript and tried to read, but big teardrops kept falling on the pages, so he put it back in the cupboard. As evening fell, Dan lay on his bed in the darkness, and soon fell asleep.

Ironic then, that he dreamt of Gloria arriving for their celebratory lunch, and her excitement when he asked her to marry him. They were both so happy. But after twelve hours, when the first rays of dawn entered his bedroom, Dan awoke to the reality and horror of the situation. His days of misery were only just beginning.

CHAPTER 45

ON Monday, Dan rang in sick. He stayed away from work for the entire week. He didn't even consider going to Gloria's funeral, but then, he'd not received an invitation. Dan wanted to remember her the way she was. The thought of her buried in a wooden box underground would haunt him forever.

Life wasn't fair. He burned with anger. His world had collapsed. He cursed the unknown hit-and-run driver, then the police, whose record promised little hope of making an arrest. Even if the police apprehended the culprit, would Gloria get justice in the courts? He doubted it.

Now he didn't need to stay in Zimbabwe any longer. He wanted to leave and leave fast. Tomorrow, he'd visit the Australian Embassy in Borrowdale. Perhaps they would expedite a replacement passport for him.

* * *

An official at the embassy greeted Dan and showed him into a room. An extensive list of questions followed. 'Why did the customs confiscate your passport? Can you explain your detention in Chikurubi Prison overnight? Were you born in Australia? No? Oh, born in Zimbabwe! Apart from your missing passport, have you any proof you are an Australian citizen?'

On and on, the questions came. It appeared the Australian official suspected him and his motives. 'We'll make enquiries about your case, though it will take time. We cannot rush these things, and we'll need to refer your case to Australia. I'll be in touch when I have something concrete for you.'

Dan left the embassy, discouraged. He'd read stories of Australian embassies and consulates being slow or unhelpful to their citizens who found themselves in difficulty in foreign countries.

Now, without Gloria, he was rudderless. His life had no direction, plans, or dreams for the future. Life seemed aimless, and he didn't like it one bit. He wouldn't go to the office, though he felt frustrated in the apartment.

Dan didn't want to see anyone, and he didn't answer the door one evening when he recognised Nikita's knock. He sat in the unlit apartment, and she would have thought he wasn't home. Neither did he want to contact Daniel Moyo. Dan didn't know what to do or how he'd ever escape his black mood.

He hated everybody and everything, and most of all, he hated himself. He'd been such a fool, putting Gloria on hold while he occupied his mind with the COU. She'd gone to her grave, not knowing how much he loved her. The most bitter pill was losing her just when he planned to propose marriage. It was everything she wanted, but it was too late now. Dan realised it was also everything he wanted, but she was beyond his reach, and the lost opportunity gnawed at his insides.

He recalled the night Eva visited and cried on his shoulder when someone murdered her husband, Victor. Now he understood how she felt.

The brilliant winter sun still shone, but for Dan, the sparkle was gone. He realised home isn't a building, city, or country. Home is where the heart lies. The rest is just nostalgia. With Gloria, Harare was home. Without her, he was a stranger in this land.

* * *

The following week, he returned to the office. Cherry and Ambrose beamed when they saw him and hoped he'd recovered from his illness. No one knew the real reason he'd been away from work.

Eunice acted as if she'd not been aware of his absence. There were rumours of a big contract in the works, and she seemed preoccupied. Cherry and Ambrose knew nothing about the rumoured job, other than it mattered a lot to the COU.

Late July. Eunice was busy, so she cancelled the debriefs for the next two weeks. It suited Dan fine, and any pretence of him being the second in command seemed long gone. That's not how Eunice saw it when he expressed that view to her at their next debrief.

'Yes, you're my second in command. I will fill you in with the details when I'm not so busy.'

'You could tell me now.'

'No, I'm too tired to talk about it now.'

Eunice was up to something. Dan soon realised she was setting him up to be the scapegoat if things went wrong with one of her contracts.

* * *

The papers overflowed with news about the Mnangagwa poisoning. The vice-president engaged in a bitter struggle with the president's wife, Grace Mugabe, to succeed her husband when the old man died.

Rivalry between the factions in the ZANU-PF governing party rose to a fever pitch. The Lacoste faction supported Mnangagwa, and the G40 faction supported Grace Mugabe. The former suspected the G40 faction poisoned the vice-president at a political rally in Gwanda with ice cream from the Mugabe's Gushungo Dairy.

Whatever the truth of the matter, the army arranged an urgent flight for Mnangagwa to go to a hospital in South Africa. He and his faction claimed it was an assassination attempt. The G40 faction believed Lacoste fabricated the whole thing to cement the army's support of the vice-president.

Many recalled the white powder incident in Mnangagwa's party office in December 2014 and his car crash with a hospital bus in October of the same year. Some members of the public saw them as attempted assassinations, while others believed they were staged for effect.

Accusations flew in both directions, and the COU benefitted from the political turmoil. The fractured political opposition added another layer of complexity to the situation. The COU couldn't afford to align itself with any one side, so accepted contributions to its cash flow from all parties and factions.

Everyone held a view about what was happening in the country. The political electricity in the air was tangible, and a spark would ignite an inferno, setting the country ablaze.

The year 2017 was an interesting time in Zimbabwe. Inevitably, it dragged Dan back in touch with Daniel Moyo and Nikita.

* * *

The next time he recognised Nikita's knock, Dan opened the door. He explained the situation and what happened to Gloria.

Nikita expressed disappointment. 'You can't lock yourself away like this. You need your friends around for support at such times. When Victor died, you comforted me, and I could have been a comfort to you.'

She was right. He found it helpful to talk about Gloria while sharing a beer or two with Nikita. A month passed since she died, and his feelings remained raw.

On Friday, Dan met Daniel Moyo at the Explorer's Bar in the Meikles Hotel. Again, he covered the recent events and once more found it helpful to talk about Gloria. As in his discussion with Nikita, he reaffirmed to Daniel his intention to leave Zimbabwe as soon as possible. Like Nikita, Daniel understood Dan's situation, but cautioned him about making any big decisions while in such an emotional state.

'I can't stay here after what has happened.'

'Yes, I understand, and you have other reasons for wanting to leave Zimbabwe. All I'm saying is why now? If you return to Melbourne at this traumatic point in your life, you might soon regret it. Throw yourself into something new. Go to Botswana or Zambia and collect more material for another novel.'

'Oh, I don't know!'

'Take a holiday to our neighbouring countries, even Mozambique. You need more time for your emotions to settle.'

* * *

Over three weeks passed since his visit to the Australian Embassy, and there was no news about his replacement passport. It was time for a follow-up.

At the embassy, the news wasn't what Dan wanted to hear. 'Mr Scott, we understand you are at the centre of a police investigation of a rather serious nature. We cannot issue you with a replacement passport until you have resolved the matter with the police or through the courts. You will appreciate, we cannot help a suspected criminal escape justice. We understand the authorities have confiscated your passport, pending the outcome of your case.'

'No, they confiscated my passport at the airport when I arrived in Harare. The police matter to which you refer occurred months later.'

'I'm sorry, but we have it on good authority the two are connected. Try to sort out your issue with the police. You don't need a replacement passport if you already have one, albeit confiscated.'

Dan was furious that the embassy doubted him, while accepting the word of a corrupt or incompetent local official. The facts of his case should be easy to verify. For now, he was stuck in Zimbabwe.

Back in the apartment, brooding over his circumstances while sipping a beer on the balcony, Dan's cell phone rang. He picked it up from the small table beside him. 'Dan Scott speaking.'

'Mr Scott, I'm Alice Ziyambi, John's wife. We wondered if you would like to visit him at our home.'

Dan sat up, bolt upright, in his chair. 'Yes, of course. How is he?'

'As well as can be hoped.'

'When should I visit?'

'Next Friday, six o'clock, if you're free. Do you have a pen and paper? I'll give you the address. Oh! And can you please keep your visit confidential?'

'Yes, I will. Please give my regards to John.'

'I will. Thank you. Goodbye.'

Dan sat back in his chair, his mind whirring. Now what? Well, at least Captain John was alive. Why would he want him to visit him at home? He understood the man was recuperating, but his wife's phone call held an air of mystery. She'd asked him not to discuss the visit with anyone. A ripple of excitement ran through him.

CHAPTER 46

Dan was curious about Alice Ziyambi's phone call. Why didn't Captain John phone him? If he was too ill to phone, was he well enough to receive visitors? Was Alice Ziyambi's request for confidentiality a question of privacy or secrecy? He imagined good reasons for both, but her manner sounded like the latter. Either way, he looked forward to the meeting. Friday couldn't come fast enough.

Was Captain John ready to return to work? In the office, apart from the Tuesday and Thursday debriefs, Eunice ignored Dan. When she spoke to him at the debriefs, she was disloyal to John. She made no secret of her intention to become head of the COU. It was obvious she believed he wouldn't return. Did she have any inside information about his condition? Might she be in touch with Alice Ziyambi or some other close family contact?

Dan cancelled his usual Friday engagement with Daniel Moyo at the Explorer's Bar. In September, the weather was warming and comfortable. Dan opened the door of the built-in wardrobe in his bedroom and surveyed his clothes. Prominent on a shelf lay the jumper Gloria made him for Christmas, and a lump rose in his throat. Too warm now for jumpers, he selected his camel jacket, dark brown trousers, and a black shirt he'd picked up in Joburg on his last visit. Black shoes and a matt-black belt would complete his dress.

A quick, refreshing shower perked him up. As Dan brushed his teeth, he looked in the washbasin mirror, and a wave of loneliness swept over him. Often, when he'd done this in the past, he'd see Gloria's smiling face peeping over his shoulder. She'd put her arms around his waist and rest her head on his back. Little things like that made him realise he needed her in his life. Now she was gone, and nothing could bring her back.

Dan finished brushing his teeth and walked into the bedroom to get dressed. It wouldn't do to be late for his engagement with the Ziyambi's. He checked the map on his computer once more to familiarise himself with the route. Borrowdale was an exclusive suburb north-east of the city centre. He wasn't familiar with the area, and he worried about losing his way in the unlit suburban streets.

The apartment block cast a shadow over the parking area, and the car's interior remained relatively cool despite the warm afternoon sun. Dan strapped on his seatbelt and opened the sunroof before backing out of his parking spot. He drove straight down to Chancellor Avenue and turned left, passing St George's College High School on the left and the Borrowdale Racecourse on the right.

Soon he arrived in Borrowdale. Dan looked at his watch. Although he'd driven at a leisurely pace, he was fifteen minutes early. He spent the spare time driving around the suburb, looking at the houses and getting his bearings.

At six o'clock, Dan drove through the open gate of Captain John's house and parked near the front door of the sprawling, single-storey bungalow. A large circular driveway filled the manicured front garden. The property was attractive without being ostentatious, unlike many of the houses in the area owned by the regime's senior politicians and civil servants. It was obvious someone with money lived there.

Dan switched off the engine and jumped out of the car. He skipped up the steps, strode to the front door, and pressed the doorbell. A tinge of nervousness coursed through him as he waited for a response. The door opened, revealing an elegant young woman. A large, friendly golden Labrador sat behind her, wagging its tail.

'You must be Dan. I'm Alice Ziyambi, John's wife. Please come in.'

For a moment, Dan hesitated. The woman's appearance surprised him. She was at least twenty years younger than John, which put her in her late thirties. She wore loose fitting white slacks and a colourful, floral, long-sleeved blouse. White sandals on her feet exposed bright red painted toenails.

'Er, thank you. Pleased to meet you.' Dan proffered his hand to Alice. Her long, cool fingers and firm handshake suggested a confident personality. It was unlikely John dominated her, as he did his employees at the COU.

'Come through to the lounge. John is waiting there for you.' As Dan stepped onto the doorstep, the Labrador stood aside as if ready to lead the way. Dan followed Alice through the entrance hall with its gleaming parquet flooring and turned right into a spacious lounge. There, in a wheelchair, sat Captain John. He looked thin and tired, with pale, grey-coloured skin. There was no mistaking his pleasure at seeing Dan. His welcoming smile exposed his perfect white teeth.

Unlike Alice's handshake, John's weak effort rested in Dan's hand as if too weary to support itself. He'd been through a tough time.

'So, John, when will you be back on your feet, playing with the dog?'

'The doctors can only guess. They hope I'll improve over the coming months, but have warned me I may be stuck in this wheelchair for good. The bullet lodged up against my spine. It was fortunate it wasn't a millimetre further to the right.'

'Do you think they discharged you from the hospital too soon?'

'No, I couldn't stand being locked up in there any longer. My best chance for improvement comes with being back home.'

'Did you see who shot you?'

'The room was dark. I just saw a female figure.'

'Well, Eva Chirau had already moved to another room.'

'Yes, so I heard. Alice, how about a couple of scotches?'

Alice brought to the coffee table two sparkling crystal tumblers, a small bucket of ice, and a bottle of Wolfburn Batch 375 Single Malt. She poured the scotch over the ice cubes and handed one glass to Dan and the other to her husband.

John leant forward in his wheelchair and clinked glasses with Dan. 'Tell me how you find this one. I suppose you've missed our scotch evenings in the office?'

'Yes, I have, though in your absence, Eunice has been calling me in for scotch debriefs.'

John grunted. 'I guessed she might. Has most of my good stuff gone?'

'I would say so because the debriefs have been less frequent in recent weeks, and she's often used cheaper brands.'

'How are things in the office?'

'A little tense. I imagine most of the staff want you back.'

John sighed. 'Well, perhaps. You remember Eric, the operative with us at the writers' festival? You thought he was the doctor's husband. I planned on promoting him to a more senior role, but I hear Eunice has got rid of him.'

'I didn't know that. The area past the strongroom door is a secret to me. I don't even go into Eunice's old office anymore because she's using your office.'

'Have you been following all this business about the Mnangagwa poisoning?'

'Yes, it's been all the news for the past few weeks.'

'Rumours are, Eunice may have organised the plot.'

'So, you're still in touch with someone at the COU?'

'No, one of my old clients suggested it to me. I warned Eunice not to take any high-profile contracts before the election. The intense rivalry within the government makes it a dangerous time to accept such contracts. A failed, high-profile assassination would destroy our business if anyone linked us to it. Now, Mnangagwa has survived, and the Mugabes are furious their Gushungo Dairy is under suspicion for the poisoning. Whoever is responsible has alienated both factions in the government.'

'Ambrose and Cherry suspected something important was going on. Eunice told me she was busy and would tell me about it later. So far, I've heard nothing.'

'In the hospital in Johannesburg, someone tried to kill me. They got the rooms mixed up and stabbed the poor fellow next door. Only Eunice knew where I was. She told Alice the office wanted to send me flowers, so Alice gave her the address. I've only realised in the last few months the full extent of Eunice's ambitions.'

'Eunice thinks the present situation is likely to be permanent. Has she spoken to you or Alice since you returned to Harare?'

'No, that one call to Alice was the only contact since the shooting. We have told nobody I'm back here. You're the only one I can trust, Dan. Though I can also trust Ambrose and Cherry, I've never confided in them. And I have a couple of operatives outside the COU. But as for the rest! I'm not sure where their loyalties lie. Eunice will have tried to entice them to her side.'

'So, we must wait for you to recover?'

'Yes, but in the meantime, be careful. The intruder at the hospital stabbed the patient next door with a screwdriver. Jonas sometimes hired a man named Gustave for his dirtier jobs down there in Johannesburg. I understand he used a screwdriver for his hits. If Eunice is now using him, who knows who his next target might be? At least he's in Joburg and not here in Harare.'

'One thing I've never mentioned, John. On my way here from Australia, Gustave tried to mug me at the Intercontinental Airport Hotel in Johannesburg.'

'Are you sure it was Gustave who tried to mug you?'

'Yes, he's the one. When I went with Eunice to Johannesburg to meet with Francis, she called Gustave in for a meeting. I don't know if he recognised me, though I certainly recognised him. Towards the end, she asked Francis and me to leave, so she could talk with Gustave in private. The next day, someone pushed Francis out of his eighth floor flat. She wanted to get rid of him, so I'm sure she organised it.'

'That is tragic news! Jonas always praised Francis.'

'Yes, he was obliging and effective in his quiet way.'

John asked Dan to pour them each another scotch, and for a time they sat in silence, savouring the single malt in their crystal tumblers. Dan surveyed the lounge with its elegant, classical, French-style furniture, and French clock collection. Clearly, John's good taste extended beyond the clothes he wore. He was an educated man, and Dan wondered how and where John gained his sophistication.

John broke the silence. 'Are you still going to the writers' club meetings?'

'Not since the festival in Bulawayo. I needed a break after all that excitement.'

'Yes, me too, said John with a rueful smile.'

'By coincidence, Mrs Olonga phoned me this week and asked if I would give a talk on punctuation at next Friday's meeting.'

'What time does it start?'

'Seven o'clock. Just after dinner.'

'I wonder if you'd do me a favour. Alice is keen to attend the meetings. Would you mind taking her with you?'

'Yes, it would be a pleasure.'

'Come as early as possible. It will give us a chance to catch up over a couple of scotches, and the cook will feed us his famous finger food.'

'Great! I look forward to it.'

'All right! Well, I better get off to bed and try to regain my energy. The doctors say I need to rest. Till next Friday, then.'

Dan said goodbye to John, and Alice showed him to the front door. She'd not been in the room while they spoke, but he assumed she knew he'd pick her up the following week for the writers' meeting. 'Goodbye Alice, see you next week.'

Alice nodded in acknowledgement.

The car tyres scrunched on the sandy drive. At the gate, Dan stopped to let a black car pass before he turned left onto the road. What an interesting meeting! Captain John hadn't spoken so openly before now. He may know more about events in the office than he disclosed, but it felt good John put his trust in him. But could he really befriend some-one who ran such an evil business? Perilous situations make for strange bedfellows.

And what about Alice? Though polite and welcoming, she never smiled. She acted more like a secretary than a wife. With the rumours of John's multiple affairs and mistresses, perhaps she just accepted the situation and led her own life. Her daughter Suzie and son, John junior, were nowhere to be seen.

Dan agreed to take the unsmiling Alice to the writers' club meeting, though it would be a bore if she didn't lighten up. She was an attractive woman but showed no spark. The way she dressed displayed money and style. Perhaps that was enough for her.

There was something familiar about Alice, though John claimed she'd never visited the office. Dan was sure he'd seen her before, but where? Then, as he neared his apartment, it hit him. That's it! The first time at the writers' club. The elegant woman in the front row, who disappeared straight after his talk. That explained John's interest in the writers' club and in his talk at the art gallery on the day he met Gloria.

CHAPTER 47

THE rivalry between the two factions of the ruling ZANU-PF party
was growing. Even casual observers of events in the country sensed
something would have to give. Grace Mugabe, the president's wife, was
hostile towards Emmerson Mnangagwa, the senior vice president, and
soon, the bitter rivalry infected all levels of the two factions.

Mnangagwa maintained the support of the army and the war veterans
who took part in the Bush War against Ian Smith's white dominated
government. His 'Lacoste faction' was so named because his totem was
the crocodile. Grace Mugabe held the support of the younger members
of the governing party, known as the G40 or generation 40 faction. The
party's youth league also supported her.

Captain John took a sip of scotch from his crystal tumbler. 'You can
see, Dan, why I'm happy to let things drift for now. We don't take sides
in politics or personal disputes. We're just a business venture offering a
professional service.'

'You took part in the Bush War. Don't your sympathies lie with the
war veterans?'

'I got involved in the Bush War for personal reasons, not because I
held strong political views. My mother's employer made provisions for
me to go to Oxford University in Britain. I even got an acceptance letter,
but then unforeseen circumstances changed everything.'

Captain John didn't expand on his comments, and Dan thought it
wise not to press him for more information. 'OK, so you're happy for
the business to coast until after the coming election, though I'm not sure
Eunice sees it that way.'

'Initially, rivalry between the factions was good for business. Now, as things have become more heated and personal, it's more difficult to avoid the impression we're taking sides. Eunice knows my feelings about this.'

John's smiling Somali chef, Yasir, interrupted their discussion with a tray of hot snacks. They included samosas, spring rolls, potato croquettes, onion pakoras, a tangy selection of dipping sauces, and one or two other dishes Dan didn't recognise.

'What a choice, John! It's hard to know where to begin.'

'All these are freshly cooked. Yasir doesn't buy any ready-made items. Somali cooks have a wonderful reputation. We were lucky to find him. And his wife is our housekeeper.'

'Where did you find him?'

'He was a refugee from the troubles in Somalia. Yasir and his wife moved to Johannesburg, but the xenophobia down there against foreign Africans encouraged them to come to Harare. If you think we have problems in Zimbabwe, you should see Somalia. It's a most dangerous country.'

Yasir entered the lounge to remove the dishes, and John poured another two scotches over the ice cubes in their crystal tumblers. 'Alice tells me the writers' club meets every fortnight. I may be in bed before you return from the meeting, so we'd better make our arrangements now. If you don't mind picking her up again, can we schedule our next chat two weeks from today? Same time, same arrangement, so don't eat beforehand.'

'That sounds great. I could get used to Yasir's cooking. It's certainly better than mine.'

Just as they finished their scotches, Alice entered the room, and Dan stood up to greet her. Earlier, Yasir answered the door when he arrived, so he'd not seen her this evening before now. She looked cool and glamourous in a white cotton dress with an orange scarf wrapped around her waist. Alice greeted him with a nod and the faintest hint of a smile. Perhaps she wouldn't be a bore after all.

Dan thanked Captain John for his hospitality and walked with Alice down the steps to his car, where he opened the passenger-side door to let her enter. At the gate, he stopped to let a couple of cars pass before turning left onto the road.

They drove for a while in silence. Dan wondered if Alice was aloof or just shy. He too struggled for words. 'I believe you have two children?'

'Yes, my daughter Suzie, and my son, John junior.'

'Do they live at home?'

'No, they're at boarding school in England.'

'You must be counting the days to seeing them in the Christmas school holidays.'

'This Christmas, they will go to my sister in Bristol. John doesn't want them here until he's had more time to recover.'

'Oh!'

That was their entire conversation, heading to the writers' club meeting at the art gallery. Dan focussed on the road and was relieved the drive was relatively short. In most situations, he found it easy to converse with others, though somehow, not with her.

At the art gallery, Mrs Olonga and the other senior ladies gathered around Alice to welcome her. It was the first time they'd seen her since before her husband's shooting in Bulawayo. Dan, meanwhile, was preoccupied with memories of meeting Gloria here at his first talk to the writers' club.

Formal presentations, including Dan's talk on punctuation, made up the first half of the evening. The second half was an informal social with tea and cakes.

Dan noted Alice seemed more sociable in the gathering of women she appeared to know well. With him, she was polite but formal. He didn't know her or have anything in common with her, except the writers' club. On their way home, it occurred to him he should have earlier spoken to her about the club and her interest in it.

'Are you writing anything or planning to write?'

'No, I'm just interested in good English, whether spoken or written. My parents always encouraged me to improve my grammar and accent.'

'You speak really well.'

'Thank you, but I can always improve.'

'Did you find my talk helpful?'

'Yes, I did. It's interesting how writing punctuation differs from the way we speak. For example, unlike the way we learned in school, we don't need a comma every time we pause for a breath.'

Earlier, he'd been stuck for conversation, but now the drive home proved a little more comfortable. Dan dropped Alice at her front door and confirmed he'd pick her up in a fortnight. She thanked him for the lift. He waited until she let herself into the house, before he eased the car around the circular drive and stopped at the gate to let a black car pass.

* * *

As the fortnights went by, Dan was a regular visitor for dinner and drinks at Captain John's house. September was hot, but October was even hotter. The weather was dust dry after the rainless winter season, and the cloudless skies promised no relief.

Dan looked forward to the evening chats with John, followed by a tasty dinner. He couldn't help noticing as the weather got hotter, Alice's dresses got lighter and shorter. He'd always considered her an attractive woman, and each time he picked her up, she seemed more alluring.

Just as one got pleasure from viewing a beautiful flower, so he got pleasure from imagining how she'd look each fortnight. With her distant manner, Dan still found it difficult to relax when talking to her. Perhaps her husband didn't appreciate her as a desirable woman and didn't recognise the jewel he possessed.

Dan sipped scotch from the crystal glass. 'John, almost every time I leave here, a black hatchback drives past. It seems odd.'

'A lot of politicians and senior bureaucrats live in this area. Many of them worry about their safety. If you look to your right at the gate, you'll see a big white house near the bend in the road, with a black security vehicle parked there. If they notice any activity, such as when you leave here, they'll drive past to investigate. They're probably checking on you, but I don't think it's anything for you to worry about.'

* * *

On Monday, sixth November, the bitter rivalry between the factions erupted. Robert Mugabe, the president, fired his vice president, Emmerson Mnangagwa. The deposed vice president and his family were in danger of detention, or worse. Two days later, Mnangagwa escaped to South Africa via Mozambique. In the COU office, there was much excitement, and Eunice relished the prospect of more business following an expected purge of members of the Lacoste faction.

The head of the army, Constantine Chiwenga, was on an official visit to China. Military intelligence forewarned him that Mugabe ordered the police to arrest him upon his return to Harare on Sunday, the twelfth. Soldiers, dressed as baggage handlers, disarmed the police paramilitary unit at the airport, ensuring Chiwenga's safe homecoming. The country held its breath.

On Tuesday fourteenth, military vehicles appeared on the roads around Harare, and the army took control of the Zimbabwe Broadcasting Corporation (ZBC).

Early on Wednesday morning, the army broadcast a statement denying it had carried out a coup. MajorGeneral SibusisoMoyo, the army chief of staff, said the president was safe, but the military was targeting criminals around him. The criminals he referred to were the leaders of the G40 faction. The sound of gunfire could be heard in Borrowdale, where Mugabe and several senior government officials lived. In a phone call with the South African president, Jacob Zuma, Mugabe claimed he was being held under house arrest.

All the talk on the street was about Mugabe's prospects of surviving the army's intervention in politics. A party atmosphere developed in Harare, and Dan wondered how Captain John was doing at his home in Borrowdale. He would find out in two days when he next saw him.

CHAPTER 48

Eva Chirau always dressed as Nikita when she visited Dan at the apartment, other than the night her husband, Victor, died. She believed they needed to be on their guard, as Eunice presented a greater threat than Captain John ever did. John's regimented approach made him more predictable than the impulsive Eunice.

Nikita thought the move against Mugabe was pedestrian, and she was concerned he might somehow wriggle out of his predicament. Chiwenga met Mugabe for negotiations and displayed a deference to the president. Rumour built upon rumour, and many people worried the coup would fizzle out.

Nothing much occurred on Thursday, sixteenth November, and Daniel Moyo expressed similar views when he met Dan at the Explorers' Bar that evening. The entire country waited to see what would happen next. On Friday, Mugabe even presided at the graduation ceremony at Zimbabwe Open University. Some thought it was a sign nothing would change.

In the office, Eunice expressed no opinion about the situation. Dan thought she may wait to see which side prevailed, before throwing her verbal support behind the successful faction. Meanwhile, he was impatient for Friday to get Captain John's opinion on events.

At last, Friday afternoon arrived, and Dan left the office earlier than usual. He returned to the apartment to get ready for his visit to the Ziyambi household. The warm day promised one of those beautiful balmy evenings that seemed to occur more often in Zimbabwe than anywhere else he'd experienced.

Five o'clock on Friday was always busy with cars and pedestrians making their way home. Today, people gathered in the streets, waiting for developments. Military vehicles guarded various points in the city, monitoring the curious and cheerful crowds.

Dan drove out on Borrowdale Road past the racecourse, before turning off towards Captain John's house. He passed two army lorries on the way. As he entered the drive, he slowed and looked towards the bend further up the road. This time, no car was parked there. It was still daylight, and perhaps too early for the security car's presence. The military activity in the area might also account for their absence.

The manicured garden looked lovely as Dan drove up the compacted sandy drive and stopped at the foot of the steps. As he got out, the house's front door opened, and a beaming Yasir emerged. He'd kept an eye out for Dan. 'Good evening, Sir. The boss is waiting for you in the lounge.'

'Thank you, Yasir.'

'There's a nice dinner tonight, Sir.'

'It's always a nice dinner, Yasir.'

'Thank you, Sir.'

Captain John, in his wheelchair with a light blanket covering his legs, gave a broad smile as Dan entered the lounge. It was clear he'd also looked forward to their discussion about the momentous happenings over the last twelve days. 'It's frustrating being stuck in this wheelchair with everything that's happening in the CBD.'

'Well, I'm glad there's no damage to your place. There was gunfire in Borrowdale.'

'Yes, we heard it. The army was giving the G40 boys a scare.'

'So, what will happen next?'

'Mugabe is finished. That's for sure. They'll go through a process to disguise the coup as a disciplined transfer of power. But it will happen. I'm sure of that. This next week should be eventful.'

The men chatted over their crystal glasses of scotch on the rocks, filling in details for one another.

As Captain John poured the second round of drinks, Alice made her appearance to tell them dinner was ready. To Dan, she looked stunning, though he tried not to show it. She wore a short, tight-fitting summer dress that ended at mid-thigh, revealing a pair of shapely legs. The dress material was a bold pattern of assorted inter-locking leaves in Msasa tree shades of red, orange, yellow, and green. Her gold stud earrings complimented her short hair, with her orange shoes providing the finishing touch.

Yasir carried their drinks to the dining table and fussed around them, revelling in their compliments about the dishes he served. Soon, dinner was over, and it was time to leave for the writers' club. Dan opened the passenger-side car door to let Alice get in, hoping she didn't notice his quick glance at her shapely, long legs. He walked around to the driver's side, waved goodbye to Yasir standing at the top of the stairs, and jumped in behind the steering wheel.

The car crunched down the driveway's hard, sandy surface. At the front gate, there was no sign of the black hatchback. Alice seemed a little more chatty than usual, and Dan drove along Borrowdale Road, trying not to ogle her legs. Seated, her short dress rode up a little, and he struggled not to stare.

In the CBD, small groups stood around chatting. It was Friday night, but that didn't explain the larger than usual number of cheerful faces. There was, it seemed, a pervasive air of expectation.

In the art gallery, the excited members of the writers' club spoke of nothing but the political landscape and whether Mugabe would go. Mrs Olonga tried to draw the members back to writing matters, but it was no use. With the first half of the evening completed, she spoke to the group. 'Well, we've completed the social part of our evening already. Many of you are keen to go home to hear the latest news. So, we'll call it a night. Remember, our last meeting of the year is in two weeks on December, one.'

The members soon dispersed, giving the gallery staff an early night. Dan and Alice walked down the front steps and along the pavement to the car.

'Do you fancy a coffee somewhere, Alice? We missed out on tonight's coffee and cake.'

'Yes, all right.'

Dan reversed the car out of the angled parking. He thought the Meikle's Hotel might be the best spot.

'Are you enjoying your stay in Zimbabwe, Dan?'

The question caught Dan by surprise. It was the first time Alice started any topic of conversation with him. 'Er, yes, most of the time.'

'Are you happy with your apartment?'

'Yes, I am.'

'John said it was nice. Where is it?'

'In The Avenues, quite close to the art gallery.'

'So, you drive out to Borrowdale, just to give me a lift?'

'Well, I also have sundowners with John and dinner afterwards, so it's not an inconvenience.'

'Could I see your flat?'

'Yes, of course. We can have coffee there.' Dan changed direction and headed to his apartment. The drive took only a few minutes. 'Here we are, on the left.'

'It looks nice.'

'Inside is even better.' Dan drove around the corner and entered the apartment's parking area. 'The parking is dirt, compacted over time, so there's little dust.' They got out of the car and walked along the ground floor passage to the stairs at the building's entrance.

As he put his key in the Yale lock, he thought it strange to be taking Alice to visit his apartment. She was the wife of the man who marked him for elimination on the Honey List—the professional assassin who'd become an unlikely friend. Dan reflected on his own morals and principals. Alice wasn't even a friend. She'd been distant until now.

They entered the apartment, and Dan flicked the light switch by the door. Mood lighting filled the large living room and kitchen area. The silver and black tones of the furnishings stood out against the white walls and blended with the closed black vertical blinds.

The expression on Alice's face made her words superfluous. 'Oh! This is a nice big room!'

'Yes, and when I open the blinds, you'll see how well the old-style wrought-iron balcony fits with the modern interior. I'll put the kettle on, then show you the rest of the apartment.'

Dan filled the black plastic kettle with cold water and switched on the power. He took out the instant coffee from the overhead cabinet above the kitchen counter, where the kettle heated with a low hiss. 'How do you like your coffee?'

'A little milk but no sugar, please.'

Dan took two mugs from the cupboard below the benchtop that separated the kitchen from the dining and lounge area of the large, open-plan room. He leant against the kitchen counter where the kettle was heating, while Alice stood opposite, next to the benchtop. It crossed his mind that it was the spot where Gloria or Nikita always stood.

'I'll show you the rest of the apartment while the kettle boils.'

A sudden loud click, and the lights went out. 'Blast! Not another power outage! And the water hasn't yet boiled.'

The room was pitch-black. The hiss of the kettle wound down, and the fridge's missing hum screamed silence. It was a moonless night. The streetlights were out, and the black vertical blinds were closed. In total darkness, they couldn't even see their own hands. 'Hold on a minute, Alice. Your eyes will adjust to the dark.' But it was so black, their eyes didn't get used to the dark.

Dan held out his arm. 'Give me your hand. We'll open the blinds and go out onto the balcony.'

As Alice stepped towards Dan's voice, her foot caught the toe of his shoe. She stumbled into him, and he wrapped his arms around her to prevent a fall. 'Whoops!' she giggled. In the blackness, balance was hard, but Dan had been leaning against the kitchen counter, and it helped to keep them both on their feet.

Neither of them moved as they stood in silence, their hearts beating a little faster at their near fall. Dan could feel Alice's breath at the vee of his open-neck shirt, and through the thin material, he could feel her firm breasts pressed against his chest. After several seconds, he realised he was holding her tight, with his left arm around her waist and his right hand on her bottom. His instinctive reaction was to hold her even tighter and pull her in to him.

Alice said nothing and made no move to separate. In the blackness, he couldn't see her face, and somehow, their lips brushed, and Alice gave another shy giggle. Several seconds passed, and suddenly they were sharing a gentle kiss. Who made the first move? It was hard to tell. In their proximity, they found each other.

Now his hands moved freely over her body as she moulded into him. Dan slowly lowered the zip at the back of Alice's dress and slipped his hands under the material onto her warm, smooth back. He sensed himself hardening. He tried to ignore it, but it was no good, so he pulled her even closer. A little voice in his head questioned his actions, but he seldom listened to it in such situations. He'd worry about the consequences later.

'You said you'd show me the rest of the apartment.'

'Keep hold of my hand, and I'll take you there.'

As they shuffled from the kitchen, Dan fumbled to turn off the light switch near the front door. He didn't want the lights turning on when the power returned. They found their way to the bedroom.

'Sit on the bed while I open the blinds.'

In the darkness, it made little difference, and Alice remained a disembodied voice.

She stood up and let her dress fall to the floor. Dan unclipped her bra and slipped his fingers inside the waistline of her panties. He eased them down until he held the cheeks of her backside in his palms. He pulled her even closer to him, and their kissing resumed with a passion. Before he undressed, the little voice returned. This time, he shared the question. 'Is this wise?' Alice didn't answer, so he took it as a yes. Dan rummaged around in his bedside table drawer.

'What are you doing?'

'I'm looking for a condom.'

'We don't need a condom.'

Her body welcomed him as he entered her. Clearly, a long time had passed since she'd last had sex.

Their passionate union was moreish, and they made love three times. They needed to make the most of their brief time together. As he lay back on the bed, Dan glanced at the luminous hands of his watch. 'Ten o'clock. I'd better get you home. We don't want you grounded.'

Dan led Alice through to the shower. Though the power remained off, the water was still quite warm. They soaped each other and hugged in a slippery embrace. The soap was fragrance-free, which meant she'd not have to answer any awkward questions when she got home. After rinsing, they helped dry each other and dressed. Coffee was forgotten, but they agreed they'd tasted something far better.

Lost in their own thoughts, they spoke little on the way back to Alice's house. She rested her right hand on Dan's thigh, showing their budding relationship held promise. They drove through the gate and pulled up at the bottom of the steps.

'Thank you for a wonderful evening, Dan.'

'No, Alice, thank you for a wonderful evening.'

She smiled.

He watched her walk up the steps. She opened the front door and waved before disappearing into the darkened house. Dan let the car roll down the drive and stopped at the gate. The black hatchback sped past.

CHAPTER 49

O<small>N</small> Saturday, eighteenth November, sizeable crowds gathered in Harare and other centres to celebrate the end of Robert Mugabe's time in power. Rowdy demonstrators converged outside his office and residence, demanding he resign. They saw the army as heroes for deposing him.

On Sunday, ZANU-PF sacked Mugabe and expelled his wife and her associates from the party. But Mugabe refused to resign from the presidency. The party gave him until noon on Monday to resign or face impeachment on the grounds he allowed his wife to usurp constitutional power.

Mugabe ignored the deadline, and the party started the impeachment process. On Tuesday, after he realised he'd lost the support of over three-quarters of his cabinet, he relented and resigned.

Emmerson Mnangagwa returned to Zimbabwe on Wednesday, twenty-second November, and was sworn in as president on Friday, twenty-fourth. It had been a momentous eighteen days since his sacking. In the last week, a party atmosphere prevailed, particularly in Harare, where excited crowds looked forward to better times.

When Dan walked into the CBD on Saturday morning, groups of excited people filled the streets. An African man slapped him on the back, saying he'd soon get his farm back. Dan just smiled. He'd never owned a farm and didn't plan to get one now. He walked past the bookshop where Gloria worked, and a dark cloud settled over him. Dan shook his head and strode out towards the Meikles Hotel, where he was to meet Daniel Moyo for coffee.

At the hotel, he found Daniel already there, seated in an armchair in the hotel lounge. They ordered coffee and raisin toast.

'Well, Daniel, everyone seems delighted. What do you think?'

'People have short memories. Everyone is excited about the prospect of change, but Mnangagwa was Mugabe's enforcer and closest ally. What makes them think there'll be meaningful change?'

'Shouldn't we give him the chance to prove he's serious and not just talking empty words?'

'Yes, sure, but don't hold your breath.'

Soon, the pair retreated to the Explorers' Bar for a beer or two. It was approaching lunchtime, so they ordered toasted cheese sandwiches. Dan enjoyed these chats with Daniel Moyo. He was the one friend with no personal issues to detract from their musings about other people's problems and the country's dire situation.

Dan noted the gathering clouds as he walked back to the apartment. Soon the rains would come. Each day, the clouds teased, only to disperse, leaving the parched city disappointed. He loved the rainy season, but now it would always remind him of Gloria. What pained him most was he never told her of the plans he'd made for their future together. She died, frustrated by his apparent lack of commitment.

Gloria came to the apartment at lunchtime on Saturdays. Now, without her, he tried to keep himself busy on Saturday afternoons, so he wouldn't sink back into his gloomy reminiscences about their time together. If he couldn't find some other distraction, he'd resume editing her manuscript, which he'd neglected recently because of the painful memories it brought back.

The warm weather led Dan to take a cooling shower around five-thirty. Refreshed, he dressed and sat on the balcony, enjoying the evening's gentle breeze. A knock on the door interrupted his thoughts. It sounded like Nikita's knock, but it was too early for one of her visits. She came only after dark. And never on a Saturday.

Dan rose from his chair and hurried to the front door to open it. A smiling Nikita stood there with her right arm raised, leaning against the doorframe, and her left hand resting on her hip. She wore a long, tight-fitting, rust-coloured dress that accentuated her tall, athletic figure. A basket covered with a tea cloth sat on the floor beside her.

'Nikita, what a pleasant surprise! You look lovely.'

'I thought you might need company this Saturday night.'

'You're welcome any night, Nikita. Fancy a beer?'

'Of course.'

'What do you usually do on Saturday nights?'

'Since Victor died, I mostly read. What about you?'

'I sit on the balcony and think.'

'About work?'

'No, mainly about Gloria.'

'Did you ever tell Gloria I visited you here?'

'No, it would have made her jealous. She never knew much about my work. Gloria would have misinterpreted our relationship.'

'Well, if you haven't eaten already, I thought I'd make you a dinner. I've brought along beef and vegetables. Do you like roast?'

'I love roast beef and vegetables.'

'It'll take a while.'

'There's no hurry. I've got no other plans for tonight.'

'That's good because it won't be ready until at least nine, nine-thirty.'

'No problem. There're plenty of beers in the fridge.'

While they waited for the roast to cook, they sat on the balcony with their beers and chatted.

'When I first came to Zimbabwe, David Jones kept in regular touch with me, but I haven't seen or heard anything of him since the writers' festival in Bulawayo. Have you seen him at all?'

'Not since the festival. With all the political tensions and activity around these days, it's probably best he maintains a low profile. People like David Jones walk a fine line. They play both sides and need to keep their heads down when there's trouble between the factions or the parties.'

The smell of the cooking roast filled the apartment. Dan salivated at the prospect of eating it. A roast beef dinner was one of his favourite meals. He couldn't recall telling Nikita how much he loved roast beef and vegetables, so perhaps it was just a lucky guess on her part. Dan took a bottle of red wine from the overhead cabinet above the kitchen counter and took out two wine glasses from the cupboard below the benchtop.

Nikita served the vegetables and carved thin slices of the roast beef. Dan studied the plate in front of him. The vegetables included roast potatoes, onions, pumpkin, and peas. A rich gravy provided the perfect complement to the meal. It seemed an age since he'd eaten a roast dinner, though Gloria had cooked it from time to time.

Dan and Nikita toasted each other and absent loved ones. It occurred to Dan he wasn't alone, though it often seemed like it. Nikita and Daniel Moyo were his two closest friends, and Alice, a fascinating distraction.

Captain John felt like a friend, but was he? Could their shared dislike of Eunice be any real foundation for a friendship? And then there was John's unsavoury business, the COU. And the small matter of sleeping with his wife. A shaky foundation at best, no question about that.

After dinner, Dan and Nikita took their glasses of wine out onto the balcony. 'Coffee Nikita?'

'Yes, please. I need coffee after all this red wine.'

They walked back into the kitchen, and as the kettle boiled, Dan noted Nikita stood in that same spot again. The spot where she, Gloria, and Alice all stood, waiting for their coffee.

It was a beautiful evening, and they sat on the darkened balcony, chatting past midnight. The sliver of the new moon sat low in the sky. The romantic setting and relaxed chatter were suddenly interrupted when Dan noticed the car across the street. It wasn't parked in the usual nose-to-kerb position but stood double parked on the verge. What caught his attention was its shape and colour—a black hatchback.

'Nikita, can you tell if anyone is inside that black hatchback across the street? It's hard to see in the dark. The streetlights don't work, and the new moon doesn't help.'

The two sat straining their eyes, staring at the black car. Then, the unmistakable red glow of a cigarette end gave them the answer. Dan stood up and stepped to the balcony edge for a closer view. Instantly, the engine started, and the car raced off down the road.

'The way he drives looks familiar. Every time I leave Captain John's house, a black hatchback speeds past.'

'Oh! Do you go there often?'

'Every second Friday, I go there for a debrief with him and pick up his wife for the writers' club meetings.'

'Ah! That must explain the gold stud earrings on your bedside table.'

'Er, no, those were Gloria's. I found them in the bedside table drawer and forgot to put them back.'

Dan saw the question in Nikita's eyes and felt his face flush. She smiled.

CHAPTER 50

THINGS were quiet in the office. Eunice hadn't resumed their twice-weekly debriefs since the last time she suspended them. Dan thought she might have run out of Captain John's scotch and the cheaper bottles she'd bought. Most likely, she waited for things to die down, following Mugabe's ousting.

Cherry and Ambrose were Dan's consolation. He enjoyed working with them because their cheerful demeanour brightened his workday, which had become otherwise tedious. The atmosphere held an ominous calm. Peace didn't fit with Eunice and the way she ran things.

Friday was the first of December and the next scheduled visit to Captain John's house. Dan looked forward to his fortnightly visits for pre-dinner drinks with John and Yasir's delicious meals. Now, he was also keen to see Alice. He wondered how she would be towards him after their intimate evening at his apartment.

At last, Friday arrived. After work, Dan prepared for the evening. He always took care of his appearance, but now he fussed more than usual. Normally, he shaved only once a day in the morning, but when he ran his fingers over his stubble, he thought he'd better shave again.

After he showered and brushed his teeth, he stood in front of the wardrobe to select his clothes. Dark brown trousers, shoes and belt, a well-ironed white shirt, and his camel-coloured sports jacket would do nicely. Dan glanced around the apartment to make sure everything looked tidy, before grabbing his keys and heading downstairs to the car.

He was excited and a little nervous about the prospect of seeing Alice. What if she regretted their last time together? He'd experienced that in the past. Alice wasn't a teenager or in her twenties, but a mature, self-assured woman. He wasn't sure how she'd react when she saw him again.

He didn't want her to greet him or behave in a manner any different from his earlier visits. Captain John would soon pick up on that. Dan also realised he needed to be careful to not pay her any more or less attention than usual. It would be a fine balancing act.

As always, it was a beautiful Harare evening as he drove out to Borrowdale. At the front gate of the house, he stopped to check for the black hatchback. No sign of it. As he parked at the bottom of the steps, a beaming Yasir appeared at the top. After greeting Dan, Yasir showed him into the lounge, where Captain John sat in his wheelchair with a blanket over his legs.

'How's your recovery going, John?'

'Quite well, really. I've been practising to stand with a walking-frame. It's painful and very tiring, but the doctors say I'll get accustomed to it. Before, my legs wouldn't support me, but now, I can stand for a few seconds. Of course, I use the frame to pull myself up, so it's my arms that are supporting me for much of the time. When I take the weight off my arms, I can stay upright for a few seconds.'

'That's wonderful news.'

'Yes, the doctors believe if I practise standing without holding on to the walking-frame, I might soon notice significant improvement.'

Before long, Alice came to announce dinner. She looked stunning in a peacock-blue, tight-fitting, knee-length dress with matching sandals. A simple string of small, light-brown, wooden beads hung around her neck, coordinated with similar-looking, mid-sized, hooped earrings.

Dan needn't have worried how Alice might behave when she saw him. She seemed back to her remote self. Polite but distant. This wasn't the woman he dropped home a fortnight ago, and instead, he worried that their intimate evening might have been a one-off.

After dinner, Dan complimented Yasir on his meal, and thanked Captain John for the evening, before escorting Alice down the steps to the car. At the gate, he looked right to check for the black hatchback. There was no sign of it. The crescent moon shone against the inky black sky in front of them. As they exited the drive, Dan was impatient to know where things stood. 'Is everything OK?'

'Yes, fine thanks.'

The exchange broke the awkward silence, with Alice quite chatty after that. They arrived at the art gallery and turned into one of the angled parking spaces. Inside the gallery, they found an excited group of club members catching up on the events of the last fortnight.

This time, Mrs Olonga kept the meeting focussed on writing matters. When the formal part of the evening ended, she welcomed two new members and announced details of the end-of-year get-together. 'Remember everyone, our Christmas party is here at the gallery on December fifteenth. It promises to be a merry night, so get a late pass. Now, we move on to our social part of the evening. There's tea and cake in the next room.'

Dan turned to Alice. 'Do you want to stay, or…?'

'Or your place? Yes, let's have a quick cup first, and then we'll slip out. No one will notice.'

* * *

In the apartment, Dan unzipped Alice's dress before they'd even reached the bedroom door.

'My, you are eager!'

Alice tugged at Dan's belt.

'And you're not?'

They switched the lights off and hurried to undress before jumping into bed. Enough ambient light came through the angled vertical blinds to avoid the inky blackness of their last encounter.

They made slow, passionate love, and afterwards, lay cuddled together. Dan stroked Alice's firm body, and she snuggled even closer into him. He sighed with contentment. 'I could get addicted to this.'

'Oh, yes! Me too! There's the Christmas party and then no club meet-ings until mid-February.'

'That'll be eight weeks before we can be alone again.'

'How will I manage that?'

'There's always John for company.'

'John and I lead separate lives. At home, we barely talk. He gets his entertainment elsewhere.'

'In my wildest dreams, I never would have imagined we'd get together like this.'

'Neither would I. John mentioned you only once or twice, but after his shooting, he was impatient to see you. That's when he asked me to call you.'

'I'm glad he did.'

'He said he wouldn't trust anyone else.'

'Well, he can trust me, except with his wife.'

'Each fortnight, I looked forward to your visit—even after the first time I met you.'

'I didn't know that. You always seemed so distant and aloof.'

'Well, how else should I have been? If not for the power outage and me tripping into you, nothing may have changed.'

'It just goes to show how tiny chance events and fine threads can change lives.'

'Enough talk for now. Let's spend more time changing our lives.'

* * *

Dan said goodnight to Alice and eased the car down the drive. At the gate, he stopped to let a car pass. A second car, a black hatchback, raced by, and Dan slammed his foot on the accelerator to follow. He never got the dimly lit registration number, nor could he catch up to it as it hurtled down the road before turning off into a side street and disappearing.

He'd accepted Captain John's explanation for its regular appearance, though the incident at the apartment, when he and Nikita sat on the balcony, seemed too much of a coincidence. Though he wasn't sure it was the same car, the driver's frantic acceleration was familiar. Might John have ordered someone to keep a watch on him? It hadn't occurred to Dan to check if the car stood outside his apartment earlier in the night when he and Alice lay in bed together.

It was only six months since Gloria's fatal accident, and Dan sometimes felt he was being unfaithful to her memory. But he spent so much time thinking about her, he welcomed any distraction to rest his mind and join the living. What niggled at him, though, was his growing feelings for Alice. It might be too soon for that.

CHAPTER 51

Dan couldn't help but feel Eunice was ignoring him. Aside from the routine administration work, things were quiet in the office. She didn't confide in him or boast of the COU's current exploits. She hadn't mentioned Captain John in a while, and Dan wondered if she was aware of his present condition. John said she'd not contacted him since his shooting, and all his information about the COU's activities came from other sources.

The quiet at work had its advantages. Unlike the struggles of writing his first novel since returning to Zimbabwe, when work was a constant distraction, he was racing through the second one.

His original plan was to wait to find out if Captain John returned to the COU. Either way, he'd intended to leave Zimbabwe as soon as John's position became clear. Now, his budding relationship with Alice was an added complication. She was John's wife, so the relationship seemed impossible. But was it?

Why did he involve himself in these complicated situations? Probably for the same reasons he remained in Zimbabwe, the thrill of danger. Dan was still single, partly because he found it difficult to resist the advances of an attractive woman. One of his former girlfriends gave him her frank opinion about where he kept his brains. Of course, he didn't agree with her assessment, though the issue hindered his prospects for any longer-term relationships.

Gloria was the one exception, and that was why her passing hurt so much. Now he was loath to give up Alice. He'd wait to see what might develop. Most often, he moved on only when a relationship came to a natural end. In the meantime, he looked forward to December fifteenth, when he'd see Alice again.

* * *

Friday, December fifteenth, the writers' club year-end social. Dan dressed in his black trousers, shoes and belt, mid-grey sports jacket, and dark grey shirt. The rain over the past three days made the weather comfortable. He drove along the Borrowdale Road in a cheerful mood with the car windows open and the radio playing.

As he drove through the front gates of John's house, Dan noticed how the rain had refreshed the beautiful garden. The smell of the rain lying on the grass was intoxicating, while the rain on the hard, sandy drive enhanced its colour to a deeper shade of rust.

When he entered the lounge, he found Captain John standing with the aid of a walking stick. 'I can't walk yet, but the stick helps me stand and keep my balance.' After a minute or two, John sat down in his wheelchair. 'Well, what do you think? I wanted to show you how much I've improved.'

'I'm impressed.'

'The next time you visit, I want to walk to the dining table with my walking stick.'

'The writers' club resumes its meetings in mid-February, so you'll have plenty of time to improve.'

'No, you're invited for dinner on Christmas Eve.'

'Oh! Thank you.'

'It's not just social, Dan. There's a job I'd like you to do for me. A friend of mine since childhood is *persona non grata* in Zimbabwe. He's battled a long illness and doesn't think he'll live out the next year. He wants to visit his old parents before he dies, but he can't return through normal channels because he'd be arrested and spend his last days in prison. I'd like you to smuggle him into the country and bring him back to Harare.'

'Er, sure. Where do I find him?'

'He's been living in Zambia. So, you must drive to Kariba and meet with Captain Moses, who runs a couple of boats on the lake. He'll wait for you at the end of Mhembwe Close at seven in the evening, next Saturday. Don't worry, I'll draw you a map.'

'Where do we meet your friend?'

'Moses will take you to the pickup point in one of his boats. My friend will use the name Elias Kachingwe. It's not his real name, so in case you run into any police roadblocks, I've got him an identity document under that name. Give it to him when you meet. If you leave the marina at eight o'clock, you'll reach the pickup point by nine, and be back in Kariba by ten.'

'And then?'

'Drive him straight back to Harare to your apartment, and someone will pick him up early on Sunday morning. The drive from Kariba is at least five hours, even more after dark, so you'll arrive home in the early hours. It will mean a sleepless night, I'm afraid, so try to get some sleep before you come for Christmas Eve dinner.'

'Right, so I'm only bringing Elias back.'

'Yes, Moses will stay in Kariba. No one must know about your trip.'

'Of course.'

'Then we can all relax and debrief on Christmas Eve.'

'That sounds wonderful.'

John poured scotch over the ice in two crystal glasses and passed one to Dan. 'Yasir has only prepared finger food this evening because Alice tells me there'll be plenty to eat at the writers' club.'

'I'm sure whatever they provide won't compare with Yasir's offerings.'

As they emptied their glasses, Alice came in to greet Dan. She wore a tight-fitting orange dress, ending above the knee. Around her waist was a purple sash, colour-matched with her sandals and amethyst earrings. The outfit set-off her unblemished, coffee-coloured skin.

'We better go,' said Alice. 'Don't forget, John, it will be an extra late night tonight.'

'OK, you two. Have fun.'

Dan escorted Alice down the steps and opened the passenger door to let her enter the car. He waved goodbye to Yasir before easing the car down the drive. With his eyes on Alice, he forgot to check if the black hatchback stood near the turn in the road. 'Do you think John realises the way you dress turns me on?'

'If he does, it would amuse him.'

'It wouldn't amuse him if he knew the consequences.'

'You mean you wouldn't make love to me if I dressed more conservatively?'

'Nothing would stop me from making love to you, but your outfits are a real come-on for me.'

'I like bright colours on these beautiful summer evenings. In winter, I dress more conservatively, especially during the day. You say you love how I look in my clothes, yet you're so keen to get me out of them?'

'So you don't think John suspects anything?'

'No, it's normal for me to dress up. We haven't slept together for ages. He sees me as a possession, not as a woman he desires. If I look good, it inflates his ego, but he's not otherwise interested in me. It would displease him if I didn't make a special effort when you pick me up for the writers' club. John would say I was letting him down.'

'Perhaps he'd also approve of your delicious performances in my bed.'

Alice laughed. 'That, I doubt!'

Dan parked the car in front of the art gallery, and he and Alice ascended the steps from the pavement in a light-hearted mood.

Mrs Olonga was delighted to welcome them and pointed out the tables full of finger food, both hot and cold. Waiting staff walked amongst the excited members with trays of Champagne and beer. Dan was glad he'd only drunk one glass of scotch with John earlier that evening.

Most of the excited chatter was about politics and the up-coming Christmas celebrations. The club committee members spoke about the plans for the following year, but kept club business matters to a minimum.

The evening was enjoyable, though Dan had his mind on other plea-
sures. When he and Alice made eye contact across the room, their
thoughts aligned. Alice made her way over to him. 'There's still a long
evening ahead. After dinner, everyone will move on to the hotels for
drinks and dancing. We could skip that and relax at your place.'

'You read my mind, Alice. Why don't we go now?'

The pair stepped out into the cool evening air. It was quiet compared to the noisy chatter inside the gallery. The sounds of another office
Christmas party came from a nearby building.

'You told John we'd be extra late, and we left the get-together early.
That means we'll have plenty of time. Much more than usual.'

'So instead of making love only two or three times, we might manage
four to six, or four times, but more slowly.'

'Don't be greedy.'

'Wouldn't you like that?'

'Yes, if I could manage it.'

'Don't worry, I have ways of helping you to manage it.'

CHAPTER 52

WITH the COU's many influential contacts, their cars were never short of petrol. Dan filled up on the Friday before his drive to Kariba. It would be a quick trip over the weekend. No one would know about it.

He was due to meet Captain Moses at seven on Saturday evening, so he planned to leave Harare at midday. The expected travel time was five hours, but he didn't want to risk being late. With a couple of hours to spare, he'd stop for a cup of tea and a quick bite somewhere along the way.

Dan retired earlier than usual on Friday and didn't set the morning alarm because the next night promised to be a tiring one.

It was ironic, Captain John trying to help someone wanted by the authorities. In normal circumstances, he'd make money from luring back or disposing of men like Elias Kachingwe. It showed John had a heart somewhere in his make-up.

Saturday dawned bright and clear. Dan rose at eight and cooked a breakfast of fried eggs and bacon. He wasn't in a hurry, with free time, until he left for Kariba. Most Saturdays he'd go into the CBD to meet Daniel Moyo or drink a cup of coffee in one of the hotel lounges. On those occasions, he'd make do with a bowl of cereal for breakfast.

It was years since Dan last visited Kariba. The place must have changed a lot. What a pity he couldn't stay over and explore the area. Still, the leisurely drive might be fun. He'd take some of his favourite cassette tapes to play on the way.

He flicked through his small collection and selected Jeff Wayne's *War of the Worlds*, Rod Stewart's Greatest Hits, and Manuel Santana's *Abraxas*. For the rest, he'd rely on the radio. At eleven, Dan made himself a cup of tea. By eleven-thirty, he'd become impatient and set off on his mission. He drove down to 2nd Street, turning left into the busy lane of traffic.

Dan drove out of the CBD into the suburbs, passing the Royal Harare Golf Course, and through Avondale, before turning left onto the Lomagundi Road. Soon, he passed through the outer suburbs and reached the open road. By ten past one, he was in the village of Banket, and twenty minutes later, he entered Chinhoyi (Sinoia). Too early to stop, so he drove on.

In front of him lay a scenic drive through the bush, greened by the rains. The deteriorating roads and signs of rural decay didn't detract from his enjoyment of the trip, but the once tidy and productive farms presented a sorry picture. Between the rutted, pot-holed roads, pedestrians, and cyclists, his progress was slower than he expected.

Just before three, Dan drove into Karoi. He felt peckish and thirsty, so stopped at a cafe and ordered tea and a toasted cheese sandwich. Refreshed after his short break, he jumped back into the car and headed for Makuti. The village lay an hour and a quarter further on, and one kilometre beyond, was the turnoff for Kariba.

By the time he arrived in Kariba, it was five-thirty in the evening. He drove through the small town to view the dam wall, always an impressive sight. But with the sluice gates closed and the river below the dam running low, exposed rocks studded the riverbed. Water stains on the dam wall betrayed the extent to which levels had fallen in recent years.

Heavy rains in Zambia were yet to have any significant effect on water levels. Many claimed three seasons of good rains would fill the dam to former levels. Others saw it as a forlorn hope in a time of climate change.

The time passed fast, and dusk was falling. Dan looked at the view, imprinting it on his mind, before heading for the fish and chip shop he saw earlier in the town centre. The shop was still open when he parked in front of it. He'd only eaten a toasted sandwich since breakfast, and now he was ravenous.

Darkness descended fast as Dan sat in his car and ate the fish and chips with his fingers. The salty meal was just what he needed after his long, tiring drive. At least on the return trip, he'd have company to keep him awake. After he finished eating, he threw the packet into a nearby rusted bin and went back into the shop and bought a bottle of water.

Dan looked at his watch. It was time to meet Captain Moses. He drove along Lake Drive and turned into Sable Drive, keeping a lookout for Mhembwe Close. He followed Captain John's hand-drawn map. Ten minutes to seven. At least he'd not be late.

In Mhembwe Close, he drove to the end of the road and parked under a tree. As he turned the engine off, someone knocked on his window. A tall, gaunt-looking African stood there. Dan lowered the window.

'Mr Scott?'

'Yes, please call me Dan. You must be Captain Moses?'

'Yes, Sir.'

Dan shook hands with the tall man. He collected his jacket from the back seat and locked the car. Captain John warned him it would be cold on the lake if the breeze blew up, even in summer.

Moses chatted away in a friendly manner as he led Dan to his boat. 'This is the one we're using tonight; in case it gets choppy out there in this weather. It's my bigger boat.'

It was much bigger than Dan expected. A wheelhouse stood a third of the distance from the bow. A broad deck ran all the way round the boat, with a canvas canopy and built-in bench seating along the rear two-thirds of the deck.

Moses boarded the boat over a plank resting on the bank and motioned for Dan to follow. 'Be careful, it's narrow and unstable.'

Dan successfully negotiated the plank and jumped down onto the deck.

'Wait for me,' someone called out in the darkness.

Dan recognised the voice at once. It was Eunice. Her sudden appearance shocked him. Had Captain John sent her? He must have.

Moses looked at Dan. 'Is she with you?'

'No. You didn't know she was coming?'

'No way, man! Captain John won't like this.'

Eunice crossed over the wobbling board, with Dan willing her to fall into the water. No such luck. She jumped down onto the deck and gave the men a sweet smile. 'This will be a different Saturday night. We better get moving, or we'll be late for old Elias.'

Dan smiled a wry smile. If she knew the purpose of their boat trip, Captain John must have told her about it. What else had he told her?

Moses didn't look at all pleased. Without a word, he started the inboard engine and reversed the boat out of its mooring. He put it into forward gear, and the boat moved off at surprising speed. Eunice walked to the stern and sat on the bench, enjoying the cooling breeze. Dan stood in the wheelhouse's doorway, where he could speak to Moses.

The boat skipper's face was set in a frown. For a time, he remained silent, staring ahead as if he didn't notice Dan. Then he turned to him. 'Are you sure you didn't ask her to come along with you?'

'No, I didn't tell her or anyone else. Captain John told me this trip was confidential.'

'That's what he told me.'

'So, he must have told her.'

'I doubt that.'

'Well, how could she have known?'

'Captain John said you were the only person I should trust.'

'That's also what he said about you.'

'She found out somehow. Maybe she followed you.'

'No, I don't think so. There was little traffic on the road. I would have noticed.'

'So what now?'

'I'll go talk to her. And see what I can find out. Technically, she's my boss.'

The engine noise and swishing of water would have drowned out their discussion. Or so Dan hoped. On the big boat, they'd spoken in lowered voices. Eunice's smile gave him the uneasy feeling she could read his mind and knew what was going on.

'So, Dan, you thought you'd go about COU business without telling me?'

'I'm not on COU business. What I do on my weekends is my concern.'

'And you never told me you visited Captain John.'

'In my private capacity.'

'I take it you are running this errand for him?'

'It's personal.'

'Are you sure? By the way, did you hear David Tawanda died?'

Dr David Tawanda was one of the three names ahead of Dan on the Honey File list.

'Died?'

'Yes, he suffered a heart attack. His escape on the Victoria Falls train must have caused it. It would have been an intense trip for him. Of course, you'll remember that because you helped him escape and made Jonas Nyandoro disappear. I don't think I ever thanked you for that.'

'I had nothing to do with Tawanda's escape or Jonas's disappearance.'

'If you say so. Oh, and I meant to tell you, we don't have to worry about Evan Garanganga anymore. Gustave handled it, just like I said he would. Some people think he's a thug, but he's a good boy, really.'

A shiver ran down Dan's back. Garanganga, another of the three names preceding him on the Honey File. After a hiatus, following Jonas's disappearance, Eunice was eating through the list at a rate of knots. That just left 'what's his name' in front of him. What was his name again? Dan couldn't remember because he'd paid little attention to it. He imagined Dr Tawanda and Garanganga would absorb a lot more time. 'Is this all recent?'

'Over the past few weeks.'

'Why are you telling me only now? I'm supposed to be your 2IC, responsible for external operations.'

'I didn't want to distract you.'

CHAPTER 53

THE boat slowed as it approached the Zambian shore. Dan left Eunice sitting in the stern and walked to the wheelhouse. Moses was all concentration. The tall skipper surveyed the shadows of the trees with his customary frown. 'Things look different at night.' Suddenly, a torch blinked three times from the shore. 'Yep, that's the signal.'

Moses approached the shore with the care of a driver trying to park in a tight space. He turned the boat, so the stern faced the shore, and started a slow reverse, listening for any scrapes, warning of sunken trees, rocks, or shallow water. About twenty metres from the bank, he stopped the boat and waited.

The sound of an oar in the water told them someone approached. With the low, setting moon, the trees on a promontory cast a shadow over the boat, making the area pitch black. They waited, straining their eyes in the darkness. A sudden thump on the starboard announced the small rowing boat's arrival alongside.

A broad smile showed white teeth gleaming in the darkness, as Moses helped the frail old man on board. Elias didn't look like a contemporary of Captain John, but then illness had taken its toll. He looked twenty years older than his childhood friend.

The effort of boarding exhausted Elias. The young man who rowed the boat passed a small suitcase to Moses. Before pushing the rowing boat away with an oar, he called out, 'Goodbye, Uncle. Travel safe.' The old man waved, but with his breathlessness, struggled to reply.

Dan introduced himself. The old man smiled. 'Ah, you are the one taking me back to Harare.' The words came in a hoarse whisper.

Eunice sat at the stern, smiling. 'Elias Tonderai, welcome aboard.'

The old man's smile evaporated, and he looked confused. He sat down on the built-in bench at a point nearest to him. It was clear he didn't want to get any closer to Eunice, whose words also hit Dan with a jolt. Elias Tonderai? Was that the name ahead of him on the Honey File? It sounded familiar, but he couldn't be certain. But it was something like that.

Dan sat down next to Elias, some distance away from Eunice. He spoke in a lowered voice to prevent her from overhearing him. 'Captain John asked me to give you this identity document in the name Elias Kachingwe. He worried we'd pass through roadblocks on the way to Harare, and you'd need to prove your identity. I passed four on the way here.'

Elias took the identity document and put it in his buttoned breast pocket. 'That woman. How does she know my real name? Captain John said no one knew I was returning to Zimbabwe.'

'I'm sure Captain John didn't tell her. If you're well known in Zimbabwe, perhaps she recognised you from photos in the newspapers.'

'I've lived in Zambia for many years. Age and my illness have changed my appearance, but she recognised me straight away.'

Dan looked across to the stern, where Eunice sat. She stared back at them. He didn't trust her, and like old Elias, wondered about her presence.

With his mind focussed on the situation, he wasn't conscious of the stiffer breeze and the choppy waves that appeared out of nowhere. But when the temperature dropped, he was thankful for the windcheater he'd brought. Lightning flashed, and a crack of thunder shook the air.

The boat he considered unnecessarily large for the trip now seemed way too small. The growing waves battered the boat, and it struggled to make headway in the strengthening wind. Dan rose and walked to the wheelhouse to get reassurance from Moses. A smile seemed to have replaced the captain's fixed frown. 'Don't worry, Dan, this old boat has survived much heavier conditions than this.'

Dan was dubious, but returned to join the anxious Elias, who sat holding his suitcase between his legs, to prevent it sliding about the deck.

Eunice rose from her position at the stern and walked past them, heading towards the wheelhouse. It was a welcome break from her fixed stare in their direction. A few minutes later, she returned to her position at the stern. Dan assumed she'd also visited Moses for reassurance as the waves crashed and the wind roared. A powerful storm with torrential rain threatened. He recalled reading somewhere to avoid being out on the water in one of Lake Kariba's storms, notorious for their sudden appearance and violence, with many fishing boats lost over the years.

Dan! Dan! Quick! The whistling wind almost drowned out Moses's desperate shouts. Something was wrong. Dan hurried to the wheelhouse, struggling to hold his feet as the boat shuddered and rocked. He reached the wheelhouse where a frantic Moses pointed through the window at flames licking the deck in front of them. 'Quick, Dan. Use the fire extinguisher! There, behind me, on the wall!'

In a flash, Dan grabbed the extinguisher, ran to the front of the wheelhouse, and sprayed the fire. At first, it kept burning. Then it appeared extinguished, only to flare-up again. He sprayed the fire again, not stopping until he was sure it was out. A blackened singe mark remained on the deck where the fire had threatened to take hold.

In the wheelhouse, an anxious Moses waited for Dan's report. 'There was a strong smell of fuel. Nothing else burned, though the fire singed the deck.'

'There's no fuel anywhere near there. Are you sure about that?'

'Yes, I think so.'

'A fire in the middle of the lake is a major problem. There's no chance of help in this weather. Especially at night.'

'How could the fire have started?'

'Who knows! I'll have to check it in the morning.'

With the excitement over, Dan left to rejoin Elias. In the panic, he'd forgotten about the heaving waters, but now he needed to steady himself as he walked along the deck. Eunice sat in the stern, but there was no sign of Elias.

'Where is he? Where's Elias?'

'Isn't he with you?'

Dan ran back to the wheelhouse. Elias wasn't there. Moses hadn't seen him. Dan raced around the entire deck. He was nowhere to be found. 'Eunice, you must have seen something. Did he stand up?'

'No. One moment he sat there, the next, he was gone. I saw nothing. The boat lurched a lot in this storm. Perhaps he fell overboard.'

'Where's his suitcase?'

'If he fell in, he might have been holding it.'

'How did you realise he was Elias Tonderai? He said he looked different from when he left Zimbabwe.'

'The old fool rang the office to confirm the rendezvous. I recognised his voice when he wanted to speak to Captain John. I told him I'd pass on the message.'

'So that's why you're here?'

'Yes, and imagine my surprise, finding you here. Though I knew about your regular visits to Captain John's house. Anyway, Elias is worth a lot of money to the COU, so now we'll be able to claim it.'

'He was John's childhood friend?'

'Yes, and I realised John would try to protect him, but business is business.'

'So, you pushed him overboard?'

'I didn't say that. Tell me, Dan, are you a betting man?'

'No, why?'

'Don't you have a copy of the Honey List? Whose name is next in line?'

'I don't know.'

'Oh, I'm sure you do. It's you. But I'm giving you a sporting chance.'

'What do you mean?'

'This afternoon, in Kariba, I posted two letters. One to Johannesburg and the second to Harare. The postal service in Southern Africa is terrible. The Johannesburg letter gives Gustave my go-ahead for Captain John. My Harare letter is to John, telling him you're screwing his wife. Would you like to bet which letter arrives first?'

'You're bluffing. Anyway, Captain John will know you're making it up to cause trouble.'

'The photos I sent him of you and his wife coming and going from your apartment will convince him. They are all date and time stamped. He'll wonder what you two were doing in there.'

'I don't believe you.'

'Friends of mine on security duty near Captain John's house have been monitoring it for me. And then you turned up. They've been telling me all your movements. About the whore who visits you, and now you've added John's wife.'

'You're jumping to conclusions.'

'Am I?'

'Are your friends the ones in a black hatchback?'

'Ah, so you're aware of my friends in the security services. You made a big mistake, refusing my offer to work with me in running the COU. I gave you the opportunity, but you rejected me.'

'I rejected your advances, that's all.'

'Did you imagine there'd be no price to pay?'

'I already had a serious girlfriend.'

'Oh, you mean that silly young girl who stayed on the weekends? It's a pity she had to pay for your stupidity.'

'What do you mean, "she had to pay"?'

'I thought with her gone, you'd see sense.'

'She died in a car accident.'

'Did she?'

'You're not saying it was deliberate, are you? A planned hit and run? Did you organise it?'

'Not exactly.'

'What do you mean, not exactly?'

'Well, if I hint at something, my boys are keen to please me.'

'So you suggested she was disposable?'

'Something like that.'

Dan felt the bile rising in his throat. He couldn't believe what he was hearing. Was it a lightning flash, a crack of thunder, or something snapping in his brain? His anger and grief erupted together in a mighty rage. He grabbed Eunice's handbag, lying on the bench seat next to her. As she stood up to retrieve it, he pushed her hard in the middle of her chest. She tumbled back over the boat's low railing into the water.

The roaring wind and splashing waves masked any sound she may have made, and in that second, she was gone. An uncontrollable shaking took over Dan's body as he stood at the stern of the boat, trying to catch sight of her. All he could see were the enormous raging waves of the inland ocean. His heart thumped in his chest as if fighting to escape.

He stumbled back to the wheelhouse. 'Moses, Eunice has also disappeared. They must have struggled and fallen in together.'

'We can't look for them in this storm. I thought you looked only for Elias?'

'Yes, but I didn't realise at first, she was also missing.'

Dan realised he still held Eunice's bag in his left hand. He rummaged through it and found a bottle of cigarette lighter fuel. 'This is how she started the fire on deck.' Next, he saw the handgun. Did she intend to use it on him, now he'd reached the top of the Honey File list? The middle of Lake Kariba, the perfect spot in a raging storm. And would Moses have heard the gunshot? Dan walked out on deck, just out of Moses's sight, and dropped the handgun into the water. Just then, the pelting rain started, drumming on the canvas canopy with a deafening crescendo.

CHAPTER 54

DAN worried about the long overnight drive back to Harare, but adrenalin made it easier than he expected. He'd never caused the death of a person before, and the traumatic finality of his actions kept him awake. He'd not intended to push Eunice over the side of the boat, but her revelation about the part she played in Gloria's death sent him into an uncontrollable rage.

It was close to midnight when they got back to Kariba. Too late to phone Captain John, who went to bed early since his shooting. Moses said he'd phone John in the morning to tell him what happened. Dan would reserve his report until he saw John for dinner that evening.

The police at the roadblocks waved him through on the drive back to Harare. Elias wouldn't have needed his identity document, after all. The poor guy missed seeing his parents for the last time, and Dan felt responsible. He'd failed to protect him, but he didn't expect the evil Eunice to push Elias overboard. The frail old man stood no chance against her.

Seven o'clock in the morning, and Dan was home. He made himself a cup of tea, ate a bowl of cereal, and got into bed. It was four in the afternoon when he woke. At first, he felt drugged, but a shower soon refreshed him. The idea of Christmas Eve at Captain John's house didn't now sound as appealing as when John first mentioned it. Not only was John's old friend, Elias, lost in the lake, but he'd need to spend the evening keeping his distance from Alice.

Dan selected his clothes with care. He was aware Alice liked him in dark colours, and she would pick up on his subtle message. He put on his dark grey sports jacket to counter the late-night drop in temperature that often followed the rain. Earlier in the day, the clouds opened and drenched the city.

In Johannesburg, Dan had bought a bottle of scotch—a Macallan 1824 Collection Whisky Maker's Edition. He was always conscious of drinking John's supply of high-priced single malts and thought he'd repay him in the way he'd most appreciate. For Alice, he bought blue topaz earrings set in silver. He would have liked to buy her the matching necklace, but such a lavish gift might raise questions. For Yasir, he bought a smart, blue, casual shirt.

He grabbed the gifts and hurried down to the car. The wet roads glistened as he drove through the streets of Harare onto the Borrowdale Road. He wondered what reception he'd get from John after hearing the news of Elias's demise. Dan assumed Alice would share his frustration at being confined to the house and making small talk all evening.

At the front gate of John's house, he checked to see if the black hatchback was in its usual spot. It wasn't. A beaming Yasir waited at the top of the front steps to greet him. Dan concluded Yasir must keep an eye out whenever he was expecting him.

'Evening, Sir. Very special dinner tonight to make you think you are back home.'

'Whatever you cook, Yasir, is very special to me.'

'Thank you, Sir. The master is waiting in the lounge.'

Dan walked through the entrance hall into the lounge to find John standing there with a walking stick. He approached Dan and gave him a warm handshake.

'Gosh! You are improving fast. It's good to see you mobile again.'

'It's still tiring, but it gets a little easier every day.'

'Did Moses phone you this morning?'

'Yes, I heard about poor old Elias. It seems his visit wasn't meant to be.'

'Eunice said he phoned the office to confirm the pickup. That's why she was there.'

'Yes, that was unfortunate. Elias must have forgotten I was recovering at home. But there's always a silver lining. It gave you the chance to get rid of her.'

'No, she must have fallen in with Elias when they struggled.'

'So you don't want to take credit for her disappearance? A pity, it could have sealed your place in the COU.'

'Now I know you're joking, John.'

John grinned and sat down in an armchair. 'Never mind, let's have a scotch.'

'Where is your wheelchair?'

'In the garage, in case I need it again. The doctors say it's likely my legs will never regain their full strength, so I've bought a car I can drive by hand. It's a used car, though in good condition. I can't wait to try it out. On Tuesday, I'll go to the office and catch up on what I've missed. Everyone is away on holiday between Christmas and New Year, so I'll be free to snoop around, disturbing no one. Why don't you meet me in the office on Friday? We can drink a couple of scotches and debrief.'

'OK, but there's more I must tell you. Eunice said she'd given Gustave the go-ahead for you, if you understand what I mean. She claimed she posted the letter to him yesterday afternoon.'

'Posted a letter? Why wouldn't she just phone him?'

'I don't know. It was some game she was playing.'

'She must have heard my condition was improving and worried I'd return to the COU. Anyway, I've got my Glock, so I'll keep it handy.'

'Eunice said those security guys in the black hatchback parked at the bend were keeping watch on your place. Perhaps that's how she found out you were improving.'

'Apart from doctor visits, I haven't been outside, so how would they know?'

Yasir walked into the room with a tray of nuts for John and Dan to nibble on while they drank their scotches. Captain John turned to him. 'Yasir, those men who park in the black hatchback near the bend?'

'Yes, Sir.'

'Have you ever spoken to them?'

'Yes, Sir. Sometimes they ask me how you are.'

'And what do you tell them?'

'I say you are getting better.'

'All right. Next time, just tell them you don't know.'

'Yes, Sir.'

The two men sipped their scotches and ate a few nuts.

'And John, there's something else I found out from Eunice.'

'Save it till Friday, Dan. Let's just relax and enjoy Christmas Eve.'

Alice came in to join the men. Dan stood up to greet her. She wore a red, knee-length dress that emphasised her trim, athletic figure. A green belt and shoes gave her a Christmas look. She poured herself a glass of white wine and sat down in an armchair.

Dan dipped into the carry bag and brought out the gifts he'd earlier wrapped in Christmas paper. 'Thank you both for your hospitality over the last three months. It's been most enjoyable.'

John raised his tumbler. 'For us too. We've both looked forward to your visits.'

Alice smiled but said nothing.

John loved his gift, as did Alice. 'Blue is the only colour I didn't have in my earring collection.'

Yasir came in to call them for dinner. At the table, John opened a bottle of Veuve Clicquot Yellow Label Brut NV Champagne. Yasir poured the Champagne for everyone, including a glass for himself. They toasted Christmas and the year ahead, before Yasir returned to the kitchen to serve dinner.

The traditional Christmas dinner included turkey and Christmas pudding, cooked with Yasir's attention to detail. The relaxed evening proved Dan's earlier fears unfounded, and all appeared to enjoy themselves. Yasir fussed about making sure everyone's glass was full. He had a knack of inserting himself into the occasion and enjoyed himself immensely. Dan's gift delighted him, and in return, he invited Dan to dinner every fortnight in 2018.

Dan's only reservation when he said goodnight and thanked them for the evening was when he'd see Alice again. The writing club meetings next year seemed forever away, and if John was driving again, would he take Alice to the meetings? Perhaps he'd say something about it when they met on Friday.

In bed, Dan thought about the pleasant evening and how 2018 might turn out. A sudden dark thought crossed his mind. Did Eunice really send a letter to Captain John? If so, would it arrive before Friday? If it arrived after Friday, what then? Whichever way he looked at it, it was a worry. Was Eunice bluffing? She liked to play mind games. There was no way of telling whether she'd told the truth. Dan's concern was how it would affect him seeing Alice. Also, how might it be for Alice if John received a letter revealing their affair? The wait for Friday would be nerve-racking.

Dan was free on Christmas Day and Boxing Day. Nikita—Eva— was away visiting her parents, and Daniel Moyo had family commitments. He'd see Daniel on Wednesday at the Explorer's Bar and Nikita on Thursday, when she'd cook dinner at the apartment. But it was Friday that loomed large in his mind.

* * *

Christmas Day was quiet and interminably long. Dan slept in, but despite this, the morning passed at a glacial pace. The Christmas Eve downpours continued into Christmas Day. Half-hour breaks of brilliant sunshine, followed by a build-up of dense, dark clouds, preceded each deluge.

Dan enjoyed Yasir's Christmas Eve dinner, and wasn't at all hungry, so he made do with a cup of tea on the balcony. It seemed like the afternoon would never end, but at five o'clock he boiled two potatoes and mashed them. For dinner tonight, he'd eat mashed potato and buttered toast, served with a sprinkling of salt and pepper. Not quite up to Yasir's standard, though better than nothing.

Boxing Day proved even longer and duller. Dan missed lunch again. He'd sat around most of the day, doing nothing much. He tried to edit a couple of chapters from the second novel he'd written in Zimbabwe, but he couldn't concentrate. The soaking downpours passed, giving him the opportunity for a walk around The Avenues. But it was too quiet. He soon lost interest in walking the deserted streets and returned to the apartment. For dinner, he ate fried eggs and baked beans on toast, a favourite of his.

Though he'd done nothing all day, he was tired and planned for an early night. Dan showered, brushed his teeth, and jumped into bed. He was drowsy, and just as he was drifting off, the phone rang. He groaned. Who could that be?

CHAPTER 55

D<small>AN</small> turned over in his bed and reached across to the bedside table, searching for his ringing phone. In the darkness, it sounded extra loud. And in his hurry to answer, his hand found it but knocked it onto the floor. He groaned and leapt out of bed to retrieve it. He picked up his cell phone and pressed the green button. 'Hello.'

'Dan, David Jones here. How are you?'

'Fine, thanks, but where have you been? It's been ages since I last saw you. I assumed you had died.'

'Ha, ha! Very funny! Merry Christmas, by the way.'

'Yeah, and to you.'

'Listen, how about us getting together on Saturday night? I've been invited to a party at The Rainbow Towers. You'll meet some interesting people there.'

'You mean people at the very top?'

'Near enough. I'll pick you up at seven. Dress is smart casual.'

'OK, it's a date.'

Dan put his cell phone back on the bedside table. He wondered about David Jones' unexpected call. The last time he saw him was at the Bulawayo Writers' Festival in June. Now, he sounded amiable, but at the conference, he seemed antagonistic and sullen. Perhaps it was because Captain John was there, making a play for Eva Chirau. Might David Jones be interested in Eva? Dan, too, felt possessive about her. A desirable, widowed woman in the company of three men stirred up competitive jealousies.

* * *

When Dan arrived at the Meikles Hotel at five-thirty on Wednesday evening, he found Daniel Moyo waiting at the Explorers' Bar. The bar tender knew them well and poured two glasses of scotch on the rocks without waiting for their order.

Dan pulled up a bar stool. 'It's been another long day. The office is closed, and I'm having trouble focussing on editing or writing. I looked forward to this evening.'

Daniel raised his glass to clink with Dan. 'Here's to absent friends and better days.'

'Have better days arrived?'

'Well, Mnangagwa is on a charm offensive, hoping to lure back white farmers and business, and hoping the West will lift sanctions against the country's leaders.'

'Is it likely?'

'They won't do it before free and fair elections.'

'The sooner the better, hey?'

'Hmm, but has anything changed? Mnangagwa was the enforcer for many of Mugabe's policies.'

'I suppose time will tell.'

'By the way, Ian Sanders and his family send their best wishes.'

'I can't help wondering if they had something to do with Captain John's shooting.'

'Oh, I doubt that. They're settled in Botswana. Why would they stir everything up again?'

'You know there was an attempt on their lives at their home?'

'That was over four years ago. There's been nothing since.'

'No, though something was developing. Captain John was dead keen for me to get Ian Sanders to speak at the Bulawayo Writers' Festival. I'm sure he intended to detain him and use him as a lure to get Sarah Kagonye back in Zimbabwe.'

'That sounds like one of your novels.'

'One of the COU's tasks is to lure dissidents back to the country to deal with them. It's all about settling old scores and silencing critics. And that's why I'm in the country.'

'Then why haven't they dealt with you?'

'That's a good question, but I don't have an answer. Given the tiny contribution I make to their organisation, I don't understand why they've not moved against me. Perhaps Captain John has protected me. We get on well, despite his gruesome business.'

'So then, what are your plans? What about Eva Chirau? She's an attractive, unattached woman, a desirable companion for any man.'

'Eva? No, we're just good friends. Why would I tie myself down?'

'You said something similar about Gloria, and losing her devastated you.'

'Now you sound like my parents.'

'Time waits for no man, Dan. You're eating up the years, so don't leave it too late.'

* * *

Dan slept in on Thursday morning to recover from one too many scotches with Daniel Moyo the previous evening. Today, Nikita would arrive just after lunch to prepare the dinner she'd long promised him. Getting up late saved him from another long, boring day. A cereal breakfast at eleven meant he'd not have to worry about lunch, and that way, he'd be ravenous by dinner time.

Just before two, he recognised Nikita's familiar knock. He hurried to the door and swung it open. Nikita stood there with a large wicker basket covered by a tea cloth.

Dan's eyes moved from the ever-attractive Nikita to the basket she carried. 'Hmm, that looks promising.'

'I wanted to be sure we had everything necessary.'

'And more, by the looks of it.'

'Well, let's get to work. You can help me prepare the ingredients.'

Dan enjoyed Nikita's visits. She put no pressure on him, and in times of stress, Nikita was a source of cool, level-headed advice. They were close friends, but their relationship didn't progress any further. She was an attractive woman, and in his sub-conscious, she was a reserve if the circumstances warranted, though he'd never thought of her romantically.

'On Saturday,' said Dan, 'I found out David Tawanda died from a heart attack in Botswana. Eunice also told me Gustave had dealt with Evan Garanganga in Joburg. Then Elias Tonderai drowned in Lake Kariba. That leaves me at the top of the Honey File list.'

'Oh no! Are you sure? I'd heard about David Tawanda, but not the others. Perhaps your copy of the list is outdated, and you're not next.'

'There's no way Eunice would promote anyone over me on that list. I'm sure I'm next. Thank goodness Eunice is no longer a problem, but I wonder how Captain John will see it. You know how regimented he is.'

'I thought you were now friends?'

'The friendship is new and untested.'

'Why is Eunice no longer a problem?'

'After we picked up Elias Tonderai on the Zambian side of Lake Kariba, Eunice lit a fire at the front of the boat. When I ran to put it out, she must have tried to push Elias overboard, and I assume they both fell off the boat in the struggle. There was a horrendous storm with enormous waves. In those conditions, it was impossible to find them, and I'm sure they drowned.'

'That's your story, and you're sticking to it.'

'Yes. Why does everyone think I pushed her overboard?'

'Who's everyone?'

'Captain John and his friend, the boat captain.'

'Perhaps because it's so convenient for everybody.'

'Well, not for me. I could never do that. And some people think I'm also responsible for Jonas Nyandoro's disappearance on the Victoria Falls train.'

'So what will you do now?'

'I'm seeing Captain John in the office tomorrow, and I'll decide then.'

* * *

Dinner was a Christmas roast. Not turkey, like at Captain John's, but roast beef, Dan's favourite. Nikita produced a traditional Christmas pudding, which was the perfect time for him to give her his present, dark green topaz earrings similar to the blue topaz earrings he'd given Alice.

'I imagined these earrings would suit you.'

Nikita put on the earrings straight away. 'They're beautiful! Thank you. I'm sorry, I didn't get you anything.'

'This dinner is more than enough, thanks.'

It was always a late night when Nikita visited. They drank Cognac with their coffee on the balcony and chatted until the early hours. After Nikita left, Dan lay on his bed, mulling over the evening. He felt it was a wonderful night. It always was with her.

Daniel was right. Nikita was a most desirable woman: intelligent, educated, and classy. Sometimes people don't appreciate what's right under their nose. But now, there was Alice to consider. A relationship with a married woman held no future. Especially one married to Captain John. But while it lasted, he couldn't see past his growing feelings for her.

CHAPTER 56

FRIDAY dawned sunny, with the promise of a warm day to follow. Dan was up early. With Eunice gone, he'd looked forward to the debrief with Captain John. He gulped down his tea and a bowl of cereal, grabbed the car keys, and raced out the door. The streets were quiet, with many city dwellers visiting their relatives back in their villages.

Dan waved to the guard on the gate as he drove into the COU premises. The office was closed in the week between Christmas and New Year, and only an unfamiliar black car stood parked in front of the building. Dan assumed it was John's new hand-driven vehicle.

He bounded up the steps and through the ornate, glass-fronted door. Because of the Christmas break, there was no Cherry or Ambrose to greet him, so he walked straight through to Captain John's office.

John sat at his desk, looking at the computer screen. Near his right hand, next to the mouse, lay his Glock handgun. 'See, your warning did not go unheeded. If Gustave, or any other unwelcome body, comes here, they're in for a nasty surprise.'

'How was the car this morning?'

'Great, just great. I'm mobile again. These old legs are steadily improving, though I'll always walk with a stick, so I'm told. But at my age, according to Alice, it makes me look more distinguished, so I'm not too fussed about it. At least I'm out of that damn wheelchair.'

'So it's back to normal when we reopen?'

'Yes, for me, but not for you.'

'What do you mean? Why not?'

'I've been looking through the invoices Eunice sent out last Friday. Have you seen them?'

'No, what about them?'

'There was one for David Tawanda and another for Evan Garanganga.'

'That's what I wanted to tell you on Christmas Eve. David Tawanda died of a heart attack. And on Eunice's instructions, Gustave disposed of Evan Garanganga.'

'So, with Elias Tonderai falling overboard with Eunice, do you understand what that means?'

'I presume you're talking about the Honey File list?'

'Yes, that's right. Ah, so you know about the Honey File?'

'Can't you change the list?'

'I'd like to, but I don't control it. I didn't put you on the list, and since you've been here, you've proved to be an asset and a friend to me. The COU receives a fifty percent deposit with each contract we accept. The person who put out the contract on you is getting impatient and wants it completed.'

'I see.'

'No, you probably don't. There are a couple of cheaper competitors offering a similar service to the COU. If we don't fulfil the contract, the person who wants you dead will demand his deposit back and go to one of them. We'd be happy to pay back the deposit, but it doesn't make you safer.'

'Who put the contract on me? The number next to my name is HMV17.'

'I can't tell from that code number. David Jones is a broker for our business and for our competitors. HMV is the code for any contract David Jones brings in, and he keeps the client's names confidential.'

'David Jones?'

'Yes. Did you notice he seemed grumpy at the writers' festival in Bulawayo?'

'Yes, I wondered about that.'

'He was upset about the time it was taking to complete your contract. His client was demanding he go to one of our competitors to get the job done. He gets double the commission if the contract comes through the COU, so if he went to one of our competitors, he'd receive less. I told him I couldn't spare you, and you weren't yet at the top of the list. That's why he was in a bad mood.'

'In Joburg, I wasn't at the top of the list.'

'Sometimes a client pays a premium for us to expedite the contract.'

'What I don't understand is what changed between Gustave trying to mug me at the airport in Joburg and my arrival here in Harare?'

'When you arrived, David asked me to park you for a while. Sometimes we delay contracts if doubts arise over the client's ability to pay the balance. He eventually gave the go ahead, but by then, I needed you here at the COU.'

'David phoned me on Boxing Day and invited me to a party at The Rainbow Towers tomorrow night.'

'That means he's making a move on you now. The Rainbow Towers is a favourite place of his. He got rid of Victor Chirau after a party there. I didn't accept the contract on Colonel Chirau, so he gave it to one of our competitors.'

'David Jones! I'd never have guessed.'

'Did you tell him where you live?'

'Yes. He's picking me up at seven tomorrow evening.'

'You need to leave Zimbabwe right now. I'll get Cherry to make the arrangements for you.' Captain John reached for the phone and made the call. 'Cherry, I'd like you to book Dan on the SA Airlink flight to Johannesburg tomorrow morning, and then the first convenient flight to Melbourne, Australia. Thank you.'

As John replaced the receiver, Dan's mind was racing. 'How can I go tomorrow? I won't be able to say goodbye to anyone?'

'Don't worry, I'll tell Cherry and Ambrose you said goodbye. I'll also tell Alice and Yasir.'

'What about my passport? I can't go without it. Even the Australian Embassy wouldn't help me with that. And Detective Inspector Tshuma said I can't leave the country without his prior approval.'

'Ah, you're in luck. Eunice changed the locks on my desk, and I had to break the drawer open. Guess what I found inside? Here's your passport, and there's a letter from Detective Inspector Tshuma saying you are no longer a suspect and are free to leave Zimbabwe. Apparently, Eunice received these in October.'

Dan was lost for words. He didn't want to leave the country in such a hurry, but John insisted he was in grave danger.

'It's a shame it turned out like this. You would have made an ideal 2IC. You did me a great favour getting rid of Eunice, and now, I'm losing you so soon.'

'John, you're not being serious. You can't believe I disposed of Eunice.'

'I don't believe, I know. And I am serious. As 2IC, you wouldn't have needed to get your hands dirty. Look at me. I don't get my hands dirty. But you would have needed to organise things and give the orders. I can see you managing that, even if you can't. Anyway, now that you're leaving, it's time for a farewell drink. I brought the Macallan scotch you gave me for Christmas. This is the occasion to christen it.'

'I can't imagine anybody putting me on the Honey File list.'

'Eunice put you on the list, but anyone might have ordered it.'

'But why?'

'Any of a hundred reasons. Perhaps your novels upset someone in government, or maybe there's a jealous husband somewhere. Who knows why? Only David Jones has the identity of the client.'

Dan's eyes flicked between the Glock and Captain John. Did he know about his affair with Alice? Dan tried to read the signs behind his eyes, but saw nothing to enlighten him.

John poured the scotch into the crystal tumblers and dropped in two ice cubes. 'Here's to your health and a safe trip.'

CHAPTER 57

CHERRY booked Dan on the next morning's eight-forty SA Airlink flight from Harare to Johannesburg. There was just enough time to connect with the Emirates one-forty lunchtime flight to Dubai, where he'd have a six-hour wait for his Melbourne connection. If he missed the lunchtime flight, he'd have to wait at Johannesburg's airport until the seven-ten flight in the evening. Either way, he faced a six-hour delay.

Dan spent the afternoon packing and phoning Nikita and Daniel Moyo to say goodbye. He implied he'd be gone for only a short time. Nikita offered to take him to the airport because early morning taxis were unreliable.

Captain John gave him less than twenty-four-hours' notice of his departure. Was the danger real, or did John just want him gone? Dan lay on his bed, deliberating on the sudden turn of events. Might John have discovered his affair with Alice? He doubted it.

Was David Jones really so dangerous? He found it hard to imagine. He pondered David's unexpected phone call and invitation to the party at The Rainbow Towers. They'd not spoken in six months, and he recalled David's churlish manner at the writers' festival. Before that, he'd been amiable, and Nikita said he was harmless.

As Dan lay on his bed, mulling over the day's events, the crunch of someone walking on the patch of gravel on the crumbling pavement caught his attention. So many times, he'd heard that sound. When he and Gloria lay in bed, late on Saturday nights, they'd try to guess how many people walked together over the patch of gravel. One, two, or more? Hard to tell.

When he lay sleepless late at night, the silence and darkness amplified the sound. It didn't worry him before tonight, so why did it catch his attention now? Slower than the normal step? But then, their pace always differed. More measured, stealthier than usual? Or may Captain John's urgent warning have spooked him? Might it be his sixth sense?

Dan strained his ears. Often, a cough, laugh, or distant voices followed the steps on the gravel. But there was no sound, no logical reason for his unease. Perhaps his imagination worked overtime. His cell phone showed two-thirty.

Then, an unfamiliar sound, a strange creaking. Dan's nerves jumped to extreme alert. What made that noise? The wisteria! Someone pulled on the wisteria. Pulling on it, or climbing it? A soft padded sound on the balcony. Might it be someone with bare feet or soft-soled shoes jumping over the wrought-iron balcony railing?

Dan leapt out of bed and shoved his second pillow under the covers. He grabbed the old, heavy, silver, six-D-cell-battery torch and slipped through the bedroom door into the lounge. The sliding doors and vertical blinds in the lounge were closed, if not locked. The bedroom's sliding door and vertical blinds remained open for the cooling late night breeze. That's where any intruder would enter.

After long minutes of silence, Dan wondered if he'd overreacted to the steps on the gravel. Just as he relaxed, two loud thumps came from the bedroom. A chill ran through his body, giving him an involuntary shudder. The hairs rose on the back of his neck. It sounded like blows to the pillow under the covers. The intruder must have thought it was his sleeping form. Dan's grip on the torch tightened as he stopped breathing and his heart raced. His ears detected a strange throbbing sound, before realising it was the beat of his own heart.

He stood to one side of the bedroom doorway, wondering what to do next. The street lights didn't work, and the moon had set forty minutes earlier. Total darkness shrouded the apartment. The sudden appearance of the bulky figure in the bedroom doorway shocked him. He'd not heard the man approach, and his presence within two feet of him was unnerving.

The man didn't notice Dan as he stood surveying the darkened room. Dan braced himself and swung the torch as hard as he could. The startled figure recoiled from the blow. The torch's head broke free and clattered across the room. Six D cell batteries followed it like tracer bullets from a semi-automatic machine gun. Dan now held the light, empty, tin casing of the torch's barrel. Useless protection against an intruder. He lunged towards the front door and flicked the light switch that turned on the mood lighting. 'Gustave!'

The big man stood holding a screwdriver, his weapon of choice. Gustave took a step towards Dan, prompting him to race to the kitchen drawer that held the carving knife. He yanked it open, exposing the confusing array of knives and other kitchen implements. He glimpsed the thick handle of the meat tenderiser and grabbed it. But he didn't fancy his chances.

Gustave stepped towards Dan, cornering him in the kitchen. To escape this trap, Dan needed to jump over the benchtop that held the kitchen sink. Too late for that. Gustave was almost upon him. He smiled, spun the handle of the screwdriver in his right hand, and made a move towards Dan. Suddenly, he stopped and shook his head, looking confused. Then he fell forward with a great slap on the tiled kitchen floor.

Dan stood stunned, uncertain of his next move. Might the big man get up again? He hurried past the prone figure, relieved he was no longer cornered in the kitchen. For half an hour, he watched over Gustave to see what might happen. Every few minutes, he prodded the body with a broom, getting no reaction. He summoned up the courage to check Gustave's pulse. Nothing he could find. The body remained warm, and Dan wondered if Gustave was dead. There was no sign of breathing, so he considered it likely.

He was catching the early morning flight to Johannesburg and couldn't leave the body in the apartment for Cherry or Ambrose to find. There was only one person to call. Dan picked up his cell phone and tapped in the number. 'Nikita, I have a problem.'

'At half-past three in the morning? What's wrong?'

Dan explained the circumstances. Nikita was silent for a long moment.

'OK, I'll be along shortly.'

Dan waited for what felt like an hour, though it was only twenty minutes. A knock on the door signalled Nikita's arrival. He swung the front door open. Nikita stood there in a tracksuit. Behind her stood three young African men, similarly dressed.

'Hi, Dan. Introductions are best avoided. My boys will handle this. Let's go out onto the balcony and talk.'

The three young men picked up Gustave's body. One took the feet and the others his arms. They shuffled out of the front door.

After the young men left, Dan switched on the electric kettle to make coffee. 'Funny how few electricity outages occur in the early hours. Where will they take him?'

'I don't know, and it's best not to ask. Those boys were Victor's men. They're professional soldiers, so they'll know what to do with Gustave.'

'Thanks, what would I have done without you? Please thank your men for me.'

'That's what friends are for. We're leaving for the airport at six, so there's no point in me going home now. Are you all packed?'

'Yep. I'll make us a cooked breakfast before I shower and get dressed. Are you OK with bacon and eggs?'

'I am. Do you know it's the first time I've visited you when we haven't drunk beer?'

'It's a bit early for me.' They both laughed.

'What did Captain John say about the car and the apartment keys?'

'He said I could leave the car and car keys at the airport, or with the apartment keys on the kitchen counter.'

Dan told Nikita what Captain John said about David Jones.

She frowned. 'So, the HMV coded ones on the Honey File list are not government contracts?'

'Some of them may be, but they've gone through David Jones, so the government can deny any involvement. David may have spoken the truth when he said my invitation to return to Zimbabwe came from the very top.'

'What did they have against you?'

'Criticising the president was a crime, and Mugabe's wife didn't appreciate it either. Remember the mysterious death of Heidi Holland. She wrote a book critical of Mugabe, and his wife, Grace, claimed she put a spell on her. It's possible they didn't like my books, either.'

Just before six, Dan was showered and Ready.

'OK, well, it's time to go,' said Nikita.

Dan checked to make sure he'd packed everything. He locked the doors to the balcony, switched everything off, and left the apartment and car keys on the kitchen counter. 'I'll miss this place. I loved it here.'

Nikita drove through the deserted streets, devoid of Harare's usual heavy traffic. 'I love early morning. It's the best time of day.'

Dan smiled. 'I agree, though I seldom experience it. Early morning is a novelty for me. Now that I'm leaving, I suppose you won't need to be Nikita anymore. You can return to being Eva Chirau.'

'Yes, it's sad. I've enjoyed playing the role.'

'After meeting you as Nikita, it's hard to think of you as Eva. I'm not sure which one I preferred.'

'If you'd stayed longer, you might have found out.'

'Yes, it's a shame. You and Daniel Moyo are my best friends.'

'You must have friends in Melbourne?'

'Not like you and Daniel Moyo.'

'After Victor and Gloria died, I thought we might have something together.'

'Why didn't you say so earlier?'

'I wanted to, but I hoped you'd make the first move. When I noticed the earrings on your bedside table, I realised it was too late.'

Dan didn't comment further, and they drove on in silence. At the airport, Nikita parked the car and accompanied him into the terminal building. After check-in, they drank coffee and chatted. Soon, Dan had to go through immigration. They kissed each other goodbye on the cheek.

'Call me when you get home.'

'Yes, I will.'

They said goodbye, and Dan passed through immigration and walked to the departure lounge. He remembered Eunice told him Gustave would deal with Captain John, and he was sure she'd also put him on Gustave's list of things to do. He thought he better check to see if John was OK.

Dan dialled the number and rang the COU office. Cherry answered.

'I called to say goodbye, Cherry. I'm going home to Melbourne for a while.'

'Come back soon, Sir. We'll miss you. Ambrose also wants to speak to you.'

'Sir, this is Ambrose. Will you come back soon?'

'I'll do my best, Ambrose.'

'I'm an old man, Sir. If you don't come back soon, I may not be here.'

'Goodbye, old friend. I'll try to return before too long.'

'I'll give you back to Cherry, Sir.'

'Cherry, is Captain John in his office?'

'Yes, Sir, I'll put you through now.'

'Hello.'

'John, it's Dan.'

'Yes, what's up?'

'Just checking. I was worried about Eunice's threat of sending Gustave after you.'

'Don't worry about me, Dan. I'll be fine. And I have my Glock for protection.'

'OK. See you then.'

Dan wondered if she sent the letter to Captain John, exposing his affair with Alice. From John's manner, it didn't sound as if he'd received any such letter. Though with the mail system in Zimbabwe, it was still early days.

EPILOGUE

Back in Melbourne, life soon returned to normal. Dan's parents were glad to see him home, especially as his communications had been infrequent and brief. Maureen, his casual girlfriend at the time of his departure for Zimbabwe, was now married. Few of his friends realised he'd been overseas for three years. So much for his friends missing him! His writing led him to lead a solitary lifestyle, and it was now more apparent than ever.

Dan mulled over his narrow escape from Gustave. He didn't mean to kill him, but the hard strike with the heavy, six-D-cell-battery torch must have caught him on the temple. What else would explain the delayed but dramatic collapse of the big man?

The question that troubled Dan was who set Gustave on to him. Eunice remained an obvious candidate. Her security guard spies followed him to his apartment, so she may have told Gustave where he lived.

Was it a coincidence Gustave appeared on the day Captain John told him to leave Zimbabwe? The sudden discovery of his long-lost passport and Detective Inspector Tshuma's letter allowing his departure from the country seemed a little too neat. If John found out about him and Alice, it would give him a motive for killing him. But then, why did John let him leave Harare?

The other uncomfortable coincidence was Gustave came only three days after he gave his address to David Jones. Captain John seemed concerned about David Jones knowing where he lived. Further, there were signs David Jones was getting close to Eunice in John's absence.

Perhaps David was impatient to claim the balance outstanding on contract HMV17. In that regard, he would have found Eunice far more accommodating than Captain John.

Jonas Nyandoro's disappearance puzzled Dan. At first, he imagined Jonas and Captain John conspired to incriminate him, but as time passed, it became clear Jonas wasn't coming back. Detective Inspector Tshuma allowed Dan to leave Zimbabwe. The police must have given up trying to pin Jonas's disappearance on him. Since his interview with Tshuma, at the writers' conference in June, Dan sensed the inspector didn't believe he was guilty of Nyandoro's disappearance or Captain John's shooting.

A plausible solution to one of those mysteries came one morning when Dan paged through the Melbourne Age newspaper. A small article in the middle pages headed, 'Meals on Wheels,' caught his eye.

Authorities in Dete, a small town on the edge of the Hwange National Park in Zimbabwe, have warned passengers travelling on the overnight train from Bulawayo to Victoria Falls to disembark only at scheduled stops.

Over the last three years, at least three passengers have gone missing when they alighted from the train to smoke, relieve themselves, or stretch their legs during unscheduled stops a few kilometres north of Dete.

Several passengers on last Friday night's train claimed they saw a leopard snatch a young woman when she exited a carriage at the unscheduled stop.

Authorities believe a leopard may have developed a taste for human flesh and taken to snatching passengers who venture from the train or stand on the carriage steps.

When he questioned the engine driver at Victoria Falls, the man said he'd seen Jonas smoking on the carriage steps. Dan gave a wry smile. So a leopard took him; a well-deserved fate for the charming assassin. How long had the police suspected this? He recalled the fuss and inconvenience it caused him.

Dan felt sorry for poor Francis. Eunice was against him from the beginning, and he never stood a chance. And what would Sally, his widowed wife, now be doing to survive the economic ills of South Africa?

And then there was Gloria. He loved her. She made him realise how a soul mate might enrich his life. She did everything for him, and he didn't appreciate it until it was too late. Dan published her book, along with the two he wrote in Zimbabwe. It occurred to him he should contact her sister, Estelle, and ask her where she wanted the royalties deposited.

The evening shadows lengthened when Dan looked at his watch. The hands showed five o'clock. In autumn, it would be nine in the morning in Harare. He'd give Estelle a ring. Dan wondered if she was still in Harare, or overseas with a new boyfriend. He looked up her number on his cell phone and called her.

'Hello, Estelle speaking.'

'Estelle, this is Dan Scott. I published Gloria's book, which is selling well. Can you please give me an account in which to pay her royalties?'

'You keep them, Dan. Gloria would want you to receive the royalties. She always said how much you helped her with her writing.'

'Are you sure?'

'Yes, I don't need the money.'

'I miss her.'

'Yes, me too.'

Alice, the lovely, lonely Alice, often crept into Dan's thoughts. She was Captain John's wife, but he ignored her as he focussed on his work and gave his attention to other women. In his hurried departure from Harare, Dan didn't get Alice's mobile phone number. He couldn't phone the house because Yasir always answered and would tell John he'd called. And he couldn't phone John and ask him for her number.

Dan made regular WhatsApp calls to Nikita and Daniel Moyo. He spoke to Nikita each fortnight, and Daniel once a month. Nikita often threatened, hinted, she would visit Dan in Melbourne one day. He resisted the temptation to call Captain John and chat with Cherry and Ambrose. He wouldn't lie to his two favourite staff members about when he might return to Zimbabwe.

Dan sat at his computer working on his fifth novel. His desk faced the front garden with its green lawn surrounded by trees. Autumn now, and with each gust of wind, a shower of yellow leaves would catch his attention as they floated to the ground. He looked at the pretty garden bordered by a high brick wall. The camellias bloomed; their splashes of pink and red, breaking up the expanse of green. But Dan found no inspiration there yesterday, and none today either. His peaceful life in suburban Melbourne was not conducive to sparking his imagination.

In Zimbabwe, he'd lived on the edge, often fearing for his safety. The scariest moment was when Gustave cornered him in the apartment's kitchen. In that moment, he thought he would die, but surviving it was exhilarating. It fired his imagination, and he charged into his next project. His plan was to moderate his behaviour and return to a quieter life. He fancied he'd pushed his luck as far as he dared.

But now, he sat, pondering the structure of his half-completed novel. Not exactly writer's block, but what some in the business call the muddy middle.

The phone rang. 'Hello, Dan Scott speaking.'

'Hello, Dan. It's me, Alice.'

MAP OF ZIMBABWE

S HOWING towns, roads, railway lines and national parks.

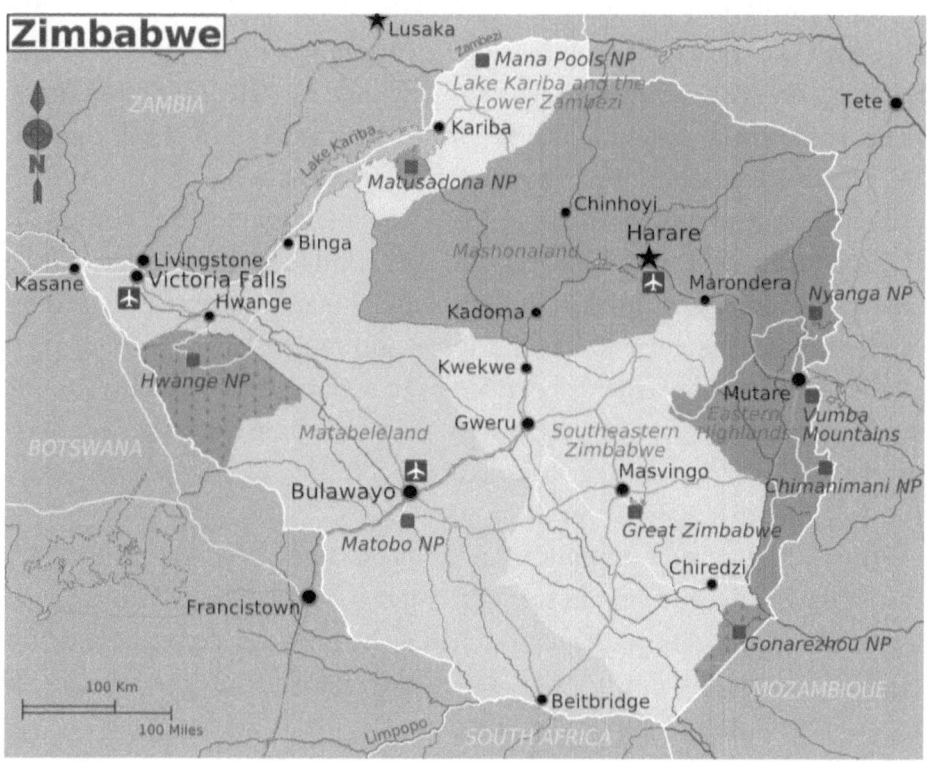

AUTHOR'S NOTE

*H*oney and *The Leopard* starts in December 2014 but is largely set in the period from January 2016 to January 2018.

The Covert Operations Unit (COU) is fictitious but sits comfortably with the factual Central Intelligence Organisation (CIO) and other shadowy branches of Zimbabwe's security services. The Harare Writers' Club is fictitious, though similar groups may exist, and the Bulawayo Writers' Festival is another figment of my imagination.

For the sake of brevity and to reflect common usage, Johannesburg's O. R. Tambo International Airport is often referred to in this book as Johannesburg airport, and the InterContinental Johannesburg O.R. Tambo Airport Hotel is referred to as the Intercontinental Airport Hotel.

Zimbabwe's infrastructure continues in a state of decay. Health, education, and roads are in desperate need of funding, and the country's utility services are in danger of collapse due to lack of maintenance, corruption, and diversion of funds.

Most of Harare's population lacks access to potable water and rely on shallow wells and boreholes, with many contaminated with sewage. Tap water is not safe to drink, and often the taps run dry. Cholera and typhoid are an ongoing threat, and in September 2018, the authorities reported yet another cholera epidemic.

Electricity outages are common, with power often unavailable during the day, coming back on briefly in the early hours.

I wouldn't like my novels to give readers the impression Zimbabwe is a dangerous place. It is one of the safest countries in Africa and well worth a visit. But like anywhere else in the world, it depends on the company you keep. If you fall in with the wrong crowd, you are asking for trouble. If my protagonists have one serious weakness, it's their tendency to associate with questionable people.

L.T. Kay
Author website https://ltkay.com

ABOUT THE AUTHOR

Bulawayo was my home town. That's where I grew up and got my first job. Anyone who has lived in Africa, even briefly, will confirm you can never really leave it. No matter how far you travel, like the grass seeds that stick to your socks, Africa goes with you.

I lived and worked in Zimbabwe/Rhodesia and South Africa for over thirty years, alternating between Bulawayo, Salisbury (Harare) and Johannesburg.

The Bush War got serious while I was living in Hong Kong, and on my return to Rhodesia, I was called up for military service in the army.

Professional qualifications in accounting and marketing helped me secure senior management positions with companies in diverse fields, including engineering, textiles, clothing and cosmetics manufacture, and service industries.

Today, I live in Melbourne with my wife Maggie and write fiction set in Southern Africa, principally Zimbabwe. Since the turn of the century that country has led a dark, surreal existence that keeps many people shaking their heads in disbelief. It would be funny if it wasn't so sad.

L. T. Kay
Author website https://ltkay.com

Other Books by the Author

The Leopard Series is a trilogy of novels set in the troubled years of Robert Mugabe's dictatorship in Zimbabwe. *Honey and The Leopard* is book 3 in the series.

Feeding the Leopard - Book 1 in The Leopard Series
It is 2008, and the global financial crisis sees Ian Sanders out of a job in Melbourne. He flies to Africa, the land of his birth, to follow his dream to write a novel set in the wilds of Zimbabwe.

In his twenty-year absence, much has changed. The country is in turmoil. A new power-sharing government is imminent, but the political situation remains volatile. People fear the police, and violent crime goes unpunished. Supermarket shelves are empty, and essential goods are scarce. Cholera rages and the Zimbabwean dollar is in free fall.

Ian plans to focus on his novel and stay out of trouble, but slowly he is drawn into a web of conspiracy and fear that pervades the lives of so many of the country's people. He is in peril, but who should he most fear: the police, the secretive COU, the wildlife or the enigmatic Sarah?

He and those around him find their values, beliefs and prejudices challenged in their fight for survival. Nearly thirty years after independence, many Zimbabweans still wait for their promised freedom.

L. T. Kay
Author website https://ltkay.com

BETRAYAL. PREJUDICE. DESIRE.
A STORY OF AFRICA

FEEDING THE LEOPARD

L. T. KAY

The Bulawayo Boys' Club – Book 2 in The Leopard Series
When there's nothing to lose, a person can afford to play fast and loose. But what if someone raises the stakes?

Alan Drake, formerly with the Australian Special Forces, drifts aimlessly, chasing the good life in Melbourne. For him, that means bars and clubbing.

When his wealthy controlling father, George, sends him on a mission to Zimbabwe, Alan has no idea what's in store for him. He regards the venture as a crazy plan and doesn't take the task seriously. Alan has no interest in Zimbabwe, and he's never heard of Mthwakazi, let alone the sinister figure known as The Leopard.

Zimbabwe is a land of shortages, and Bulawayo lacks the bright lights that so appeal to Alan. He can't wait to get back home. He soon discovers the city can generate more than enough adrenalin to keep his blood racing, but not in the way he might have hoped.

The mission takes Alan into the national parks where he sees the plight of the wildlife and the hardship endured by the nearby rural population. It leads him into an unintended war with an unknown foe. How can he fight a faceless enemy? People are relying on him. Has he left it too late to leave?

Alan soon realises someone wants him dead. And to make matters worse, the people he's come to help are now also on a death list. The ambitious project has become a fight for survival, with unexpected consequences. His father never warned him of the dangers of the mission.

How could his simple role in the venture lead to this?

Can he extricate himself and his colleagues from the mess he's created?

What can he salvage from the fiasco?

Can Alan resist Africa's many temptations?

L. T. Kay
Author website https://ltkay.com

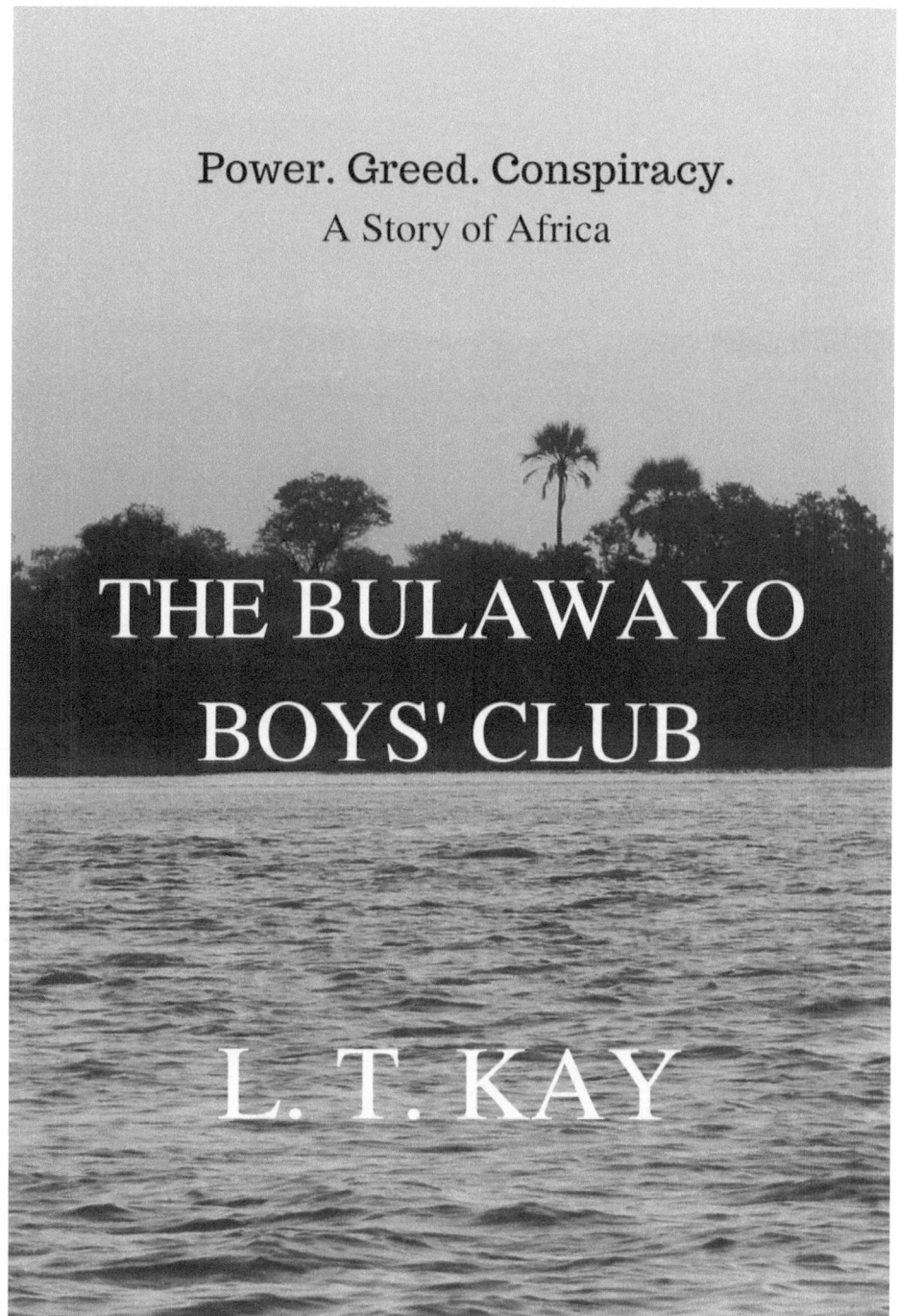

Power. Greed. Conspiracy.

A Story of Africa

THE BULAWAYO
BOYS' CLUB

L. T. KAY